MURDER UNDER THE PALMS

A gripping crime mystery packed with twists

PAULA LENNON

Preddy & Harris Book 2

Revised edition 2022
Joffe Books, London
www.joffebooks.com

First published by Jacaranda Books in
Great Britain in 2018

Cover art by Nick Castle

ISBN: 978-1-80405-138-2

For Montego Bay,
Still Jamaica's diamond despite the rough

CHAPTER 1

The last time Detective Raythan Preddy looked into the eyes of the Honourable Everton Wrenn was across the courtroom in the Western Regional Gun Court in Montego Bay. Then those eyes were brown and shining, with a glint of humour. Today those eyes were grey, dull and unseeing, inside a cold body which lay on the tiled verandah floor of his home. The body of Judge Everton Wrenn was clothed in a colourful dashiki and knee-length shorts. Preddy had never imagined the judge as a dashiki and shorts sort of man. Until today the detective only recalled seeing him clad in the long black robe of his profession, grey whiskers brushing against a starched white collar, favouring a true Jamaican statesman of integrity.

The silent Caribbean Sea lapped lazily against the short pier metres away from the verandah. Looking up Preddy noticed a catamaran sailing by in the distance. Tourists out on their early morning exploration of the western side of the island would be unable to see the body or the bright yellow crime tape. They would just see an unidentifiable mass of people crowding a stunning waterfront property on an expensive stretch of pristine sandy beach, part of the exclusive

1

Wynterton Park gated community. The carefree revellers could probably glimpse flashes of white light as the police photographers did their thing, but that would be about all. No flashing blue lights. The tell-tale vehicles, all parked in the front driveway which abutted the busy highway, were hidden by the sprawling houses and towering walls preventing the road-bound commuters from seeing the activity beyond. Preddy was well aware, however, that rumour and gossip were quite adept at scaling high walls.

Wynterton Park was a well-established residential neighbourhood with side-by-side entry and exit points, separated only by the small brick hut that provided the security guard with somewhere to shelter from the elements in between raising and lowering the giant iron barriers. Thirty properties, each occupying a third of an acre, consisted of an architect-designed Mediterranean-style villa with arched windows, crested by orange clay tiled roofing lined with integrated solar panels. Miniature versions of Royal Palm trees, interspersed with lilac hibiscus flowers sprouting yellow stigma ran the length of the wide communal driveway, which was flanked on either side by perfectly maintained green lawns.

As Preddy watched the waterway traffic he wondered if the assailant had arrived via boat and fled the same way, or whether the attacker was still right there on the premises, watching the Pelican Walk detectives. He turned and glanced around. The bright red hair of Detective Sean Harris stood out amongst the locals and seemed to have acquired its own audience. It was not unusual to find local people studying the white officer as there were no others operating in the parish of St James. The Scotsman was on the beachfront questioning a male resident who was forcefully shaking his braided head from side to side while staring at his foreign inquisitor. Harris closed his notebook and turned his attention to the sand, studying it for clues.

Preddy took the few stone steps down from the verandah onto the sand and beckoned towards Harris. "Get anything?" asked Preddy.

Harris shook his head. "He was so eager tae talk tae me I thought he must have seen something." He pushed his damp fringe from his forehead exposing a greying hairline. "He kept saying 'say dat again' and 'repeat dat', even though he understood me."

Preddy nodded. The accent might be unusual, but Harris was highly capable of making himself understood, and his Patois was coming along at a good pace. "A new member of de fan club."

"Just what I need," said Harris sarcastically, returning his gaze to the sand. "Looks like a lot of people were on the scene before we got here. There's footprints in the sand all over the place, different sizes."

"I know. Not surprising though," said Preddy. "People get up and go swimming and fishing long before six. Dey've had more dan two hours to mess up any evidence."

"Did a good job," murmured Harris.

"Detectives!" The forensic pathologist's voice interrupted them and they headed up the steps onto the verandah. "You asked me for my initial thoughts so here goes. I think our victim was strangled."

"Strangled?" repeated Preddy.

Doctor Sewell nodded as she looked up from beneath her copper tinted dreadlocks. "Someone throttled this man with their bare hands."

"Rass." Preddy inhaled deeply, drawing in salty sea air. He stared at the deceased's temple. "But dat mark on de forehead, not a blow wid something hard? You see it, Harris?"

Harris peered closely. "Aye, he definitely got a knock."

The doctor tilted her head sideways in thought. "Maybe, but he was strangled."

Detective Kathryn Rabino approached them from inside of the house. "Mrs Wrenn is at the dining table sir," she said. "I think she's ready to talk."

"Okay, good. I'll get back to her in a minute," said Preddy. He pointed at the mark. "What dat look like to you?"

"I'd guess Judge Wrenn fell and hit the corner of the coffee table, sir." Rabino tucked her weaved ponytail under her blouse collar and crouched down beside the table. "This thing feels like solid marble. Not a mark on it, but then again his skin wasn't broken."

Doctor Sewell pointed a finger below the deceased's chin. "See here, the bones on the front of his neck are broken. Can't see any ligature marks though."

"So dey strangled him and he fell, or he fell and dey finished him off by strangling him," mused Preddy.

"Unusual eh?" asked Harris.

"Very," said Preddy.

In nearly two decades on the force, Preddy could not recall dealing with a death by strangulation involving the use of bare hands. Even those killed with a ligature were few and far between. The preferred method of murder for the local clientele was the gun followed closely by the blade, be it a knife or machete. Stones were a distant runner-up. His first thoughts on seeing no sign of blood on the body was that Judge Wrenn had been bludgeoned with one perfect blow, but now he learned that someone had literally squeezed the victim's life out of him.

"Sounds a wee bit personal," said Harris as he leaned over the body.

"I'll say," Rabino nodded.

"Time of death?" asked Preddy.

"On appearance, I'd say he's been dead since around eleven o'clock or midnight . . . give or take an hour on either side," replied Doctor Sewell with a grimace. "Poor man."

Preddy scanned the floor around the body and turned to a crime scene officer. "Bag dat for me, please," he said, pointing at the remains of a cigarette butt on the floor.

"If it's alright with you, detectives, I'll take him back to the lab for some more tests?"

"Yes, sure doc," said Preddy. "I guess dere is nothing else he can give us."

The pathologist gestured with her hands, and the waiting white-clothed officers set about placing the corpse in a blue body bag. Preddy followed behind them walking through the wide halls of the house to the front of the property where he could see Detective Javinia Spence near the open doors of the ambulance.

"Get back, me say!" she shouted as the paramedics approached with the gurney. Her arms were spread wide against the concerned neighbours who had postponed going to work in order to watch the unfolding spectacle on their doorsteps. Whether it was her tone or the gleaming weapon holstered in her belt, the neighbours obeyed. Spence turned and headed towards Preddy, her face a picture of annoyance.

There were at least twenty people staring at the departing ambulance as it crawled up the long driveway, some straining their necks towards the tinted windows. Preddy did a quick sweep of their faces; males and females, old and young. It was not unknown for the killer to return to the scene of the crime and witness the aftermath of the destruction caused. In this case, maybe the killer never even left. Rarely did killers' faces give anything away. Preddy watched as the security guard raised the exit barrier and allowed the ambulance to leave. If the crime was not committed by a resident, the murderer either had to pass through the security checkpoint, or climb over the ten-foot high walls, navigating strategically placed barbed wire and broken glass. Not an easy feat by any standards and certainly not when flustered or in a hurry. The only other entry point would be by sea.

"Damn people," muttered Spence. "You would think people on dis complex would have better behaviour, but dem rubber-necking like any old cruff."

"Fear of death and disbelief of death does dat to people," said Preddy. "Although, for all we know one of dem is a murderer."

As he turned towards the house Spence said, "Hold up a minute, sir." She reached up and brushed something from his shirt collar. "Hominy corn porridge for breakfast?"

"Dat bird," he muttered. "Can't let it starve."

"You good!" she said with a smile. "Me woulda run it 'way long time. If de puss never eat it first."

As Spence and Preddy strolled back through the house he admired the local paintings that adorned the magnolia walls, of the national heroes, of court houses, and memorable scenes of atrocities and disasters. The rustic terracotta ornaments and flowery china vases on the shelves and alcoves which lined the passageway he attributed to the woman of the house.

Rabino was standing beside Oleta Wrenn who sat motionless on a wicker chair in the spacious dining room with her elbows on the table and fingers on her temples, staring intensely at the brown wood. She was about sixty years old, with plaited grey hair flattened under a hairnet. Her forehead was slightly indented at the hairline, evidence of wearing too-tight wigs. She wore glasses, which gave her a look of studious concentration, fitting for her occupation as principal of a flourishing high school. Her face had remained impassive even as she had let Preddy in earlier, and the detective had wondered at her apparent calm in light of the tragedy.

Judge Everton Wrenn was a pillar of the Montego Bay community. A legal stalwart with impeccable credentials and unquestionable judgment. A man more widely known outside of the judicial family because of his popular judgments rendered in English and summarized in Patois for the local newspaper. A faint smile crossed Preddy's lips as he remembered Judge Wrenn's most recent conclusion: "*If you no stop murder people pickney, me nah stop give you place fi park you backside fi de next thirty years!*" Yes, Judge Wrenn was a man after Preddy's own heart who must have collected a lot of enemies in his illustrious career, which may have cost him his life.

The judge's death was sure to strike fear into the good citizens of the parish of St James, and be particularly alarming to Montegonians. Wynterton Park was classed as one of the safest neighbourhoods in the city. Here the middle-class families with good jobs or successful businesses could live in peace. If murder could visit Wynterton Park, murder could stop by anywhere.

Oleta Wrenn coughed to clear her throat but said nothing. Rabino patted her shoulder gently. Preddy studied the widow's appearance. Oleta was a slim woman down to her waist which then extended to broad hips giving her an avocado-like shape. Her hands seemed slightly swollen and she wore no jewellery of any kind. The detective's eyes focused on a broken index fingernail just as she looked at him.

"It broke off when I was shaking Everton, Detective Preddy," she said, her voice steady as she followed his gaze. She rubbed the edge of the damaged nail with the forefinger of her left hand. "I can assure you that I didn't kill my husband."

Preddy raised his eyes to hers. She reminded him of his long gone Sunday School teacher who used to place sweets in eager tiny hands following his word perfect recital of Bible verses. "You find anything missing, Mrs Wrenn? Anything valuable? Phones, money, jewellery?"

Oleta glanced around her. "A few artefacts — very old coins that were in a jar on the coffee table, and, yes, his phone. I haven't noticed anything else."

Detective Spence moved towards Oleta. She reached into her trouser pocket for her own phone and said, "Give me de phone number, Mrs Wrenn, make me try call it."

Oleta reeled off the number and then said, "I already tried, it didn't even ring. Not a sound." She shook her head. "It's relatively new, a Galaxy Edge, silver."

Harris wandered over to the coffee table. "Were the coins worth anything, Mrs Wrenn?" he asked.

"Everton seemed to think so. Said he was going to get them appraised. I think he got them from an auction at Harmony Hall in St Mary. Seemed to think the auctioneer was mistaken over the true value." She rubbed her throat. "I'll probably never find out now."

"Ye'll have tae give us a full description of them," suggested Harris. "And if ye have any photos that would be good."

"What about cash?" asked Preddy.

Oleta gestured with her head. "His wallet and watch are over there."

Preddy moved to where Oleta had indicated; a huge mahogany desk with a laptop computer which was covered in newspapers, documents and files. Partially hidden by a plant pot was an expensive looking watch lying beside a black leather wallet which was thick with credit cards and cash. He flicked through the wallet, noting that it contained a few hundred Jamaican dollars which bought nothing, and plenty of US dollars which bought a lot; as well as two credit cards which bought peace of mind. The watch was a designer brand, but as with most watches these days it was almost impossible to tell the fake from the real.

"He was a smoker," stated Preddy, glancing at an opened box of cigarettes balanced on a folder. "Do you smoke, Mrs Wrenn?"

She shook her head. "Never touch the things. Hated that Ever did."

"I understand," said Preddy. "I see a cigarette butt and some ash on de verandah. No ashtray?"

"Should be there," replied Oleta. She looked beyond Preddy and pointed. "See that pot on the shelf? Please take it down for me." Preddy lifted down a decorative vase and peered inside as he handed it to her. She pulled out the contents. "Petty cash, Detective . . . just a few thousand dollars, but it's all here."

"Didn't take much," said Spence as she glanced at the blue bills with former Prime Minister Michael Manley on one side and Jamaica House on the other.

"Came here for one purpose," said Preddy slowly, "not to steal."

Nine months had passed since Preddy's last high-profile murder case, which resulted in the incarceration of one of the city's most prominent residents, Lester Chin Ellis, as well as a former Pelican Walk police officer. The many cases since then had attracted little media attention except as worryingly growing crime statistics. Some victims remained unidentified. Some were named yet unclaimed by relatives who had had enough of their kins' misdeeds or could not afford to bury them anyway. Just last week the Jamaica Constabulary Force's media communications unit had issued a plea to the family of a deceased gunman to come collect his body from a funeral home. No one responded to the appeal. Living in Jamaica was expensive for ordinary people. Dying even more so. Nobody was willing to take on any additional expenses if they were not obliged to.

Preddy preferred to conduct investigations out of the spotlight and he worried about the level of scrutiny that would once again fall on Pelican Walk. Voices urging the government to declare a state of emergency were already growing louder like a rumbling earthquake. People desperately wanted to see violent crime retreat to tolerable levels and were pushing for soldiers and police to be given temporary control. The detective was thoroughly against the idea which he saw as equivalent to admitting that the criminals were winning. He was convinced that crime could be controlled with smart policing: seizing the guns, imposing mandatory fifteen-year sentences on those found with illegal firearms, monitoring shipments, installing more CCTV cameras in strategic areas, filtering out the rogue cops and gaining the co-operation of a suspicious public. And parents, he thought, needed to get a grip on their children, guide them the right way, know where they were, the friends they were keeping. Too many parents expected their children's teachers to do their jobs for them, and turned a blind eye when their offspring were fraternising with undesirables and lingering on the streets.

Oleta shivered involuntarily. "I can't believe I was upstairs in bed with the patio doors wide open all night. The murderers could have come up for me too."

"Yer husband sent down a lot of bad people, Mrs Wrenn. Do ye know if any of them ever threatened him?" asked Harris. Ginger hairs protruded from the Scotsman's face as if he had missed an appointment with a razor blade, and he rubbed them self-consciously. The early morning phone call had caught him off guard and his stop in the bathroom was too brief.

Oleta shook her head. "He never showed any fear of any of the criminals he put away. I wanted him to do only commercial and civil cases, but he wasn't interested in those. When I asked him about the danger, he just said it was his vocation and someone had to do it. He was of the opinion that good must triumph over evil no matter what." She wrung her hands as she spoke. "He wasn't interested in the idea of bodyguards, but he wasn't a careless man. There were places he wouldn't drive to or through, and he changed his routes quite often. Or rather, Tuffy did."

"Who name Tuffy?" asked Preddy.

"He's sort of a part-time driver," said Oleta. "I'm not keen on driving, although I can. Ever didn't like to drive either. He preferred to do his paperwork while in the car so he hired a driver." She hesitated before adding, "you may as well know, detectives, Tuffy is an ex-convict. Had a long stint in prison too. Everton wanted to give him a second chance. My husband believed in second chances. More than me."

"Real name?" asked Harris, pen poised over his well-worn notebook.

"Antwon Frazer. A-N-T-W-O-N. He's been working with us for around a year now. Takes Ever wherever he needs to go. I don't use him so often."

"Where can we find Mr Frazer?" asked Preddy.

Oleta glanced up at the silver clock on the wall. "He has our car. He doesn't know about the murder so I would expect him to turn up at around nine-fifteen as usual to take Ever to work."

Preddy raised an eyebrow. "Maybe he knows more dan you think."

Oleta frowned and seemed confused. She placed her hand on her chest. "You think he could have something to do with it? Tuffy? After all my husband did for him? After

10

we treated him like family. Family is everything to me. Everything." Suddenly the tears that had been so noticeably absent began to cascade down Oleta's cheeks. Once they had started there seemed to be no stopping them.

Rabino hugged the lady's shoulders. "You let it all out, Mrs Wrenn," urged Rabino. "I know this is very hard for you, but we have to get as much information as possible as quickly as possible."

Oleta sniffed and patted the detective's hand. "You remind me of my baby girl, Maria," she said. "She's devastated."

Rabino pressed a packet of hand tissues into the widow's shaking palms. Oleta removed one with difficulty and dabbed at her eyes. She clutched the packet tightly as if it gave her strength.

Preddy did not believe such hands could ever close around a man's throat. In his experience it was unheard of for Jamaican stranglers to be female. Women tended to stab their victims. "We need Tuffy's phone number and address," he said.

"Yes, sure." She rose, helped by Rabino, and moved into the adjoining sitting room. "Tuffy has never been late though. He's usually well early . . . like all half hour and just sits outside in the car listening to music. If I notice him, I bring him a cup of mint tea."

Mint tea. It could hardly wake anyone up let alone put a pep in the step, thought Preddy. The drink for that was ganja tea. He could still feel the energising benefits of that infusion tingling through his body.

Oleta retrieved her phone from the mantelpiece and read the phone number out loud. "He lives in the Ancona area, but I don't know his actual address. He's said before that it only takes him about twenty minutes to get from Ancona to Wynterton Park, so we could always call him at short notice."

"We'll give Tuffy a while to turn up," said Preddy. "If him don't come we'll go look for him."

Preddy watched as the crime scene officers went about their work swabbing items of furniture. The chance of finding fingerprints anywhere was slim, but he hoped for some

DNA. It would be nice if the cigarette butt could be linked to an identifiable third party. He could see nothing that the murderer would have needed to touch in order to get to the judge. The verandah was completely open access with no external iron grill. The sole security grill was on the inside of the solid wooden door which opened onto the verandah and both had been left wide open last night.

Nine-thirty came and went with no sign of Tuffy Frazer. Detective Spence glanced at her watch impatiently. She then keyed on her phone before placing it close to her ear. The phone rang unanswered. She tried again with the same result. "What car Tuffy driving and what is de registration?"

Oleta rubbed her brow. "It's a red Toyota Camry. I can't even remember the plate number. My brain is gone, Detective. See some documents for it leaning up on the bookshelf."

Spence moved towards the bookshelf. "You want me go look for Tuffy, sir?"

"Good idea," said Preddy. "Reel him in."

"I'll go with her." Rabino gave Oleta a comforting pat on the shoulder. "If you need anything, just call."

"Thank you, Detective."

"De press will be climbing de gates by now, " warned Preddy. "We can confirm dat Judge Wrenn is deceased, nothing else at de moment. No cause of death, nothing."

"Yes, sir," Rabino nodded.

Oleta Wrenn rose as Rabino and Spence left. She headed towards the kitchen. "I am forgetting my manners, officers. Can I get either of you gentlemen a cup of tea? I have mint, ginger or moringa?"

"Naw for me, thank ye," said Harris.

"Don't trouble yourself, Mrs Wrenn. I'm fine, too," said Preddy, following behind her.

She beckoned towards the Scotsman. "Come away from the window, Detective Harris. The sun is getting hot over there and the air con isn't working. It can't be good for you."

Harris shuffled forwards with an embarrassed smile. "I'll survive, thank ye."

Preddy felt his pain. No matter where they went people always expressed concern over the imagined fragility of the pale white man who could not tan brown, and instead acquired various shades of red and pink. "What time you last see your husband?" asked Preddy.

"Must have been around eight o'clock. I asked him if he was coming in and he said he soon would. I went upstairs and was laying on the bed watching TV . . . CVM news. I must have dozed off because when I next looked at the clock it was just gone ten."

"And no sign of him?" asked Preddy.

"No. I went to the top of the stairs and shouted down to him. Told him to come in and lock up. He just said 'coming' and that was it. I turned off the main light over the bed, but left on the bedside lamp on his side, then went to sleep." Oleta took a deep breath. "I woke up around six and realised he wasn't beside me. At first I thought he must be in the bathroom, but I couldn't hear anything. I went downstairs. That's when . . ." Her speech was briefly halted by sudden tears but she continued, "that's when I saw him."

"Never got de chance to defend himself," said Preddy. "Him have a gun?"

"Yes. It's still there. Look in his desk drawer."

Beside Judge Wrenn's desk were many shelves full of well-used legal tomes, cases and statutes, and journals. Preddy flicked a glance at them as he headed towards the desk. He opened the top drawer which slid out easily. A gun was partially concealed under a mass of papers.

Preddy looked at Harris. "9mm Beretta," he stated.

Harris nodded. "Pity the judge couldnae get tae it."

"It is licensed, Detective," said Oleta peering around his broad shoulders. She cradled her mug, seeming to gain comfort from inhaling the hot minty aroma.

"I don't doubt it," said Preddy, and closed the drawer. "Did your husband ever suggest he was being followed or watched by anybody?"

She shook her head. "He wouldn't worry me with such things. He confided most things in Lawrence. The two of them live like brothers, tell each other everything. Oh God! I have to tell Lawrence."

"Lawrence?" repeated Harris.

"Lawrence Guthrie. My husband's best friend. He's also a judge," she sipped her tea.

"I've heard dat name before, but I can't picture de man," said Preddy.

"They went to UWI together and then to Norman Manley Law School before Lawrence went abroad for a few years. Must be a good forty years since they've been friends, from before I even knew Ever. They have their little arguments from time to time, mainly about points of law. Sometimes it's funny to listen to them." She stopped rambling and stared off into the distance.

Preddy walked into her line of vision causing her to blink as she refocused. "We going need to talk to Lawrence Guthrie, Mrs Wrenn. Phone number?"

"He'll be heading to work at the Parish Court," she said before reciting his telephone number. "You may not get a chance to speak to him if he's on the bench. Can I call him first, Detective? I want the news to come from me."

"Yes, go ahead, although I expect de news has travelled and reach him already," said Preddy.

"Did ye or Judge Wrenn have any disputes with any of yer neighbours?" asked Harris.

She shook her head. "No. Everybody in Wynterton is friendly. Not necessarily, stop-and-chat friendly, but you know, 'how are you?' sort of friendly. The only time I've even seen any inkling of fuss between the neighbours was when a foreign man two doors up painted his house a greenish colour which is against the strata board rules. All of the houses must be white, yellow or beige . . . pastel like. Inside we can do whatever we want, not outside."

Preddy noted that these were pretty much the rules at his own Ironshore apartment complex. The outside walls were so sacrosanct that a poster of a missing pet rabbit was shredded in less than a day by the zealous property manager. "Was your husband on de Wynterton board?" he asked.

"No, we're represented by eight homeowners, including a property manager. The management repainted the house white in foreign man's absence. The man did curse and carry on when he returned, and Ever had to go try quieten him down. He threatened to sue the board, but he never did. No point really, because we have a written set of bylaws and he broke them." She screwed up her eyes deep in thought. "Other than that I don't know of any time my husband has raised his voice with anybody here."

"Is there a possibility he would've had a fight with a neighbour and naw told ye?" asked Harris. "Ye did say he didnae like tae worry ye?"

"I guess so." Oleta stared at Harris, visibly irritated and gripped her cup. "No neighbour murdered my husband, Detective. It's one of those low-life criminals he put away that did it for revenge, I can feel it in my bones. I don't know if people in your country murder their next-door neighbours in the middle of the night, but we don't do it in Jamaica."

Preddy was surprised at the strength in her voice. Maybe the mint tea was more efficient than had proved to be his experience. She was wrong though, he thought. Maybe she was fronting false pride or didn't want to believe that whether in Jamaica or elsewhere neighbours would indeed murder neighbours in the middle of the night, even in broad daylight if the urge took them.

She caught him studying her. "I'm sorry to sound so angry, detectives, but our children, Maria and Martin are abroad and not taking the news well. Their father is gone. Our family is destroyed and I'm here alone. My whole life has been turned upside down overnight."

"Dinnae apologise," said Harris, with a wave of his hand. "This must be terribly hard for ye." He glanced back towards the judge's desk. "Do ye mind if we take yer husband's laptop? Might have some useful information."

"Take it, man, take it," she said. "He didn't really use it that much."

"We going do everything possible to find out who did dis," Preddy sought to assure her.

Oleta nodded. "Thank you, Detective. I promise you if anybody in particular comes to mind I'll let you know, immediately. Right now, I just can't think of anything that will help you. Please get the man who murdered Everton off the street detectives, before he murders again."

CHAPTER 2

Tuesday, 2 May, 10.20 a.m.

The Western Regional Gun Court formed part of the St James Parish Court on Meagre Bay Road close to the Montego Bay coastline. For a courthouse it was not much to look at: a bland, two-storey, flat-roofed property taking up a large part of the road, but the surrounding blue sea did help somewhat.

Only two other buildings occupied the short street. Next door was the city's main Post Office, a garish salmon pink building where residents queued in long lines for everything from letters to pension payouts. In this venerable institution all records were still made using pen, paper and carbon since nothing was computerised. Immediately opposite the court were the extensive well-kept grounds of the St James Parish Library. Although short, the road still managed to be one of the busiest thoroughfares for pedestrian and vehicular traffic. Meagre Bay was once the setting for Jamaica's first squatters' camp and scene of the very first civilian uprising. It was still a place of unseemly behaviour where motorists and law enforcement alike, unable to find parking space at the rear of the court house, or in the designated spaces immediately in front of it, parked on the adjacent pavements. Frustrated pedestrians were forced to abandon the pavements and brave the swerving vehicles on the potholed roadway.

A newspaper vendor sat on an empty beer crate outside the Post Office with a stack of sunburnt local and national newspapers. Beside her sat a woman selling colourful, stale-looking sweets from a range of cloudy glass jars. A heavily pregnant stray dog lay metres from her feet. It would soon move on when the nearby fast-food outlets began serving lunch and customers began disposing of well-seasoned bones.

Preddy's vehicle mounted the uneven pavement and he gave an apologetic smile to a female pedestrian who glared daggers at him as she was forced to manoeuvre her voluptuous frame around his vehicle. Through the rear-view mirror he watched her swaying figure for a few seconds and once she had breached cursing distance he shut off the engine. He was here on serious business and did not fancy a showdown with anyone, particularly when he was clearly in the wrong.

More than the usual number of people seemed to be mingling outside of the courthouse. It opened to the public at 10 a.m. and most people, whether witnesses or parties to the cases, would shelter inside from the sun, waiting for their names to be called. Many were inappropriately dressed in bright clothes as if going to a party rather than into a sombre setting. People with no court matters lurked in the vicinity because they had nothing better to do, no jobs to go to. Although hot and busy, it had become a place of sociable convenience where people could amass to discuss the ills of the world when there was no computer or nobody at home.

As Preddy approached the building, the blurred faces began to take shape. He recognized a few of them as court staff, mainly long-serving clerks, also two parish judges. Voices were raised, accompanied by a lot of gesticulating. Soon it was clear that the topic of animated discussion was the murder of Judge Everton Wrenn.

"We are going to shut down this place!" insisted one of the judges. "We are not going work like this. It is foolishness!"

"We have no protection," his nodding colleague added. "The justice minister has to do something before we're all murdered. If not, we'll just have to stay away from court business."

"Dat's right!" proclaimed a woman in a floral mini-skirt two sizes too small for her. "Crime outta control. Dem a murder every one a we, old naigger and judge alike. Dem no business. Dem no care!"

"We fi block dis road!" said an under-dressed man beside her. He clutched at the waistband of his shorts with one hand while waving a clenched fist in the air. "Lock down Meagre Bay Road and mek Police Commissioner come open it up back, if him bad!"

Preddy frowned and raised himself to his full height, which was way over six feet. He towered over the speaker. "Nobody not blocking any road round here, sir."

The man spun around and faced the detective. "Ah who you?"

"Police officer." Preddy flashed his badge. "And if you put you finger near me face again I going break you hand."

The man quickly took two steps back. "Sorry, officer. Me never did a go box you. Me just vex, you know? We cyah take de murder every day so!"

"Neither can we," said Preddy. "Talk what you know instead of blocking road. De doors of Pelican Walk are always open."

The opinionated woman stared hard at Preddy. "Pelican Walk? But no dis man shoot up and kill off de bwoy dem a Norwood?" she declared. "No him name Raythan Preddy? Dat's why him quick to wah bruk you han'. Mek me tek 'way meself from hereso, cause me know wha' him will do!" She beat a hasty retreat down the road, followed by the potential road blocker.

Preddy shook his head as he stared after them. Road blocking was the in thing. Since disgruntled locals had learned that stacking old tyres, rusty fridges and broken chairs in the road was a sure-fire way of getting their concerns aired on television news, it had become an epidemic.

"Detective Preddy? I'm Judge Bailey."

Preddy turned to face the speaker, a short grey-haired man in a black suit.

"Hello, sir."

"This is serious, Detective." The man shook his head as he spoke. "I'm going to speak to my colleagues. We will not block roads, but I can assure you that we can get the judicial system to grind to a halt from here to Kingston if nobody will pay attention to our cries."

Preddy had recognized the judge even though he had not remembered his name. The relationship between the police and the judiciary had been fraught from as far back as Preddy could remember. To him the judges were quite similar: powerful people who were quick to chide the officers for shoddy police work and lack of satisfactory evidence. These same officials would allow court cases with irrefutably strong evidence to drag on for up to ten years. Meanwhile the perpetrators were set free on bail. Free to commit further atrocities which inevitably they would.

Preddy inhaled and said, "I hear you, sir. De murder investigation has just begun and believe me it is our priority. If you know anything or hear anything please call me any time, day or night." Preddy handed the man his business card.

"I'll take one." The other judge reached out for a card too. "Sad to say, but if Jamaica was still the white man's island all this couldn't be happening."

"Ah whe you ah talk 'bout?" asked a vendor woman staring at him indignantly. "Den people nah get murder a foreign too? White man ah murder white man ah foreign every God day! Dem more wicked dan we!"

"But dem ketch more murderer a foreign," said another dissatisfied spectator. "Jamaica police cyah do nutten! And some a dem police corrupt too! Dem need fi weed dem out. Bring in some man from foreign who noinna Jamaica police clique. Make de foreign man dem sort out de murderer dem."

Preddy cut off the interloper with a deathly glance. The man quickly lowered his eyes. Although it was well known that the clear-up rate for murders on the island was hovering around fifty percent, Preddy was not in the mood for any comparison with wealthy nations. Clearing out the bad apples in the JCF was a good idea. The brass just needed to find the will to start that process and to date it seemed like no one was even looking for the rotting apples, while the bruised ones decayed at pace. Bringing in men from abroad to sort out the JCF was a refrain he was tired of hearing.

The presence of Detective Harris might have been useful at this very moment, but Harris was busy inspecting Judge Wrenn's laptop back at Pelican Walk. The sight of Harris would surely help reduce the judges' ire and encourage their co-operation, yet foreigners were not going to solve the country's problems and yearning for the return of the white man was a fallacy in itself.

"I would urge you to go back into court, sirs," Preddy pleaded. "De parish needs you and you must know dat."

The judges mumbled to each other but did not move.

"If you'll excuse me, gentlemen." Preddy bowed in frustration and bounded up the stone steps where he entered the drab grey lobby. To the left were bored customers sitting and waiting to be seen at the civil claims counter. Here they could file claims or make enquiries about doing so. Each person held a numbered pink ticket and waited for their number to light up and buzz on an overhead screen. The clerks behind the counter seemed absorbed in their own discussions. The overhead ticket display remained rigidly fixed on number one. For the waiting civilians it would be a long day.

"Dey're expecting me upstairs," said Preddy as he was waved through the metal detector by the female officer who stood guard. "Court going hold today?"

The woman shrugged. "Not sure if any session start, sir. Only a couple of judges upstairs. Some came in and went right back outside."

Preddy was met on the second floor by Judge Wrenn's distraught clerk. She was a tiny dark female in an oversized trouser-suit and towering heels. Her once perfectly made up face was spoiled by streaks of mascara-stained tears. She opened the door to the Judge Wrenn's chambers and allowed Preddy to precede her.

"Thank you for your assistance," said Preddy gently. "I know today going hard for all of you."

She nodded and dabbed the corner of her eye. "That black book is his court diary. It goes back about a year. The upcoming cases are in there too."

"Thank you."

Preddy sat at the judge's cluttered desk and waded through the roster of past and upcoming cases. Some of the names rang a bell, others did not. All of these cases had to do with guns, and yet the judge's murder was not perpetrated with a gun. Maybe the killer wished to prove to Judge Wrenn that guns were not the only way to remedy a prickly problem. Preddy raised his eyes towards the clerk. "Can I get copies, please?"

The woman tucked her tissue into her shirt sleeve, took the papers from him and left. Preddy poked around the remaining paperwork on the untidy desk checking the scrawl on multiple Post-it notes. The main bin beneath it was empty. A recycling bin beside it contained a heap of carefully sorted empty plastic cups and plastic bottles. Family photos were all over the walls and desk. In one, the judge posed with Oleta and their son and daughter, two good-looking grown-up children. There was a large framed picture in which a whole host of judges were assembled, glasses raised, celebrating something momentous. Another, a graduation picture from university days, showed a much younger Everton Wrenn and his ambitious classmates. He was much slimmer then with a firm waistline and no wrinkles.

Certificates of his many achievements were proudly displayed in a cabinet behind glass, together with debating trophies. All around was clear evidence of the judge's successful career, leaving no doubt in the minds of anyone who entered his chambers that this man had reached a great height. The female clerk duly returned and handed the bundle of warm photocopied pages to the detective.

"Thanks. Is Judge Lawrence Guthrie here?" asked Preddy.

"He's in session at the moment, sir. His courtroom is way on the other side of the building," she replied. "Judge Bailey is just about to start too."

"Okay. Judge Guthrie is who I really wanted to see." Preddy tucked the papers under his arm. It surprised him that Judge Wrenn's best friend was capable of holding court on such a tragic day. "Please have him call me."

"Judge Wrenn was a really nice man," she whispered.

"So I hear," replied Preddy. "Some people he jailed might not think so though. You know if he ever mentioned anybody who might want to see him dead?"

"No, sir." She shook her head emphatically. "You never know either, Jamaica is getting to be a strange place. Some people want to murder you if you don't let them jump the queue in front of you."

"Call me if you think of anything else I need to know. Or if you overhear any conversations you think would help us, pick up de phone."

"I will, Detective. You have to catch the murderer." She forced a tiny smile. "Heng him rass!"

* * *

Preddy sat in Superintendent Brownlow's office listening to one side of a conversation. It was unusual for the superintendent to beckon him in when he was on the phone, so Preddy knew it was a conversation he was meant to hear and more than likely was about his major case. From past experience, this had rarely proved good for Preddy. The detective popped a mint into his mouth and gazed at the certificates and plaques behind his superior while trying to figure the conversation. The superintendent carefully placed the phone in the receiver and clenched his fists. Preddy said nothing as he watched him. Let the super speak first when he was in a bad mood.

Superintendent Brownlow stood and began pacing the floor with his hands behind his back which caused his shirt

23

buttons to strain. His ample jowls wobbled as he pursed his lips. Tiny beads of sweat appeared on his forehead despite the quietly oscillating desk fan. "Just when I think we're about to see a change in course, something happens," he spat bitterly. "Judge Wrenn's murder has really kicked off a fire storm. Commissioner Davis is coming under attack, and you know that if he gets hit with a fist I get hit with a sledgehammer."

Preddy crunched on his mint at an inappropriate time and the superintendent gave him a sharp look. Mints had never sounded so loud before, but then they were never crunched in such sudden silence before. The detective regretted picking up the sweet but he had drained a much-needed flask of ganja tea before venturing in to report to his boss and it was important to disguise the odour.

"I've put you in charge of this one because you're the best person for the job Preddy. You know the way the murderers work better than anyone else at Pelican Walk. Make no mistake about it this cannot become a cold case. We need results and we need them now!"

"I understand, sir," said Preddy, painfully swallowing the remains of the crushed mint. "Rabino, Spence and Harris are working closely wid me on dis."

"You know the judges are threatening to strike?" stated the superintendent as he paced . "Can you imagine, civil disobedience from those meant to enforce law and order? It would be just the signal the criminals are looking for to run amok."

"I think de idea is to get de Minister of Justice to improve deir working conditions." Preddy wished he could retract his words almost as soon as they had left his lips.

The superintendent wheeled round and eyeballed his detective. "You think I don't know what their intention is? Well, Detective, you better ensure that there are no demonstrations and no civil disobedience by catching the judge's killer fast, hadn't you?"

"Yes, sir. Priority number one."

"Good." The superintendent appeared to calm down. "It's not that I don't sympathise with the judiciary. I do."

"We need more resources, sir," said Preddy carefully. "More officers, more CCTV throughout the parish, better weapons. Look from when we were promised more staff and not a thing. It's like de old saying. We're being 'given basket to carry water'."

The superintendent sighed. "I know, man. I know. Maybe Judge Wrenn's murder will be the catalyst we need, but nothing is going to happen overnight. The killer needs to be caught fast."

"We're on it, sir," Preddy assured him. "We're not going to let up until we find who did dis."

"Fine." The superintendent moseyed over to the window and stood staring out towards the distant blue coastline. "Send Detective Harris in to see me."

Preddy slowly rose to his feet wishing he could see Browlow's face. "Detective Harris, sir? Him gone out to buy mosquito spray."

"Oh." The superintendent still did not turn around.

Preddy eyed the rolls of flesh on his boss's neck, which reminded him of bread dough. "You sure you don't want me to give him a message?"

"Yes, I'm quite sure, Detective." The superintendent bristled and turned to stare at his inquisitor.

Preddy decided to face down the wrath. "Sir, is it something do wid my case, er . . . our case?"

"Lord, Raythan man!" The superintendent flopped down in his chair and thumped the table. "No, it has nothing to do with this case. And it has nothing to do with you."

"Yes, sir. I mean, no, sir."

"What's wrong with you?"

Preddy chose his words carefully. "I just thought dat maybe you forgot what we agreed, sir."

"I didn't forget a damn thing," snapped the superintendent. "At no point will Detective Harris be given any information that has not first been shared with you."

"Sorry, sir."

Preddy gave a short bow as he left the superintendent's office, frowning. Detective Harris's swift return from Glasgow

25

had taken Preddy completely by surprise having imagined he had gone for good last summer. The Scotsman had been packed off with his wooden Rastaman head, many tins of Blue Mountain coffee and a good quantity of white rum, and that was supposedly the end of that. Two months later he was back and seemingly keen on serving at Pelican Walk instead of seeking a top posting elsewhere on the island. Harris had hinted that there were marital issues at home, but refused to be drawn on the subject other than to discuss his three bairns, all teenagers, who he clearly missed. Preddy had to admit that the foreigner was a good detective who coped well with the scarcity of tools for modern policing. It still unnerved him that Harris had a direct line of access to the superintendent, even though Brownlow had sworn that Harris would never be put in charge again. That promise had allegedly been rubber-stamped by Commissioner Davis, yet Preddy would never forget last year's stitch-up with the Chin Ellis case. The brass just couldn't help themselves sometimes when it came to foreigners, leaving Preddy unsure of whether he could ever totally trust Harris. He had never met a foreigner without an agenda and he expected no difference with Sean Harris.

Preddy returned to his own office, closed the door and pulled the blinds down blocking the view of any passersby. He punched a button on his CD player and the air was instantly filled with the calming sound of leaves rustling in the wind. This would last for fifteen minutes followed by a track of a babbling stream, transporting him into deep thinking mode. He stared at the mound of photocopied pages on his desk. So far the evidence relating to Judge Wrenn's murder was sparse. A longlist of some of St James's most notorious criminals was as good a place to start as any. Spence and Rabino would help to narrow the list down, and maybe Officer Timmins could help. In reality he could do with a dozen officers for the task, but Pelican Walk's resources were, as usual, already stretched thin. Footsteps echoed along the corridor. Preddy hoped that they would keep going. He ignored the first somewhat timid knock on the door. He answered irritably to the second.

"Come."

"A gentleman downstairs in reception demanding to speak to you sir," said the secretary, pushing the door slightly ajar.

"I'm well-busy at de moment, him going have a long wait," snapped Preddy. "Dis is a mad morning, what wid Judge Wrenn's murder."

"Well, he says he wants to know what you're doing about that same murder. Says he's Judge Lawrence Guthrie."

Preddy lowered the pages. "I'll be right down. Oh, and see if Detective Harris has finished fighting de mosquitoes for me."

* * *

Preddy recognized the visitor as one of the young men in Judge Wrenn's graduation photos. Much older now, Lawrence Guthrie was tall and light-skinned with a strong build. He rose as Preddy and Harris entered the meeting room and immediately held out his hand.

"Detective Preddy? I'm Lawrence Guthrie, Judge Lawrence Guthrie."

The man's voice was as powerful as his handshake, Preddy noted. "Pleased to meet you Judge Guthrie. Dis is my colleague, Detective Harris."

Harris nodded. "Judge Guthrie."

"Lawrence, please." The judge shook Harris's hand energetically.

"Oleta told me what happened. I'm devastated, detectives. Everton and Oleta are the nicest couple I know. He was a very great man. The best man I have ever known." His words came in a torrent and his clipped English accent indicated that he had spent many years abroad. "I heard you were asking for me at court. I just had to come and see you. Please let me know if there is anything I can do."

"Thank ye Lawrence, have a seat," said Harris pointing to one of the four chairs arranged around a scratched wooden table.

Preddy watched as the judge lowered his statuesque frame onto the plastic seat.

"You have to catch the murderer, detectives, you have to," insisted the judge.

"Dat is certainly our intention, Lawrence," said Preddy. "Did Judge Wrenn have any known enemies?"

"I've been thinking about that all the way here, Detective." Lawrence clutched his large hands together and leaned forward earnestly. "We have to encounter some very nasty individuals on a daily basis. The work of a judge is very dangerous."

"Very dangerous?" repeated Harris.

"Yes. And I do mean that." Judge Guthrie stared at him with a pleasant expression. "You're from Scotland, Detective Harris? I did some of my post-graduate training in Scotland, way back when . . . at Edinburgh University. Did a year at the School of Divinity. Great place. Not really where I wanted to go though. I wanted St. Andrews."

"Och, Glasgow suited me fine," replied Harris politely.

"Ah! Not as prestigious as Edinburgh or Andrews," Lawrence warmed to his topic, "though I guess you did manage to churn out a couple of prime ministers so it must have had some things going for it."

"Och, I daresay Edinburgh and Andrews have churned out their fair share of pricks too," said Harris with an easy smile.

Lawrence chuckled. "Quite so."

Preddy glanced from one man to the other. He had a feeling that Lawrence was also one of those judges who would favour foreign policing so, for now, Preddy was content to let Harris do the bonding.

"I understand that my name originated in Scotland and I believe it, based on history," Lawrence gave a wide smile. "Got my complexion from the sixteenth century Scots who landed in St Elizabeth, no doubt. Sex starved men chasing the locals about."

"Maybe naw something tae tell the grandkids about, Lawrence," said Harris warmly.

"I guess not," Lawrence leaned back in his chair and crossed one leg over the other. "So what is Scotland like nowadays, Detective?"

"Still cold," replied Harris, "which is one of the reasons why I'm happy tae be here. I only wish the circumstances were more pleasant."

"Indeed." The judge nodded soberly.

The anxieties of the superintendent burned in Preddy's mind and he asked, "Did Judge Wrenn express any fears or concerns about any of de cases he was involved wid, upcoming cases or past ones?"

"No, not really." Lawrence looked thoughtful. "Everton wasn't a fearful sort of man, never has been. As far as he was concerned he had a job to do and he was going to do it well. It wasn't that he wasn't aware of the need for personal safety. He has a licensed firearm for protection, most of us do. There are many people that could have wanted Ever dead, because judges and lawyers are just not popular people."

"They should try operating on the front line," mumbled Harris.

"You last saw him, when?" asked Preddy.

"Yesterday afternoon. We had lunch at Mosino . . . down Catherine Hall, then we went our separate ways. He was in good spirits throughout, arguing his case forcefully as usual." Lawrence's jovial features disintegrated into a frown. "I still can't believe that mere hours later he was murdered."

Preddy stared at the judge's firm hands. "Arguing about what?"

"Oh not that type of argument, Detective." Lawrence held up the palm of his hand as if to shield away an accusation. "Just about the law and human rights. Those sorts of things. He and I agreed to disagree on numerous things."

"Where were you last night?" asked Preddy.

Lawrence looked astounded then laughed. "You mean I have to provide an alibi?" He waited, then looked towards Harris for reassurance. As neither of the detectives smiled nor spoke he continued. "Okay, so I have a girlfriend, detectives.

I'm not proud of it. My wife still lives in St Elizabeth, you see. I go home most evenings, but occasionally because of work I stay in Mo Bay overnight, with Jacqui. After I finished dining with her, on the Houseboat Grill, I dropped her off then went back to the Ambassador West Hotel alone around 11 p.m. The concierge saw me, by the way." He paused and stared into the air. "Let's see, I read a book, *Brothers in Blood*, great Asian crime tale, then went to sleep."

"In bed, alone," said Preddy, watching Lawrence's twinkling hazel eyes. The twinkling had begun when he stated he was not proud of cheating.

"Alone. It may be said I lack morals, detectives, but I'm not a murderer."

"Forgive us," said Harris. "Only in the movies do people straight off say 'I did it.'"

Lawrence took a small diary from his trouser pocket, tore out a blank page, wrote on it and handed it to Preddy. "I'm going to save you some trouble. Jacqui's phone number."

"Thanks." Preddy glanced at it before placing it in his notebook. The morals of the judiciary were not his concern, but there was just something about Lawrence Guthrie. He oozed over-confidence as if he was the smart one and the detectives were amateurs. Until his alibi was corroborated, the man would have to be a suspect, friend or no friend. "You ever see anyone threaten Judge Wrenn?" asked Preddy.

Lawrence leaned his head to one side and considered this for a moment. "Not a serious threat really."

"We'll decide if it's serious or naw," said Harris.

The judge nodded. "Sometimes after cases when defendants hear the sentences they'll shout out things in frustration or anger. You know . . . 'You fi dead!'" Judge Guthrie's Patois sounded strangely affected to Preddy's ears. Even Harris's attempted Patois sounded way better. "Everton got that sort of thing from time to time over the years, but as far as I know no one ever tried to attack him." The judge sat back in his chair. "Even in my court I get threatened sometimes with similar words and my cases are purely civil."

"Oh, you don't do criminal cases?" asked Preddy.

"No, Detective. I do sometimes work out of the court rooms that hold criminal trials, but on mainly debt disputes. Still highly contentious though. You know, landlord and tenant matters, overdue debts, that sort of thing."

"Sounds really dangerous," said Harris.

Something resembling annoyance flickered across Judge Guthrie's face. "You'd be surprised at how violent people can be when it comes to money and property matters, Detective Harris."

Preddy studied the judge. His stature did not reflect that of a man who did small cases at all. Judge Guthrie was quite overbearing. The way he had taken control of the meeting suggested a man of inflated power used to dealing with complex matters and being in charge.

"Thank you for coming in Lawrence." Preddy got to his feet. "Call us if anything springs to mind. Even if you don't think it's important, we want to know."

"I will, Detective," replied the judge. "And I must ask you to do the same. Everton was my best friend and I'd like to be kept informed of how the case is proceeding."

"We cannae give anyone details of our investigation," said Harris, "naw even judges."

"Of course, I understand," Lawrence nodded. "I'll find my way out."

Preddy closed the door behind the judge.

Harris said quietly, "He doesnae understand. He thinks he's above being treated like a layman."

"A bit pompous dat's for sure, but you'll find dat wid many people in his profession." Preddy stared at Harris. "One would think you two were fraternity brothers de way he chatted to you."

Harris nodded. "Aye, and his friend's just been murdered. He tried tae sound earnest, but what I got from him wasnae compassion at all. It was more like remote fascination."

"Hard to know what to make of him. Some people are not easy to figure out." Preddy moved to open the door. "By de way Super wants to see you. He didn't tell me what it was about." He waited expectantly for his colleague to fill in the blank, but Harris just eased past him and nodded.

"Och, better go make sure all is well."

CHAPTER 3

Tuesday, 2 May, 4.50 p.m.

Ancona district was a place where zinc fences abounded, creating physical divisions in a community already overwhelmed with invisible ones whose roots lay in political allegiances. The metal barriers were relatively easy to move unlike the mental barriers of hopelessness which solidified the idea of no-go zones and exclusive territories. Districts like this emerged from squatter settlements populated by people who over the decades had seized the land and built foundationless homes while renouncing the notion of paying taxes. No real infrastructure existed. All types of waste was disposed of in trenches overgrown with weeds that led to no one knew where or cared. Inevitably the detritus would make its way into the Caribbean Sea polluting the crystal waters. Respective political parties, afraid to dislodge the illegal dwellers for fear of losing all-important votes come election time, continually turned a blind eye to the environmental debacle.

On the opposite side of the city a complete reversal of fortunes. The Spanish, the Americans and the Chinese had plenty of faith in the parish of St James. Multi-million dollar investments continued unabated. Three new all-inclusive hotels, two private health care facilities offering state-of-the-art facilities, and a burgeoning BPO sector. Starbucks and Ashley Furniture Homestore were the city's newest arrivals. Plenty of photo opportunities for desperate vote-seeking politicians and ambitious dignitaries. There were more visitors arriving on the island than at any time before, over four million debarked last year. For the first time ever, Poland was laying on direct flights to Montego Bay, while Germany was increasing its direct flights. Meanwhile the locals just wanted to feel safe within their own homes and relaxed while walking the streets. It was not too much to ask.

As Preddy pulled into the driveway of the Zed Bar a powerful burst of high powered noise hit his ears and his hand instinctively went towards his weapon, his heart palpitating. Within seconds he realised that the noise was a passing car backfiring and not automatic gunfire. He sank back in his seat and wiped his palms on his knees. Gunfire always did this to him. This was the effect of his ill-fated incursion into the volatile Norwood community. He had led his six-man team in search of wanted men deemed responsible for shooting an officer weeks before, and leaving said officer in a persistent vegetative state. The plan had been to surround the house and encourage the men to leave peacefully, but his infuriated officers were unable to contain their rage. Preddy closed his eyes and gripped the steering wheel. He barely remembered the door being kicked off, but he could not forget the bullets flying, the brain matter splattering and the men dropping dead. Three of them, one of whom he held in his arms until his dying breath while blood poured from the gaping wound in his neck.

Preddy took a deep breath and exited the vehicle. The Zed Bar was a single-storey wooden building that had seen better days. Rusty zinc slats hung loosely from the roofing. It was a lair that many police officers would not visit without back-up, fraternised as it was by people with little respect for law enforcement and even less fear of them. Amateur paintings of gunmen adorned the external walls along with slogans of worship to these kings of the bullet whose nicknames announced their trade. Hazard, Lick Shot, Bullet. These were the false idols relied on by the impoverished majority for food, money and protection. Good, hard-working people did live in Ancona. Good people trapped for reasons beyond their control and forced to see, hear and speak no evil.

In front of the bar were two cars in need of extensive bodywork. Preddy wondered if they had been dumped or if the owners still hoped that by some miracle they could be made to function. A motorbike with a missing headlamp was propped against the building and looked heavy enough to bring down the bamboo walls. The third car was an empty red Toyota Camry which stood out because of its good condition. A few feet behind it was an unmarked police car belonging to Detective Spence, whose figure Preddy could just make out in the driver's seat behind her tinted windows. Spence could always be relied on for a stakeout as she enjoyed the thrill of taking down an unsuspecting fugitive by any means necessary.

As Preddy entered the bar Rabino gestured with her chin towards the shaven headed man clad in a string vest sitting in a corner. His complexion was stained an unmistakable purplish pink tint, a clear indication of skin bleaching, and his neck was covered in tattoos. His muscled arms too showed evidence of intentional skin lightening which were the hallmarks of the Benbow Crew.

Preddy walked towards him. "Antwon Frazer? Or you prefer Tuffy?"

The man's eyes widened as he glanced up from his beer.

"I'm Detective Preddy. Mind if I sit down?" Preddy lowered himself without waiting for an answer. In a flash Tuffy Frazer ducked beneath the table and went scrabbling across the floor. The table fell, temporarily hindering Tuffy's flight, but he kicked it off and started running. His speed and agility took Preddy completely by surprise. Preddy leapt to his feet. Rabino, perched on a stool near the doorway, stuck out a jeans-clad leg which Tuffy was unable to dodge.

"Rass woman!" Tuffy sailed through the air and came to rest with half of his body outside of the ramshackle building.

Preddy grabbed the back of his slender neck and hauled the man to his feet.

Tuffy glared at Rabino who returned the look. "Detective Rabino," she said. "Not 'rass woman' or whatever other nasty names are going through your mind."

"Get offa me!" Tuffy struggled unsuccessfully to break away from Preddy.

"Retake your seat, Mr Frazer," warned Preddy pushing him back to his recently deserted spot.

The only other patrons in the bar were two males. Grasping their beer bottles the men silently headed for the exit appearing as nonchalant as possible. The bartender, an elderly-looking man, approached the detectives with a mop, eyeing the spilled beer. He picked up the bottle. "I don't want no trouble, officer. Look how everyting did peaceful. Now it gwine mash up!"

"It will soon be peaceful again, sir," Preddy assured him. "We won't be long." Tuffy was shoved into his seat with a jolt. Preddy picked up the table and pulled it close before sitting down next to him. The bartender finished mopping around the area and retreated to the bar. Rabino took up a seat on the other side of the reluctant interviewee restricting any movement. Tuffy scowled as he looked her up and down. She maintained his gaze unblinkingly.

"Over here. Let's start again," said Preddy clicking his fingers to gain Tuffy's attention. "Detective Preddy, Pelican Walk police."

"I know you is who." Tuffy brushed the dirt from his vest while trying to disguise the repeated heave and fall of his chest.

"And yet you running?" asked Preddy.

"You kill off de man dem a Norwood to blood claat! Of course me run! Wha' you want wid me?"

Preddy had no intention of informing Tuffy that he had not fired a single shot or killed a single soul that fateful day. "Profanity is punishable by a fine. You know dat?"

Tuffy stared at him in confusion. "Wha'?"

"Cussing claat," explained Rabino.

"Sorry, sir, mam," said Tuffy quickly. "You surprise me, man. Me no usually cuss bad wud."

The detective shook his head. "Where have you been? Didn't go to work dis morning. It's like you knew you wouldn't be needed?"

"How you mean?" Tuffy glanced nervously at Rabino. "Lady, don't make dis man shoot me, you know!"

"Shooting people is an unfortunate part of the job, Mr Frazer," stated Rabino coldly, "and it's 'Detective.'"

Preddy placed his hands together and cracked his knuckles. "Make sure your answer is believable Mr Frazer, or . . ." Tuffy drew back from Preddy and his shoulder hit Rabino's, ". . . I'm going to throw you inna lock-up for theft."

"But see here now! Wha' me tief officer?

"A red Camry parked out front," replied Preddy.

"You wrong! A Judge Wrenn car wha' him let me drive, me no tief it!"

"We know whose car it is. And we also know dat you did not go to work dis morning," said Preddy. "You were seen driving in de Wynterton Park area, before we even got dere."

Tuffy's shoulders sagged and he stared at his sandals. "Me did go a work you know. At least, me never turn into de Wynterton gate." He licked dry lips. "Me see whole heap a police car when me get near de entrance, and me stop de newspaper bwoy outside and ask him what happen. Him say dem murder Judge Wrenn. Me say 'bumbo cl . . . !' Oh, sorry officer! Me drive 'way same time."

Rabino eyed him in disbelief. "So a boy told you that someone murdered your employer and your response is to flee? Who does that?"

"Lady, me watch enough TV to know dat me is de first person police gwine come rough up!" retorted Tuffy. "You think me ah eediat?"

"And rather dan get it over wid, you ran?" said Preddy in exasperation. "You know how long we out here looking for you?"

Tuffy's eyes pleaded for understanding. "Me frighten you know, bredda?"

"I'm not your bredda," warned Preddy. "Talk."

The chauffeur shuffled uncomfortably in his seat, annoyed that his personal space was reduced to nothing by the detectives. He could not even spread his legs apart to catch little breeze. "Me don't have nutten to do wid Judge Wrenn murder, officer! Not one ting!"

"You better have a good alibi for last night," said Preddy.

Tuffy pulled a hole-riddled face flannel from his pocket and dabbed his sweating brow. "Me never go back to Wynterton Park after me drop off de judge around five o'clock yestideh evening. Ask your officer dem down a Trojan Street station. Dem see a group of we playing domino outside one shop and haul we up, carry we go station. Dem question we, fi me no know how many hour. Dem say me have outstanding warrant fi traffic violation and carry me a Night Court. Ask dem!"

"We will," promised Rabino. "And God help you if you're lying."

"Jah nah help me. If him did a help me, you wouldn't in here now a squeeze me up so."

"Don't blame anybody else for your behaviour," said Rabino. "We all have choices, Mr Frazer. You made your own."

"Police always a harass people," grumbled Tuffy. "Even woman a get in pon it now. All white man me see pose up inna newspaper, come a Mo Bay fi come run Pelican Walk!"

Preddy tensed. "No white man not running Pelican Walk, whatever you see inna paper."

Tuffy was undeterred and continued, "Bet is a whole bag a money dat white man a get too, and Black man nah get it!"

"You never pay a dollar of tax so don't concern yourself about taxpayers' money," said Preddy.

"Quite," agreed Rabino. "And why are you keeping such close tabs on appointments at Pelican Walk anyway? You planning on joining the JCF?"

Tuffy mopped his brow again. Preddy glanced up at the dilapidated overhead fan whirring noisily above Tuffy's head. "It's not dat hot in here. You have a temperature or something bothering you?"

The fugitive kissed his teeth. "Me no know what you talking 'bout. You jus' a fight 'gainst poor people."

"Don't bother try dat," said Preddy dismissively.

"Lots of poor people are good and honest. We're fighting against criminals," said Rabino. "If they happen to be poor so be it. If they're rich we'll take them down, same way."

Tuffy scowled. "A how you so *Hinglish*, Lady? You a gwaan like you ah no Jamaican like we."

Rabino shook her head. "Jamaican born and bred, but definitely not like you, Mr Frazer. Not at all. And if you don't tell us what we need to know I'm going to show you just how not like you I am." She removed a pair of handcuffs from her trouser pocket and placed them on the table.

Tuffy wiped his damp palms on his vest. "Look Lady, me . . ."

"Detective," Rabino corrected him again. "Don't let me tell you again."

"Detective Lady, gwaan a Trojan Street go talk to dem wicked officer. Dem will tell you! A Night Court me deh last night till late-late."

"Next time you hear your phone ringing answer it," ordered Preddy as he put away his notebook. "Get out of here. Go on, get out."

"Me hear you, boss!"

Rabino turned her knees to the side and allowed the flustered man to exit. She followed him to the door and waved a thumb, a signal to Spence. As Tuffy peeled away in his employer's vehicle Spence fired up her car and set off in his dust.

"Spence is on his tail, sir."

"Good. Dat man knows something," said Preddy. "Innocent people don't run and hide, and dey don't sweat so. It's like him have a timebomb ticking under him shirt." He thought for a moment before adding, "Get Oleta Wrenn pon de phone."

"What's on your mind?"

"Not sure. We need her to formally report de Camry stolen. Tell her not to take any calls from Tuffy. We need to search dat car from top to bottom. Spence better not let it out of her sight."

* * *

Oleta Wrenn was pleased to hear from Detective Rabino. She liked the sound of her sympathetic voice and professional tone, not brash like the other female detective who appeared to be all about business. The police seemed to be making some progress. She had heard tales, some from her own husband, of police neglecting to get on the ball quickly enough. Maybe they had no choice but to act immediately in Everton's case, because the public and the media were outraged at the killing. Added to that they had a Scotsman on board who had publicly stressed his determination to help the parish of St James reduce the alarming murder rate.

Maybe if Everton had not been sitting on the verandah last night he would still be alive. If he had just come indoors and upstairs when she had called him, they would probably have sat and talked at length before falling asleep together. Oleta's eyes filled with tears. If the police did not want her to communicate with Tuffy Frazer they must have good reason. Tuffy was used to spending time in prison. She wanted to believe in prison rehabilitation, but she did not. People who went to jail, particularly hardened criminals, just came out even harder — angry and consumed by revenge. What they didn't learn on the outside they learned on the inside and were thrust back into society eager to show off their newly acquired skills. It seemed Tuffy had nothing to contribute to society. Another long stint would neither do him harm nor set him straight.

She wondered what Everton would make of the knowledge that Tuffy was under investigation for his murder. Would he think his own murderer deserved a second chance?

Would he want revenge? No matter what the outcome of the investigation she knew that Ever was not a vengeful man. She closed her eyes. Theirs had been a good life. Yes, they had their ups and downs like any other couple, but her husband was a good man. She needed him. Their children needed him. The grandchildren to be would need him. He should not be dead.

* * *

Spence followed discreetly as Tuffy drove erratically through the winding potholed roads heading south to the small farming district of Montpelier. The sun was beginning to set at a rapid pace as if racing to get some much-needed rest. Tuffy's neck was leaned at a ninety-degree angle and she could see that he was cushioning the phone perched under his ear. Definitely not the form of driving sanctioned by the road code.

As Tuffy began to slow down Spence switched off her headlights and crawled at a good distance behind him. He turned onto a grass verge and alighted in front of a small half-built house, unpainted, with breeze blocks on show and pieces of steel foundation clearly visible. Some of the windows were boarded up; a few had panes of murky glass. No lights were on. A streetlight bulb remained defiantly intact and blinking, although the protective glass surrounding it had long been shattered. To the untrained eye the house appeared to be uninhabited, but to Spence it was clearly a den of some sort. Nothing good ever happened in these hovels and there were way too many of them spread out all over St James. If she had her way they would all be razed to the ground.

Tuffy closed the car door and moved swiftly towards the house. He rapped on the front door glancing over his shoulder before disappearing indoors. Still the lights did not come on. Spence reached for her phone.

"I don't know how long him going stop for. Get de wrecker here right now," she whispered urgently at the screen. "Yes, Montpelier main road. It getting well-dark, man. Tell dem to make haste."

She hunkered down in her car keeping her eyes peeled for signs of life from the house or the surrounding bushes. Her loaded gun lay on the passenger seat. Montpelier, a relatively quiet leafy area, commanded huge crowds for its famous annual agricultural show, yet you never knew who could be wandering the streets at nightfall. She believed in shooting first whenever no back-up was available and if any criminal challenged her, tonight would be no different. Her husband Mikey and the girls prayed for her to return home safely every day and she intended to keep her promise to do so. When the squad car arrived, Spence was instantly out of her vehicle walking towards them and waving them down. A female alighted with two males behind her.

"Didn't know you were coming, girl." Spence said when she spotted her colleague.

"See, I told you those tarot card readings are a waste of time," replied Rabino. "Pure charlatans."

"Oh ye of little faith," said Spence.

Rabino adjusted a Nikon camera that dangled by its strap from her neck. "Tuffy and I are not quite best friends," she said. "He's going to lose it when he sees two women. Wouldn't miss it for the world."

Spence squinted past her colleague's shoulder. "Is who dat? Oh, Blagrove and Mitchell. How are you gentlemen?"

"A-Okay, madam," said Officer Mitchell with a smile.

"Always at your service," said Officer Blagrove. "The wrecker is just behind us."

The rattling of the tow-truck's engine could be heard in the background. "Okay good," Spence pointed at the Camry. "Dat's de car. Haven't seen any movement inside de house from Tuffy went in. Not sure how many people in dere or what dem doing."

The four officers approached the house quietly. Rabino placed an ear close to the door and shouted, "Antwon Frazer! Police! Come out now."

Behind the door came the instant sound of scrabbling feet. One thing was certain: there was more than one person inside. The sound of splintering glass sent the two male officers running around the side towards the rear of the property. Spence kicked the front door which easily dislodged from its poorly maintained hinges and crashed to the floor. She and Rabino entered, guns drawn. A tiny kerosene lamp flickered in a corner. The odour of marijuana was strong and a grey mist clouded the air. Beer bottles littered the dirt floor. A pack of dog-eared cards lay scattered, some upturned, some face down.

"Antwon Frazer!" shouted Spence.

"Me deh ya, officer! No shoot!" The trembling man rose up from behind an overturned table with his hands above his head.

One of the male officers re-entered through the back door. "Gone deep into de bush. "Couldn't see how many of dem and it dark-dark back dere."

"It's alright," said Rabino. "The person we really want to speak to is right here anyway."

"Whe' you wah speak to me fah? You no jus' speak to me likkle while?" Tuffy stared at Rabino's gun as if he was speaking to it and not to the detective.

"Aren't you de lucky one to have us showing you so much love?" said Spence.

"Me no want no love from no blasted police woman!"

"You hear that noise outside, Tuffy?" asked Rabino. "That's our truck taking the Camry away. Oleta Wrenn reported it stolen."

"A lie dat! An' you know seh a lie!" shouted Tuffy, taking two steps towards Rabino.

"If you come any closer I'll put a bullet through your leg," said Rabino, tapping her weapon against her side.

"And me will give you a matching one," promised Spence.

Tuffy's chest began to heave and fall. "Leave de car! Me a go call Miss Oleta!" He took out his phone, punched the keys desperately and put it to his ear. His face grew more agitated as he failed to connect to Mrs Wrenn. "Dat car is not stolen! Me get permission fi drive it. She never tell me fi bring it back. You a liad!"

"Come we go outside, Mr Frazer," said Spence, waving a hand at the gaping front entrance. "We'll let you pop de trunk."

CHAPTER 4

Wednesday, 3 May, 9.20 a.m.

Preddy brushed at his shoulders and checked his collar for corn crumbs before he walked into the pathologist's cold dimly lit laboratory. He wondered what his children Roman and Annalee would make of his new-found feathered friend when they arrived on the weekend. That is, if the parakeet chose to return. At first it had turned up maybe once a week, but since Sunday it turned up every single morning, sitting on the window ledge staring at him, refusing to budge until he opened the window. Yesterday it had climbed onto his shoulder, its light weight adding nothing to the heavy burden already lodged there, and he fed it corn on the cob while explaining that he had to go to a crime scene.

Doctor Sewell wheeled the gurney towards the detective, her lab coat stretched across her generous figure. She turned on a long-armed lamp causing the law man to blink as his eyes adjusted. She removed the white cloth exposing Judge Wrenn down to the chest and brought the light closer to his face.

Preddy stared at the corpse. He would never feel apathy towards dead bodies. He had seen many of them throughout his career, some riddled with bullets, others chopped up with machetes, and then some like this with barely any marks. Whether they were newly dead and warm, or long dead and cold, the bodies had the same effect on him, leaving him lamenting the loss of life.

The beautiful parish of St James was spawning residents who served no discernible purpose but to cause major stress to law enforcement officers and terrify innocent citizens. Someone had to reach the youths while they were still young enough to be guided. Too many were left to be educated on the streets in a way of life that had a career trajectory straight to Hell via the cemetery.

"I want to show you something." The pathologist pointed at the darkest spot on the judge's neck. "It was death by strangulation all right, but you see right here? Severe damage. Fractured larynx."

Preddy bent low and stared at the area just above the collar bone. "What cause dat?"

Doctor Sewell frowned. "Not sure. Could have been done by something other than fingers. Like, I don't know, maybe a sharp elbow to the throat?"

"I see," said Preddy. "And we're sure it wasn't accidental?"

She nodded emphatically. "An elbow blow could have been accidental." She used her right elbow to demonstrate a sharp jab. "After that, no. This was no momentary grip, Detective. Somebody squeezed really tightly here and held on. I scraped under his nails and tested it. There are no cells from another person. No signs of him mounting any self-defence. My feeling is that he was taken totally by surprise."

Preddy straightened up. "He was sitting on de verandah facing de sea when his wife left him and went inside." Preddy turned his body to the right and looked over his shoulder then made the same motion to the left. "I'm trying to work out how de person got to him without him fighting back. He must have been asleep."

"Maybe he was impaired after a few drinks?" said the doctor. "There is a high level of alcohol in his system, although I wouldn't say he was drunk."

"He did have a few drinks earlier in de afternoon wid another judge friend of his. Didn't see any wine glasses or bottles on de verandah though, so I doubt if he had a nightcap."

"Drinking early afternoon is consistent with the level of alcohol," she replied. "You're right, he could have fallen asleep. Maybe he didn't know what was happening to him — which would be a blessing."

"If he was reclining wid his neck tilted back it would be an open target."

The doctor grimaced and rubbed her own wide neck. "Ouch!"

"He fell forward, was knocked out on de table and dey finished him off," theorised Preddy.

"Either way it was very quick and clean. No more than two minutes of pressure and the judge was gone."

"Angry and personal," said the detective. "Dis is not going to be easy without any evidence. Nothing else you can tell me about de body?"

"I wish I could, Detective Preddy," she replied. "I don't see many strangulations. Usually the murderer has killed his wife, girlfriend, baby mother, and always in a momentary fit of rage." She gave a wry smile. "Some of us badly need anger management training in this country."

"Serious thing," murmured Preddy.

She replaced the covering over the judge. "Let me know if you need any further help from me. I loved reading Judge Wrenn's legal columns. The man had a great way with words. It's such a shame to see him come to this."

* * *

Detective Harris stood waiting for Preddy on the sands near the Wrenn's beachfront at the Wynterton Park complex. He wished that the waters near Glasgow were as clear blue and as warm as the magnificent Caribbean Sea. Maybe then he might have been able to withstand the urge to return to the beautiful island with its crime figures trending the wrong way and a police service that did not embrace reform. Boden Boo and Erskine Beach were nice but not like this. When he first joined the Scottish police service over two decades ago the administrative systems currently used in Jamaica were long obsolete. No one was prepared to invest what was needed to bring the island up to speed with modern policing methods. Although Superintendent Brownlow seemed quite willing to discuss the matter he was either unwilling or unable to take appropriate action. No, instead he had another little job for him. Another job which he would have to do without Preddy.

Harris mopped his brow as he waited. Yes, Jamaica was hard going, but there was no country in the world that did not have policing problems and there were few countries as beautiful as this. His white cotton shirt clung to his body and he tugged at the hem for brief respite. The heat could be all-consuming at times, but he revelled in the fact that he no longer needed a coat or gloves. He waved at Preddy as the detective approached and wondered why his colleague seemed to be looking elsewhere.

"What's up?" asked Harris.

"You see anything different here?"

"Naw." Harris scanned the coastline. "What am I looking for?"

Preddy indicated a warning sign next to the Scotsman, painted in red on a white background. Harris tilted back his head and read it. It was not the usual sign warning swimmers of dangerous currents or high tide that one might expect to see. This one warned of pollution, yet there were no washed-up black scandal bags, plastic bottles or Styrofoam containers to be seen. Nothing like the detritus that plagued the gullies in city centre and the urban areas, which were collected in huge environmental drives each year only to be replenished within months.

"Pollution." Preddy popped a mint into his mouth as he studied the waterfront carefully. "De water touching de sand is browner dan it should be. Look out to sea, too. It's too brown."

Harris removed his sunglasses and stared at the water which would be considered pristine back home. "Looks pretty clean tae me."

"Let's have a look further up," suggested Preddy.

The detectives continued on up the beach and passed at least a dozen stunning properties. Some of the neighbours waved at them relief evident on their faces because the police had not deserted them. Preddy acknowledged them with a brief nod while Harris waved back politely. Some neighbours were out for the morning, their patio doors closed and iron grills padlocked. Either that, or they now trusted no one and had decided to secure themselves indoors while working from home, all previous confidence in security dashed by the murder of a prominent resident.

"Any one of these neighbours could easily have walked this route on Monday night and ended up in front of the Wrenn's home," said Harris.

"Dat's why you shouldn't wave at dem," said Preddy. "De murderer could be mocking us."

Harris glanced at him. "So, naw making friends tae get information? That's the way I usually do it."

"We're doing it my way," said Preddy curtly.

Harris could feel his temples pulsating and wished he could train himself to avoid that reaction. It was annoying to actually feel the blood rising in his cheeks. "The judge would probably naw have been startled tae see them. The two could have been talking calmly before the attack. The judge, easy in the company of his visitor, settled back eyes closed, maybe still talking when he got jumped."

Preddy nodded. "I could see dat happening."

Harris inhaled deeply. "It's hard tae imagine murder in a place like this." He gazed around him. "The water, the trees, the sun, the air. It's amazing."

"It is. We have to get dis parish back to what it used to be." He glanced at Harris's flushed face. "You game?"

"Absolutely. I'm in for the long run, for the greater good." Harris was emphatic, although he remembered

Preddy's prediction that he would eventually be overwhelmed by it all and opt for a quieter parish like Portland or even just return to Glasgow. The Scotsman was determined not to give his colleagues the satisfaction. He intended to remain part of the Major Crimes team and ensure that law-abiding citizens of St James felt safe. Besides, the Super was unlikely to allow him to be reassigned until the Police High Command was good and ready.

"So you think you'll ever get divorced and settle here?" asked Preddy.

Harris continued to take in the panorama. "It's a possibility."

"Which one? De divorce or living here permanently?"

"Either. Both."

Preddy glanced at his side profile. "Just wondering, you know?"

Harris smiled wryly. "Aye, I know, Preddy. Yer dying tae throw me a going away party and pack me off with a crate of Appleton Estate Special."

"Appleton? You'd be lucky," said Preddy. "Let's go see Oleta."

The detectives turned and set off back down the beachfront towards the Wrenn's villa.

"So, another possibility is that this guy came by sea?" suggested Harris.

Preddy said, "Someone, known or unknown to de Wrenn's, could have arrived by sea, pulled up on de jetty, murdered him and sailed off again. Dere is no easy way of finding out who was on de water dat night. We have no restrictions on night sailing. De Marine Police and Coastguard are out on an irregular basis. We don't have enough officers or vessels to cover de entire Western coastline twenty-four seven."

Harris looked out to sea. "Hell of a lot of water tae cover."

"Oleta said de houses are all yellow, beige and white. At night it would be almost impossible to tell what colour de house was."

Harris nodded. "A killer who arrived by sea would have tae be a regular visitor tae the Wrenn's or someone who knew the route like the back of his hand."

"Agreed," said Preddy. "Anyway, whether by land or sea I don't believe dis murder was de result of a chance encounter or a robbery gone wrong. Dere are far easier places to infiltrate and rob dan Wynterton Park, and less sturdily built men to attack dan Judge Wrenn."

"I've naw found anything of interest in his computer files yet. Nothing tae suggest why he may have been a target."

The detectives climbed the verandah steps. Oleta welcomed them inside of her home, and brought them each a glass of ice-cold coconut water. Preddy drained his glass in a few gulps while Harris slowly savoured his.

"Thanks," said Preddy wiping his lips. "Do you get boats going past de complex after dark or night visitors who arrive by sea?"

Oleta took the glass from him. "People sail by all the time even in the pitch black, from small boats, to catamarans to yachts. You'll just see a little light moving and know that someone is on the sea. Most times you don't even hear a sound."

"What about regulars?" asked Harris.

"This is a regular route for members of the Yacht Club too. They don't stop by to call on us in de night though. The jetty is small and isn't well lit so if you don't know it's there you could be in serious trouble." Oleta frowned. "When I called out to Ever there was no hint that anyone was out there with him."

"You absolutely sure dat he was on his own though? Dat he was de one who answered you?"

"Well, he was the only person downstairs so I wouldn't have noticed anyway. All he said was 'coming' like I said. His radio was on when I left him although it was really low. If I had even heard voices I would probably have assumed they were from the radio. He was listening to a talk-show last night — discussing whether the government was right

51

to reject the British Prime Minister's offer to build a prison here." She fell quiet and appeared to be lost in thought.

"And what do you think de judge would have thought of David Cameron's offer?" asked Preddy.

"Everton said 'yes, why not accept the offer?' But I said, 'no way, no damn prison.' Let them build a school instead!"

Her words were spoken forcefully. Preddy glanced at her through the corner of his eye while flicking for a blank page in his notebook. "We do need a new modern prison though," he said. "Ours are ancient and falling apart. Human rights campaigners are all over us."

"We need new schools even more," she replied with passion turning to Harris, "and hospitals."

Harris looked slightly embarrassed. "I'm afraid I'm naw yet well-informed about the prison system or the school system. I would imagine that we havenae got great budgets for either."

Oleta shook her head. "Educate the kids then we won't need to be sticking them in prison ten years down the line!"

Preddy eyed the widow. Oleta was over sixty and ageing well, but she was much shorter than the judge and did not seem physically capable of even clasping her hands together tightly. Not that an argument over a prison should constitute a motive for murder where a happily married couple was involved. He could imagine her giving her husband a playful elbow to the ribcage in a heated disagreement, but nothing carrying force.

"What happen to your wedding ring?" he asked.

"Oh, my hands not so good again. Any little thing . . . they swell up, so I haven't worn it in over a year."

Preddy leaned over the verandah wall and used his notebook to point along the beach. "Dere is a sign over dere about pollution. What's dat about?"

Oleta's eyes narrowed. "Nathaniel Mexell is the cause of it. You should have seen the place when we moved in five years ago . . . lovely water, pristine. Now look at it." She indicated an enlarged photograph on the wall adjacent to the judge's desk. "Look inside. That was taken on the beach soon after we moved in. That's me and Ever with our kids Martin and Maria. Look at that blue! You ever see anything so lovely Detective Harris?"

Harris followed her gaze. "It's stunning." He glanced across at Preddy. "I see what ye mean now about pollution. Naw so blue anymore."

Preddy took a few strides indoors and stared at the photograph of Oleta and the judge, and their adult children which was similar to the one in Judge Wrenn's chambers. He guessed that both offspring were in their early twenties. The glowing, happy family celebrating their new home, displaying pearly teeth just like a Colgate advert. All four sitting on deck chairs on the beach with the sun bearing down on their raised glasses. The water shimmering behind them was a clear aquamarine blue.

"Big difference," said Preddy.

"It's that new housing scheme in the hills," she said firmly. "NatMex started work about a year ago and since then we've noticed the difference. A lot of silt washing down whenever it rains and it collects on the beach front."

Preddy recognized the name of the construction company NatMex. It was still a relatively new and small company, but the thirty-something owner Nathaniel Mexell had already made a name for himself. His recently designed solar project on a hundred new-build apartments in the neighbouring parish of Trelawny had attracted international accolades. Mexell had moved on to his latest project here in St James and named it Montego Hamlet. By all accounts the current apartments would surpass the first set by including underground water storage facilities to state-of-the-art interiors.

"Didn't ye complain tae NatMex about it?" asked Harris.

"The strata board took it up with the company. Last thing I heard was that Mexell said they had all the necessary environmental permits and were not doing anything wrong." Her brow knitted into a deep frown. "Everton was not happy about it at all. More letters were sent to them, but I'm not

53

sure what response we got after that, if any. You'd have to check with the manager, Mr. Ingram. He's supposed to be in his office. It's on the far side of the pool, just below the bar."

Harris continued to study Oleta's many photographs of the extensive waterfront complex.

"We'll do dat," said Preddy. His eyes flicked over the judge's desk. "I see you did find de ashtray?"

"No, that's just the box."

"Nice looking thing," Preddy picked up the empty box and glanced at a paper receipt tucked inside before pushing it back in. He stared at the picture on the box. "What's dat engraved on it?"

"It says 'For Ever'. I gave it to him last month for his sixty-third birthday. He nearly didn't get it on time," explained Oleta. "The maker emailed me a copy of the proof and had put 'Forever' on it thinking I had made a mistake having written 'For Ever' — two words. Had to get it changed pretty quickly."

Preddy replaced the box and gazed around.

Harris turned and asked, "What did ye do with the gun, Mrs Wrenn? Ye might want tae put it away somewhere safe."

"It's still there." Oleta hugged her upper arms and rubbed them. "I'll probably put it by my bedside table, just in case he . . . in case they come back."

"If ye hear any sound in the night, please call us," urged Harris. "Do ye have anyone who can stay with ye?"

"Maria and Martin will be here as soon as they can. They live and work in Toronto, you know, not too far from each other."

Harris nodded. "Okay, that's good."

Preddy moved towards the front door. "If you can think of anything we need to know, anything at all, you can contact either of us or any of my detectives. Rabino and Spence will always be on hand to talk."

"I will," Oleta nodded. "What's happening wid de Camry?"

"It's secure at Pelican Walk. We going inspect it later," said Preddy. He decided not to share any information about the contents of the Camry's trunk and her tone did not suggest knowledge. "Thanks again for your help last night. We shouldn't have the car more dan a day or two at most."

"There's no rush, Detective. Whatever it takes."

Preddy and Harris made their way to the management office, a stand-alone single-storey structure in the middle of the complex. Through the windows a dark well-dressed man could be seen bent double over his desk writing. Preddy rapped on the window and the man adjusted his glasses as he looked up. The detective waved his badge and watched as the man pushed back his chair and made his way to the door. Behind it the key turned in the lock.

"Mr Ingram? I'm Detective Preddy, Pelican Walk. Dis is Detective Harris."

"Good morning, gentlemen." Mr Ingram held the door open wide and beckoned. "Come in, come in. I did see you yesterday, but I spoke to another detective."

They entered and took up the seats offered in front of the manager. Photographs of the grand opening of Wynterton Park lined the yellow painted walls. A prominent photo of the previous mayor adorned in his gold ceremonial finery cutting a ribbon at the entrance. Balloons hanging from the palm trees tied with thin pieces of colourful string. A new calendar hung on top of an old one so that the dates of both sets of years were displayed. Both were well circled and marked. There were photos and phone numbers of the eight-strong management team. Preddy cast a keen eye over them. Mr Ingram seemed to have used a professional photographer for his head shot, or had had it taken when he was much younger. Without the glasses he looked quite different back then.

"What a terrible, terrible thing to have happened." The manager went around his desk and resumed his original position, pen poised mid-air. "We have never seen anything like this before. Wynterton Park is such a quiet, safe community. I still can't quite believe it."

"Ye have our sympathies," said Harris, nodding sagely.

"It's always a shock when violent crime hits any community," said Preddy, "but I want you to understand dat we are determined to take back St James."

"I'm glad to hear it, Detective. This crime thing will bring us down if we don't stem it." The manager glanced at Harris. "How are you finding it, sir? Is this what you expected?"

"It's a challenge that I'm up for," replied the Scotsman. "Like Detective Preddy says, we cannae let the criminals have St James. We'll have their balls first."

Preddy opened his notebook. "Do you know whether any of de residents were being threatened by anyone, whether by other residents or external figures?"

"Not that I know of. This is a peaceful place, Detective. At least it was until now." Mr Ingram shook his head. "The little spats that happen here happen at all strata complexes, and I've managed two before this. You know — complaints about where others hang their clothes or put their rubbish, that sort of thing."

"And about people painting houses the wrong colour?" said Harris.

Mr Ingram smiled. "You've heard about that. Wasn't too bad. Judge Wrenn got Mr Simms to see reason and calm was restored quite quickly. The white paint just looks better."

"What about de NatMex pollution issue, was dat handled by de judge as well?" asked Preddy.

"We did discuss it with Judge Wrenn as a board, you know? It's always good to have a lawyer you can refer to when these sort of things crop up," said the manager. "We approached it as a united body. Mind you, Everton was getting pretty impatient with NatMex. Said he was going to warn Mr Mexell personally."

Preddy leaned forward in his chair. "Oh?"

"Well, Everton was determined that Wynterton Park wouldn't end up like Old Fort Bay in Ochi. Not nice." Mr. Ingram grimaced. "He said that if we didn't get a response to our last letter soon we would get tough. Said we would get an injunction and lock down NatMex until they cleared up the place, or at least put some barriers in place to divert the silt away from the beach." Mr Ingram pulled out a drawer and rooted around in its depths. "Let me see . . . the last letter we wrote was two weeks ago."

"Can I see dat?" Preddy reached across the desk and took the whole file. He skimmed the pages and flicked through photographic evidence. He handed the file to Harris who scanned the letters. "Doesn't say anything about an injunction. Did de judge draft dese letters?"

"Mainly, and the chairman signed them off. Judge Wrenn said he would personally talk to Nathaniel Mexell first and see if he would see reason. If not, then he would seek the injunction."

Harris interjected, "So naw response tae any recent letters? Ye sure that Mexell even received them?"

"I sent a bearer to hand-deliver each communication to the company. They received them."

Preddy frowned. "What, all de way to Jackson Town, Trelawny?"

"No man, you mad! No disrespect officer," the manager added quickly. "Mexell has a house in the Meadows of Irwin Hills. An easy bicycle ride for the bearer, twenty minutes at most."

"Can we copy dis file?" asked Preddy.

Mr Ingram shook his head. "The copier isn't working, detective. You can borrow it still, and drop it off when you've finished. I know you won't lose it."

Preddy rose and said, "Thank you, sir."

"Do you know if the judge ever did speak tae Mexell?" asked Harris as he tucked the file under his arm.

Mr Ingram shrugged. "If he did he never reported back to me so I don't know. The judge was a man of his word though. If Everton Wrenn said he was going to do something, he did it."

"Ye know, ye really need tae arrange a security assessment. Get some CCTV cameras set up around here, particularly covering the gates and perimeter fencing," Harris advised him as he got to his feet.

Mr Ingram threw up his hands in exasperation. "It comes up in the minutes month after month, but there are so many other things on the grounds that have a call on the management fees. The board cannot agree on how and when to get the security cameras."

"Guess it will be top of de agenda at your next meeting," said Preddy.

* * *

Preddy switched off the air con as he turned into the driveway of Pelican Walk police station and crawled towards the blue and cream building with its faded exterior. All police stations on the island shared similar colours, either blue and cream or blue and white. Some, like Pelican Walk, could do with improvements to the brickwork, new guttering and a good lick of paint. Some stations were crumbling death-traps which should really be bulldozed and rebuilt from scratch, but no government or opposition ever saw police welfare as a vote winner.

Harris triggered the control which retracted the window. He leaned out and waved to two officers who were chatting under the laden mango tree, their pockets bulging with ripe fruit. "Let me out here, Preddy."

"No way. Too many mango equal diabetes," said Preddy.

"Thanks, doc."

"We're wanted in de evidence room and we're late."

Preddy continued on and pulled into the front car park. He noted that the commissioner's parking spot was already taken although he didn't recognize the car.

Harris noticed too. "Nice wheels," said the Scotsman as he exited the passenger door.

"For real." Preddy ran his eyes over the vehicle. A brand new grey Pajero with sparkling rims. No one would dare to park in that spot even though Commissioner Davis rarely visited the station. No doubt the commissioner had been able to find some spare millions in the budget for a new vehicle for himself. None for a new water tank though and certainly none for a new roof.

Preddy checked that the Wrenn's red Camry was secured under the tarpaulin at the rear before heading indoors behind Harris. Waiting for the men in the evidence room were Rabino and Spence, standing before a plastic table spread with weapons. Two UZI sub-machine guns, four AK-47's, a MAC10, and twelve cartridges of ammunition.

"Fuck!" said Harris.

"Rass!" breathed Preddy.

"Dat's what I said last night!" Spence chimed in.

Rabino smiled. "Actually, that's what Tuffy said too, although it wasn't said in surprise — more in resignation."

"Ye know Antwon Frazer is going tae deny all knowledge," warned Harris.

"Oh he did. As soon as he opened the trunk, I photographed every piece of metal right in front of him," said Rabino. "Closed it back right in front of him too. For someone who didn't know what was in the trunk it was interesting to find a plastic bag with a six-pack of bottled water and a receipt for purchase that morning, all nestled in there."

"I just hope we've got his fingerprints on one of those weapons," said Harris. "We can at least do him for possession."

"It will take a while to get de results back from de lab," said Preddy. "Let's make dat a priority."

"Yes, sir," Rabino nodded.

"Where is our Mr Frazer?" asked Preddy.

"Downstairs in a holding cell," said Rabino. "His lawyer's stuck in court, but says he'll be on the way. I tried to speak to Tuffy, but he won't speak to us. Said he's not speaking to anyone and we should, I quote, 'go chuck offa house top.'"

Spence looked at the Scotsman and explained helpfully, "Dat just means 'go dead.'"

"Och, thought as much."

"Nice," said Preddy. "Tuffy have time to polish up him social skills."

"Tuffy managed a smile for me," Spence pointed out as she headed to the door. "Those lovely gold-capped teeth."

"I think you'll find it was a grimace," offered Rabino. She moved towards the table. "Better get these pieces bagged and tagged."

"I'll do it," said Harris, getting to his feet and offering her a warm smile. "Thanks for the brochures by the way. I'll look at them later."

"No problem," she said, returning the look. "See you later."

As the door closed behind her Harris spread his arms, placed his palms on the table and leaned over the weapons. "It's scary tae think there are many more of these out there."

Preddy scanned the tools again. "We have to get dem off de streets. One by one is not going to do it. We need to go after de gangs instead of waiting on dem to strike. Otherwise we'll always be chasing our tails."

Harris picked up the MAC10 and held it at eye-level. "Ye really wouldnae want tae be at the wrong end of this would ye?"

"And yet we are," said Preddy. "We have to start disrupting deir business right now. De Benbow Crew is as good enough a place to start as any."

"Is that naw what would happen in a state of emergency? Police get pro-active and go intae the problem communities?" asked Harris. "I thought ye were against that?"

"I am. You don't need to declare a state of emergency for dat. Probable cause and reasonable suspicion will do," replied Preddy. "Maybe one day it will come to dat: police and soldiers embedded in hot communities for God knows how long. And what happens when dey leave? Temporary solution to a permanent problem."

Harris studied the weapon closely. "The brass seem tae think we can get a good deal of the guns in by asking for them. I understand another 'Get The Guns' initiative will be held later in the year? Apparently the first one was quite successful?"

Preddy snorted. "No matter how many get handed in de murder rate not going down. Most of what we get are what dey don't mind losing. Old stuff. Another boat load is on de way."

"It's a start though," suggested Harris.

"It's not an anything," said Preddy.

"So have ye told the brass of yer concerns?"

"What do you think?" Preddy gave him an icy glare.

"Maybe ye need tae stress yer concerns more forcefully?"

Preddy had been heading towards the door, but he turned around and faced the foreigner. With effort he kept his voice as even as possible. "You think dey care about what we think. Sorry, I shouldn't say *we*, I should say *I*."

Harris narrowed his eyes. "Meaning?"

"Meaning what I said," replied Preddy. "Some people's opinions are more respected dan others."

Harris rested the gun on the table. The veins on his temples stood up and began to throb. He inhaled and seemed to be silently counting. "Look, I'm pretty sure we're all after the same thing here. Everybody wants tae see the city cleared up."

Preddy continued on his way. "You know sometimes I think you get it, and den I realise, you really don't."

"Care tae elaborate?"

"You're in it for de long run," Preddy threw over his shoulder. "You'll learn."

Harris scowled in frustration as he tagged the weapons. It was not his fault that Superintendent Brownlow, in particular, had taken to asking him for his opinions on various policing strategies often within earshot of other Pelican Walk detectives. It would have been remiss of Brownlow not to pick his brains for information on what methods worked in the fight against crime, yet he wished the Super would consult him in private. After all, it was not as if he did not have plenty of opportunity to do so.

CHAPTER 5

Wednesday, 3 May, 7.50 p.m.

Preddy reclined on a well-cushioned chair in his home office with his feet up on the tidy desk reading Judge Wrenn files and sipping coconut water. Yet again he had failed his New Year resolution to stop working from his Ironshore apartment. At the end of last year he had removed all case files, documents and notes and returned them to Pelican Walk vowing to leave work at work. Within a month or two, other paperwork had taken their place filling up the drawers and nestling on the bookshelf beside his textbooks. Crime solving was in his blood and if that passion had not been diluted over turbulent decades of pain and pleasure it was unlikely to happen now. The apartment was completely silent apart from the whir of the air conditioning unit. An untouched plate of cooked food sat on the coffee table beside him. It had been microwaved hot about an hour ago, and now was in a tepid state.

His phone rang and he frowned as he glanced at the name. Damian was a good guy. They had worked together many years ago and maintained a good friendship despite the fact that Damian had abandoned the JCF to work in airline security. No doubt he was calling to suggest they grab a drink soon, but he would have to wait. Voices were a distraction he could do without at this minute.

Within minutes the phone rang again. This time he smiled as he glanced at. He could handle this distraction. This was a voice he was always happy to hear, one that chided him when he deserved it and encouraged him when he needed it, his scientist girlfriend of two years.

"Hello beautiful," he said.

A throaty laugh entered his ear. "Hmm, I wonder what favour you going ask for now?"

"Not a thing. Just hearing your voice is exactly what I need." He wished she was there with him, but it was just as well that she was in her own apartment elsewhere in the city. He needed to keep on top of this murder case from the outset. In a competition between reading files and Valerie, the latter would always win if she was present.

"I love you too, Detective," said Valerie. "You been quiet today, understandably. Judge Wrenn's murder still dominating de news. What a thing eeh? Finally de Prime Minister has opened his mouth."

"You see dem talking about Zones of Special Operation now? ZOSO. Dat's a new one. I guess dis murder has made de government go all imaginative."

"I saw it." Valerie sighed. "So we going get teams of police and soldiers taking up residence in certain hotspots for sixty days. Will it work though?"

"We can only watch and see," said Preddy. "Dey haven't given much detail yet about which communities will be declared ZOSO. De plan is to restrict movement of gang members as dere will be curfews as well as searches. My hope is dat dey swamp all known communities at once and don't just select one or two."

"Political selection you mean?" said Valerie.

"You done know how it go, already," he replied. "Police work will not get any easier without a bipartisan approach. Frustrates de hell outta me."

"You can only do what you can do, Ray," she said sympathetically. "You have any thoughts on de judge's murder?"

Preddy wished he could reply positively, but without any evidence the road ahead would be rough and slow. "Dis one has me worried. I mean, dere are numerous criminals who would be happy to see de judge six feet under. De method of murder is just so unusual though, strangulation."

"You have dat Scottish man working de case wid you?"

"Yes, my girl. Detective Harris says he's in it for de long run and de greater good." He paused before adding. "We'll see."

"You sound like you don't believe it?" Her tone was playful. "He must love dis job, and thankfully your bad company hasn't put him off."

"Well, thank you for dat vote of confidence, Baby," Preddy laughed. "He and I get along just fine, so long as he stays in his lane and stops sneaking around. De judiciary will welcome having him on board for Wrenn's case."

"Well Harris must know more dan most about dat type of murder," she proclaimed. "People in Scotland don't have illegal guns like we. Dem more likely to go strangle each other."

Preddy chuckled despite himself. "Dat is de least scientific thing I have ever heard come from your lips, Val." He laughed again. "I get your point though, you're not fooling me. Look, I promise I will make good use of de team and not over-exert myself. How's dat?"

"No getting past you is dere, Mr Detective?" Her voice was soothing to his ear. "No joking though, Ray, you really have a problem wid delegation and you need to get over it. Your mental health will not improve if you don't share de burdens wid other officers."

"Yes, Boss." These were words he had heard before as she never missed a chance to remind him that he was not alone in his goals.

"Dat parakeet come back?" she asked.

"No sign of it. Dey're daytime birds though so I wouldn't expect it to turn up."

"You sound like you miss it?"

Preddy pictured the tiny bird and gave this a few seconds thought. The little yellow beak moved when he spoke to it, and its head bobbed. It did not answer back or judge him in any way. "I admit I did look at de window earlier expecting to see a green bunch of feathers waiting for me. Nothing."

"He'll be back. You been feeding him, he'll be back," she said. "And speaking about food, make sure you eat dinner tonight."

"I've already polished off a snapper and roast yam, honest," Preddy lied, glancing at his uneaten meal. The reminder to eat was also advice he was used to hearing, but there were many times when his tastebuds could not respond to grisly photographs or news of dead bodies. "I just have a few more papers to finish off den I'm done wid work for de night."

"Okay, and don't stay up too late, Ray."

"I won't, Val. Love you, baby."

"Love you too."

Preddy hung up the phone and took up the plate of well-seasoned fish and yam. He headed for the kitchen where he covered it up with a plastic lid and shuffled around in the fridge making space for the dish. He remembered reading somewhere that it was not wise to reheat food, store it in the fridge and reheat it again. That advice would just have to be ignored when it came to his snapper. It had never hurt him before. He frowned as he poked around the cold shelves. So many other things that needed to be thrown out. Some of them belonged to his children and would probably spoil before the weekend. He opened a margarine tub to see bits of corned beef and cabbage which he recognized as their leftover breakfast from two weekends ago. He flinched from the odour and covered it again. There was a skinny cat lurking on the ground floor somewhere who did not appear too discerning. He would feed it in the morning.

Preddy retrieved his pile of papers, locked his office door and headed to his sitting room where he sank into the sofa and turned on the television. Now the talking heads were all at it. Debating the crime situation islandwide with the focus on Montego Bay. Judge Wrenn's murder featured prominently, complete with video of the gloriously blue backdrop against which he had met his fate. It was impossible to identify any signs of sea pollution from the TV screen, not least because the local news media often suffered poor picture quality on broadcasts. Only those people who lived or worked at Wynterton Park would find the sea discolouration obvious.

Preddy set aside the judge's roster of criminal cases and picked up the strata manager's file of correspondence. It crossed his mind, not for the first time, that Judge Wrenn may have been looking over the wrong shoulder. Criminals were always going to be the judge's main concern, but a businessman like Nathaniel Mexell was never going to be a fan of the judiciary either. Not if the judge was a threat to his growing successful business and might slow down the march of his property development. Preddy sat and read the papers for hours before he found himself stifling a yawn. He glanced at the clock which revealed that it was nearly midnight. His temples pulsated so he swallowed some stress tablets and gulped down another bottle of coconut water before making his way to bed.

Within minutes the familiar images began to sweep though his mind and he was wide awake again. The ghosts of Norwood just would not go away. For a few seconds the images remained vivid, blood and grey matter and screaming. Flashes of bullets everywhere, pockmarked walls all around. One young man begging not to be slaughtered as his compatriots fell beside him. Preddy bolted upright, heart pounding and wiped the sweat from his brow. He eyed a bottle of sleeping tablets, but decided against taking them. He had no idea what different medicines did in the body when mixed and he had no intention of crippling his mind. Superintendent Brownlow had offered him the opportunity to attend counselling sessions, which idea Preddy had listened to and nodded enthusiastically, but had not done much more than that.

Harris had encouraged him to go to, but he had ignored the advice. The Norwood raid was something that Preddy just did not want to talk about whether with family or with strangers.

* * *

Antwon Tuffy Frazer surveyed the dark grey walls surrounding him. Time moved slowly when you were confined. Yet again he was detained by the wicked Babylon who were surely on a mission to get him this week. First the ruffians of Trojan Street station and now the hooligans of Pelican Walk. He did not know which set was worse in reality, but since he was now detained at Pelican Walk it was those officers who held the title of Most Evilous.

Tuffy sat on his hard mattress-free single bed and drew his bony knees up under his chin. They weren't even his guns. Transporting weapons was just something he did to earn a few extra dollars, well a lot of extra dollars if he was truthful. It wasn't as if he fired them anymore. He was long done with that side of the business. Other people were not done, and it was not his business to try and convert them.

As a driver for Judge Wrenn he had never been targeted by law enforcement before. Even if the car got stopped the traffic officers would recognize the judge and just wave them on. The judge's death made him a police target and he had foolishly neglected to calculate the speed in which that would happen. It was careless not to have emptied the Camry and handed it back to Miss Oleta the moment the judge's death became news.

He wondered why Oleta was proving so difficult to contact. The heartless Babylon must have upset her. She was a nice lady who did not deserve to lose her husband in such a manner. Judge Wrenn was a nice guy too who was happy to chat about normal things. They would talk about the weather, sports, women, the cost of living, anything at all. Sometimes when court was over the judge would take the car and go about his business, but when he returned he always handed over a good tip and a cold beer. Everybody had to die though, young and old. When the time came there was just no getting away from it, ready or not. He would use Oleta as a referee for his good behaviour. They got along quite well. She was a caring lady who always checked that he had tea and breakfast before he took Judge Wrenn to work. Much nicer than his own mother who was too busy taking care of his father to worry about what her sons were up to. Part of him could hardly blame her though. If she made a misstep his father used his fists to help her walk straight.

If the officers had arrived just one hour later the purchaser would have taken possession of the weapons, Tuffy would have collected his money, and he would have been back at home in Ancona. He cursed himself beneath his breath. His crew had fled from the squatted house up into the impenetrable terrain as soon as the police knocked on the door. He had thought about running too, but the good weed had made him a bit heady. There was no point in running anyway, since the car was evidence of his presence. That damn police woman with the false hair and the long eyelashes who chatted like a TV newsreader was back again. The other hoggish female with the braids he did not recognize. She had spoken to him like he was the lowest of the low. Bumbo claat women. That's why they had to get their dead. Should stay indoors and mind the pickney, not get involved in bad man business and then want the public to cry over them when they got shot up.

Tuffy kissed his teeth as he struggled to get comfortable. To make it worse for him, no lawyer had turned up. Even though he had been promised more than once that his attorney was on the way the dutty lawyer-man never showed up. At this time of night he was hardly likely to make an appearance either. It was true that Tuffy owed the lawyer some money from last year. Lawyers were not poor people though so he could afford to wait. The law man surely couldn't be malicing him over any inflated bill? He had to know he would get his money. Sometime.

Tuffy closed his eyes and lay curled in a fetal position, not that he was going to get any sleep. Maybe it was just as well he was behind bars. This Benbow Crew business was all well and good and had stood him in good stead over the years, but now he was getting too old for it. This was young boy business and the young boys were getting younger and harder to control. Gone were the days when there was a fifty-something in charge, with a reasonably sound head on his shoulders. Now it was every youth for himself. The owner of the weapons was going to be very unhappy and Tuffy did not relish the thought of explaining how and why the deal did not take place. The lawyer might be able to work his magic with the court, but there was no one to work any magic with the owner of those guns.

CHAPTER 6

Preddy hid behind the ajar door of the empty room and peeped at the closed conference room door immediately opposite. He and Harris were due to meet in the car park in ten minutes and the Scotsman had said he was headed to the canteen first, yet Preddy had seen him enter the conference room and immediately draw the internal blinds down. As the door opened, Preddy straightened up and watched Harris leave closing the door behind him. The man carried a small bronze laptop which was nothing like Judge Wrenn's laptop and not one Preddy had ever seen him with before. When he could no longer hear the foreigner's footsteps Preddy crossed the corridor and entered the conference room. Even the blinds covering the external windows were down. Quickly he scanned the room. No one was else was inside and the tables were bare. Not a cup, file or a piece of paper anywhere. Preddy frowned and closed the door. He headed down the rear staircase leaping the stairs two at a time and climbed into his car not a minute too soon. He barely closed the door before Harris appeared, minus the bronze laptop. Instead, he held two bottles of cold water one of which he handed to Preddy.

"Och, here ye go."

"Thanks," said Preddy, and placed it on the dashboard.

Preddy crunched on his mints as he drove. He had long decided against introducing Harris to ganja tea, although he felt sure it would give the Scotsman added energy particularly now that he had joined an over 40's football team. There was no mistaking the health benefits derived from the brew and ordinarily he would have been happy to share that information. It was bound to get to back to Superintendent Brownlow though and Preddy knew better than to light that fuse. Explaining where he got the green plants from was not in his plans, not least because of his wish to protect the industrious farmer. Besides, he knew with certainty that Harris was secretly up to something and he did not fancy the idea of sharing anything private with him.

Harris reached towards the dashboard and turned on the radio. The soothing low sound of instrumental jazz music filled the car. He turned the dial a few times pausing briefly each time he located a station. Finally settling on one he liked he turned it up a notch.

"Wha' de rass is dat?"

Harris smiled. "Miley Cyrus."

"Find something better, man."

"She's quite good when ye really listen tae her. My daughter likes her."

"Not listening to her, find something else."

"Och, it willnae kill ye Preddy." Harris reached for the knob and searched for another station. "This sounds like Eminem."

"Sounds like it needs to be turned off."

Harris tried again. "Michael Bolton? Nobody can object tae Michael Bolton?"

Preddy gave him a deadly side-eye. "I object."

"Hmm, naw sure who this one is? Nice tune."

"Leave it right dere," said Preddy. "A real vocalist, Gregory Isaacs, de Cool Ruler."

They turned off the highway dubbed the Elegant Corridor and onto a winding road which lead up into the new upmarket housing scheme of Montego Hamlet. NatMex was clearly spending money on the development and for once a building company seemed to be following the artist's impression of the site that was available online. A huge archway marked the entrance with a sign welcoming visitors and warning them to take care. Preddy slowed down as he drove under it. The wide driveway had been carved out by a digger and the compacted marl made the road perfectly smooth. The laying of the tarmac was for another time, preferably before the rains came. Half-built sentry positions at each side were large enough to hold a bed and he wondered whether this was the intention. Newly planted Bull Thatch Palm trees lined the route on either side, each with their spiny green leaves gracefully spread into the shape of a giant fan. Huge white stones separated the tropical trees from the road protecting their stout trunks from bad drivers.

Two liveried NatMex Construction vans were parked in the open yard, their muddied tyres propped up by stones to prevent them rolling down the hill. Workmen in high-visibility vests were sprinkled throughout the premises, some carrying blocks, others mixing cement. Two storeys of the buildings had gone up already and it was clear from the erect steel protruding from the top that more storeys would be added.

The owner was expecting the detectives, but so far Preddy could not pick him out. From that distance they were all just men in orange tops and matching hard hats. He guessed that the black BMW X6 belonged to Mexell. It was always the first thing that successful young men bought to show that they had arrived. Preddy pulled his car up alongside the top of the range vehicle.

"Ye're a bit close ye know," warned Harris as Preddy manoeuvred into the narrow space.

Preddy backed out slowly and was jolted by a sharp toot behind him. He glanced through the rear-view mirror and was surprised to see another black X6 behind him.

"A whe' de rass him come from?" he mumbled.

"Guess this is the BMW fan club convention and we didnae get the memo," mused Harris.

Preddy straightened up his car and climbed out, followed by Harris. The man who had just arrived parked behind Preddy blocking him in and stepped out too. He was a slender young man no more than thirty, smooth-shaven, and over-dressed for a building site in long-sleeved shirt and tie with polished leather shoes.

"You're in my spot, you know, man," he said glaring at Preddy. His voice was cultured and assured while also bordering on impolite.

"Yer in ma spot, Detective Preddy," Harris corrected him, "but it's naw problem, Detective Preddy. I'll just move ma car over here."

"Yes, dat," said Preddy.

"Oh! Detectives." The man had the decency to look embarrassed. "Just a minute."

He re-entered his car and reversed, backing it quite some distance into an empty space. He removed a briefcase from the footwell, closed his door and seemed to concentrate for an inordinate amount of time on fiddling with the door handle, even though Preddy knew it locked electronically. Eventually, he walked back to where the detectives were standing and looked at them expectantly, seeming to have regained his composure.

"Me, you now know," said Preddy. "Dis is my colleague, Detective Harris." Harris nodded in the man's direction.

"Stephan Channer. How can I help you, detectives?" He held the briefcase in one hand, the other went firmly into his trouser pocket.

Preddy recognized the name from the strata manager's correspondence. Stephan Channer was NatMex's company secretary and a qualified lawyer. Before Preddy could answer a voice boomed from above the hillside.

"Hey! Detective Preddy, up here!"

It was still too far away to identify the person, yet it could only be Nathaniel Mexell who stood waving energetically at them.

Channer frowned. "I guess you're expected, although Nat didn't mention it to me."

"Should he?" asked Preddy casually.

"Not necessarily, but being a lawyer I always advise clients to have a lawyer present when police come knocking, even if they're asking the most innocuous of questions." He stared pointedly at Preddy as he spoke.

"Lead the way, Mr Channer," said Harris, placing his sunglasses over his nose. "We're right behind ye."

They headed up the slope towards the worksite, negotiating around white plastic pipes and reels of electrical wire that lay scattered on the ground. Nathaniel Mexell strolled down a pedestrian pathway made out of tree trunks and carefully laid to resemble debris that just happened to have beached there. Preddy liked the natural feel to the place. There was no questioning it this company had taken a holistic approach to property development.

Mexell was a handsome dark man, dressed in jeans tucked in Timberland boots with a long-sleeved shirt hanging loose over his waist. He was over six feet tall and almost on eye-level with Preddy. He held out his hand and gave Preddy an easy smile.

"Boy, I hope I'm not in any trouble, Detective." Mexell tilted his hard hat back slightly. "I've seen you on TV before. Heard all about the Norwood . . . .umm, issue."

"Likewise." Preddy shook the man's hand while staring at him with a faint smile. "I mean, I've seen you on TV, too. Posing wid clean shovels and even cleaner boots, cutting ribbons."

A bit of the spark went out of Mexell's eyes. "I'm trying to be a good productive citizen, Detective, raising the profile of Montego Bay and its offerings."

"I commend you on dat," said Preddy before gesturing towards his colleague. "Dis is Detective Sean Harris."

Mexell turned to the Scotsman. "Detective Harris. I know who you are, too. Saw you in the local newspaper when you just joined Pelican Walk. We don't have any foreign policemen in Mo Bay, well, not that I know of. You have quite a . . . distinctive look."

"I've had worse things said about me, Mr Mexell," said Harris, shaking the owner's outstretched hand. "Most of which cannae be printed in a family paper."

"Call me Nat. Not even the workers call me Mr Mexell." He regained his beaming smile. "They tend to call me boss or bossie, although I'm sure they call me some other choice words when I'm not in earshot."

"Now that the bonding is over, is this an official visit Nat?" Stephan Channer said icily.

Mexell held up his hand in a conciliatory gesture. "Got a call last night, Stephan. Sorry. Should've mentioned it." He looked at Preddy and made a point of rolling up his sleeves as if he was a labourer. "You've picked a really busy day though, detectives."

"Continue working, dat's fine," said Preddy, using his hand to shield his eyes from the sun. He studied both of Mexell's hands and arms. "We just have a few questions to ask. We're investigating de death of Judge Everton Wrenn."

"And why would Nat know anything about that?" snapped Channer.

"Naw one said he did, Mr Channer," said Harris studying the company secretary.

Mexell gave a husky laugh. "It's alright Stephan. You cannot hide the lawyer in you, can you? Ask whatever you like, detectives."

"Within reason," added Channer.

"You didn't come here to get your hands dirty den, Mr Channer?" asked Preddy, running his eyes over the irritant. "No hard hat, no protective vest, no work boots? Just come to drop something off?"

"I came for a meeting with a surveyor actually, and it's a good thing I did," replied Channer. "The surveyor can wait. My presence is clearly needed right here."

"Let's walk. We can talk as we go, Mr Mexell," suggested Preddy. He had no intention of doing first names with his suspect regardless of his geniality. "We can go back up dere, to where you were working."

"Sure," said Mexell, turning slightly to point out the danger. "No handrails yet so be careful how you go. I'm waiting on some sisal rope from Mexico."

They started back up the hill and Preddy gazed around the premises. The new Montego Hamlet residents were assured of a spectacular sea view, and from the looks of it all of them would enjoy a very comfortable standard of living. "You've imported a lot of stuff for dis place?"

"A fair bit, but I'll make it back, Detective." Mexell looked across at Harris's pink face. "If the sun is too much for you, Detective Harris we can go inside the show home to talk?"

"Naw it's just fine," mumbled Harris, dabbing at his trickling brow.

Preddy glanced at the red-headed Glaswegian who looked as if he was about to pass out. He refused to wear a hat of any kind even though he had been gifted one upon his return to Jamaica. A nice panama with a blue ribbon which he had accepted graciously and promised to wear, but only when off duty.

As they walked Mexell happily spoke about his successful Falmouth development and his determination to make an even bigger success of Montego Hamlet apartments. He pointed out where various units would go and what would be built into them — a gym, 24hr convenience store, bar, swimming pool and children's play area. He seemed a perfectly amiable young man and Preddy wondered if he was also a consummate actor. His hands showed no sign of injury and his body language was not that of a person with anything to hide. So far Mexell had maintained eye contact, displayed no nervous tics and wore not even a ripple of perspiration.

"I understand you were in dispute wid de Wynterton Park community residents?" Preddy watched the russet coloured eyes for signs of agitation, but there were none. The group stopped at a long workbench that was covered in sawdust and A3 papers.

"True, they did complain." Mexell brushed away some of the dust. He picked up a pencil and T-square and leaned over a blueprint of the property. "All a fuss about nothing really."

"Funny, Judge Wrenn didnae seem tae think so," said Harris.

Mexell kept his head down, but Preddy noted that the pencil stopped moving.

"You had a meeting wid de judge, Mr Mexell. Something about an injunction I understand." Preddy made it more of a statement than a question, and it achieved the desired result.

"Yes. Yes, I did." Mexell blinked rapidly as he looked up at the detective, pencil poised mid-air.

"What does that have to do with anything, Detective?" asked Channer, aggression in his stance and tone.

"It's okay, Stephan," said Mexell. "I didn't realise our little meeting was public knowledge, Detective?"

"Shows how two-faced Wrenn is," said Channer. "He said we would have time to consider his request before seeking an injunction, but the fact that you detectives know about it tells me he lied."

Harris glanced in his direction. "And of course, lying is a completely new phenomenon tae lawyers, Mr Channer."

"We won't even go there," said Mexell, his smile reticent. "Anyway, yes we discussed what he called 'pollution' and what I call 'run-off', although I'm pretty sure it wasn't ours anyway. We have not broken any laws, neither criminal nor environmental." Mexell stretched across a work bench and removed a paperweight fortifying some drawings from the light breeze. "In the site office, over there, are all of our building permits. You're free to inspect them. Everything has been done by the book and continues to be done by the book."

"No law breaking at all." Channer placed his briefcase on the bench and pulled out a stool. He perched on it with one leg crossed over his knees, arms folded on his chest and stared at the interrogators.

"Maybe some laws were not as adequately adhered to as dey should have been?" said Preddy. "I doubt if Judge Wrenn would threaten you wid de laws unless he was sure he had good grounds."

Mexell put his hands on his hips and looked sceptical. "It's called string-pulling, Detective. Everton Wrenn and his cronies would no doubt be successful in court because the judges are all friends. Scratching each other's backs and all that. This one appoints that one who in turn appoints his friend and they rule like the mafia. They might have got rid of the horsehair wigs, but they kept the black robes and secretive rituals."

Preddy raised an eyebrow. "Where were you on Monday night, Mr Mexell?"

"Come on now, Detective Preddy! You can't really believe I have anything to do with Judge Wrenn's murder?" Mexell's face remained incredulous, but his pencil snapped. Startled he quickly bent to retrieve the pieces and remained staring at the ground after he had done so.

"If you have any evidence then lay your charges, Detective," said Channer, getting to his feet and glaring at Preddy.

"Naw one is being charged with anything at this stage, Mr Channer," said Harris, moving closer towards the angry man. "The question was a simple one."

"And I'm happy to answer it," replied Mexell, looking impatient. "Take it easy, Stephan."

"You don't have to tell them anything," remarked Channer, frowning.

Mexell gave his partner a look of displeasure. "But I want to," he replied through gritted teeth. "I was at my parents' home, which is just a few doors down from mine in Irwin Village. I had dinner with them at about 7 p.m. — pork and hard food, great stuff — then had more than a bit to drink with my dad then fell asleep on my old bed. Woke up, maybe around tenish, got up and went home. Girlfriend was asleep when I got back. Snuck into bed, woke up probably around 5 a.m. when I heard our dogs barking."

Preddy was unable to assess Mexell's truthfulness from his face. "When did you last see Judge Wrenn?"

"See him?" Nathaniel Mexell cocked his head to one side. "Let me think now . . . probably on Saturday. Yes, it would have been Saturday."

"Saturday? Where did you meet?" asked Preddy.

"We didn't, not really," said Mexell. "Passed him on the waterfront and waved to him. A few of us from work were on my yacht, you see."

Preddy tried not to show obvious interest. "You sail by Wynterton Park quite often den?"

Mexell shrugged. "Not often. Well, we've been practicing for the upcoming regatta so I've done the route about once a week over the past two months."

"The regatta?" repeated Harris.

"Yes. The race will go from the Freeport to Salt Marsh Bay and back," replied Mexell. "I patched up my uncle's old boat, reconstituted the motor, painted NatMex on it and decided to see what it can do. Need to keep marketing and advertising by all means, detectives. As long as we don't come last I'll be happy."

"We won't come last," said Channer confidently. "The motor isn't great, but the boat moves well as long as the sea is calm and we have a good wind behind us."

Preddy stared at the lawyer. "So you sail, too."

"Sure. Why not?" said Channer. "And before you ask where I was, I can tell you that I was at home in bed with a cold. Alone. Nobody was with me. I took a few ibuprofen and was in bed by nine o'clock with a box of tissues."

"Glad tae see ye made a speedy recovery," said Harris dryly.

"So, you waved at Judge Wrenn. Did he wave back, say anything?" asked Preddy.

Mexell shook his head. "He didn't indicate that he noticed me, but he must have recognized the boat. Probably just ignoring me because he was annoyed."

Preddy pointed at a culvert. "Is dat where de water is supposed to be running down to de sea?"

"Not 'supposed', Detective," said Channer.

Mexell followed Preddy's gesture. "That is where the water collects. Regardless of what Judge Wrenn believed our water system works well. It does not go anywhere near Wynterton Park beach. They're just looking for someone to blame and I happen to be the wealthy target."

"Come now," said Preddy. "I've seen de letters between de strata board and yourselves going back more than a year. Dey seemed to have a legitimate concern and tied de pollution to your building work. I didn't see any outright denials in your replies."

"You could trace water impurities to any number of places along the coastline," said Mexell. "I told them before to try the Lime Ridge tyre factory further up the road. All that ash about the place. As far as I'm concerned, they are the most likely cause of any alleged pollution."

"And did dey, try Lime Ridge?" asked Preddy.

Mexell shrugged. "Judge Wrenn said Lime Ridge has been there forever and nobody had ever found them to be a nuisance. Anyway, I told him it was his problem and he shouldn't try to foist it on me."

"That's naw very sympathetic, Mr Mexell," said Harris. "Sounds as if ye were very angry with him."

"If there's nothing else we can help you with? We are rather busy detectives," said Channer quickly. "Some notice of an appointment would be preferable next time."

Preddy glanced at Harris. "I think dat will be it for now," he said before turning to glare at Channer. "If I think of anything else I'll be sure to stop by, wid or widout an appointment. Dis is a murder investigation not an inquiry about a property."

"You do that, Detective," said Mexell with an expression that reflected relief. "I really hope you catch Judge Wrenn's killer."

"I intend to," said Preddy holding his gaze.

Mexell blinked first. "There are many things I might do to keep my company alive, Detective, but not that. Never."

"Never," echoed Channer.

Harris tucked his notebook into his pocket. "I hope I live tae see the day when a murderer puts out their hands straight off and says, 'Ye got me.' I keep praying."

* * *

As Preddy drove quietly his frown deepened. Harris finally said, "Spill it."

"Hmm? What?"

"Well ye look like yer crunching on a cockroach."

Preddy gave Harris his deepest side-eye. "Find a better analogy next time, man." He stopped at the red traffic lights. "You did notice how him sit down and how him get up? Channer I mean?"

"Come again?" mumbled Harris.

"Very smoothly," said Preddy. "Sits without using hands, gets up without using hands."

"Naw sure what ye're getting at, but if ye're thinking he's gay I'll buy it. He seems tae be in love with his boss. Not sure that Mexell knows it though."

Preddy clenched the steering wheel tightly and finally only moved at the incessant tooting behind him when the light changed to green. "Not gay," he said quickly. "Not gay, no, not what I was thinking at all, at all."

It was Harris's turn to look concerned. "Okay, calm down, Preddy. What were ye thinking then?"

Preddy cleared his throat. "Well he moves like my son, Roman."

"Och, aye?"

"I don't like how you said dat." Preddy kept his eyes firmly on the road. "My kids do karate. My son has dat sort of smooth movement. Doesn't use his hands to sit or to stand. He puts his hands in front of him for balance, or sometimes to the side, widout touching anything."

"So Channer does karate, so what?"

"So he could disable de judge with one quick kick or elbow to de throat. Dose guys move fast. He doesn't look like a strong man, but you don't have to be strong to strangle someone to death once you've disabled dem," explained Preddy. "Doctor Sewell said it would take only two minutes of pressing on de larynx."

"Ye think Channer could have done this, with his boss or at least with the boss's knowledge?" asked Harris.

Preddy sighed deeply. "I think we have to look more closely at both of dem. Channer has no alibi, seems uptight, lot of animosity. Mexell's alibi isn't sound either. How convenient dat his woman was asleep when he got in."

"Ye know, Channer could naw be using his hands because he hurt them when strangling the judge," ventured Harris.

"Good point, though he held his briefcase comfortably enough." Preddy turned the car off the side road and onto the main road heading towards Pelican Walk station. "We need to find a way to interview dese men separately, see if one of dem will slip up. Mexell is de more likely of de two to give us anything."

Harris nodded. "I'll look intae him."

"In de meantime, let's go see what Tuffy has to say."

"Aye, that's a story I want tae hear," replied Harris. "Apparently he says he's naw talking tae any 'bumbo claat woman.'"

"Your accent is coming on," Preddy smiled. "Let's see if he has any clean words he can teach you."

* * *

The half-smile on Nathaniel Mexell's face vanished long before the detectives had disappeared from view. His cheek muscles hurt from the effort. He watched as their car wound its way down the hill on his freshly laid marl, past his newly planted hedges. The only visitors he wanted in Montego Hamlet were the ones who were coming to sign a contract before placing a hefty deposit, yet all sorts of officials were landing on him. Today it was police detectives. Last week it had been the nosey environmentalists from the National Environment and Planning Agency. The NEPA reps had inspected his pipework and poked around in his culverts and drains. He had tried to distract them with ice-cold fruit punch and cupcakes, but they had been more interested in following the pipelines.

He cursed himself inwardly for allowing himself to be in this position. If only he had followed his own mind and done what he had wanted to do. Yes, it would have cost him hundreds of thousands of dollars, but the money was coming in at a steady rate. Everybody wanted a part of Montego Hamlet. He could afford to do the right thing. Instead he had let himself be led into behaving in a way that could land him in jail for a long time.

Mexell closed his eyes briefly. The very idea of spending his days amongst the dregs of society was enough to send his stomach plummeting. He would have to be very careful around these detectives. The local one was known to be a dogged trigger-happy cop and the white one was probably weeks from morphing into the same. No foreigner ever successfully managed to teach Jamaican cops anything: they either adapted to the island cops' bad ways or escaped on a one-way plane ticket back to the First World. The fact that this Scottish one had returned meant he planned to become as badly behaved as the rest of them and he had an expert teacher in Raythan Preddy. Mexell removed his hard hat and tucked it under his armpit. Montego Hamlet was practically sold out off-plan with less than a dozen units left. The quicker he completed the development and left the area the better.

CHAPTER 7

Preddy and Harris arrived back at Pelican Walk and strolled into the lobby area. In front of the reception desk, two people were seated on the solid wooden benches: a young lady with eyes glued to her phone, who did not notice their presence and an elderly gentleman who was busy filling out a form balanced on his knee. He looked up and smiled a weary smile beneath his grey moustache.

"You alright, sir?" asked Preddy patting him lightly on the shoulder.

"Yes, man. De paperwork nuff though!"

"Tell me about it," murmured Harris.

"Is you name Misser Harris, no?" asked the old man. "Me see you pon TV!"

"Aye, that's me, sir." Harris placed one hand on his hip, straightened his shoulders, tossed back his head and twisted his body from side to side. "Much prettier in the flesh, ye'll agree?"

"Ha hiiiiy!" The old man laughed out loud revealing a good set of dentures, then swatted a back-hand in Harris's

84

direction. "You gwaan 'bout you business Misser Harris, 'bout you pretty!"

Preddy grinned at the cheery gentleman. "If you need any help, Officer Wilson will help you, you hear?"

"Yes, man. Thank you!"

Harris winked at him. "Look after yerself, young man."

"Me hear you, sah." The pensioner guffawed and slammed a wrinkled hand on the bench. "Me no quite ready fi dead yet!"

The detectives approached the front desk and greeted Officer Wilson. "Which room for Antwon Frazer?" asked Preddy.

Officer Wilson ran a finger down his register. "Interview Room 3, sir. His lawyer is with him."

The detectives headed up the stairs. "Damn, should have worn an orange shirt for Tuffy," said Preddy as they climbed.

Harris looked at him quizzically. "Orange shirt?"

"Socialist colour," explained Preddy. "Tuffy is from a madly orange district. Ancona. People's National Party or die."

"Ye have orange shirts, Preddy?"

"More dan one. Me have some green one too."

"Aah, Jamaica Labour Party," said Harris.

"Dat's right. Some of our people are tribalists. Dey'll give a kidney for JLP or PNP, both kidneys if it wouldn't kill dem."

"Ouch." Harris grimaced. "What would ye give for them?"

"Not even my fingernail clippings, for none of dem," said Preddy forcefully. "Sad to see poor people building up deir hopes every four years only to get zip. De IMF is our master."

"Got it."

They turned down the corridor and stopped outside Interview Room 3 which had an occupied sign hanging against it. "You can make friends wid Tuffy," Preddy whispered. "I grabbed him by de neck on our first meeting so he may not feel dat warmly towards me."

"Aye, first impressions."

Inside the room sat Tuffy Frazer with a young man whom Preddy assessed as being straight out of law school. The lawyer already had that disenchanted look of someone who had fallen out of love with the practice of law and wanted to be anywhere but confined in an airless interview room with grey stone walls and scratched plastic chairs.

"Gentlemen." Preddy nodded at them. "Detective Raythan Preddy and Detective Sean Harris."

"Haldin Newman, Caldecott Chambers." The lawyer made no attempt to shake hands, but sat stiffly with his elbows on the table and a tablet in his hands.

"Mr Frazer, we meet again," said Preddy.

Tuffy sat up straight. "Me glad you no bring dem two bad-mind woman wid you."

"We've naw need for any women today," said Harris, smiling in a friendly manner at the suspect. "They're at their desks where they belong."

Dat's right," said Tuffy nodding emphatically.

Preddy made a mental note to warn Harris never to run that line even in jest in front of Rabino and Spence. Rabino would admonish him and let it go, but Spence would hold a grudge until The Second Coming.

Tuffy's dishevelled appearance was the result of having spent a sleepless night in considerable discomfort. His eyes implored Preddy. "You haffi help me out, me boss."

His lawyer rolled his eyes. "Mr Frazer, please. We have to do this properly and protect your rights." He turned his attention to Preddy. "Please read my client his rights. As you can see he is keen to be co-operative."

Preddy read Tuffy his rights which the suspect quickly acknowledged. Harris tapped on his notepaper. "Is yer name really spelt A.N.T.W.O.N?"

Tuffy's craned his neck and tried to see what Harris was writing. "Yes, a wha'?"

"Unusual, that's all," said Harris.

"You think my modda cyah spell?"

"I wouldnae dream of questioning yer ma's spelling abilities, Antwon," said Harris politely.

Tuffy narrowed his eyes. "Me sure know say a S.E.A.N. write inna paper and a Sharn me hear dem call you, not Seen. My modda spell better dan your modda. Same way my name spell it pronounce!"

Preddy winced. Harris was not to know that any statement which invoked a slight against a Jamaican's mother was likely to incur wrath. There would be no bonding between Tuffy and Harris now. Preddy quickly intervened. "Antwon, what can you tell us about de murder of Judge Everton Wrenn?"

A deep frown etched on Tuffy's forehead. "No gun you wah talk to me 'bout?"

"My client has a point, Detective," said the lawyer. "Illegal guns and ammunition is what I heard he's being detained for."

"Dem two *hugly* woman bring me in here for dat! Gun and ammunition dem seh."

Harris offered Tuffy a no hard feelings glance. "We'll talk about what we say first, Antwon, and worry about what the women say later."

"Wait," Tuffy's frown grew deeper. "Me no like how dis white man talk. Sound like you no like Jamaican woman? You no like wha' dem do or wha' dem seh? Wha' dem do you?"

Preddy was surprised by Tuffy's sudden abandonment of his hitherto staunch misogyny towards Spence and Rabino in favour of their defence, however he declined to intervene while waiting for Harris to answer.

Flushes of crimson appeared on the Glaswegian's cheeks. "I'm naw sure how ye drew that conclusion, Antwon, but yer wrong. I like Jamaican women just fine. I work with some of the best."

"Eeh-eeh?" Tuffy voice oozed sarcasm.

"We're naw here tae talk about that though are we? We're investigating Judge Wrenn's murder."

"Look from when me done wid bad man business?" Tuffy raised his voice. "Me no inna Benbow Crew again. Me cyah answer question 'bout no murder. You just mek me angry and miserable right ya now!"

"Sorry tae be the cause of yer misery, Antwon," said Harris, "but I bet Oleta Wrenn is feeling angrier and more miserable than ye. And aye, I like Oleta just fine. She seems like a lovely lady."

"Miss Oleta nice, yes. Me never do a ting to her husband," said Tuffy.

Preddy leaned forward. "You're facing some very serious weapons charges Antwon, I'm sure your lawyer already explained dat to you. If you want us to try do anything for you, you have to tell us what you know about Judge Wrenn's murder."

"Me no inna de murder game," declared Tuffy. "You can gwaan talk 'bout you illegal possession of firearm. Me no possess nutten! Nobody no see me possess nutten! Inna house a Montpelier dem come find me. Dem don't find me wid my han' pon no gun!"

Preddy stared at him. "Seriously, you need to start talk. For Miss Oleta's sake, talk."

"Me no know nutten!" insisted Tuffy.

"My client knows nothing about the murder, detectives," said lawyer Newman. "Move on."

Tuffy looked from one detective to the other, but could find nothing encouraging in their features. "Me wah witness protection, a dat me a tell you. And a dat me tell Misser Lawyer-man here, but him nah listen!"

"Och?" said Harris. "Well let's talk about witness protection after we hear what ye have tae offer, Antwon."

"I'm all ears," added Preddy.

"Mr Frazer, please be quiet," said the lawyer impatiently. "Detectives, my client cannot speak on any murder as he knows nothing about it. He knows very little about the weapons and ammunition. It's not his car as you well know. He was wearing very dark shades when he threw a bag of bottled water into the Camry without noticing anything untoward. The first he knew about the content of the car trunk was when Pelican Walk officers dragged him out of a house in Montpelier and forced him to open it."

"*Hexactly!*" cried Tuffy. "Dat me trying to tell dem, long time!"

Harris scowled. "We'd like yer client tae tell us in his own words."

"As you can see, my client is very agitated and distressed," replied the lawyer smoothly. "He slept in a vest and shorts on a very hard mattress with a thin sheet. It's little wonder he can speak at all."

"Yer client has suggested that he wants witness protection, so he must have something that he wants tae say," said Harris, whose temples had begun to pulsate. "Something that might soothe his agitation and distress. We'd like tae hear it and see how we can help."

The lawyer glared back at the Scotsman. "Mr Frazer was given only dry bun and water yesterday evening. My client has not been offered a morsel this morning. Only a cup of bush tea without even a spoon of sugar and you want a coherent conversation with him. Trust me I intend to register a formal complaint. You cannot starve inmates all night and all morning and then interrogate them. It's unconscionable. I'm pretty sure you could never get away with that in Scotland."

Tuffy began to massage his temple and moan. "Whoy! Me head a hurt me."

Harris cast a look of disdain in Tuffy's direction.

Preddy assessed the lawyer. Young he might be, but clearly he was no pushover. "Sorry about dat. Antwon should certainly have been fed. We'll make sure he gets a good breakfast when dis interview is finished." Preddy looked at the detainee. "We going get you some saltfish and dumpling, how about dat?"

"Thank you, boss!" said Tuffy warmly. "Mek sure dem don't over-fry de dumpling dem, cause me no like dem dry-dry."

Harris leaned back in his seat. "Antwon, ye must realise ye're facing a very long time in jail? Dry dumplings are the least of yer worries. We'd like tae help ye tae help yerself. I'll be the first tae agree with ye that a police cell is naw a nice place tae spend any time, let alone days or weeks."

The lawyer scrolled on his tablet computer. "As we speak my colleague is preparing the papers for a bail application. There's no way my client is staying in here until a trial."

"Yer client had a large cache of weapons. A judge is dead. He's staying in his cell," predicted Harris.

The lawyer's smile was smug. "We'll see. You have absolutely nothing to tie my client to Judge Wrenn's murder, and as I said, Mr Frazer was oblivious about the contents of the car. As far as I'm concerned: Wrenn's car, Wrenn's weapons. My client happened to be in the wrong place at the wrong time." The man got to his feet. "Detectives, there is nothing to be gained by continuing this conversation, so my client is done. Any further questions will result in 'no comment' responses."

Harris and Preddy exchanged glances. "Have it your way, Mr Newman," said Preddy. He tapped the glass and beckoned to an officer outside who opened the door. "Take him back to de cell." The officer entered and Tuffy stood up.

Preddy shook his head. "Well Antwon, I guess we'll see you in Gun Court in de near future."

"Me a get my dumpling dem now, boss? Me hungry bad!"

"Aye, ye'll get yer dumplings," seethed Harris. "Naw too dry-dry."

CHAPTER 8

Thursday, 4 May, 2.05 p.m.

Preddy balanced the tray of drinks and slowly walked across the canteen floor to where his team were sitting. He lowered the tray and glanced at his watch. Lunch was late and it would have to be quick so he could fit in a trip to the Parish Court. The chef's assistant followed behind him with four plates of food expertly balanced on two trays.

Rabino rubbed her hands together as a plate of jerked chicken and seasoned fries was placed in front of her, with a side dish of mushy greens. Spence was handed barbecued chicken and fried rice with a large dollop of the same crushed greens. Harris had an identical plate, and eyed Spence as she ravenously cut piece of chicken and scooped the greens onto her fork. She closed her eyes and chewed while making an appreciative murmuring sound.

"Well, I recognize Preddy's greens as callaloo, tasty stuff, but what's this?" Harris poked at his greenery with his utensil. "Looks a bit like mushy peas?"

"Susumba Surprise," said Spence, continuing to make happy sounds. "Can't believe you no get none from you inna Jamaica. It nice, you see!"

Harris put a chunk of chicken breast into his mouth followed by a huge forkful of greens. A split second later his eyes began to water and a look of revulsion crossed his face. He snatched a paper napkin and spat the mouthful into it. "What the hell is that?" he spluttered, rapidly shading dark pink.

"Susumba," declared Rabino.

"Surprise!" yelled Spence simultaneously.

Preddy chuckled as he tucked into his steamed snapper fish and callaloo. "I don't know how anybody eats dat either. Some people call dem 'gully bean'. Bitter and disgusting!"

"Ye said it." Harris shuddered and dabbed his streaming eyes. "Ugh!"

"Big baby," muttered Spence as she chewed in contentment. "Eat dis stuff and you can do ninety minutes on any football field and not break into a sweat. Your new team will be proud of you."

"Really." Harris gulped down a mouthful of water and wiped his lips with the back of his hand. "Ye know, Detective Spence, I get the distinct impression ye knew I wouldnae like that."

Spence widened her eyes, the picture of innocence. "Now why would you ever go say a thing like dat, Detective Harris?"

Harris stared at her. "Maybe it's ma Spidey . . . I mean ma Anansi senses."

"What you know about Brer Anansi?" asked Preddy with genuine curiosity. The realisation that the Glaswegian had taken to reading Jamaican folk tales was a pleasant surprise.

Harris grabbed his water bottle again and took a few more gulps, shuddering as he did so. "Jeez! That is really awful!"

"No it's not," said Rabino, scooping up another mouthful to savour. "It's an acquired taste, I guess. I acquired it when I was about two. Loved it ever since."

Harris winced. "Any mother giving her bairn that doesnae love the wee thing."

"I born eating susumba," said Spence. "Straight from breast milk to susumba."

"Why is it that I dinnae find that hard tae believe?"

Spence paused her fork in mid-air. "How you mean?"

Suddenly Harris clutched his throat and began to cough. "Och God! I think I'm allergic tae . . ."

Harris rolled out of his chair onto the floor, his face growing redder by the second. His eyes rolled back in his head displaying white insides. His hands flailed weakly at his neck. Preddy sprang out of his seat which clattered to the ground and he set about undoing Harris's shirt collar. Spence grabbed her bottle of ice-cold water and poured some onto a napkin. She lifted his head and cradled it then began to wipe his face. Harris writhed and struggled for breath then went completely still.

"Detective Harris!" shouted Rabino, patting his cheeks. "Sean!" She snatched his wrist and felt for a pulse.

Other police officers deserted their food and began to make their way to the scene.

"Backside! Him alright?" asked one concerned officer, quickly falling to his knees.

"Hope him no come here come dead!" announced another officer, peering around Preddy's back. "God help we if white man come dead pon we!"

Spence dispensed with the napkin and started to pump on Harris's chest. Suddenly Harris opened his eyes and grinned widely at her. She sat back on her heels. The Scotsman brushed off his shirt. "Your face, Detective Spence!" He began to laugh as he got to his feet. "Thank ye for the water, that was very calming, but the pressure on the chest needs tae be lighter next time. I need tae take ye through resuscitation techniques again. Ye clearly dinnae know yer own strength. Damn near broke ma rib cage."

Spence rose clutching her own chest. "Blasted man," she muttered. "You nearly give me heart attack." Rabino helped her to her feet.

Preddy stood up and shook his head. Detective Harris had not come to Pelican Walk to die, but he was well on his way to making himself a possible target for murder.

Another worried officer stared at Harris and then at Preddy. "Him drop down a ground 'boof!' and him a laugh so?"

"Don't worry about him," Preddy exhaled as he studied Harris. "He's a bit . . . strange. Very strange."

"Guess he knows a whole lot about Anansi," noted Rabino with a hint of what sounded to Preddy like admiration. "The undisputed original ginnal."

Harris straightened his trouser legs and checked for signs of dust, before retaking his seat. "For future reference, I dinnae like susumba," he said as he spiked his chicken. "I dinnae like surprises either."

Dat makes two of us, thought Preddy.

* * *

Preddy had been on his way to the St James Parish Court, when he reminded himself that he was being neglectful and that one divorce under his belt was enough. There was time to run an errand and so he had diverted to the flower shop in the city centre. Now he was outside of Valerie's lab impatiently waiting for her to exit the building. Busy admiring the luscious looking clusters of ripe naseberries on an evergreen tree he did not hear when the side door opened.

"Hello stranger!"

Preddy spun around and pulled Valerie close to him giving her a kiss and a warm hug. She had on a white coat over a floral dress and kitten heel shoes.

"Mind you crush me flowers!" She took the roses from him and inhaled deeply. "At least I imagine dey are mine and is not some other woman you going to see?"

Preddy smiled. "As if."

"Dey are lovely, Ray."

"Like deir owner," said Preddy. "I'm running away though. Not sure if I'll see you later."

"Okay, baby." She drew back and pointed downwards. "Dere's something on de back of your leg, look like mud, near your right calf."

Preddy bent and brushed it off. "Mexell's mud. I was up at his development in de hills dis morning, Montego Hamlet."

"Oh," said Valerie with a grin. "Looking to buy us a luxury property are we?"

Preddy laughed. "Unfortunately, not. Looking to ask Mr Mexell a few questions about his business dat's all."

"He seems like a nice sorta guy."

Preddy had been entering his car, but now he paused and looked back at her. "Didn't know you know him?"

"Not really know him," she replied. "He came by here more dan once wid some water samples he wants tested."

"Tested for what?" asked Preddy.

"He seems to think dat de tyre factory up by Lime Ridge is polluting de water all de way downstream." Valerie frowned. "Not sure where him get dat idea from."

"Interesting," said Preddy. "And what do you say about de samples?"

"I haven't gotten around to looking at dem yet, Mr Detective. We have a whole heap of backlog. He'll have to wait another couple of days. I told him dat."

"I'll let you get back to it," said Preddy, smiling as he settled into the driver's seat. "Wouldn't want you to blame me for your late nights."

"Later. Bye baby." She blew him a kiss. "Love you."

"Love you, too."

* * *

The courthouse lobby was thankfully not busy in the late afternoon, most customers having been processed by lunchtime. Preddy covered the court steps two at a time and followed the signs. He strode down the corridor towards Judge Lawrence Guthrie's chambers. On the door were two worn wooden plaques one bearing Judge Guthrie's name, the other Judge Bailey. He knocked on the door.

A familiar voice said, "If that's you, Detective Preddy, come in."

Preddy pushed the heavy door open. The rectangular room was a good size with plenty of space for the two judges. Judge Bailey's section was vacant, his chair tucked well under his neat desk. Judge Guthrie's desk was on the opposite side of the room. It was full of brown manila files. A throne-like chair was too big to fit under the desk and was wedged against it. In the corner was a small table with an ice-box and plastic cups. The judge was standing with his back to the door, staring in the mirror while fixing the collar above his robe. An oscillating fan whirred away beside him delivering much-needed cool air.

"Good afternoon, sir," said Preddy.

The judge mumbled a greeting through pursed lips as he tilted his head back and checked his stubble. Preddy closed the door and walked towards the man's desk. Some of the photos around Judge Guthrie's space were similar to those in Judge Wrenn's office. Lots of university shots strategically placed for visitors to see. Old boys unwilling to put away photographs that harked back to their youth. Photos of what appeared to be Judge Guthrie's family, a wife and children; two boys who looked like young teenagers, and a girl who could be in her early twenties, all laughing and smiling. A prominent one of the whole family at a dinner table was framed and formed the centrepiece of the judge's desk.

"Nice kids," remarked Preddy leaning in towards the photos.

"Great kids." The judge smiled into the mirror. "Nobody's interested in practicing law though. My daughter's training to be a vet. My wife's glad about that. She's the animal lover in the family."

"Never been one for pets myself, but a little bird is changing my mind," said Preddy. "What are de boys going to do?"

"That's to be decided. They change their minds more often than I change my robes."

"Thank you for seeing me, anyway, Judge Guthrie. I know you must be very busy."

"Anything to help, Detective. I will always try to make myself available." He turned his head from side to side making sure that his collar was straight. "I've allowed my court to rise so the lawyers can go get some additional evidence faxed to them, but it will be recalled in about half hour."

"It won't take long, Judge," Preddy assured him as he surveyed the room. Beneath the table a piece of cloth had become dislodged from a cardboard box it was covering. There were empty glass bottles inside with the recognizable insignia of Wray & Nephew.

"As long as you need, Detective." Judge Guthrie smiled at his reflection. "There."

"Did Judge Wrenn ever talk to you about getting an injunction against a company . . . a personal matter?"

Judge Guthrie frowned and turned to face the officer. "No, not at all. Personal, you say?"

"Yes, it's alleged dat de beach at Wynterton Park was being affected by a development up in de hills," explained Preddy. "It's my understanding dat Judge Wrenn was planning on seeking an injunction to stop de works."

"Aah!" Judge Guthrie nodded, recognition having dawned on him. "That would be NatMex? Ever . . . sorry, Judge Wrenn, did tell me of his frustration that they'd destroyed his beautiful beach. It used to be really blue down there you know, absolutely glorious."

"I've seen some pictures," said Preddy. "De suspicion is dat it has something to do wid deposits of silt. Did he ever mention de Lime Ridge tyre factory to you?"

The judge shook his head. "No, never. Only NatMex."

"Only NatMex," echoed Preddy.

"Wait a minute," The judge stared closely at Preddy. "You don't think Nathaniel Mexell had something to do with Everton's death? Jesus Christ!" The judge flopped down on the corner of his desk, hands gripping his knees.

"We're following up all leads, sir," said Preddy. "How easy or how hard would it have been for Judge Wrenn to get an injunction against NatMex?"

"Well, I hate to give away our secrets, but it's a fact that any request for help from a member of the judiciary would be moved up the roster of the relevant judge hearing the matter. That's just how it goes."

"I understand, but would the injunction actually shut down NatMex completely, I mean cripple Montego Hamlet?"

The judge looked thoughtful. "Quite possibly, Detective. Of course, it would depend on the terms of the injunction sought. Everton would not just ask for a cease and desist type of ruling which would prohibit them from continuing the building work. He would want them to remedy the situation and insist that they show proof that no further pollution would take place," he explained. "NatMex would have to do some remedial works to channel the silt away from the beach. Not easy, because they removed a lot of trees to do the building work, and remember, it's the trees that collect a lot of the silt water."

"So, it could be very costly for NatMex," said Preddy.

"Very. Time and money. And then there's the publicity as it must come out. Buyers would want to know what was causing the delay and preventing them from moving in. News would spread. Mexell wouldn't like that." He paused. "Everton wouldn't like that either."

"Why would Judge Wrenn care about publicity?" asked Preddy. "Surely, his sole interest would be in getting de matter resolved, getting a clean beach?"

"True, but when you're up for promotion it doesn't look good if there's anything . . . external going on at the same time. I know that from personal experience." The judge smiled wryly. "It's best to stay under the radar in your private life."

"Judge Wrenn was up for promotion?"

Judge Guthrie seemed to be distracted and stared at the wall. A wall littered with his own certificates and diplomas encased in gaudy gold frames. "Sir? You say Judge Wrenn was due to get a promotion?"

Judge Guthrie blinked twice. "Yes, to the Court of Appeal. He'd applied and was on a short shortlist. He would've made a great Appeal judge. He was a very gifted, intuitive man. Very sharp, a stickler for right over wrong."

"It's a shame when we lose people like dose." Preddy said, shaking his head. "We need more of dem in dis society.

"I agree. What happens next, Detective?"

"We continue wid our investigations," said Preddy noncommittally.

"You do know that the judges are agitating towards industrial action don't you? We're fed up with a lot of things . . . salaries, antiquated working conditions, and now a murder practically on our doorstep. I don't see how we can avoid even a go-slow. It's inevitable."

Preddy gritted his teeth and silently counted to three. It was not as if the rank and file of the police service had it any better than the court staff, yet the officers continued the daily grind and did not strike. "I can assure you we're doing our best."

The judge leaned forwards, his hazel eyes searching. "Do you have any strong suspects, Detective?"

Preddy met his gaze. "Every lead will be followed up, I promise you dat."

"It would be good if you could find the murderer quickly, put everyone's mind at rest."

"Yes, it would."

The door knocked and Judge Guthrie's clerk put her head in the room. "You ready, sir?"

"Yes, I'm coming right now." The judge indicated that Preddy should precede him and the detective obeyed. The two men followed behind the clerk who tottered on her heels towards the courtroom, past benches of weary people in the waiting area some of whom perked up when they saw the judge approaching. It was standard court practice that people waited and waited. Waited for their lawyers, waited for the other side's lawyers, waited for the judges.

The judge nodded at Preddy as a court officer held open the door to the courtroom. "Do contact me if you need any further help, Detective."

"All rise!" bellowed the court officer.

Preddy watched as the judge strode along the aisle to his bench. The audience members downed their newspapers and turned off their phones, standing silently in an orderly manner. Judge Guthrie was an extremely commanding presence and it was little wonder that the crowd were in awe.

"You joining us, sir?" asked the court officer.

"No, no," said Preddy and backed away from the door leaving it to close. "I've seen enough."

* * *

Judge Lawrence Guthrie gave a brief bow as he took up his seat on the bench. Maybe people did commit murder over such things as pollution, but he had never come across anybody who had been accused of such a thing, let alone convicted of it. Tensions could run high when it came to valuable property and he could see how the police could conceive that Everton Wrenn and Nathaniel Mexell might literally come to blows. Detective Preddy was clearly covering every angle he could think of. He had heard that Preddy was one of Mo Bay's finest lawmen and he believed it. Like a good detective he was unlikely to share any information unless absolutely necessary, which was unfortunate as he would have liked to follow the detective's line of reasoning on every suspect he came across.

Everton's worthless ex-con driver Antwon Frazer was in custody, that much he knew. That man would always be a prime candidate for a prison sentence. Now it seemed they were going after Nathaniel Mexell. Either one would do. Judge Guthrie stifled a smile. It would not do to appear to be in a good mood before the court. The judge surveyed the courtroom taking in the solemn faces of people who shuffled uncomfortably on the hard wooden benches. He had to get his mind back on the job. He ran his eyes down his roster. These people were relying on him to adjudicate their disputes. They hung onto his every word and each desperately wanted him to find in their favour. It was his duty to pay attention to their pleas even as they irritated and bored him, even as he wished that he could get away from them for good. There would be time enough later to think about who could be nailed for the murder of his beloved friend, Judge Everton Wrenn.

CHAPTER 9

The detectives were assembled in the evidence room with the door closed and the blinds down. On the long table were individual notebooks, handwritten papers and mounds of bottled water. An overhead fan delivered enough air to ruffle the pages if not to cool the room. The faint odour of mosquito repellent lingered. Preddy stood at the busy whiteboard writing down pertinent comments. He noticed that Harris was using his usual tablet computer and he wondered what the Scotsman had done with the bronze one.

"So how did dis person get so close to Judge Wrenn?" asked Preddy.

"He knew them?" suggested Harris.

"Nobody really know nobody," said Spence bluntly. She had neither forgiven nor forgotten the Scotsman's earlier performance, which had done little to reduce her suspicion of him that had existed since his very first day in Pelican Walk. "We no see no evidence dat anybody climbed de walls of Wynterton Park. No torn pieces of clothes, no blood on de perimeter fencing. I'm guessing de murderer was already on de premises, or crept under de security barrier unseen by de guards."

"Or came by sea," added Preddy.

"Or came by sea," nodded Harris. "I spoke tae various property owners on the waterfront. There are people who sail at all hours of the night and early morning. The majority seem tae be law-abiding citizens just enjoying the sea."

"Inna dat black dark, though?" said Spence with a look of incredulity. "Dat person would be brave. Tuffy don't look like a brave man to me. I never see a man nervous so!"

"That's probably the effect you had on him," Rabino grinned. "Mind you when the Camry trunk opened I thought he was going to pass out. When my camera started flashing he backed up like a vampire avoiding sunlight!"

"I backed up when I see dat thing flashing! Not keen on being a muse for you and your amateur photography," Spence chuckled. "Anyway, if Tuffy did it he never arrived by sea."

"De coastguard weren't patrolling on Monday night." Preddy flicked over a page of his notes. "De marine police have looked through deir records too, but de few people dey saw were sailing around sunset. One fisherman who swore he was fishing, although dey saw no catches in his boat. A catamaran who dey waved to — said it looked like some white tourists were on it. Another catamaran followed shortly after wid just de captain."

Spence frowned. "Dey can't cover de entire coastline though, so somebody could have got past dem."

"It would have to be somebody who knew de judge's house and could pick it out in de dark," said Preddy. "Not an easy feat."

"The security guards swear their records show everybody that came or left the premises on Monday straight through to Tuesday morning," said Rabino. She waved a handful of papers in the air. "I took copies of the register. There weren't many visitors and we've spoken to everyone on the list. A couple of delivery men, a plumber, a JPS meter reader and a mobile hairdresser. No one had an appointment that would take them near the judge's villa. No suspects."

Harris twirled his pen. "Those security guys didnae look so alert tae me. I'm more inclined tae go along with what Spence said. It's possible that someone got past them on foot, just crawled under the barrier. And it's naw clear what happens when they change shifts . . . timekeeping naw being a great thing and all in this place." The silent hard stares that greeted the latter statement resulted in a swift correction from the foreigner. "Timekeeping in general. Present company excluded of course."

"Of course," echoed Spence.

Preddy nodded. "And de residents come and go widout being signed in and out either. Speaking of residents, what do we think? Anybody we specifically need to focus on?"

"Logically, we start at de beginning with Oleta Wrenn," declared Spence. "Family are always top of de list."

"Unless she's a great actress, those tears were genuine," observed Rabino. "I could feel her whole body shaking. I purposely squeezed her hands, but she didn't flinch or anything. Swollen fingers, sign of water retention maybe? Not a bruise on them."

"Broken nail dat she has an excuse for," added Spence. "Sounds plausible."

"Can't see her hiring anyone to do it, either." Rabino tapped her pen on her notepad. "There's no motive we can ascribe to her. She and her two children are Judge Wrenn's sole beneficiaries. She has a good job as a high school principal. The children work abroad and have good jobs. By all accounts they were a happy loving couple."

Harris shrugged. "She has naw alibi and we have naw motive or evidence against her."

"Antwon 'Tuffy' Frazer?" said Preddy, running a black marker under his name. "Mr Fried Dumplings."

"Naw too dry-dry," quipped Harris.

Rabino gave him a quizzical look, but Harris just smiled.

"Tuffy is my prime suspect. Judge Wrenn must do him something," said Spence. "Dat abandoned house where we caught him is apparently well used by him crew men.

Neighbours see dem coming and going all de while, but dem too frighten to confront dem. You know how it go."

"Tuffy's crew seem tae be quite productive businessmen," said Harris. "Guns and bullets for all who want them."

"Wholesale and retail," said Preddy. "De Benbow Crew are major producers of violence. So far dey don't export it to other parishes. It stays in St James. We can only hope dat dey don't think of expanding. Now might be a good chance to curtail deir activities once and for all."

"Dem never shoot Judge Wrenn though," Spence reminded them. "No bullets involved here."

"True. Who strangles anybody nowadays anyway?" asked Rabino. "I mean, come on. We could cover Jarrett Park from end to end and have a gun show with the amount of weapons laying around in the squatter communities. I can't see anybody in the Benbow Crew deciding to put their hands on someone's neck."

Spence nodded. "Take too much energy. Dem lazy worthless bwoy no have time for dat. Unless dem gun misfire or something and dey did have to use dem hand?"

"Possibly," said Preddy. "Improvisation brought on by necessity. And if dey went dere to murder de judge dey were not going to leave him alive just because dey couldn't shoot him."

"They could have left him alive and just shot him another day," suggested Harris.

"Not if he saw the killer's face they couldn't," said Rabino. "Particularly if it was Tuffy. I've asked Trojan Street police to check their records if they picked him up Monday night. Can't even find out who was on duty that night. Who's running that mess of a station now?"

"Dat would be Superintendent McCallum," said Preddy. "Dat place is an embarrassment to dis parish. I can only hope de Minister close it down one day."

Rabino continued, "I'm trying to check Tuffy's alibi about being at Night Court, but none of the court clerks are returning calls. It's like those guys have already started some sort of informal strike action."

"Hmm. Speaking of courts, what about Lawrence Guthrie?" asked Harris. "His enthusiasm for the case could be because he genuinely wants tae be helpful, but it's also a trait of people with a lot tae hide."

"Judge Guthrie," stressed Rabino, shaking her head at the very thought. "Judge Wrenn's best friend since forever."

"One of de last persons to see de judge alive though," remarked Preddy. "And dey were arguing, by Lawrence Guthrie's own admission. We don't really know what dey were arguing about. He suggested it was just a normal healthy debate."

"The death of Judge Wrenn must have created a vacancy in the judiciary for somebody?" mused Harris.

"Not for Lawrence Guthrie," said Preddy thoughtfully. "Maybe for another prospective judge. Lawrence is way down de judicial food chain. Judge Wrenn was up for a promotion to de Court of Appeal. His death might benefit another candidate, but not Lawrence Guthrie."

"Maybe Judge Wrenn's death came about as a result of jealousy," suggested Harris. "Guthrie's friend was moving out of his reach up the career ladder and he wanted tae take him down a peg or two. The death was accidental."

"That would be some accident," said Rabino.

"Dat would be some jealousy," muttered Spence.

"I'm not going to discount Guthrie," said Preddy. "He has quite a few white rum bottles dat he attempted to hide in a box in his chambers. Who knows what a drunk would do?"

"Drunk and jealous — good mix for murder," said Harris.

"You don't like de man at all, do you Detective Harris?" asked Spence. She drained a bottle of cold water and watched him. "I know how it is though. Sometimes it hard not to think bad things about certain people, no matter how decent dem seem."

Preddy quickly said, "Check out Judge Guthrie's alibi with his girlfriend Jacqui Morgan." He took a piece of paper from his notebook and held it out towards her.

Spence tore her eyes away from Harris. She stretched and took the piece of paper from Preddy. "Yes, sir."

"Nathaniel Mexell," said Preddy, circling the businessman's name. "Owner of NatMex Construction. Looks like Judge Wrenn was about to shut him down, paralyse his operations in Montego Hamlet. Apparently remedying de pollution issue is a very expensive thing. And den of course he wouldn't be able to complete de apartment sales."

"I'll buy that motive for murder," said Rabino.

"Mexell certainly wouldnae have Judge Wrenn on his Christmas list," agreed Harris.

"Mexell was a bit over-friendly and unduly relaxed," said Preddy. "Tried to make it seem as if an injunction is no big deal, which we now know it would have been."

Harris nodded. "And he has that company secretary, Stephan Channer, who seems willing and ready tae do anything tae protect his boss. With all his cultured tone he's full of aggression. Naw a nice man at all."

"Yes, Channer does bother me," admitted Preddy as he underlined the name. "I don't know if dat's de lawyer in him. Very antagonistic and defensive. And he has no alibi . . . went to bed with a bottle of ibuprofen."

"That he wished was Mexell," added Harris.

"Huh?" said Rabino glancing at the Scotsman.

Preddy turned from the whiteboard. "Yes, Detective Harris thinks Mr Channer is gay."

"Eeh-eeh?" Spence gave this information a few seconds to sink in. "Oh well, if battyman commit murder dem fi go jail too. Dem not going get no special treatment."

Rabino threw the top of her pen at Spence who grinned as she narrowly avoided being hit. "Moving swiftly on," said Rabino with an exaggerated eye-roll.

"Quite," said Preddy. "Do what you can do dis evening, people. We have a lot of work to do tomorrow. Lots of alibis to follow up on." Preddy began to collect his paperwork, then looked up at the still seated detectives. "Wait, you people still here?"

CHAPTER 10

Rabino cruised along the highway in her jeep with Spence in the passenger seat. Eventually they navigated the busy airport roundabout and headed towards Gloucester Avenue, the famed Hip Strip. Rabino pulled up outside of a clothes boutique in a new shopping plaza overlooking the Caribbean Sea. The boutique's neighbour on one side was a cambio with a queue of customers waiting to exchange foreign currency for the rapidly depreciating Jamaican dollar, and on the other a restaurant selling bland fast food at tourist prices. The boutique itself was a floor to ceiling glass structure. Pink mannequins with tiny waists posed in the windows advertising the latest lines of fashion. Some were bedecked in outlandish outfits geared towards the adventurous, the daring and the downright lewd. Others looked more staid yet fashionable, designed for women with conservative tastes.

"Look at de split pon dat skirt," remarked Spence. "Might as well go naked."

"Some do," Rabino smiled. "Our good ex-stripper friend Zadie Merton would love it."

"Ah Zadie. Me hear dat she doing tourism management at college now."

"Really? Good for her. She's not dim so I think she'll make it." Rabino stared at the outfit again. "You sure you don't fancy it for the office summer party?"

Spence laughed. "Heh! If me ever try leave my house inna dat Mikey would carry me to go mental asylum! Why you walking around wid you crotch out-a-door if you not at beach? Madness, my girl."

"Madness indeed," agreed Rabino. "Needs a pair of shorts at least."

"Your figure could manage dat wid shorts. Me? I would need to drop ten pound first and me not giving up my banana bread. I going bake a whole heap next weekend!"

Rabino closed her eyes briefly and kneaded her temples. "Let me look into your future without you having to pay me a cent. I predict you will burn the banana bread like last time."

"You ungrateful, eeh!" Spence chuckled. "You nyam it down like you never see food for a week! Anyway, is not me burn it. Is de kids dem. Dat's my story and I'm sticking to it."

A bell on the door tinkled as the detectives entered and a young sales assistant in a tiny skirt and bright make-up made her way towards them.

"Good day, ladies." She spoke in a sing-song voice showing clean teeth and dimpled cheeks.

Rabino peered at the name tag brooch on the assistant's chest. "Good day, Marsha. I'm Detective Rabino. This is Detective Spence, Pelican Walk police."

"Oh wow!" Marsha's eyes widened. "Detectives."

"Is de owner here?" asked Spence.

"I'm here!" The voice came from above them. Jacqui Morgan was on the mezzanine floor peering down at them. She was a slender lady with a long neck and tightly coiled copper curls pressed close to her scalp. Long African earrings dangled from each ear. Her eyes were perfectly done using the latest shadowing technique and she resembled a gracefully ageing model. Jacqui was in her late forties, determined to never look fifty.

"Come on up the stairs, detectives," she said. "Marsha you're on your own for now. Watch the front door. I saw some boys walking past earlier with rucksacks, looked like real thieves."

"Yes Ma'am, will do."

"Thank you for agreeing to see us, Miss Morgan," said Rabino as she followed the woman into a small room that seemed to serve a dual role as office and display area.

Spence pulled out a chair without an invitation. Rabino stood next to her, eyes fixed on the glamorous owner.

"It's Mrs, actually. And yes my husband is alive, but we live totally separate lives." She smiled as she spoke through burgundy lips. "I'm seeing Lawrence Guthrie now, as you know." Her face glowed with intense pride as if she could not believe her good fortune.

"Dat's nice," said Spence. "Where were you on Monday night, Mrs Morgan?"

"Call me Jacqui, please." Jacqui rubbed her perfectly manicured hands together applying invisible hand cream. "Monday night, you mean the night they murdered the judge?"

"Dat's right," said Spence her eyes flicking from the woman's face to her hands and back again.

"Lawrence and I went to dinner on the Houseboat Grill. Such a unique place in the middle of the water beside the mangroves. You have to ring a bell and they send a little raft to collect you from the shore. Have you guys ever been there?"

"No," stated Rabino flatly. "Sounds delightful."

"We're not after recommendations for a dinner venue though," said Spence.

Jacqui studied the unsmiling detectives beneath her heavy lashes. "I know he must have told you this already, and it's true. He picked me up here when I locked up the shop, which must have been around six-thirty . . . seven."

"And after dat?" pressed Spence.

"He dropped me off at home, must have been around ten-ish."

"Seems like an early night for both of you?" said Rabino lightly.

Jacqui responded with a bright smile. She pushed back in her chair, settling comfortably. "He couldn't come inside, because my husband was home. Yes, we still live together at present, but we lead separate lives, as I said. I never stay out really late in the week anyway as I don't want to disturb the kids who should be in bed sleeping. I have two teenagers, you know. You ladies have children?"

"Two," said Spence, staring at her with no hint of sisterhood in her gaze.

"Maybe, some day," replied Rabino.

"Well don't leave it too late, Detective," warned Jacqui pursing her lips in disapproval.

Rabino folded her arms across her chest and forced a smile which did not reach her eyes. "Not everybody makes a good mother. Some mothers are just plain selfish. Some use their kids as pawns. Some are neglectful and only had the kids because they could, not because they really wanted them. I see the evidence every day."

Jacqui scowled while sizing up Rabino.

"So, you don't know where Lawrence went after he dropped you off den?" Spence asked.

Jacqui shrugged. "He went back to his hotel. No reason for him to lie about that. He stays there at least two nights a week. On weekends he goes back home to St Elizabeth."

"Expensive hotel, de Ambassador West," said Spence. "I wouldn't have thought most judges could afford it?"

"Paid for by taxpayers, not by Lawrence," offered Jacqui. "Nice place, but I want us to get a place together at some point, maybe in Reading or the Fairview area. Enough of this hiding away from the spouses business. We're too mature for that now."

"Yes," said Rabino. "And it wouldn't set a good example for the children either."

"Let he who is without sin . . ." quoted Jacqui.

"Did you ever meet Judge Everton Wrenn?" asked Rabino.

"No. Lawrence talked about him all the time, but I never met him. They were best friends, but I'm not sure what Lawrence told him about me." Her eyes fluttered giving her a sheepish look. "I got the impression that he wanted to make sure we were solid before introducing us. We've only been together for three months . . . three great months though." She delivered another radiant smile of contentment. Spence rolled her eyes and glanced around at the various items of designer clothing hanging from the rails.

"Do you know whether he and Judge Wrenn had any arguments recently?" asked Rabino.

Jacqui shook her head. "Not that he mentioned. They're best friends, Detective. Whether they argued or not Lawrence would never hurt his best friend."

"You think he would tell you if he did?" asked Spence. "Are you two really dat close, dat quickly?"

"Yes, we are." Jacqui stood and adjusted the sleeves of a cotton dress hanging near her table. "And yes he would. We talk about everything."

"Eeh hee," muttered Spence, her tone one of amused disbelief as she rose.

Rabino handed Jacqui a business card. "Please call us if you think of anything that could help our investigation."

"I'll do that, Detective. Sure you don't want to have a good look around before you leave?" Jacqui eyed Rabino from head to toe. "You're quite slim. I have some nice floral pieces that would suit your shape. Look at this one." The businesswoman removed a slinky dress from a hanger and held it up in the air.

Rabino was quite satisfied with the normal womanly figure that swimming and yoga classes had moulded, but that low-necked clinging jersey dress would have her thighs on parade. "That's not quite to my taste," she said. "I prefer clothes that breeze can pass through."

Jacqui turned her attention to Spence. "You know you have great ankles. This cream skirt suit would be good for you if you're going to a formal do. We can find a nice pair of heels to go with it. What you think?"

"Smart suit." Spence pulled out the carefully hidden price tag and scrutinized it. "No wonder you don't want anybody to see it. Dis suit cost more dan my fridge."

"I can offer you a discount?" suggested Jacqui, hopefully. "Fifteen percent off?" she pressed, after affecting a mental calculation.

"It nice still, but I'll pass." Spence started down the stairs and Marsha hurried towards the bolted door. "Maybe when de annual bonus pay out."

As they walked back to their car Rabino asked, "What annual bonus? Don't tell me those online ginnals you consult have predicted a bonus?"

"Heh! No sis." Spence grinned. "Never once have dey predicted dat I will come into money."

"Damn, maybe one day."

Spence glanced at her. "You must have plenty of money coming your way when de old folks pass on since is you alone dem have?"

"They're not going just yet, I hope." Rabino smiled. "I've told them to spend their money and enjoy doing whatever makes them happy. I'll get by just fine. Dad used to do so much foreign travelling as a diplomat, but it was all work. Now he can take mom cruising on the seven seas which is what she's always dreamed of doing."

"Alright for some." Spence opened the car door and climbed inside. "Dat Jacqui is a woman in love. Her eyes just a shine!"

Rabino mimicked Jacqui Morgan's voice. "'Three great months.' Hah! Mrs Three Great Months is totally in awe of her darling Lawrence."

Spence shook her head. "So much so dat she leave de two pickney a yard and gone sport wid him. Damn hypocrite!"

"Same thing I was thinking. Mother Of The Year."

"Good luck to her hoping dat dey soon move in together," said Spence. "Guthrie have him wife and she have her husband. Mr Morgan might well be on board wid his wife's foolishness, but I bet you Mrs Guthrie don't know a thing. Cheating men love dat type of set up."

"True talk," said Rabino as she started the engine and put it into reverse. "I get the distinct impression from Preddy that Judge Guthrie is used to deception, a master of it." A pair of plump tourists sauntered behind her vehicle clutching their lunch and she waited patiently for them to pass. She wondered why anyone would pay so much money and fly so far to buy the same greasy burgers they could buy at home. They should try jerk chicken and bammies instead.

"You think he could be involved in de murder and Jacqui know 'bout it?" asked Spence.

"Hmm, not sure. She's so in love I believe she would accept anything he told her though," replied Rabino. "And it's not a crime to love somebody else's man. Not yet anyway."

"Courthouse would a full!" Spence grinned. "Jailhouse even fuller!"

* * *

Stephan Channer drove to the marine park docks and skilfully eased the BMW into a reserved parking space. The space was meant for dock management, but he knew that no one would ask him to move. Most people were leaving anyway, heading off to lunch before the decent restaurants ran out of the most popular selections. He turned off the gently purring engine. He loved how the vehicle moved with smoothness and precision. It was almost a shame to climb out, away from the soft leather seats. He smiled as memories flooded back of his very first vehicle. His treasured and battered rust bucket of a Hyundai that he washed down every single morning. It had been *the thing* back in the day, got him to exactly where he needed to go even though the floor was so deteriorated he used to fear it would give way when he pressed down on the accelerator or the brakes.

If it was down to those Pelican Walk detectives he would lose all of this hard-won wealth and he was not about to do so. It was his time for creature comforts. All those years of studying, not to mention the money spent by his struggling parents to get him onto a decent career trajectory. Then there were the boring years of learning the ropes through a varied mix of practice areas and it was compulsory to get involved in all of them. Crime, civil law, litigation, wills and probate, as well as corporate and real estate matters. He had found it difficult to get really interested in any of the subjects when he merely touched the surface of each area.

The decision to become an in-house lawyer, and have only one master, was swift. It was much easier to concentrate on learning everything there was to learn about conveyancing, and the truth was real estate was one area of law robust enough to stand the test of time even during a recession. When he had heard that Nathaniel Mexell was looking for a company secretary he saw it as a good opportunity to move on to something prestigious. Now, a mere three years later, he was doing well. Now he was the owner of a lovely house that he was expanding. He drove a highly-coveted car that he had so far not contributed a cent towards, and he was able to sail in a nice yacht whenever it took his fancy.

Channer nodded at the dock hand and gave him a brief wave. The man returned the greeting then bowed his head back into his newspaper. Channer rolled up his sleeves and stood with his hands on hips studying the NatMex boat. He narrowed his eyes and peered at the hull. Moving closer he dragged a finger along a mark on it. He wondered when it got there and how he had not noticed it before now. There was always a chance that something or somebody had knocked against it over the past few days. He frowned. There was no point in taking any chances.

He filled a bucket with water from a nearby keg and used an old rag to rub down the area. To his relief, the mark disappeared after a few strokes. Channer stood up straight and admired his handiwork. Police had a bad habit of seeing everything and he had a feeling that if the yacht ever came across the detectives radar they would be all over him like curry on goat. Not that the detectives should come near it. As long as Nat kept his mouth shut there was nothing to be afraid of. A frown crept across Channer's face. There was a lot to be said for the mantra that the only way to keep a secret was for nobody else to know. If a second person knew, you were always in danger of the whole world finding out.

He set about cleaning up the rest of the boat and then inspected every inch of it. Once he was sure it looked pristine he returned the bucket and rag to the below deck storage room. With another wave to the dock hand he made his way back to his vehicle. He cast a final glance at the NatMex yacht as he drove away. It was ready for the regatta, and ready for any inquisitive eyes that might focus on it. He was determined that NatMex would stay winning.

CHAPTER 11

Friday, 5 May, 2.05 p.m.

Preddy leapt into the police jeep and set the siren shrieking as Harris climbed into the passenger side. Preddy gunned the engine and screeched out of Pelican Walk car park and onto the main road, barely avoiding a collision with an oncoming car. The aggrieved motorist swerved out of the detective's way and Harris waved a placatory hand at him. Ahead, other cars quickly moved aside to avoid being bumped off the road. This was a busy time of day on the road for Montegonians. Many would be finishing lunch and returning to work, others would be leaving the second city for an early start to the weekend. The tour buses and coasters took up a great part of the roadway carrying excited sun-worshippers from one immaculate beach to another. Whichever way you looked there was traffic merging uncomfortably with pedestrians, leading to tooting horns and heated verbal confrontations. The detectives sped along Top Road towards the St James Parish Court with no opportunity to appreciate the magnificent views of the waters and hills all of which were now a merged blur of blue green.

"Do we naw have bomb disposal experts?" asked Harris.

"Yes, dey're on de way," replied Preddy. He glanced at his perspiring colleague through the corner of his eye. "In de meantime, we're it."

Harris raised an eyebrow. "I dinnae think so, Preddy. Ma kids wouldnae appreciate it. We'll clear the area, but we're naw dismantling any bombs."

"No sir," said Preddy flatly. "Absolutely not, sir."

Harris flushed. "Sorry, I didnae mean tae sound like that."

Preddy concentrated on manoeuvring around the traffic. "I'm wid you. Dere's no way I'm going near any bomb."

"Are ye sure we should be going at all? I mean, an anonymous caller specifically asking that ye be told. Could be a ruse tae get ye down there?"

Preddy was grim faced. "I know. But I have to take dat chance. We rarely get bomb threats — no more dan one a year and none has ever turned out to be de real thing. Dere's probably something else going on here."

"I'm ready for action whatever it is." Harris checked that his weapon was loaded before re-holstering it. "They've got metal detectors at the courthouse. Would someone even be able tae get a bomb inside the building?"

"Not everyone goes through de detectors. You and I don't have to. Other police officers don't have to, neither do de judges for dat matter. Everybody else including court staff is supposed to."

The closer they got to downtown Montego Bay the worse the traffic became with impatient drivers trying to jump the queues. By now most of the roads in the immediately vicinity were in the process of being cordoned off and traffic officers were diverting vehicles away from the city centre.

"Ye see," said Harris. "That's why I said we should get motorbikes."

"Feel free to go look bike," replied Preddy. "Not for me. If I'm doing ninety on de roads I appreciate solid metal armour around me."

"We'd have been there already. Ye could knock fifteen minutes off easily with two wheels."

"You could also get knocked off easily, and den your fifteen minutes would be up," said Preddy.

Harris looked wistful. "Ye can even lease them for a weekend. I've done Mo Bay tae Negril a few times now. Nothing beats being on a bike with the rubber burning, carving up the miles with the wind rushing through yer hair."

"In case you haven't noticed my hair is two millimetres tall."

"Och, ye've got naw sense of adventure, Preddy."

"Got less grey dan you, though."

As they reached their destination Preddy noted that some drivers had not removed their cars from the court car park, fear of losing their treasured spots being greater than the threat of damage from an explosion.

The courthouse had been evacuated under Preddy's instructions by the time the law men arrived. Court staff, recently returned from their lunch break, were mingling with the evacuees and discussing the strange turn of events. The traffic police had stretched yellow and black caution tape around the entrance. The crowd remained way too close to the premises for Harris's liking and as he climbed out of the jeep he shouted, "Ye need tae stand right back!" He gesticulated with outstretched arms. "Naw one wants tae go flying through the air without a parachute!" The crowd murmured and grudgingly moved further back.

"Nice touch," muttered Preddy.

"I do ma best," said Harris.

Preddy slammed the car door shut and adjusted his bullet-proof vest. "A white man wid outstretched arms. You know what dat means to some people?"

Harris looked genuinely intrigued. "What?"

"Jesus Christ."

"Jesus, Preddy." Harris shook his head.

A court clerk walked towards the detectives, looking agitated.

"Everybody out of de building?" asked Preddy.

"Yes, sir. All rooms are cleared," he replied.

Preddy nodded. "You have any criminal trials on today?"

"No, sir. And we only have a few civil hearings set for this afternoon."

Preddy looked up at the facade. "Do we know exactly where dis bomb is supposed to be located?"

The man pointed upwards. "They said it was on a bench just outside of court room two, first floor, in the waiting area."

"Who said?" asked Harris.

"The security guard on the front desk went to look when we got the call from Pelican Walk," explained the clerk. "Said he could see a large red plastic bag."

"I'd like tae question him. Where is he?" asked Harris.

The clerk looked at Harris pityingly, "Run gone, long time."

"Nobody went near de bag though?" asked Preddy while mentally trying to picture the floor layout. He had a vague idea of where the suspect package could be.

"No. Once the guard started shouting everybody came running out. A lady said she heard ticking coming from the package but didn't pay any attention to it. A gentleman said he saw the bag and assumed it belonged to someone else on the bench. Then another man said he was standing right beside it and saw it moving."

Preddy was pretty sure that if he spoke to a dozen people he would hear a dozen different tales about who saw what, but everybody would claim to have been in the immediate vicinity. A traffic officer walked towards the detectives and greeted them.

"We need to get de fire brigade on stand by," said Preddy.

"Yes, sir. They're on the way," said the officer.

"Try and find out how close de bomb disposal unit are."

"Will do, sir." The officer walked away with his phone at his ear.

"Where is de lady who heard de package ticking?" asked Preddy.

"See her over there," the clerk waved in the woman's direction. "Hi! Lady! Lady!"

"It's okay, we'll go talk to her." Preddy quickly walked over to the old woman followed by Harris. She was smartly attired in a navy blue dress with flat shoes. Her thick grey hair was plaited in two with each plait dangling behind an ear. Preddy smiled at her. "Detective Preddy, Pelican Walk police. And dis is Detective Harris."

Harris murmured a greeting.

"Me name Miss Ruby." The woman gave a nervous smile. Although her dark skin was barely lined she could be no younger than eighty.

"You saw a red package and heard it ticking, Miss Ruby?" asked Preddy. "Like a clock?"

"Yes, Officer." She eyed Harris swiftly, before returning her gaze to Preddy. "Just like a clock."

"Was it loud, ma'am?" asked Harris gently.

"What you say?" she asked. "Me don't understand your accent."

The sudden siren wail of an approaching fire engine pierced their ears making Preddy flinch, yet the old woman showed no reaction to the sound or the vehicle's presence. Preddy gave her a stern look. "You understand his accent just fine, Miss Ruby. You didn't hear any ticking did you? You didn't hear a thing?"

"How you to tell me what me hear, officer?" Her tone was defiant, but Preddy detected a wobble even so.

With his notebook partially covering his mouth Preddy tapped his lips. "So was it a quiet ticking or a loud ticking?"

The woman narrowed her rheumy eyes and stared at him. "What you say?"

Preddy repeated the question with the notebook still covering his lips. The woman shot a look at Harris again.

Harris smiled at her kindly. "Miss Ruby, ye hearing's naw up tae much is it. Ye didnae hear a thing did ye?"

She stared at him meekly. "No, but me see a red package though. Big like so." She held her frail hands apart indicating about one foot in length.

"Okay, Miss Ruby, you stay right here," said Preddy. He turned and walked a few paces with Harris at his side.

"Sweet old thing," muttered Harris. "I wish ma grandma was still alive."

"Dis would probably kill your grandma. Did she know you became a detective?"

"Aye, she was happy enough about it. Sees it as being all noble. My mam, naw so much. I was a keen gardener as a teenager. I think mam would rather I stuck tae that."

Preddy glanced at his watch impatiently then walked to the fire engine and spoke to one of the firemen. A few minutes later a long ladder was raised close to a first floor window. Preddy retrieved a pair of binoculars from the jeep and began to climb the ladder.

Harris looked on in alarm. "Preddy, for fuck's sake did ye forget what we said? The bomb squad are coming."

"De caller said it would detonate at two-thirty." Preddy continued his way up. "We've got a few minutes till two-thirty and I want to see what Miss Ruby saw and what de security guard saw."

"It might be the last thing ye see!" warned Harris.

"You're a great comfort, Detective, you know dat?"

Harris turned and surveyed the watching crowd, looking for anyone who appeared suspicious, anyone who might be planning to use Preddy as target practice. His right arm hovered around his holster as his eyes panned the observers. A vehicle resembling an army tank breached the police cordon causing Harris's heart to skip a beat. He studied it keenly as it approached and then began to breathe more easily. The experts had arrived. They were dressed from head to toe in heavy protective suits and hard hats. They proceeded to push the spectators even further back and barked orders at them warning them of their impending demise.

Preddy could hear all this while he remained trained on his goal. He had spotted the package. It was red, but it was not plastic. He was not sure what the material was although he recognized it as a designer sneakers bag. No ticking sound could be heard. Preddy moved the binoculars back and forth covering the long wooden bench. He then lowered them and studied the area beneath the bench. One of the bomb disposal experts called up to him, warning him to come down. Preddy heard the man and ignored him, focusing instead on what appeared to be a pair of old shoes beneath the bench. Well-worn scuffed brown leather shoes. The detective made his way back down the ladder.

"I don't think dere's any bomb," said Preddy glancing down at the man.

The expert glowered at the detective. "And you know that how, Detective?"

Preddy shrugged. "Well, I'm not sure. But I would say someone changed deir shoes for new sneakers and decided to leave de old ones same place."

The expert waved at the other officers in his team. "We'll take over from here, if you don't mind, Detective?"

"He doesnae mind," said Harris quickly. "At all."

Preddy followed Harris across the road where they stood and watched in silence as the bomb squad entered the courthouse. Preddy's heart pounded as he waited, trying to imagine what would happen if he was wrong. Supposing the whole building went up like Hiroshima and everything and everyone around went up with it? A few minutes later a heavily padded arm waved out the window and a voice shouted, "All clear!"

Preddy was surprised to find himself exhaling as he had not even realised he was holding his breath. Harris too let out a deep sigh. "I really hope we dinnae get any more days like this."

"Me too." Preddy frowned as he watched the experts exit the building. "Somebody phoned in a bomb threat, but why?"

Harris said, "Tae make sure their case was postponed?"

"Possibly, but it seems like overkill for a civil matter and dere were no criminal cases."

Harris wiped his brow and donned his sun glasses. "Maybe somebody just wanted tae start the weekend early? The person who did the shoe swapping?"

Preddy started walking towards the jeep deep in thought. "Hmm, maybe."

"So who do ye think would've done something like this?"

"I have no idea, Harris. No idea."

CHAPTER 12

Friday, 5 May, 4.20 p.m.

Preddy hovered at Superintendent Brownlow's door waiting for another officer to leave. The detective took some comfort from the sound of the voices that his superior seemed to be in a good mood. Then again it was Friday afternoon, when officers tended to be at their most jovial. The door opened and the departing officer was a man who Preddy recognized from the Fraud Squad.

The man lightly punched Preddy's arm on the way out. "Wait, Raythan? Is you dat?"

"Me same one, Vern," said Preddy with a grin. "Getting greyer by de day."

"No man, you look better dan most a we!" he replied. "Can't get my belly flat like yours. What's your secret?"

"No secret," Preddy sighed. "A murder a day keeps de fat away."

"I hear you, Ray. Next time."

"Come in, Preddy." The superintendent called out. "So, it was a hoax eh?"

"Yes, sir," said Preddy wearily as he entered. "Some idler wasting our time."

"I must say I'm relieved to hear it. We would have sunk to a new low if people start putting bombs in the courthouse."

"I doubt if we'll ever get to dat stage, sir. Our people are too afraid dey might blow demselves up."

"I hope you're right, Preddy. Anyway, I'm leaving here in ten minutes so I hope you have something good to tell me that will make my journey home more pleasant?" Superintendent Brownlow pointed at the chair opposite his.

"It's messy, sir." Preddy lowered his athletic frame into the chair and hid a frown. As lead detective, he did not have the luxury of dreaming about pleasant journeys home while Judge Wrenn's murderer was on the loose. "De evidence is sparse. We have a number of people we're working on at de moment, people who we know saw Judge Wrenn in his last hours and some who we think saw him."

Superintended Brownlow nodded. "My mind tells me that it's the Benbow Crew man that he had working for him. Bad idea. What's his name again?"

"Antwon 'Tuffy' Frazer, sir," replied Preddy. "He seems to be de most frequent visitor to Wynterton Park, although Oleta Wrenn didn't see him dat night. We're looking into him for guns and ammunition offences . . . might get some information about de murder."

"Well look into him good, Preddy. Those are some of the most evil people I've ever come across and the fact that Judge Wrenn put a few of them away has made them even worse." The superintendent frowned darkly. "They seem to be cloning themselves or something. Out of all the gangs in St James they are the one giving us overtime problems."

Preddy sighed deeply. The Benbow Crew were as firm a fixture on the city landscape as the palm trees themselves. Multiple violent robberies and murders had been attributed to them, including the slaying of children and young women. Getting witnesses to come forward was always the issue when it came to investigating their crimes as people were genuinely terrified. A few of the members had been put away, languishing now in the maximum security Tower

Street General Penitentiary in Kingston. Some just could not be nailed. Preddy recalled that a local woman who refused to testify had once told him that, "You cyah protect me. Dem will kick off me door long before you even jump inna your jeep let alone start de engine!"

"Detective?"

Preddy drew himself away from his thoughts. "We've been talking to Tuffy, sir. Seems keen on witness protection. He has information, but is how to get him to share dat information."

"Where is Tuffy Frazer now?"

"Still in a holding cell, sir. Him lawyer not too happy. Tried to get Tuffy bailed earlier, but de judge adjourned de hearing for a behavioural report. Tuffy has an arrest record a mile long, even before he was put away last year. Him also have a bad reputation for breaching previous bail conditions. De prosecutor told de judge dat he would have a report by Monday."

Brownlow looked satisfied. "So we've definitely got him for the weekend, good. Let him sweat down there."

"In de meantime we'll see what else we can dig up on him. We're awaiting fingerprint tests on de guns we seized. I want to make sure he doesn't make bail. I'm going to have another chat wid de lawyer about what leniency we can offer him for information."

"Okay. Keep me informed. Anybody else on your radar?"

Preddy gave himself time to think before answering. "We're looking at all de last known people to see Judge Wrenn alive, sir. He had lunch wid Judge Lawrence Guthrie late dat afternoon. Guthrie doesn't know of any threats against de judge's life other dan de usual threats people throw at him at court after a guilty verdict."

"Is Guthrie really a suspect?" Brownlow leaned back and frowned as he studied Preddy.

Again Preddy considered his reply. He knew Brownlow and his social climbing. The man would not want to rock the boat with the judiciary unless there was firm evidence of their involvement in wrongdoing. "Can't rule him out yet, sir. He and Everton Wrenn seem to have been great friends, bar a few social arguments. Dey go way back according to Oleta, and I've seen evidence of it in both of deir offices."

"Doesn't he have an alibi?"

"We're investigating his alibi — Spence and Rabino are on it. Seems he's a bit of a gyal-man and was wid a woman, who isn't his wife, dat night."

"I see." The superintendent gave a wry smile and his heavy jowls quivered. "And what would be his motive?"

He's a jealous drunk who flipped, Preddy thought, but averted saying by clearing his throat. "We're working on dat one, sir."

Brownlow scowled. "You do know that the judges are threatening not to work next week? From what I hear, some of them didn't even turn up for court today, called in sick."

"I've heard rumblings, sir," replied Preddy.

"We have to stop the rumblings from becoming an earthquake, Detective."

"Yes, sir. We're also looking into Nathaniel Mexell. You know dat guy who heads de NatMex construction company?"

"Ah yes. He's the one with the flashy solar development in Falmouth?"

"Him same one," said Preddy. "Seems dat his company is responsible for polluting de waters of Wynterton Park and Judge Wrenn took great exception to de blight on his community. A huge swathe of water close to shore is deep brown instead of bright blue."

The Superintendent looked thoughtful. "A civil matter, surely?"

"Yes, but de end result could be very expensive and could close him down," Preddy explained. "We going look into Mexell's alibi too, sir. He doesn't seem to have much of one. Says he dined wid his parents den crept into bed wid his sleeping girlfriend and was dere all night."

The Superintendent glanced at the clock on the wall. He hauled his ample body up and began to gather his belongings.

"I'm going to get into a domestic myself if I'm not home within an hour, so I have to get on my way. Put together a written report for me by Monday, because the Commissioner is already hounding me on this one."

"Yes, sir." Preddy rose and straightened his cramped legs.

"We have to tread carefully or we'll be in the firing line," muttered Brownlow as he turned to shut his blinds.

"Yes, sir. We've got dis." Preddy moved towards the door. The superintendent must be talking about the royal 'we', he thought, knowing that the blame would be conveniently placed on the Major Crimes detectives if the murder was not solved.

"Detective Preddy, how are de counselling sessions coming on?"

Preddy blinked a few times before turning around slowly. "Coming on well, sir. Everything is good."

"I'm glad to hear it. Sleep is an underrated part of our jobs. It's hard to make headway at any career if you're not getting enough sleep." The superintendent picked up his briefcase. "Let me know if you need anything."

The two men exited the room and Superintendent Brownlow locked it behind him. "So, how are you and Detective Harris getting on?"

"Fine, sir." Preddy wanted to know what Brownlow and Harris were up to and he itched to fire the Superintendent's question right back at him. "Just fine."

"Good. Harris is keen to stay and work in Jamaica. Wouldn't mind if we could hold onto him for a few years. He seems to have some pretty good ideas about managing the crime situation."

Preddy had heard some of Harris's master plans for solving the country's problems, all of which involved a few million pounds sterling that no one had placed on the table. "I know he's keen to stay and work at Pelican Walk though I don't know why," mumbled Preddy, aware even as he spoke that this comment would not be well received.

"Well, Detective Preddy, you want to make an appointment with Commissioner Davis and discuss it with him?"

"No, sir."

"How about the rest of the team?" asked the superintendent. "Everybody pulling together?"

"Spence and Rabino are totally on board for dis investigation too, sir."

This was not entirely true, particularly in the case of Spence, but Preddy did not think it would go down well if the super realised that Spence would rather transfer to another team than ever take orders from the Scotsman. Even Rabino, who was always game to make the best of every situation, had railed against the idea of working on anything other than an equal footing with the foreigner on any investigations.

"That's what I like to hear." The superintendent threw his jacket over his shoulder and began his march towards the stairs. "Now, don't hang around here too late, man. Get home and get some rest."

"Yes, sir. I will."

Preddy headed back to his office. There were plenty of things to do before he could head home to the comforting silence of his four walls. Detective Harris approached him just as he reached his door.

Harris said, "Ye alright, Preddy?"

"Sure, my nerves have settled now. How 'bout you?"

"I'll be dreaming of sneaker boxes for a while," Harris smiled. "Anyway, just tae let ye know, I couldnae find anything suspicious on Judge Wrenn's laptop. Naw threats or incriminating emails. Naw searches on any search engines tae cause alarm."

Preddy desperately wanted to ask him what was on the mysterious bronze laptop. "Okay. Always a good idea to check."

"He does have an encrypted Word folder that I cannae access. Mrs Wrenn says she doesn't know anything about it, but thinks it must be confidential court work."

"Dat would make sense." Preddy placed a hand on his door handle. "Still, see if any of de guys downstairs know anything about encryption. I doubt if you'll get any help before Monday now."

"Do ye . . ."

"Before you ask, no we don't have any dedicated technology experts you can call on."

Harris frowned. "That wasnae what I was going tae ask. I was going tae ask if ye needed any help with anything."

It was an invitation that Preddy was tempted to accept. He could ask the Scotsman to explain the occasions when he could not be found, why he was skulking around the meeting rooms and what was on the personal laptop, but part of him was still hoping that Harris would volunteer to tell all without being pressured. "No, but thanks, I'll soon be off myself. Sometimes it's easier to concentrate at home."

"I try tae avoid taking stuff home, maself," replied Harris. "It can make yer home life a right mess. It's a slippery slope, Preddy."

Preddy pushed his office door open. "Don't I know it. Gotta do what I gotta do, though."

"Aye, sir," Harris nodded and walked away.

Preddy entered and closed the door behind him. He had no doubt that Harris's offer to assist was genuine, but Preddy had no intention of leaving Pelican Walk police station for a good few hours. His destination for later that night was a place where Harris would be all too visible. He did not want the Wynterton Park security guards to change their behaviour which they were likely to do if they caught sight of the white man.

CHAPTER 13

Friday, 5 May, 10.50 p.m.

Tiny stars sparkled in indigo skies as Preddy left Pelican Walk. He drove along the illuminated highway past food vendors rolling out their illegal carts of pungent jerked chicken to satisfy the tastes of the city's late night revellers. Not a food-handlers permit in existence amongst them.

Preddy thought about the missed counselling sessions as he headed towards Wynterton Park. He had lied to Valerie when she asked, told her the talks were going well before abruptly changing the subject. Surprisingly the doctor had not reported his absence to the superintendent. The first and only counselling session had annoyed Preddy. It was not that he could not appreciate the necessity of the counselling, but the psychologist seemed more interested in discussing Preddy's childhood. There was nothing wrong with his childhood; growing up had been good fun so there was no need to discuss it. The problem was all the bullets, blood, bodies and screaming at Norwood that remained the worst shootout he had ever been involved in, notwithstanding the fact that he fired no shots. He would return to counselling only if the doctor agreed to start where Preddy wanted to start — with that bloody day.

Preddy parked at a distance with his lights off and stared at the well-lit Wynterton Park guardhouse. The guard about to go off duty was packing up his belongings. The man took off his blue long-sleeved shirt and replaced it with a T-shirt. He tucked his cap into his knapsack and walked towards the roadside. The streetlights highlighted the frustration on his face as he looked up and down the road. For a few minutes he stood there impatiently. Eventually he returned to the hut and pulled the door firmly shut. He raised the iron bar to allow the free flow of vehicular traffic and then began to walk up the road. Preddy glanced at his watch and cursed under his breath as the departing guard grew smaller.

A white vehicle turned into the Wynterton Park grounds and Preddy kept track of its tail-lights until they went off outside a villa. He wound up his windows, turned his car onto the premises and drove down the long immaculate driveway before making a U-turn. He parked under a low-hanging mango tree and continued to study the security guards' hut. A full eighteen minutes elapsed before the replacement guard arrived.

The tardy man lowered the iron barrier, went inside the hut and scribbled something on a paper stuck to the wall. Preddy waited another two minutes before putting on his headlights and driving back towards the exit. The guard hastily raised the barrier as the detective's car approached and made no attempt to try and identify Preddy.

The detective turned onto the main road and drove on a few metres before parking. His phone rang and he glanced at it before pushing it into his pocket. Valerie. No doubt hoping he was safely indoors resting. He headed on foot back to the guardhouse. "Excuse me, man," said Preddy forcefully, as the guard busily tied his sneaker laces. "Hey!"

The young man looked up with a start and quickly straightened up. "Yes, sir?"

"Detective Preddy, Pelican Walk. I have a few questions."

The man stared at him keenly. "Oh yes, me remember you from de other day."

Preddy leaned into the hut and looked at the page the man had written on. "Look like your watch not working?"

The man swallowed and stared at his feet. "A dat we always do."

"A dat you always do?" repeated Preddy. "Now is quarter past eleven, not eleven o'clock. You didn't tell my officers dat's what you always do. One of you leave five minutes early, one of you arrive fifteen minutes late. Who know what happen Monday night?"

The man scratched his jaw. He glanced at the piece of paper with its recorded lies then back at Preddy. "Sometimes it hard to get taxi a night time you know, sir. And if de boss man know we late, we inna trouble. We have to write it up like dis."

Preddy skimmed the list. "You signed in at eleven on Monday night too!" Preddy thumped the wall with his clenched fist. "A murder took place right here. A judge was murdered and instead of talking de truth you busy hiding your lateness from bossman?"

The guard drew back startled by the ire flowing in his direction. "Must be about dis same time me reach here Monday," he mumbled.

"You remember if you see anybody leave de premises, whether on foot or car, resident or visitor?"

The man began to rifle through the pages of his A4 loose-leafed book. Preddy scowled as he watched him. "I hope dat book isn't a work of fiction too, you know? I just left here and you didn't make any note of my details."

The guard's shoulders sagged as he lowered the book and admitted, "Is truth you telling. Most times when visitors leaving we no too worried to check dem. Is when dem stay and won't exit we go check on dem. Dey not supposed to park in residents' spot because dere's a visitors' area further down."

"Even after a murder nobody is checking?" The detective shook his head. "I better have a chat wid de property manager. He can take it up wid your supervisor."

The man's eyes widened. "Me a try help you you know, Boss." He pushed the book towards the detective. "Look, you can see all what we write down! I was here right until eight in de morning."

Preddy made no move to take the book. Spence and Rabino had been through the list before and interviewed all of the named individuals so he expected no surprises. "I want you to cast your mind back. Forget about de damn log book for a minute and picture Monday night."

The man closed his eyes briefly. "Sometimes people come over here to drink at de bar. I believe a Monday night when I did see a man leave here late, late. Drive one criss black Bimmer. It nice you see!"

"And you noted de registration, of course?" Preddy did not try to disguise the sarcasm.

"No, but me know is who because me see him in dat car before," replied the guard. "Is an X6 him drive. Him name Mexell."

"Nathaniel Mexell, de construction man?"

"Dat's him." The man nodded eagerly. "Him come here more dan one time already, come drop off letter. Me see him when me use to work day shift, but dat was like late last year . . . or coulda even early dis year. Me don't remember ever see him at night time though. Dat night me just believe say him must come for a drink."

"You speak to him?"

"No, me and him never talk. Him window tint and him never roll it down. Me just see de car and open up de barrier. Even in de night it look good under de street lamp. Den me watch it go down de road." The man shook his head from side to side in obvious admiration. "A one a dem me want. Nice you see!"

"If you tell me dat de car was nice again, I going fling you and your damn book a rass ground! You think dem pay you to study whether car look good? People want to sleep peaceful inna dem bed think say security out here looking after dem and you out here, coming to work late and coveting people car?"

"Me know say it look a way still," murmured the guard.

135

"It look more dan 'a way', youth man," growled Preddy. "It look bad. You going have to change you behaviour."

"I gwine try do better sir, leave home half hour earlier."

"Dat's a good idea," said Preddy. "What time Mexell leave?"

The man shook his head. "Late-late, long after me come, but me never look at de time. Just a guess, could be about twelve-thirty . . . one."

"You see anybody else hanging around here Monday?"

The man frowned. "Me no believe so. Is not like week-end, Mondays usually quiet."

"You did see Tuffy Frazer, Judge Wrenn's driver?"

The guard thought for a moment. "No. If Tuffy was here dat night him did gone before me come to work. Him is a friendly guy still. Will stop and say hello and chat wid we sometimes."

"Oh? And you have a lot to chat to a Benbow Crew member about?"

"No, sir! Wow!" The man's hand flew to his heart. "Me nuh into no gang business. Me know Tuffy did go a prison for it, but me nuh know if him a gwaan wid any bad tings now. We just talk about music and girl, tings like dat."

"When you last see him?"

The guard stared up into the air. "A long time me nuh see Tuffy to talk to. Me did glimpse him Tuesday morning a drive past, but I believe dat was after de police was already here. Him stop beside a little bwoy, den him drive off again. Me nuh see him from dat day."

"You sure?"

"Yes, sir."

"You know if him ever get a boat and sail past here?"

The guard shook his head. "Me no know 'bout dat. Me never hear him talk 'bout no boat. Him is a man what love him fish still . . . love a fried fish, so maybe him and de fisherman dem go out. Dem will sell you fish cheap-cheap if you go help dem ketch it." The man suddenly moistened his lips. "You feel say a Tuffy and dem Benbow bwoy kill off Judge Wrenn?"

"I haven't come to any conclusions one way or de other," said Preddy in an unfriendly tone. "And when people like you don't keep proper records it make my work even harder. In future when police officers ask you questions concerning a crime you answer dem truthfully. Dere's no way we can clean up dis city if ordinary citizens will not help us. You hear me?"

"Yes, Boss. Me sorry, man."

Preddy drove slowly to his apartment with Nathaniel Mexell firmly on his mind. Mexell who had denied being at Wynterton Park and denied being a murderer was clearly a liar. Preddy did not doubt the guard's observation. The watchman might not care about doing his job, but he certainly cared about ogling expensive cars.

A thought crossed his mind. Tomorrow there would be an ideal opportunity to bump into Mexell without an appointment and maybe he could convince the man to speak. It was nearly midnight, but Preddy did not hesitate to make quick phone calls to Spence and Rabino. He replaced the phone on the dashboard and drummed his fingers on the steering wheel as he drove. Soon he reached for it again, dialled another number and waited.

"We're going to a regatta in de morning, you coming?" asked Preddy.

"A regatta?" Harris sounded sleepy. "Och that thing at the Yacht Club? Is it tomorrow?"

"Yes, we'll be on de water for a few hours wid de marine police," said Preddy. "Might get a chance to see one of our suspects in social mode, see if he'll let him guard down."

Silence at the other end of the line.

"Detective Harris?"

"Sorry, if it was Sunday I'd be okay. I'm actually tied up on Saturday," Harris stuttered. "Prior engagement that I cannae get out of I'm afraid."

"You sure 'bout dat?"

"Aye, quite sure."

"I see. Go back to sleep." Preddy hung up abruptly. Harris would probably spend the weekend at a function that the Police High Command had arranged. He was not scheduled to work on Saturday and Preddy would never force anyone to do so unless it was a life or death situation. The Glaswegian had wanted in on the murder case from the beginning and should have been willing to break a frivolous date to be with the team.

Preddy turned into his apartment block and pressed the security code which opened the gates. He crawled through quietly and pulled up in his spot. Valerie had left him a voice-mail and he wanted to get in, get something to eat and ring her back. She would be annoyed and disturbed to know he had worked a fifteen hour day and he decided to keep that information from her. Inside he opened the fridge and belatedly remembered that it was purposely depleted. He took out a plate of sliced pineapples and began to munch hungrily on the pieces. Roman and Annalee would descend on him tomorrow morning and he would let them pick up whatever they wanted at the supermarket. As usual they would choose plenty of processed foods full of preservatives, while he would source the fruits and vegetables. Anything he could buy that would help to keep them onside was fine by him. Any mention of Valerie to the teens was met with silence or monosyllabic responses, even though they had all dined graciously together a month ago. Valerie herself remained unconcerned and saw their behaviour as normal. "Give dem time," she had said.

Preddy kicked off his shoes and sank onto the sofa to make his call. "Hello beautiful. You okay?"

"Tired, Ray. Is not too long I get back in you know?"

Preddy frowned. "What happen?"

"We had to secure de premises a bit better, dat's all," said Valerie. "Looks to me like somebody was trying to break into de lab. At first, I thought maybe de back door wasn't locked properly and nobody came in, but den it looks like somebody was trying to force something — like a screwdriver — into de lock of an internal door."

Preddy straightened up and placed his plate on the arm of the sofa. "You want me to go over dere and look at it?"

"No, baby! You stay home. De place secure now. Everything important has been put away." She paused and he could hear a smile in her voice. "My knight in shining armour."

Preddy grinned. "My armour is always at your disposal. You feel like coming over? I can send a taxi for you?"

"Hah! I'd love to, but I want to be up for five a.m. No rest for de wicked."

"You working tomorrow?" he asked in surprise.

"No, I'm heading to Kingston, remember? Knutsford Express style."

Now he did remember. Valerie usually finished work early on Friday afternoon and headed back to what was once the family home in Kingston. The family now consisted of only her teenaged son since her husband, from whom she was soon to be divorced, had moved out.

"Of course, baby. Of course," he said.

"Back on Sunday night, or Monday morning, not sure yet," she said.

"I'd better let you go to your bed den," said Preddy. "I'll be taking de kids out tomorrow. Set dem lose at de regatta while I do some work."

"I'd tell you to say 'hi' for me, but dat might earn you a couple of icy glares."

Preddy was happy to note the hint of laughter that remained in Valerie's voice. She was dealing with a similar response from her own teenager, equally unenamoured with the idea of his mother having a new partner.

"Wish you could come too, baby," he said.

"Me too," she sighed. "How's de judge's murder investigation going?"

"It's early days yet, though you wouldn't know dat from speaking to de super," replied Preddy. "He wants answers yesterday. I'm hoping it will move significantly ahead by

Monday, though. I just need to convince one or two people to speak to me."

"Well, remember what I said about delegation. Don't try to be Superman and do everything yourself."

"As long as you're around woman, I can deal wid pretty much anything Mo Bay can throw at me."

Valerie chuckled. "Hmm, dat is something to tell de Commissioner. He's seeking a way to curb crime on de island. You can tell him to provide all officers with loving and supportive partners and he'll be on de way to Utopia."

"I don't think I'll try dat one out on him, but thanks for de suggestion." Preddy smiled. "He doesn't want to hear a thing from me other dan names of murderers. Shout me in de morning when you get to New Kingston so I know you arrived safely."

"I will. Goodnight, baby. Love you."

"Love you, too."

CHAPTER 14

Saturday, 6 May, 11.25 a.m.

The morning sun blazed with a force and intensity that promised a sweltering day. A gentle breeze spread the familiar aroma of warm salty water, but made no dent on the temperature. Preddy and Rabino were on the waterfront admiring the swathe of marine traffic at the Freeport. Today there were no giant cruise liners carrying thousands of enthusiastic tourists, and no cargo ships weighted with sixty-foot containers which were the usual clientele of the busy commercial area. Instead, yachts of all sizes were lined up on the crystal waters surrounding the Yacht Club.

Every competing vessel was the standard white, but each had unique markings. Some boats, ostentatious in their design, were purely for show and had obviously cost their owners a great deal of money. Then there were the smaller vessels crewed by men with their sleeves rolled up who looked eager to challenge the competition, even though they could not possibly overcome the mightier ones.

Food and drinks were on sale in abundance. Long tables covered in red table cloths and spread with fruit punch, rum and wine, as well as jerked chicken, sausages, fried fish, fried plantains, rice and peas, and hard dough bread. The delightful mixed scents made Preddy's stomach growl. Earlier he had managed an energetic one hour jog followed by a cup of ganja tea and creamy cornmeal porridge, and without the current temptations he would not usually feel hunger pangs. The parakeet had not shown up for breakfast even though he had opened the window and whistled and waved a saucer of crushed corn grains. Roman and Annalee had eaten before they arrived at his home and had turned down his offer of food, correctly predicting that there would be plenty to eat at the waterfront. Preddy noted a large glass cooler stocked with Chinchillerz desserts and smoothies. The iced fast-food company continued to thrive under new management, remaining true to the ideals of founders Ida and Terence Chin Ellis who still held a majority stake in the business.

Preddy took off his sunglasses and hooked them over the pocket of his cotton shirt. He raised his binoculars and watched as Nathaniel Mexell and Stephan Channer pulled into the pier in a white boat with the name NatMex painted in bold red. A huge Jamaican flag fluttered from its mast. Mexell had on a baseball cap with its peak pulled down firmly over his forehead, and a white T-shirt and black jeans. Channer wore a brown panama hat and a long-sleeved khaki shirt with matching trousers. Preddy pointed them out to Rabino. Neither man appeared to notice the detectives and Preddy decided against attracting their attention.

As usual, Channer was close to his business partner's side and Preddy wondered whether Harris was right and Channer was besotted with Mexell. Whether Channer was present or not, Preddy was determined to confront Mexell before the day was over. Again the detective noted Channer's smooth movements and frowned. Maybe he would do anything necessary to protect his boss. The two businessmen could well have committed murder together, one distracting Judge Wrenn while the other strangled him. The security guard did not see who was in Mexell's car when it left Wynterton Park on Monday night and it could easily have contained two occupants.

Preddy swung his binoculars around the rest of the competitors. Most of the monied class were on site, the white and brown folk who held the most clout in society, connected people who knew other connected people in commerce and in government. People who ensured that the prime business opportunities stayed within the clique and the wealth remained unshared with the ordinary man on the street who was left to make do with low wages or street hustling. Although Preddy recognized a few of the participants as local business owners, male and female, most were new faces. From a glance at the competitors' list it appeared that many came from Kingston and St Andrew, uptown people happy to get away from the busy capital city for a leisurely day on the water.

Rabino reached into her bag for her DSLR camera and began changing the settings while muttering to herself.

"Dat thing look expensive," said Preddy. "It not working?"

"It's fine. Just me trying to remember what I was taught in class about focusing on a target and blurring the background," she replied. "Looks easy when the experts do it, but I'll need to practise every day."

A man on a passing boat waved and yelled at her. "Kathryn!"

"Hi, Len!" Rabino waved back enthusiastically. "He owns an electronics shop on Barnett Street. Fixed my tablet a few months ago," she explained to Preddy. "I was going to ask him to look at the CCTV cameras for us at the same time, but then Detective Harris waved his magic wand so I didn't need to."

"Some still need looking at," replied Preddy. "And Harris didn't pay for it."

Rabino smiled and gave him a disapproving look. "It's a great start though, sir."

Although Preddy was grateful that many of the Pelican Walk CCTV cameras had been upgraded and replaced, he was not prepared to publicly shower Harris with praise. The Scotsman was getting enough of that from other people. A delighted Superintendent Brownlow eulogized Harris and his colleagues in Glasgow for their generosity and Preddy could not help but feel riled that the foreigner, who was supposed to be under his jurisdiction, had this sort of influence. Preddy was convinced that the national security budget could cover many of the essentials needed by Pelican Walk if the people holding the purse strings would allocate the funds properly.

"Maybe we'll get a few air-con units out of him one of dese days," muttered Preddy.

"Now, that would be fantastic!" agreed Rabino. "Sometimes I feel like the heat is welding my clothes to my skin. If I could dress like this all the time though . . ."

"Good luck wid asking Super to add coloured long shorts and T-shirts to de dress code."

Rabino bowed in his direction. "With your support of course, sir."

"I'll stick to my chinos, ma'am. You're on your own."

"Spoilsport." Rabino raised her camera and began clicking the boats.

"Ah, I see de judiciary is represented," said Preddy as Lawrence Guthrie clad head to toe in white sailed by with a female. There was no mistaking his imposing frame which was quite firmly built for a man in his sixties. His muscles stood out against his polo shirt as he pulled at the mast.

"That's not Jacqui Morgan by the way, sir." Rabino informed him as she focused her camera. "Could possibly be Mrs Guthrie, although that lady looks a bit young."

"I've seen Mrs Guthrie's photo." Preddy trained his binoculars on the pair.

"I can envision Mrs Guthrie in a twin-set and pearls, a respectable judge's wife," said Rabino. "She wouldn't be propping up her breasts in a tight tank top like that."

"Bwoy, you women! You're right it's not his wife . . . or daughter either." Preddy lowered the binoculars and grinned at his colleague. "If I had dared say something like dat though, I wouldn't hear de end of it."

Rabino chuckled. "You can say anything you like in front of me, sir. You know that."

"Dat man behind him is a judge too, you know," said Preddy training his lenses to the water again. "I forget his name, but he's one of dem dat would be happy to join industrial action."

"Hmm. It's good to see that the judges aren't barricaded in at home, terrified to leave because the worthless police aren't doing their jobs," replied Rabino dryly. "Everyone knows we're the cause of all the ills in Mo Bay."

A familiar female voice shouted. "Hello idlers!"

Rabino turned and waved. "Hey Mummy!"

Detective Spence had her hands occupied with two energetic young girls. All three were dressed in light floral dresses. Spence wore a broad-rimmed straw hat with her braids dangling around her ears and looked nothing like a police officer. She looked like any other proud mother enjoying a day out with her happy offspring. Preddy was in no doubt that her loaded gun was in the low-slung bag on her side. The girls were struggling to escape their mother's hands and get closer to the sea. Spence gave her colleagues a wry grin as she eventually lost the battle and let her daughters run free.

"Welcome, fellow idler!" shouted Preddy. "Look like tings a run you, not you a run tings!"

"She can handle all kinds of vicious criminals, but not those two mad girls," said Rabino.

Spence waved back and hurried after her children. "Me can hear you, you know!"

"Good! Meet us back here around two!" shouted Rabino.

"Will do!"

"Where have your two got to, sir?" asked Rabino scanning the pier.

Preddy glanced around him. There were many children of all ages running unchecked amongst the adults, but his teenagers were nowhere to be seen. "God only knows," he replied with a smile. "Probably trying to talk deir way onto one of de boats, although I told dem not to try it."

"You think Detective Harris will make a showing?"

Preddy shook his head. "No, I think he'll stick to his so-called prior engagement. Sounded adamant dat he couldn't be here."

"Hope he's not vexed with us over his susumba surprise," said Rabino with a smile. "Would have thought he'd have jumped at the idea of a day on the water. He's always talking about how wonderful the sea looks and he goes swimming quite often too."

"Maybe it's de company he's not too keen on," said Preddy.

Rabino arched a well-shaped eyebrow. "I don't know, he's usually okay around me?"

Preddy pointed at the approaching marine police vessel whose captain was waving at them. "Looks like dis is us." A small grey motorcraft with police identification painted in black letters on both sides was headed in their direction. The two detectives made their way down the long pier as their colleague steered the boat closer and stalled the engine. He was a young officer with a ready smile dressed in navy blue uniform. They climbed on board, greeting the man warmly. He turned the boat towards the other competing vessels which were assembled close to the pier jostling for space while trying to avoid breaching the tow rope which served as the starting line.

"Detective Preddy," called a booming voice. "Didn't know you were a sailing fanatic?"

Preddy looked to his side and acknowledged Lawrence Guthrie with a bob of his head. "Just checking out de water today, judge."

"Is that your wife?" Judge Guthrie removed his shades for a better look.

"My colleague, Detective Rabino."

"Ah." The judge frowned and replaced his glasses. "See you later. Enjoy the trip!"

The judge barely acknowledged Rabino's wave which did not escape Preddy's attention. The woman beside

Guthrie smiled and waved causing her tight attire to ride up. She did not adjust it and left her slender midriff exposed.

"I guess Judge Guthrie is not dat interested in female detectives," remarked Preddy.

Rabino seemed amused. "I'm not offended. He probably recognized my name. Dad being a diplomat and all, he tends to be mistaken for a politician and you know what our politics is like. You're orange or you're green. Either way somebody hates you."

The unexpectedly loud bark of the starting gun caused Preddy to flinch and his heart to skip a beat. Whether he heard guns in the day or at night the end result was always bloody images of dying youths encroaching on his mind. He took a deep breath and tried to relax again. The chance of anyone taking a shot at anybody else in this genteel seafaring community was minimal.

The breeze had started to pick up sending small white-crested waves bouncing against the boats. The yachts pulled away from the dock followed by resounding cheers and the clinking of glasses on the shore. The waves were not strong enough to cause any difficulties for the competitors. Some vessels moved more slowly than others, knowing that they had no chance of winning anyway. For many it was the participation that counted. Their names were on a list, the list. Being seen amongst wealthy, elite Jamaicans was victory enough for the privileged few who would delight in seeing their faces plastered over the social pages in the Sunday newspapers.

The race was estimated to take three hours from the Freeport to Salt Marsh Bay in Trelawny and back, for those who intended to complete it. Many would give up within the hour. An enthusiastic race official with a massive megaphone shouted out the obligatory health and safety instructions to the eager participants. Orange buoys dotted the route for as far as the eye could see, and the competitors were advised to stay as close to them as possible. They were also warned about keeping a safe distance from their rivals. The race officials were surprised at Preddy's offer to patrol the race route, yet they were quick to accept the show of support. Anything that would help to make the well-heeled participants feel more comfortable was good.

Preddy waited until the competitors had set off and were a healthy distance ahead before nodding at his captain who set the engine to a gentle throttle and followed at a leisurely pace behind them. Preddy could not remember when last he had been on the sea. It was a sad reality that, like many of his fellow Montegonians, he rarely found time to be on the water although it occupied a major part of his vision every day of the week. He would take the children swimming at the beach when they had school holidays and occasionally join them in the water. Most times he would drop them off, watch them for a while, and either disappear back to work or take up residence under the nearest almond tree and work silently from there. Sailing was something he just never found the time to do. The last time he had boarded a boat, it was anchored at the dock, and that was to arrest a would-be stowaway and murder suspect over a year ago. Life was always work, work and more work. He vowed to get the children onto a glass bottom boat for the holidays, maybe bring Valerie with them.

He closed his eyes and enjoyed the vessel's gentle rocking motion. He inhaled deeply and allowed himself to savour the salty sea air. The sun bore down on his head and he wished he had worn a baseball cap like some of the other sailors.

"You alright there, sir? Not sleeping are you?" teased Rabino.

"Just enjoying being alive," said Preddy wistfully.

"You look like you're envisioning Paradise. A prosperous Mo Bay full of happy smiling people getting along well — whichever community they're from — picking fragrant flowers for window vases, not wreaths for family caskets."

Preddy opened his eyes. "I'm getting worried about how good you are at reading my mind."

The journey towards the Trelawny parish border was largely uneventful. They passed a few catamarans travelling in the opposite direction towards Montego Bay bearing rowdy tourists who seemed thrilled by the mass of traffic. The scantily clad tourists danced to up-tempo soca music and eagerly filmed the competitors as well as the police boat. They waved vigorously and cheered the officers holding aloft transparent cups of alcohol. Preddy and Rabino waved back at them. Preddy thought their captains should have known better than to have the vessels on the water, particularly as the regatta had been advertised well in advance. Some hustlers just would not postpone or give up the hustle if they found willing tourists to serve. The chance to get hold of much-needed foreign currency was too good to let slip.

Long before they neared Salt Marsh Bay they were met by returning vessels actively heading back to the Freeport. The police boat maintained a safe distance to allow them easy passage. Soon Preddy instructed the officer to bring their boat to a halt. This was as good a place as any to await the return of the man he particularly wanted to speak to, and whose vessel he had picked out of the line-up of those returning.

"You watching to see who's cheating, officers?" yelled a young man as he guided his vessel past the police.

"Something like that!" shouted Rabino.

"Or is drugs you looking for?" asked another youth on the same vessel, showing his teeth.

"Not today," said Preddy. "Unless you know something dat we don't?"

"No, sir!" The youth chuckled. "Just joking, sir!"

Soon they were passed by Nathaniel Mexell who gave the officers a cursory glance and then kept his head straight. Stephan Channer glared at them and shook his head in an open display of disgust at their presence. Preddy ordered the captain to turn their vessel around. Within minutes they had edged closer towards the NatMex vessel which was lying in about tenth position.

"Looking for a race, Detective?" shouted Mexell raising his cap slightly while steering the boat expertly with one hand. "You do get around."

Preddy raised his voice, "I could say de same about you, Mr Mexell."

Channer glided effortlessly to his feet and leaned over the starboard. "Having another lazy day out, Detective?" he bellowed. "Must be nice to have a crime-free parish like St James to police."

"Ouch!" Rabino whispered as she lowered her binoculars. "You must have really rattled his cage, sir."

"Him like me really," Preddy murmured. He raised his voice again. "Mr Mexell, we wouldn't mind a word wid you. Maybe later on?"

"Why later on? Why not now?" shouted Mexell.

"Because now is inconvenient to both of us," yelled Preddy. "You're racing, we're supervising and I don't want to lose my voice."

"Oh, I don't know . . . seems fine to me. I can hear you quite well." Mexell said something to Channer who moved forward and took over the wheel. Mexell moved closer to the stern so that he could eyeball the detectives. "What do you want to know? Shoot. Actually, don't take me literally Detective Preddy."

"Boy," whispered Rabino. "I'm going to enjoy visiting these two in jail."

Preddy cleared his throat. "We need to discuss Monday night again. Seems you left something out de last time we spoke."

Channer leaned sideways and said something to Mexell. Preddy raised his binoculars for a closer view of the men's lips, but could not work out what was being said. The two men appeared to be arguing. Channer's face was contorted in rage.

"I wonder what that's about?" said Rabino.

"Knowing Channer it's about telling Mexell not to speak to us about anything," replied Preddy. "Dere's no way around dis for him though. He's going to have to explain de lie about his movements."

The NatMex boat swayed, moving away from the buoys. Mexell re-took the steering wheel as Channer straightened the masts. The boat regained its safe position. "I'll see you on dry land, Detective," shouted Mexell in an apparent change of heart. "Must concentrate on our place in the race! Besides, the sea can be a dangerous place if you're not too careful!"

"See you there," mumbled Preddy.

Preddy allowed the police boat to fall behind again and it was soon overtaken by all of the competitors, even the stragglers at the back. The noise of cheering from the pier floated far out to sea. Hundreds of people crowded the pier waving banners. Each boat was welcomed back enthusiastically by the punters regardless of how well or how poorly they performed.

Once back on dry land, Preddy noted that even more food had been laid out. He could see Roman and Annalee chatting with other youths and holding plates of what looked like chicken wings. His stomach rumbled jealously, but he ignored it. The teenagers looked animated and were completely oblivious to the presence of their father. He smiled wryly to himself. The days of clutching at daddy's hand — particularly with Annalee — were long over. Now he was practically invisible when they saw people of their own age. Now they revelled in their space and if he was honest with himself it was not a bad thing.

He spotted Spence beckoning to him and pointed her out to Rabino. They made their way to the well-stocked table where Spence sat eating with her daughters. The girls, who were six and eight were too busy stuffing their mouths with chicken nuggets to do anything other than smile and wave.

"Where's mine?" asked Rabino, before tugging the braided plait of the older daughter who squirmed and grinned.

"I can see mine," said Preddy pretending to reach for a nugget from the younger girl's plate.

"Nooo!" she squealed and moved the plate out of his reach. "Take Mummy's, not mine!"

"Oh, okay, madam!" Preddy reached over and took a cocktail sausage from Spence's loaded plate. "You see dem?" he asked as he chewed.

Spence nodded. "Mexell went straight to de bar, but he's down at de back behind de bamboo divider so you won't see him unless you go right in. Channer went in de opposite direction," Spence indicated two covered up plates of food. "Dat one is yours, sir. Kathryn take up de other one."

Rabino obeyed and instantly started munching on chicken. "Mmm," she murmured as she reached for the ketchup bottle. "I really need this. Sailing makes you hungry. You see Judge Guthrie and his new side piece?"

Spence grinned. "Me see dem, yes. Poor Jacqui Great Three Months!"

"Cast aside, so the judge could cast off with someone else," said Rabino shaking her head. "Mind you, maybe he has the two of them on the go."

"Gyal in a bungle," sang Spence. "Gyal from Rema, gyal from Jungle."

Preddy uncovered his plate and admired the array of savoury finger-food. He picked up a handful of plantain chips then re-covered his plate. "Soon come. Maybe I can have a brief chat wid Mexell before him bodyguard get back."

"You need me, sir?" asked Rabino, hastily swallowing a French fry.

"No, man. Stay and eat," replied Preddy quickly. "If either of you see Channer advancing wid a metal pipe held over him head and a mad look pon him face you better be behind him."

Spence jabbed her fork into a sausage. "I woulda bruk him head wid my bottle long before him reach you!"

"Thank you." said Preddy, before whispering, "bullet make too much noise."

Preddy walked through the chattering crowds negotiating the clusters of wicker chairs and glass tables. He briefly acknowledged a few people who recognized him, mainly local businessmen and expatriate professionals. The well-stocked bar was quite full of chattering expensively dressed and stylishly coiffured patrons wearing fine jewellery. Sitting at the many tables ensconced in conversation were adoring couples as well as large groups of friends. In front of all customers, bottles of imported white and red wine with grand sounding names were cooling in ice buckets. The low music playing in the background was instrumental reggae and some giddy voices were singing, making up their own lyrics to the tunes.

Spence was right, it was impossible to see past the chiselled bamboo divider at the end of the bar space. He purchased a Red Stripe beer at the counter and snapped the top off with his fingers. He sauntered behind the boundary. This was an open-air space with a picturesque view of the sea and hills. A broad leafed almond tree provided respite from the sun allowing narrow slits for yellow light to pass through. Only three men were seated, each on a separate glass table which rested on natural stone paving slabs. The tables were separated by rows of neatly trimmed potted hedging which ran like green troughs between them creating a feeling of private zones. The hedging only came up to shoulder height of the seated diners so the privacy was somewhat limited, allowing for friendly interaction if desired. Nathaniel Mexell was at the furthest table staring out at the sea with a cigarette dangling from his fingertips and a bottle of Dragon stout in the other hand. The peppered shrimp on his plate did not appear to have been touched.

Preddy settled onto a stool directly in front of him, blocking his sea view. Mexell blinked a few times before focusing on the intruder. "Detective Preddy," he said, curtly. "You found me." He dabbed his cigarette out in his plate and reached into his breast pocket for another.

"You were hiding?" asked Preddy. He took a mouthful of beer as he watched the man light up. The brand of cigarettes was the same as that smoked by Judge Wrenn.

"No, I was not hiding. Just getting far from the madding crowd." Mexell scowled and pocketed his lighter. "Besides, they don't like when we smoke near the kids."

"What dey don't like is de possibility of getting fined up to a million dollars. You must know dat smoking in a public place is not allowed?"

Mexell dabbed out the newly lit cigarette and returned it to the packet. "Don't know why they let kids in the bar anyway."

Preddy shrugged. "It's billed as Family Day. What else are de parents going to do? Moor dem to de bollards?"

Mexell moved his stool to the right slightly so that he could once more gaze at the sea unhindered and tilted his head back. His fingers were thin with no marks or rings. Preddy wondered whether he was looking at a man who could place those fingers around the neck of another man and squeeze him dead. "Beautiful colour isn't it, de Caribbean Sea," mused Preddy. "Such a shame when it gets polluted. Spoils other people's pleasure. Forces dem to take action against de polluters."

Mexell grasped his glass bottle as if trying to break it with his bare hand. "Just cut to the chase, Detective. What do you want? I already told you I did not kill Everton Wrenn!"

"You did tell me dat," agreed Preddy. "What you did not tell me was dat you were right dere at Wynterton Park dat night."

"What?" A flicker of fear passed through Mexell's eyes.

"Tell me what happened, Mr Mexell."

The businessman removed a handkerchief from his jeans pocket and dabbed at his rapidly watering forehead. "You've made one hell of a mistake," he croaked. "I wasn't there!"

Preddy slammed his beer bottle on the table making Mexell's hand jump. "Don't lie to me! You were dere dat night. Drove your black Bimmer. You were seen, Mr Mexell."

Each of the men on the other tables raised their shoulders and glanced with interest in the direction of the detective and the interviewee. Mexell gave an embarrassed nod at one of them and took a long swig of the bitter stout. Preddy glanced beyond Mexell's head and frowned as the unmistakable voice of Stephan Channer carried from the distance. The bodyguard was returning.

"Talk to me, Nat," coaxed Preddy as the urgency of the situation hit him. "Dis could be your last chance."

"He was alive," whispered Mexell.

"Tell me about it. Talk to me!"

"I swear he was alive." This businessman's eyes had glazed over and his mouth curved downwards. His shoulders slumped and his fingers trembled as they traced an imaginary mark on the table.

"Detective Preddy!" called Channer as he negotiated the maze of hedges with juice glass in hand. His eyes blazed as he looked from his business partner to the detective and back again. "Couldn't wait for me? How dare you!"

Rabino and Spence were right behind him. "Everything alright here?" asked Rabino. She walked up to Channer and stood so that their shoulders were almost touching.

"You tell me," said Channer. He looked Rabino up and down dismissively. "Who are you? The wife?"

Spence moved to take up a position on the other side of Channer and stared up at him. "She is Detective Rabino. I am Detective Spence, Pelican Walk police."

Channer turned towards her his lips curled in a snarl. "The cavalry arrives and with ovaries! Bravo for Pelican Walk and its equal opportunities!"

"De JCF is very inclusive. All lesbian and gay can apply to join too," said Spence. "You're welcome."

The lawyer recoiled. His face contorted and his hands trembled causing orange juice to spill from his glass. His left hand inched toward her, but he halted as if scorched by her fiery aura. He spun and redirected his ire at Preddy. "And where is the white man? The Massa actually let you lot out on your own for the day did he?"

"But a whe' de rass," breathed Spence her jaw dropping. "A must drunk dis man drunk?"

"I don't drink," sneered Channer.

"You soon start," predicted Preddy as he clenched his fists into tight balls. A red mist had begun to descend before his eyes and it took some mental effort to push it away.

Mexell seemed to have climbed out of his stupor. He got to his feet shakily and drained his bottle. "Come on, Stephan. Let's go."

"Stay away from us detectives," snarled Channer. "Don't try this again."

"I'm not under arrest for anything am I, detectives?" Mexell did not wait for an answer. "Good. Nice to have met you, Detective Rabino, Detective Spence." He wiped his brow and strode away with Channer close on his heels.

"I shoulda bruk de damn bottle over him head fi real!" said Spence staring daggers at the departing duo.

Preddy exhaled and unfurled his fists. "You might still get de chance."

"I guess Mexell didn't confess then, sir," asked Rabino.

"Not exactly," muttered Preddy. He turned his attention to Mexell's vacated table, eyeing the cigarette butt and bottle. "Might be some prints we can use. You have a couple of evidence bags in your purse?"

CHAPTER 15

Saturday, 6 May, 4.52 p.m.

The dedicated parking area at the Freeport had long been breached and the adjoining roadway was lined with badly parked top of the range vehicles. A frazzled looking parking attendant did his best to clear a six feet wide space through which motorists could escape. Preddy tooted his appreciation as he carefully navigated his way through and drove away from the congested dock leaving the Yacht Club behind. Annalee bounced around in the passenger seat to earphoned music, humming while chewing on gum. Roman was in the back seat, head down, eyes glued to his flickering tablet.

"I hope Spartan come back by now," said Roman.

"I well want to see him," said Annalee as she pulled out her earphones. "Spartan cute."

"Who's Spartan?" asked Preddy.

"Look." Roman pushed the tablet over the front seat and Preddy cast a quick glance at the parakeet's photo he had shared with them.

"So him have name?" Preddy was amused. The tiny creature had not shown up this morning, probably put off by the unfamiliar noisy voices in the apartment. "Why Spartan?"

"You don't see dat little crest on him head top? Look like a Greek Spartan helmet to me."

"Guess it does," said Preddy. "Don't get too attached to him, he may never turn up again."

"We can get a cage for him," said Annalee.

Preddy turned his head and gave her a hard glare. "And is who going clean out cage?"

She twirled her ponytail around her finger and smiled sweetly. "You just put clean newspaper in de cage every morning and throw it out every night."

Preddy was unmoved. If left to them his place would be full of cats, dogs, rabbits and tropical fish. "De bird does not belong to me. Him not going in any cage. Just like how you want to be free to run up and down and go where you want? Same way him feel."

Roman chuckled. "Him tell you so, Misser Officer?"

"Don't need to," replied Preddy. "How would you feel if you had to sit inna cage all day wid barely enough room to move?"

Annalee turned halfway in her seat to face him. "You lock up people inna cage a Pelican Walk all de time whether dem like it or not."

"A true," agreed Roman. "A six by six cell is not much room."

"Nobody get locked up at Pelican Walk for stealing bulla," said Preddy. "Terrorize de city, get locked up. Every adult knows de likely penalty for violent crime. People who want to live free lives don't go around murdering people. De bird has clean hands . . . wings. No cage."

Annalee sank back into her seat defeated. "Dad, what happen to Detective Harris?" she asked. "Why you only bring Spence and Rabino?"

"You don't like dem?" Preddy glanced at her through the corner of his eye.

"Of course!" She poked her father in his side. "A what kinda question dat?"

Roman raised his head. "De sort of question Dad will fire back at you when him don't want to answer whatever you ask him! You don't know dat yet, girl?"

Preddy smiled and pointed a warning finger at his son's reflection in the rear-view mirror. "Watch your YouTube or whatever it is you shouldn't be watching."

"I still want to hear de answer to Annalee question though," said Roman. "Where's Detective Harris?"

"Minding him own business, I guess," replied Preddy pointedly. "I don't get to tell him where him can go on weekends you know? Even detectives are entitled to time off. Unless he was scheduled to work on Saturday or it's an emergency he can be wherever him like."

Roman was not put off. "Look from when we telling you to bring him to dinner and you won't bring him."

"Is true. You shoulda bring him today," Annalee propped herself up sideways and studied her father. "Den we could all have dinner."

Preddy gripped his steering wheel. "I've never brought Spence or Rabino home for dinner either."

Roman piped up. "Well Javinia husband woulda kill you!"

"Shut up, man," Annalee grinned. "Eeh Dad? Him alone in Jamaica. You no say him wife and pickney dem still in Scotland?"

"Dat's right," mumbled Preddy.

"And him cyah bring Kathryn because she have boy-friend," said Roman, discarding his tablet to concentrate on his father. "Or because of what-she-name-again? Valerie?"

Annalee smiled and peeped over her seat at her brother. "Heh! Valerie woulda come fight her and try beat her out of de apartment!"

Both Annalee and Roman began to chuckle. "A dat me woulda want see!" said Roman. "Who you think would win Kathryn or Valerie?"

"Well, we no know how Valerie set, but Kathryn a police, she must win!" concluded Annalee. "Easy thing dat!"

Roman began to make chopping motions at Annalee who spun around and began blocking them. Preddy ground his teeth and tried to concentrate on the traffic. He wondered whether in his absence his offspring had been busy guzzling alcohol or smoking herbs at the Freeport. He inhaled deeply but could not detect the smell of anything untoward, just cherry flavoured gum. They were under eighteen, but minors could get their hands on anything they wished if they set their minds to it. Still, he had never seen either of them express a wish for any form of drugs.

"Who you think would win, Dad?" asked Annalee. "Definitely Kathryn, no?"

"Turn around and fix you seatbelt," warned Preddy, as he reached for the radio dial. "Next time de two of you going walk home." He turned the knob, desperately trying to find something that would drown the teens out, but the music was even more irritating than the voices. No Gregory Isaacs or even Beres Hammond to soothe his soul. An overhead red and orange billboard caught his attention and he was never more grateful to see a Chinchillerz branch.

"Just what I need," he said. "I feel like some mango and grapenut ice cream."

"Valerie like mango and grapenut?" asked Roman snidely.

Preddy wondered what prior discussion between his offspring had taken place behind his back that had led to this baiting. The orange and red sign was thankfully getting closer. He kept his eyes on the road. Soon they would be eating. Then there were less than twenty-four hours to go, as their mother would come and collect them tomorrow afternoon.

"Answer no, Misser Officer!" demanded Roman.

Preddy tried not to grind his teeth. "Okay, go for it. Let's hear it. What is it about Valerie dat you don't like?"

"How you mean? We had a nice dinner wid her," said Annalee sweetly. "We did nice to her."

"Who say we don't like her?" said Roman. "I'm sure we like her just as much as you like Detective Harris. She even better looking dan him."

"Him not bad looking," said Annalee. "Dat hair though, you shoulda tell him to dye it brown."

"I'm not telling him any such thing. Nobody is coming to dinner. Nobody is fighting and guess what? Nobody is getting ice cream either." Preddy turned into the Chinchillerz parking lot and shut off the engine. He pointed at the building next door. "You two can go to de supermarket and discuss everybody's social life. Go easy on de MSG products. Call me when you reach de checkout. I'll go get myself something to eat."

"No Dad, you mad!" Annalee laughed and instantly popped her seat belt. "Coconut and sweetsop cream I want!"

Roman was already out of the door. "You know what would be sweet?" he said, striding away. "If de white man decide to take up wid Kathryn. Can you imagine! Kathryn Rabino Harris."

Annalee seemed delighted at this suggestion. "Den Dad would have to invite de two of dem to dinner!" She followed behind her brother, blissfully unaware that the equivalent of a hand grenade had been tossed behind her.

Preddy leaned against the driver's door watching them enter Chinchillerz. A deep frown etched in his brow. It was true that Harris rarely spoke about his wife, but he did talk about his 'three bairns' whom he clearly loved. He had not mentioned another woman. Preddy prised himself off his vehicle and slowly walked forwards, annoyed that their casual banter about Harris and Rabino should bother him. Rabino had said Harris could be nice. She was always the first to laugh at his jokes and was quite friendly towards him. What were those brochures she had given him the other day? She had not brought boyfriend Clive with her to the regatta. Now that he thought about it, he was not sure when last she had mentioned him. Surely, never Harris though. Spence would not welcome the pairing for starters and she was sure to let something slip.

Preddy shook the thought away as he pulled on the heavy glass door. He had enough on his plate worrying about murderers and did not want to consider the possibility of anything that would complicate the dynamics of his team. Something way stronger than mango and grapenut ice cream was needed. He wished Chinchillerz would eventually devise a marijuana ice cream. A marijuana and lemongrass blend would be good. Maybe he should stick that in their new customer suggestions box.

CHAPTER 16

Monday, 8 May, 11.12 a.m.

Preddy had done his weekly run to a homeless shelter and was now leaving having delivered a pot of red peas soup to the indigents who despite their pitiful circumstances always enquired after his health. Most of the residents now recognized him on sight and smiled their relief as soon as his vehicle appeared. They wanted to help him carry his huge pot into the kitchen, but past experience led him to reject that offer and let the charity's chef assist instead. A whole pot of food had once been lost to willing arms weakened by lack of nutritious food. Usually he would stay and help serve them, while they engaged him in chit chat. It was good to talk about anything but crime sometimes. Today's brief debate was on the topic of whether chicken back soup was nicer than chicken foot soup and he regretted having to leave before he could properly defend his corner. Chicken foot was good, but chicken back had the edge. Superintendent Brownlow was expecting a written report and was never going to accept any distraction even to engage in important culinary conversations with needy Montegonians.

Preddy was grateful for the cool interior of his car which provided welcome relief from the blazing morning sun. He slid in a 'sounds of nature' CD and listened to a babbling brook as he drove. As he turned into Pelican Walk police station he noticed Harris in the parking bay clutching a hefty Julie mango and speaking to another officer. Preddy rooted around in his glove compartment for his pack of mints and popped two into his mouth. Harris had once accused him of smoking weed, which Preddy had truthfully and vehemently denied, but he had a feeling the Glaswegian remained suspicious. He did not smoke weed he steeped green leaves in boiling water and drank it, and the odour did tend to linger. Harris spotted Preddy and acknowledged him with a brief nod.

The two men strolled together towards the building entrance.

"Good weekend?" asked Preddy.

"Aye. Out and about . . . ended up refereeing some wee laddies playing five-a-side football."

"How were dey?"

"They'd do well tae take up rugby."

Suddenly, Preddy stopped in his tracks. Heading out of the station were two men. He stared at Antwon Tuffy Frazer as if he was a ghost. Tuffy smiled displaying slivers of glinting gold crowns as he strode past with his lawyer Haldin Newman. The lawyer had a smug look on his face, the look of a man who found this all in a day's work and could now go find better things to do.

"Whe' de rass?" said Preddy.

"What the fuck?" said Harris.

Preddy's phone began to ring. Spence was on the line. He pressed a button as he spun to watch the departing men. "Yes, me see him. Right here on de way out."

Harris came around the side of his car and stared at Tuffy's back.

"Bye Sean Paul!" teased Tuffy over his shoulder. "You never ask me how fi spell Frazer, but it spell F.R.E.E."

"They let him go?" said Harris. "He had enough ammunition tae take out a dancehall full of people and they let him go?"

Preddy covered the phone speaker with one hand. "Walked out of de courthouse half an hour ago. Came straight back here wid his lawyer to make a complaint . . . about our culinary failures which apparently amounts to mistreatment."

"Should have cremated the damn dumplings." Harris shook his head. "I dinnae get it."

Preddy continued to speak to Spence before finally hanging up. "Seems de judge agreed wid lawyer Newman dat Mr Frazer was no danger to anybody and will report for a hearing in three days."

"Naw danger?" repeated Harris. "For all we know he's got another stockpile of guns and bullets somewhere ready tae start a war in Mo Bay."

"Denied knowing any weapons were in de car. I cannot believe de judge bought dat nonsense about dark sunglasses obscuring his view." Preddy dug his nails into his palms. "Apparently de judge concluded dat Mr Frazer is rehabilitated as he's been gainfully employed since leaving prison and hasn't been in any trouble recently."

Harris's face flushed. "He'll be off intae the wind long before any court hearing."

"Den we'll have to fly right behind him."

* * *

Tuffy smirked as he climbed out of his lawyer's car following the short journey to the Montego Bay Transport Centre. Freedom felt nice and smelled nicer. On each side of the entrance to the bus park were vendors selling oranges, naseberries and all varieties of mangoes next to giant ice buckets filled with boxed and bottled juice drinks. A man rode past him balancing a glass casket on a bicycle. The aroma of hot beef patties and cocobread went past with him. Tuffy inhaled in appreciation. Lunch would have to wait an hour more.

Inside the park were taxis, coasters and mini-buses heading to all areas of the island, some illegally blaring music from speakers fixed under the seats. The larger coasters were bound for the capital city, Kingston. Tuffy walked past the smaller mini-buses which were on course for the parishes of Hanover, St Elizabeth, Westmoreland and Manchester. Sweaty young loadermen wandered the park raucously shouting out the destinations of particular vehicles, hoping to claim a cash tip from the drivers for directing commuters to their buses. A rotund newspaper vendor waved her copies of the *Western Mirror* at the commuters. Some bought papers to shield themselves from the fierce sun which tried to melt the tinted windows. An old lady carried a huge plastic bag full of iced bag juices of all colours which she pushed hopefully towards the long-suffering passengers.

At a taxi stand, Tuffy surveyed the many rows of taxis which plied the local routes. He had no plans to leave the parish of St James. It was a pity that Judge Wrenn's car was no longer available. He was not a fan of these public passenger vehicles as he suspected that many of the drivers had bought their licences without ever having sat a driving test. He could not afford to be choosey since he did not have his own set of wheels and no taxi driver was going to furnish his driving licence on demand. Tuffy sighed heavily. If the bumbo claat police had not taken the hardware out of the Camry he could have earned some extra money for making the delivery. Plenty of extra money. Now he had a lot of disappointed customers on his patch and one particular unhinged thug to placate. A thug who knew where he lived. The longer he took to go home to Ancona the safer he would be.

Tuffy climbed into a taxi bound for the Pitfour district. He had friends to see, fried fish to eat and white rum to drink. Calm guys who did not bother with the gun business, preferring to do carpentry and masonry instead. They were doing an exceptional trade in coffins, caskets and headstones. One way or the other, someone ended up prospering from the proliferation of guns and ammunition on the island. Two other passengers climbed into the taxi. The driver was waiting on one more before he would move. He tooted his horn and waved a questioning hand at people who wandered by. Tuffy settled more comfortably into his seat. His attorney was good to have secured his release, particularly as he still owed him money. True, he would have to be back in court on Wednesday to face gun charges, but there was no way the cops could pin the guns on him. No fingerprints belonging to him on any of the weapons, of that he was sure. As far as his lawyer was concerned the guns belonged to the car's registered owners, Judge Everton Wrenn or his wife, Oleta.

Stupid detectives thinking they could nail him for any guns or any murder. He was not afraid of the police, men or women. He was not so sure that the Norwood murder cop would not try to do him some harm, so he vowed not to provoke him. The white man was another matter. The foreigner was unlikely to come to Jamaica and try to rough anybody up. Those days of white man lynching and whipping Black man were long gone. Tuffy smiled to himself. He would show Detective Spelling Bee a thing or two about how business was run in Mo Bay. The white man would learn how to spell and pronounce a lot of names in that strange twang of his. The Benbow Crew would continue to run their corner and, yes, people would continue to get murdered if they would not listen to sense. Anybody who came ran the risk of being taken out, be it a rival gang member, a community resident, or even a Supreme Court Judge.

* * *

Preddy increased the length of his strides along the corridor when he saw Superintendent Brownlow, and veered to the right, pretending not to notice him.

"Oh, Detective Preddy!"

Preddy closed his eyes and slowed to a halt. He did not want to hear Super talk about the restless judges or the go-slow at the courthouse. Slowly he turned around and forced his lips to curl upwards. "Sir," he nodded. "I left de report wid your assistant, you know?"

"Yes, I'm going to look at it." Superintendent Brownlow gestured towards a doorway and Preddy followed him with some surprise.

"Is Detective Harris alright?" whispered Brownlow. He made no attempt to open the door and the two stood leaning against it.

Preddy wondered if it was a trick question. "Yes, sir. As far as I know him fine. Well, he's a bit mad about Tuffy's release, but him alright."

"If anything was wrong with him, you would tell me?" asked Brownlow.

"Yes, sir. What happen?"

"You tell me." The Super put his head out of the archway and looked back and forth before reeling it in. "Word just reaching me that something happened in the canteen last week. That he was flat on the ground writhing in agony! What happened?"

This time Preddy did not need to force his lips to do anything. They curled obediently. "Oh, dat sir. He just fell off his chair, easily done."

"But it sounded to me like something far worse than that. And nobody told me." Brownlow viewed his detective with undisguised suspicion. "You wouldn't be lying to me now would you, Preddy?"

"Of course not, sir!" Preddy looked indignant. "He went to sit, misjudged where de chair was and fell down. He was slightly winded, but was up on his seat again in seconds, none de worse for wear." Preddy tried to sound reassuring. "You know how de officers are anyway, sir, dey just love to create excitement around any little thing."

"Oh, good." The superintendent seemed to breathe more easily. "You know, if something is wrong with the chairs down there maybe I need to see if any money's in the budget to change them?"

You guys already gave Harris a new mahogany desk and chair, thought Preddy. "Dey are pretty strong plastic, sir. As long as people look before dey sit dere is no reason for any accidents."

Preddy stared at his superior and said with a degree of hopefulness, "Better you use de money for something else, sir, like replace some bald tyres?"

"Hmm. Well, we'll see," said Brownlow. "In the meantime, keep an eye on Harris. Sometimes people come from foreign and can get . . . a bit strange."

"I'll say," agreed Preddy. "You really want *me* to keep an eye on *him*, sir?"

The superintendent bristled. "He reports to you doesn't he?"

Preddy wanted to ask, *And what is Harris reporting to you?* but decided against it, choosing instead to say, "Yes, sir. Of course, sir."

The Superintendent seemed to change his mind about saying something further.

Preddy watched him carefully. "Everything alright, sir?"

"Sometimes Harris goes to events, er, where the commissioner and the security minister may be present." Brownlow coughed. "Just wondering if he needs a check-up that's all. Would be a bit embarrassing if he collapsed in front of them, you know?"

"I see, sir." Preddy spoke slowly savouring this confession of favouritism. "I don't think you have anything to worry about on dat line, sir. If he wasn't fit for de job I'd be de first person to notice. And tell you. Him mind active and intelligent, like Anansi. De sun stop bother him long time. De mosquito and him will never agree, but him coping." Preddy paused momentarily, before adding. "Him love de food and drink too, sir. You'd be surprised to see what him eat wid absolutely no complaint."

"Oh." Superintendent Brownlow seemed to be thinking deeply.

An officer walked past and Preddy nodded at him. The man looked back over his shoulder at the two of them. Preddy cleared his throat. "You know if we don't move out of dis doorway soon, sir, people going think we plotting to take down de Commish or something."

"Yes, sorry Preddy. See you later."

The superintendent stripped his burly frame away from the wood support and strolled off down the corridor. Preddy strode purposefully in the opposite direction smiling to himself and bounced up the stairs two at a time.

* * *

Preddy pushed the door of the evidence room and greeted the other three detectives who were seated at the table and mid-conversation. The sweet smell of banana bread wafted in the air from the open plastic storage container in front of them. He walked up the whiteboard and looked around for a marker pen.

"Well, dat a your business," said Spence. "If you put in for any motorbike, don't call my name."

Harris shook his head pityingly. "Och, ye dinnae know what yer missing."

"Not missing a damn thing," said Spence. "And if you get one and you see me pon road, don't bother stop and ask me if me want a ride."

"I don't know, might be fun," said Rabino as she took a bite of banana bread.

"Eeh hee? Fun?" Spence looked her up and down. "Fun for other people when your hair blow offa your head gaan a road!"

Rabino laughed and elbowed her in the side. "Your concern is touching, I'll get a helmet."

Preddy grinned. "Should have brought my popcorn."

Rabino continued, "That's what you're supposed to be worrying about, woman, my delicate skull!"

"Of course me worried 'bout dat too," said Spence belatedly. "Don't climb pon no bike, girl."

"Hmm, so I guess it's just one for a motorbike," said Harris as he reached for a slice of the sweet dessert. "I'll stick tae hiring one for pleasure only." He waved the container at Preddy.

"Don't mind if I do," said Preddy as he helped himself. "I guess dis is Spence and not you?"

"Aye, I cannae bake tae save ma life," said Harris. "Cannae cook much either. Glad tae see cookshops and restaurants all over the place."

"Thank you, Detective Spence." Preddy chewed appreciatively. "Now, where are we?"

The four detectives turned their discussion to Judge Wrenn's case. Almost two hours elapsed and Preddy was feeling considerably frustrated. It was rare to have an active murder case with absolutely no physical evidence and no eye witnesses. Usually there were bullets or shell casings or guns or knives. All they had were a list of names on a whiteboard and a deep suspicion about each person. Tuffy still topped the list and Preddy hoped to get a phone call from the trailing officer concerning the suspect's movements soon. Mexell and Channer had moved up the list and now resided above Judge Guthrie. Mexell had seen Judge Wrenn that night. The businessman now ignored all calls Preddy made to his landline and cell phone, no doubt under advice from Channer.

Preddy looked up when a knock came at the door. The blinds were down obscuring his vision of the corridor outside. It was not unusual for people to knock and go away when they sensed that the occupants did not want to be disturbed. Preddy decided to ignore the person and continued speaking.

The door was pushed open. It took a brave person to do this without Preddy's permission and he fully expected to see the face of either Superintendent Brownlow or Commissioner Davis. Instead, Officer Timmins put his head into the room. Preddy had had one run in with Timmins last year, but now he trusted the young officer and found him to be a diligent law man.

"Sorry to interrupt you sir."

"What is it?" asked Preddy impatiently.

Spence glanced up at Timmins. "It better be good, because I was just about to seek permission to go shoot a man named on dat whiteboard." She pointed a finger as she spoke. "Him no have any damn manners!"

"And she isn't joking," added Rabino.

"Super send me to call you." Timmins stared at the whiteboard and gulped. "Backside," he whispered.

Preddy stared at the frozen officer and began to feel decidedly uncomfortable. "Speak man!"

"Officer Timmins?" said Harris quizzically staring at the officer's stunned face.

"Dem shoot up a man." Timmins gestured towards the whiteboard with his chin. "De person who dead? Right dere on your list!"

CHAPTER 17

Monday, 8 May, 5.20 p.m.

The police photographers moved back as the Pelican Walk detectives approached. Harris stared at the bullet-riddled corpse which lay on its back next to a grass verge in front of a small unpainted concrete house. The eyes, wide open, were staring at the sky. A bullet created a third eye right in the middle of his brows. His arms were spread-eagled, a partially consumed bottle of cream soda just beyond the reach of his fingertips. Bullet holes punctured his torso and blood soaked every inch of his once blueshirt. The last time Harris had glimpsed the man he had been smiling, revealing his prominent gold-capped teeth in a taunting manner. Those teeth were sunken now, barely visible through silenced purple lips.

Some of the Ancona residents leaned over the decaying walls which separated their board houses from the road and watched the scene from afar. Despite the police presence not everyone felt safe enough to venture out. A young woman with baby in arms stood between the clothes billowing on her clothes line, hushing her screaming child while craning her neck to catch sight of the body. A boy was perched high on a stack of empty beer crates providing commentary to his shorter friends below.

Harris glanced at the onlookers who had felt comfortable enough to converge on the scene, smartphones in the air. "Too many people around here rubber-necking and none of them are admitting tae seeing anything. Can we naw get an evidence tent or something tae shield the body?"

"Haven't seen a decent one in around five years," said Preddy, struggling to suppress his irritation and anger. The man who he believed was key to Everton Wrenn's murder was dead, executed mere metres from the man's own front door.

Spence glanced at the foreigner, "Please add dat to our Christmas list, Harris. Crime scene tent."

Harris made a mental note to do just that, sooner rather than later. He and his colleagues back home took their crime fighting tools and equipment for granted. Each day it became more apparent how little the Jamaican detectives had to work with, yet how dedicated they were to the task.

"De caution tape will have to do," said Preddy. "Dey know not to cross it."

"I reckon Tuffy Frazer lasted all of three hours," calculated Harris. "I understand that the prosecutor had argued for him tae be kept in custody for his own safety, but his argument was rejected."

Preddy rose from his haunches and shook his head. "And tomorrow's front page will show de court just how sound dat argument was."

Harris stared down at the body. "Tuffy dodged the man we had on his tail, but he couldnae dodge a killer's bullets."

"At least de shooter left us wid something," said Preddy, nodding in the direction of a gun which lay in a clump of grass with a yellow marker tag next to it.

Rabino walked towards the gun. She crouched down and frowned before beckoning to Spence. "That looks like blue paint on the handle," she whispered.

174

"It look so," said Spence using a latexed index finger to poke the weapon. Then as recognition dawned on her, her eyes met Rabino's startled ones. "No man. Couldn't be?"

Rabino took out her camera and zoomed in for a few shots of weapon, watched by an official photographer who looked displeased to see an amateur encroaching in his space. Rabino moved back and gestured to the photographer to take over. She scrolled through her older photographs and turned the screen to Spence.

"Rass Kathryn," murmured Spence. "Say nothing yet."

"I have to!" insisted Rabino.

"Not now," Spence hissed. "We need to check first." She straightened up and walked back towards the corpse. Rabino followed reluctantly behind her.

Harris was examining the body closely. "I count six holes in him so far," he said. "The killer came right in front of him and lit him up."

"Dere are plenty of shell casings around, way more dan six," said Spence as she held up a transparent bag displaying the evidence. "Dis gunman was not leaving until Tuffy was one hundred percent dead."

Harris patted Tuffy's shorts pockets and removed his house keys and a few hundred dollar bills. "He had more than this when he left Pelican Walk. He's spent a few hundred already, probably on food and transport."

Preddy glanced at Tuffy's last remaining belongings. "Apparently, he was just dropped off by a Pitfour taxi and bought a soda at de corner shop at de end of dis road. He's a regular customer dere. So far, dat's all we know."

"As annoying as he was I wouldnae wish him dead," said Harris shaking his head.

"Just hope he hasn't take our case wid him," muttered Preddy.

The sun was going down and soon it would be dark. The Ancona neighbourhood was like so many others in the parish. It was never easy to get the gunmen's victims or would-be victims to speak to police officers. Victims of St James gang violence were usually younger men than Tuffy, men in their twenties, although in the last few years death had ceased to be so discriminatory. Now everybody was fair game.

"Okay, let's try again." Preddy whipped his notebook out of his pocket. "See if we can get somebody to talk and bring an end to dis."

Spence reached into her pocket for pen and paper. "Easier getting lime juice outta rum punch."

Rabino seemed subdued. "Might get a few people to call us back when they're not in plain view of the whole community. I'll hand out a few cards." She wandered off towards the crowd. Some people jostled for position as she approached, eager to gain her attention. A young man with missing teeth leered at her.

"Wha' happen, baby?"

Rabino stared at him. Her usually calm persona suddenly deserted her. "Call me that again. Go on, call me that again."

The man's confidence faded although he tried to maintain his smile. "So me cyah talk to you?"

"If you have information about Antwon Frazer's death, talk to me. If not, don't play with me. Not in the mood."

Tuffy's body was duly covered with a white sheet while awaiting the arrival of the coroner. The detectives spread out and spent the next hour immersed in the horde who asked more questions than they offered answers. As expected, community members in fear for their lives preferred to deny all knowledge of the gunman rather than risk having their homes sprayed with bullets while they lay in their beds.

There was no doubt in anyone's mind that this was no random shooting. Tuffy was murdered because of what he knew. Whether that knowledge concerned Judge Wrenn's murder or the stash of illegal firearms or both was something Preddy was determined to figure out.

* * *

Haldin Newman hung up his phone and sat staring at the walls of his high street law office. Most people expected a lawyer's office to be glamorous with light decor, avant-garde art work and designer chairs. Those were TV soap opera law offices. His was that of a Montego Bay criminal lawyer and he was pretty sure that even the Kingston criminal lawyers could not afford to pose. His work space consisted of one large room and a reception area. The reception area was divided in two by strategically placed plyboard behind which his assistant could work when she was not manning the reception desk. Whenever the front door buzzer beeped she would race around the plyboard to see whether the person seeking entry was someone her boss would care to admit.

For the umpteenth time Haldin noted that the walls were greying and needing lightening up. Maybe bright yellow: a nice cheerful colour, anything to help take away the bleakness of days like this. Days when his many criminal clients were making his head hurt. Some days he was running all over the island behind them, trying to find out from unhelpful policemen where they were locked up, writing reports to convince senior police officers or judges to release them. Then there were days spent purely on the task of chasing them for money. A few willingly paid up; mainly the lottery scammers who always had a ready supply of US dollars at their fingertips. Others dragged their heels about paying and some even became so openly hostile that many a time he would give up the pursuit. If they ever sought his services again he would just be unavailable.

And then there were clients like Antwon Tuffy Frazer. Tuffy was a dead client. Not just any dead client either. Clients had died before and life went on for the lawyer. Either he would get his money from the estate or he wouldn't. But in this case the Crown prosecutor would have to give up on prosecuting any crime the dead client was charged with committing. If the deceased was a witness the police would have to abandon the idea of getting any useful testimony.

Haldin closed his eyes tightly. A prominent judge was dead. Tuffy was dead. Something told Haldin to mind his own business. That was the best thing to do. After all he was under no duty to disclose a thing. Let Detective Preddy and the Scotsman go do their thing with what little information they had. The phone rang and he let his assistant pick it up. He hoped it was something she could deal with, but within seconds she had buzzed through. Haldin picked up his phone and listened.

"Put her through," he said wearily. There was a click down the line and Haldin announced himself in the most professional and upbeat manner he could muster. He listened as the voice of a distraught lady flowed into his ears. "Tell him not to speak to the police, ma'am." He sighed and reached for a pen. "What station is he at and what is the officer's name."

His clients would always keep him in business. If only he could shake his conscience. Criminal lawyers with a conscience was not good for business and he would need to toughen up considerably to survive amongst the sharks.

* * *

It was late evening when Preddy's mobile phone rang disturbing the complete silence in his home office. Leaning forward he glanced across a pile of papers at the electronic display. He did not recognize the number and at first did not recognize the voice of the person asking to meet him.

"Sorry, who is dis?"

"Haldin Newman. Antwon Frazer's lawyer, Detective."

Preddy sat up straight. "Mr Newman, of course." The man sounded nervous, nothing like the assured tone that he used in their initial meeting. Preddy's heart beat increased. "We can meet any time you like, sir. Tonight is good."

Silence came from the other end of the phone and for a moment Preddy was afraid that the man had changed his mind. "I can come and meet you if you prefer? Just name a place and I'll be dere."

"You know where the August Bar is, on Sunset Boulevard?"

"Yes, man. Right by de car rental place."

"Meet you there in half hour. Just you, you know Detective Preddy?"

"Just me," Preddy repeated getting to his feet. "I'm setting out right now."

Preddy raced along the highway, bullying his way through fellow motorists at the busy roundabout that separated Top Road from Bottom Road. He ignored their toots of outrage and sped along the lower level, eventually turning into the large carpark of the August Bar. An open-air social spot, he could see most of the patrons from his vantage point. They stood close to the bar counter drinking and talking, middle-aged conservatively dressed people. None of them resembled the lawyer. The music was relatively low and a decent type of reggae, Michigan and Smiley old school tunes, not the raucous foul-lyrics that dominated the airwaves.

Preddy drummed his fingers on the steering wheel, frequently glancing at his rear-view mirror as cars entered and left the premises. He was just about to ring the lawyer when a car drove past him and he recognized the man's silhouette. The detective climbed out of his car and leaned against it watching Newman park his vehicle. The lawyer came towards him hastily and indicated that they move out of the spotlight. Preddy followed him around the side of a low wall where a few customers sat on cushions drinking alcohol. The lawyer made no move to take a seat and instead glanced over his shoulder.

"Thank you for coming, Haldin," said Preddy warmly. "Okay if I call you by your first name?"

"Yes, sure. I prefer Hal though." The lawyer wiped his brow with a face flannel. "I'm tired of hearing Mr Newman barked at me all day anyway. Some even have the nerve to call me 'dat bwoy Newman.'"

"I know de feeling, Hal," agreed Preddy. "Sure you don't want to go in and grab a drink. I hear dey do a mean pina colada?"

"So, I look like a pina colada man?" The lawyer gave him a rueful smile. "No, thanks, I'm good. Heineken is my thing for future reference though."

"Registered and understood." Preddy smiled back and studied him carefully. "Listen, any information you can give me about your client will be gratefully received. We have a gun dat we're pretty sure was used to murder him and a good description of de killer."

"I've been thinking about this all evening."

"Okay," Preddy nodded. "You can talk to me, Hal."

"What I have to tell you is off the record." Haldin took a deep breath. "If it's not, I intend to walk away now."

Preddy frowned. "I have no idea what you're going to tell me. Let's see what you have first before we agree anything. I promise if I can keep your name out of it though, I will. Trust me on dat. It would take a court order for me to reveal a confidential source to anyone."

The attorney pondered for a moment, watching as a bar customer lit a cigarette and strolled past him. "I realise you might say that my client was purely trying to deflect attention from himself." He paused and glanced at Preddy. "He told me something that led me to believe he was not involved in Judge Wrenn's murder."

"Talk to me," urged Preddy.

"Well, he swore blind he didn't do it. He said he couldn't prove that no member of the Benbow Crew did it either, but he felt pretty sure that they hadn't. They discussed it you see, as criminals do, and nobody took responsibility for it."

"Maybe de killer just wasn't ready to admit to it yet?" suggested Preddy.

"Believe it or not most of them had a love-hate relationship with Judge Wrenn. Seems they actually enjoyed the lectures he gave them, particularly when delivered in Patois."

Preddy's face grew critical. "Well dat's all nice and cosy and all, but tell me you're not expecting me to just take Tuffy's word for it?"

"No, of course not," said Haldin quickly. "Tuffy said something else. I think he was very wary of the person he does think is involved, almost afraid." He looked at Preddy hesitantly. "And this is where I don't want to get involved. He's an important man."

"Go on."

"Tuffy said he drove Judge Wrenn to lunch that Monday. Said he took him to Catherine Hall and dropped him off then picked him up a couple of hours later. Nothing happened at the drop off. When he came to pick him up the judge was in the car park arguing with another man."

A couple exited the August Bar and walked in the direction of Preddy and his informer. The lawyer instantly stopped speaking and pretended to be checking something on his phone. The departing pair climbed into a vehicle near to Preddy's, seemingly oblivious that they were being watched. The headlights went on as the vehicle backed up, blinding Preddy momentarily. He turned his head to one side and blinked a few times. Soon the car park was back in semi-darkness.

"Who him see?"

Haldin tucked his phone into his pocket. "Judge Wrenn and Judge Lawrence Guthrie. You know him?"

"I've come across him a couple of times," said Preddy carefully.

"They're good friends I understand from Tuffy. It wasn't the first time he'd driven Judge Wrenn to meet Judge Guthrie, whether at lunch breaks or formal occasions. Sometimes he drove both men together when they were going out. He'd heard them argue before, friendly arguments. The argument down at Catherine Hall? Not friendly."

"What was it about?" Preddy tried to keep any hint of excitement out of his voice.

The lawyer shook his head. "He didn't hear really. When he arrived he had his windows wound up, air con on and music playing. It was their body language that he saw. He said Guthrie was clearly furious, pointing his finger in Judge Wrenn's face and shouting. Judge Wrenn was backing up with his palms up, but he was shouting too. Tuffy said he had never seen Guthrie look like that before, his eyes were black and his face all screwed up. Tuffy said he honked the horn to get Judge Wrenn's attention and Judge Wrenn quickly climbed into the car." The lawyer looked around him again before continuing. "And then here's the thing, he said Judge Guthrie's face went back to being calm as day and he said 'See you around Ever,' and waved them off. Tuffy said he asked Judge Wrenn what it was about, but the judge just laughed it off and said his friend had got the wrong end of the stick."

"And he wasn't able to get anything more out of him?" asked Preddy.

"Not a word. Tuffy said he could tell from Judge Wrenn's demeanour that all was not well. He wasn't his usual chatty self on the drive back to court . . . seemed preoccupied and was staring at pictures on his phone."

"Thanks for letting me know dis, Hal," said Preddy patting the lawyer on the shoulder. "I owe you one."

The attorney exhaled loudly. "I didn't know what to do. Certainly didn't expect my client to get murdered. He did express fear about what the Crew would do to him when you confiscated the guns, but I think he was also scared of Judge Guthrie." He turned and stared at Preddy. "You think Guthrie could have killed Judge Wrenn and Tuffy?"

"In twenty years at dis game I've learned never to reach conclusions too quickly," replied Preddy. "Everyone is a suspect until dey are not."

The man nodded. "Makes sense."

"I can promise you dis, though. Tuffy's death will be investigated wid de same vigour applied to Judge Wrenn's case."

"Glad to hear it." He straightened up and shook Preddy's hand.

"Thank you. I'll do my level best to keep your name out of dis," promised Preddy.

"Thank you, Detective. Good luck."

CHAPTER 18

Monday, 8 May, 11.57 p.m.

Preddy soaked his tired body in warm bath water full of mineral salts infused with aloe vera, a present from Valerie. Showers were great but he really needed this. It was a long time since he had laid down in herbal water for any length of time, but he felt the distinct need to do so tonight. He lay perfectly still for ten minutes and his aching muscles gradually began to thank him. His phone rang, forcing him to open his eyes. It was nearly midnight, but he knew undoubtedly it had to be work. He wondered if Haldin Newman had remembered something else. He snatched a towel, dried his hands and grabbed the phone perched on the laundry basket next to him. A familiar name flashed on the screen.

"What happen?" asked Preddy.

"You're not going to like this, sir." Rabino's voice was hesitant which was unlike her and at once set Preddy's mind racing.

He stood and climbed out of the bath, water dripping on the tiles as he tied the towel around his waist. "Talk to me."

"That gun, the one that we located near to Tuffy's body? I've seen it before, sir. Saw it on Tuesday night in the Camry."

Preddy blinked but was unable to remove the mist from his mind. "I'm not following you?"

"Sir, that gun is one of them seized from Judge Wrenn's Camry in Montpelier where we arrested Tuffy." Her words sounded as if they were being forced reluctantly from her throat.

"You cannot be serious?" Preddy felt as if his breath was being squeezed out of his lungs. "How is dat even possible?" He padded across the floor and sat his damp body on the edge of his bed.

"I'm sorry, sir. I screwed up. I don't know what happened, but I'm one hundred percent certain that it's the same gun," she said. "I photographed everything on Tuesday night in the trunk. That gun had a bit of blue paint on the handle so it stood out in my mind. I didn't count the weapons though. It was late, I was tired. I just thought that was something to do in the morning — which I did. Didn't notice any guns missing. The Camry was left covered up under tarpaulin when Spence and I left Pelican Walk that night."

"Oh rass," murmured Preddy.

"The guns and ammunition were laid out in the evidence room the next morning by us. I just assumed they were all there. It was plaguing my mind today because I remembered that the gun used to kill Tuffy also had a blue mark. Hoped it was just a coincidence, but then I checked it. The photographs are pretty conclusive. It's the same gun, even has a dent on the barrel that you can just make out in the photo."

Preddy clutched the towel to his head and rubbed his wet scalp. "So wha' de rass happened?"

"It was taken sometime during Tuesday night, sir." Her panic was quite evident to Preddy's ears despite the phone static.

"Dat would suggest one of our officers took it, because nobody else could get access to de rear car park," said Preddy. "De only officers who would know dere were guns in dat car would be de ones who were wid you."

"Blagrove and Mitchell," murmured Rabino.

"Blagrove and Mitchell?" repeated Preddy. "Never. No way would dem do something like dat."

"I agree, sir."

"Okay wait." Preddy stood up and started pacing his bedroom. "Just wait. You sure exactly when you last saw it?"

"Well . . . I can't be sure. Maybe . . . I think maybe when I took the photo, sir!"

"Calm down, Kathryn. Just think. You think all de guns made it to Pelican Walk dat night? Is dere a possibility dey were removed enroute?"

"Could be," replied Rabino with less panic in her voice. "They were photographed all spread out in the trunk while we were in Montpelier. Spence locked the trunk. The Camry was covered in tarpaulin. It was picked up and brought to the station on the wrecker." She paused as she recollected. "In the morning Spence and I unlocked the trunk. Now that I think about it, it unlocked quite easily. We brought all the tools up to the evidence room and spread them out on the table. I didn't notice that the gun with the paint mark was missing."

"Okay, go back a bit," ordered Preddy. "Picture dat night. Who was where, doing what?"

Rabino inhaled and exhaled loudly. "I sat in the passenger seat and caught a ride back with Spence. Tuffy was handcuffed on the back seat. The wrecker with the Camry on board was behind us. Blagrove and Mitchell left together just before we set off."

Preddy stopped pacing. "You see anybody else following you?"

"No, sir. I just spoke to Spence about it and she's none the wiser either," said Rabino, before adding. "This is my fault, not hers. She did suggest we log the weapons that night. I was tired and didn't want to."

Preddy frowned. "In de morning I need you to get de names of de men who operated de wrecker. See if Blagrove and Mitchell can remember deir faces if you don't."

"I can get onto it right now, sir," said a dejected Rabino. "And I will remember their faces. I'll try and speak to the wrecker company owner. Wake him up if I have to."

"No, don't," said Preddy. "I don't think we should alert anybody tonight. We can do dis in daylight."

"Oh fuck! I feel like such a fool."

"Tuffy was a dead man walking from de minute he lost dose guns," said Preddy. "Whoever killed him was going kill him anyway, don't beat yourself up about dat."

"But with a gun that we had . . . that I had in my possession. How the hell am I going to explain that one to Brownlow?"

"I'll deal wid it. You don't have to explain a thing to him." Preddy tried to sound reassuring. "Dose guys in de wrecker? Either one or both of dem know exactly what happened to dat gun. Trust me, we will make dem talk."

"Yes, sir," she murmured.

"And remember, one eye-witness said de shooter had on a light blue hoodie wid de right sleeve rolled up and a distinctive tattoo on his right arm. She specifically remembered dat de tattoo was like a lizard or crocodile."

"I swear to you, sir, if one of the wrecker workmen meets that description, I'm going to shoot him on the spot."

"Dat's the spirit." Preddy forced a smile into his tone, knowing that Rabino would never shoot unless she felt threatened. "Look, try and get some sleep now. We need you well rested for tomorrow."

"I'm going to try and remember everything about that night," she promised. "Sleep isn't going to happen for me. And it's not like there's anybody here for me to disturb with my restlessness, anyway."

Preddy frowned. Now was not the time, but he did want to ask about the absent Clive. "We going fix it, Kathryn. We going get Tuffy's murderer," he insisted. "I have to make a stop at de Parish Court before I get in, but I'll be at de station. Don't worry about anything."

"Thanks. Goodnight, sir."

Preddy hung up the phone and rested his hands on his knees. It was one thing for him to tell Rabino to get some sleep and quite another when it came to himself. Keeping this gun debacle from Superintendent Brownlow until he had all the answers was not going to be easy, and would probably be impossible if Detective Harris found out. Until he knew what Harris was really up to the less he was willing to confide in him. Preddy uttered a sharp groan. Get the guns. Not get the guns from one set of criminals and hand them to another. He pulled on his boxer shorts and lay stretched out on his back, hands folded under his head, eyes wide open. Not even the bloody Norwood images would get a look in tonight.

CHAPTER 19

Tuesday, 9 May, 9.12 a.m.

Preddy crammed the remaining paperwork into his briefcase and picked up his keys. He scoped out the apartment as he always did making sure that all possible entry points were secured. Although Ironshore was a safe and relatively affluent area there were always opportunists on the lookout for easy pickings, knowing that the Neighbourhood Watch was vision impaired. Above the ticking of the dining room clock his ears detected a gentle sound like someone drumming a pen on a desk. He doubled back and spotted the yellow beak tapping with determination at the window. A pair of tiny dark eyes in a bright green crested head watched him and moved from side to side.

"Hello Spartan, you come back?"

Preddy glanced at the front door and then at his watch before his eyes went back to the insistent bundle of feathers. The Parish Court wasn't open yet anyway. He put down his things and unlocked the window. The parakeet instantly flew onto Preddy's shoulder clutching the cotton shirt beneath its delicate feet. It seemed like a young thing and was about six inches high. He smiled and slowly walked towards the kitchen.

"Corn done," he whispered. "Hope you eat leftover rice and peas."

He grabbed a spoon and opened the fridge. The bird cheeped and held on as he stooped to uncover a small pot scooping up a heap of rice. The impatient bird scrambled down his long sleeve to his cuff and began eating the grains before he could shut the door. He closed it with a soft back heel.

"Dat's right, be quick Spartan, I have a murderer to catch," he murmured. Using his left hand he stroked the top of the creature's tiny head. The bird paused to give him the side-eye and he quickly lowered his hand. "Okay, you eat in peace. I know how it is, boy. If you're not a boy, forgive me. You look like a boy wid dat hairstyle."

As its craw began to bulge the parakeet slowed its furious pecking and relaxed into a more leisurely snatch and grab scattering a few grains onto the floor. "Cho, Spartan man!" Preddy chided him. "You remind me of dem old drunk. Can't raise a liquor glass to dem mouth widout spill it and still calling bartender to bring more."

He stooped to pick up the grains, careful not to dislodge the bird. "I remember when drunks used to be my problem, Spartan, many many moons ago. My problem now is people who like to kill people and think dey can continue to share space wid normal people in society. Not going work at all."

When the rice was gone Preddy tossed the spoon into the sink and the bird flew back onto his shoulder. It pecked him lightly on the cheek. "Hey, I hope dat was a 'thank you' and not a 'where's my corn?'" He headed towards the window with his contented companion. "Don't worry, more corn soon come. See? Now you have double incentive to come back."

Preddy stroked its chest, ruffling its feathers, expecting the parakeet to take flight. Instead the bird clutched onto his shoulder reluctant to let go. He knelt down beside the window sill and leaned towards it gently rocking his shoulder until the bird got the message and hopped off. It gave him a quick look of appreciation or annoyance, he could not tell which, before spreading its wings and soaring high, vanishing into the greenery of a lime tree.

* * *

Preddy crunched his mints as he sat parked outside the Parish Court watching the security guard remove the padlocks from the shuttered iron grill. The media had been warning people for days of delays in court proceedings due to unofficial industrial action in Montego Bay. He could see a few court staff waiting outside, but no sign of any judges. Still, it was early and there was plenty of time for the judges and the usual loiterers to show up. Preddy waited for a few minutes after the three employees had gone inside before heading for the door. The officer manning the metal detector had not yet switched it on. He recognized Preddy immediately and waved a hello as the detective walked past.

"Thanks for your help Friday, Detective. We thought the place was going to be blown sky high!"

"Not a problem, man," replied Preddy as he sprang up the stairs two at a time. "My business is to keep everybody safe."

At the top of the landing he stood looking up and down the corridor. Most of the doors were closed and there was a heavy silence and emptiness that enhanced the mouldy smell of the building. Many people had entered these hallowed halls seeking justice or revenge or both. Some left of their own free will, others were carted off in the back of a police truck. From behind him came the clicking of heels.

"Can I help you, sir?" a woman asked. As Preddy spun around and looked at her, she said, "Oh, Detective Preddy, isn't it? I'm Ivy Dixon, a court clerk."

He had noticed her outdoors; a fleshy woman with a wide mouth and pleasant appearance. A ring adorned every finger. She was the first person to enter the building, which Preddy hoped counted for dedication and conscientiousness. "Yes, please Mrs Dixon. You know I'm investigating de murder of Judge Wrenn?"

"Are you though?" She stared at him blankly. "From what I hear the police are not doing anything at all."

Preddy was about to give a sharp retort before he noticed her wink. His face relaxed into a smile. "Dis is a thankless job as I'm sure you know. Plenty is going on dat we can't talk to de public about."

"Trust me, I know," she nodded. "I've asked my colleagues who else we're going to turn to if we decide to fall out with the police. I mean, look at what happened with the suspect package! We can't stop returning police phone calls. We can't stop updating case files. Let's take up our safety and pay concerns with the government, I say."

Preddy nodded his appreciation. "I'm really glad you feel dat way."

"You guys have a hard job to do," she replied with a deep sigh. "I couldn't do it. Tell me what I can do to help."

"De Night Court records. I'm looking for Monday, de first of May. Where are dey?"

"The night Judge Wrenn was killed." She inclined her head. "Follow me." She turned and led the way towards one of the courtrooms. Inside she picked up a thick black register. "I did a shift on that night. This is the record of the cases. Court only sat on two nights last week." She flicked through the pages and then stopped. "We had a horrible set that Monday: all sweatsuits and hoodies and gold teeth and bad attitude."

Preddy took the book and frowned. Lawyer Newman had never alluded to his client's presence at Night Court, but there was his name, Antwon Frazer. The name below Tuffy's rang a bell too. Rohan McNeary alias Steely Vicious was a notorious member of the Benbow Crew. The last man's name was unknown to Preddy. Jevon Collins. If he too was a Crew member he would have an alias which might be more recognizable. Preddy shook his head. Their parents had given them decent respectable names and they had opted for names calculated to instil fear and force respect.

The clerk stood at Preddy's shoulder looking at the book. "Judge Guthrie warned them to find something productive to do with their lives."

Preddy drew back. "Judge Guthrie? You mean, Judge Bailey? It's his name I see here."

"They swap from time to time if necessary. I think Judge Bailey was due in, but Judge Guthrie was definitely here. That guy Collins swore at him. He's a right nasty looking man they call Devil Head. When he took off that hoodie? Man! Two thick dreadlocks stood up like horns! His skin is purplish pink and he's full of ink. Looked like the real Devil himself." She gave an involuntary shiver. "He said he was just playing dominoes with his friends not committing any crime."

"What time was dis?"

She leaned her head to one side. "Well, we were open between eight and ten. Could be closer to ten."

Preddy's temples began to throb. "You sure you couldn't be mistaken, about de judge, I mean?"

"Positive, Detective," the clerk replied. She chuckled. "Judge Guthrie took on Antwon Frazer. Asked him what he did for a living. Antwon said he was a respectable person 'a community organizer.' The judge asked if it's him organizing all the robberies and murders in St James. He made me laugh, but you know you can't laugh out in court or he'll reprimand you. Judge Guthrie is very serious about his courtroom."

Preddy wondered if some subliminal message had passed between Judge Guthrie and Tuffy. The judge already knew Tuffy's occupation, having been chauffeured by the man before, and having seen him that very afternoon. "Did Antwon Frazer have a lawyer wid him?"

The woman shook her head. "No, none of them had legal representation. All three of them were warned and let go. Judge Guthrie told them that he never wanted to see any of them again, they should learn a trade or get jobs."

Preddy handed her the register. "Thanks."

They left the courtroom and headed towards the stairs. "Everything alright, Detective?"

"Yes," replied Preddy. "Do me a favour though? Don't mention to anyone dat we've had dis conversation. Certainly not Judge Guthrie."

She beamed at Preddy. "I won't. And don't tell anybody that I didn't log the right judge's name."

"Is Judge Guthrie due in today?"

"No, not today, sir. Tomorrow."

As he drove towards Pelican Walk police station a number of questions ran through Preddy's mind. Judge Guthrie had lied. It was not beyond the realms of possibility that the judge could be in league with the gangsters. The public shaming of them that night could have been a sham to deflect suspicion from his relationship with them. The judge seemed to have released the notorious Crew without much of a hearing. Preddy squeezed the steering wheel and frowned. Wherever Judge Guthrie was he would find him and confront him, but first it was best to break down the girlfriend, Jacqui Morgan. His phone rang and he snatched it off the dashboard.

"I was just about to call you," he said, before the caller could speak. "You find him?"

"Something like that, sir," said Rabino.

Preddy was relieved to hear her voice sounding calm and even. A distinct voice shouting in the background did not sound calm. "Dat sound like Spence? What happen?"

"We have an incident here, sir. If you've got some time I suggest you come and meet us at the wrecker company."

"On my way."

* * *

A truck was backing out just as Preddy was turning into the extensive compound of the automobile cemetery. The premises also operated as a haulage yard and contained many shipping containers as well as disabled vehicles all amassed around a gigantic workshop. Rusting body parts and broken chassis were stacked up as far as the eye could see. The piercing beep of the reverse indicator played on the detective's nerves. He drummed his fingers and waited, impatient to reach the heightened voices. It did not take him long to figure out where the commotion was coming from. His vehicle crawled towards the back of the yard and stopped under a large awning. The group of people had their backs turned to him. As he started to walk towards them he spotted Spence and Rabino among them. Everyone was showing keen interest in a towering guango tree.

"Hello people," murmured Preddy.

"Oh hello, sir," said Spence with a quick glance at her superior. "See de damn ass up dere!"

"Still refusing to come down," added Rabino. "Adamant that he's done nothing wrong."

Preddy walked closer to the tree and looked up. "And yet he's twenty feet off de ground clutching onto a thin branch." A man dressed in red floral shorts and white merino was high up, yet the whites of his eyes were clearly visible. His long bare feet dangled beneath him.

"The tree hugger goes by the name of Deano Miller, sir," said Rabino. "The owner says he's only worked here for two weeks. He was definitely one of the two men who hauled the Camry. The other guy — the driver — is over there." She pointed at the driver who immediately held up the palms of his hands.

"Whatever happen — a no me! Me never do nutten, Boss!" he swore.

"Come down, Mr Miller!" shouted Spence slamming a fist against the tree trunk. "You think we have time fi waste?"

"Me not coming down! Lef me alone!"

Preddy looked at Rabino. "So Miller is our man?"

"I'd bet my life on it," she nodded. "When Spence and I pulled up nobody moved a muscle except our Miller. He took one look at us and started running. Took me totally by surprise, I must say. By the time we ran round here we couldn't see him. Thought he'd hopped over the fence and gone, and I was just about to jump it too. Then Spence spotted the red patches disappearing up the tree."

"Guilty conscience, eh?" suggested Preddy.

Rabino nodded. "He did it. Some Mission Impossible business was going on behind us that night and we didn't see."

"I going kill meself!" shouted the man.

"No, don't do dat, Deano!" Preddy bellowed.

"Dat a your business!" shouted Spence simultaneously.

Preddy shot Spence a disapproving glance. "I think we better do dis my way."

Spence kissed her teeth and took a few steps back. "Anyhow him want to come down dat is his business," she mumbled. "All head first. Me will take him how me can get him."

Preddy shielded his eyes and looked up the tree. "I'm Detective Preddy, Deano, please come down and let's talk. Dis is not doing you any good."

"You want borrow a ladder, boss?" asked one of the workmen.

"It not going reach dat far," warned another. "You need to be a good climber to go up dere."

"I'm certainly not going up after him, but thanks," said Preddy, "bring de ladder come."

The two men headed in the direction of the workshop entrance.

"What did de driver say happened?" asked Preddy quietly, not taking his eyes off the rough dark soles above his head.

"We were in front of the wrecker. We stopped briefly at a traffic light," Rabino explained in a low tone. "Deano Miller told him the tarpaulin was coming off the Camry and climbed out ostensibly to fix it. The light changed, the driver drove off again and after a few minutes Miller climbed back in . . . while the vehicle was in motion. For some reason the driver didn't think there was anything strange about this behaviour." She paused then added. "We haven't told him or any of the others why we need to talk to Miller. He's probably guessed that something's been stolen though."

"Maybe Spence have de right idea," whispered Preddy. "Let him come down head first since him think him a Tom Cruise."

The workmen returned with a long ladder and placed it firmly against the tree.

"Look Deano," shouted Spence. "Look how we get ladder fi you!"

The man's suspicious eyes peered through the leaves, but he made no move to descend.

"Deano, you know you can't stay up dere," said Preddy. "We're not leaving until you come down. We only want to ask you a few questions."

"What you wah ask him 'bout?" asked one of the men. "Eeh hee, is what him do?"

"Whatever him do, me no want him inna me place!" said the business owner in a loud voice. The man waved a bunch of keys in the air as he spoke. "You know how long me a run my place without any trouble? I gwine fire him today!"

"We'll take him off your hands, sir," Preddy assured him. "Deano, you coming down?"

The fugitive shifted, trying to lessen his discomfort. A shower of sticky black pods cascaded towards Preddy who took a step back and brushed at his shirt. More spots to add to Spartan's claw marks.

"But wait, is police you a throw things after?" asked one of the men incredulously.

"Me never throw a ting," insisted the suspect. "Is drop dem drop down!"

"I believe you, Deano," said Preddy gently. "Come down, man. Dis can be sorted out. Sometimes people do things dey didn't plan to do, and wouldn't usually do. We can talk about it."

No response from up the tree. The workmen muttered among themselves, each giving their opinion on what wrongs they believed their colleague had committed, hoping that one of the detectives would interject. Their theories ranged from theft and burglary to rape and murder.

"Ssh!" Preddy hissed. "Deano, come down man. Let's talk."

The owner walked forwards. "Look here Miller, you damn blind or something? You no see is which Babylon dis! Remember Norwood? Is an assassin. Him will light up your arse if you no come down!"

Preddy was about to chide the man for his interference when to his surprise he saw that Deano Miller was actually moving, and in the right direction. The Norwood episode brought Preddy countless nightmares, yet it also brought him co-operation.

"Don't shoot, Misser Preddy! Don't shoot! Me a come!"

"Yes, move you backside!" Spence encouraged him.

The labourers cheered as Deano started his descent, digging his fingers into the bark until he reached the top of the ladder. Spence grabbed the waistband of his shorts long before his foot hit the last rung of the ladder.

Rabino gave him an icy glare. "We meet again Mr Miller."

Preddy said, "We meet for de first time."

"I know you remember me, don't you?" asked Rabino.

The man did not reply and studied the dirt between his misshapen toes.

"Okay, we going sit in my car and have a chat," said Preddy taking Miller by the arm. "And if you don't want to talk dere we can provide you wid a bed at Pelican Walk."

"And no bother wid de running again," warned Spence. "Me can't take de running inna dese shoes cause dem new and just hurt up me toe."

"Me have exhaust pipe to fix dis morning," grumbled the man.

"Not at my place." The owner said, shaking his head vigorously. "Find some other work somewhere else. Look from when me working wid police and dem never come here looking to question nobody. You can gwaan leave!"

"There see," said Rabino. "You're now unemployed, so you're free to come and talk."

The detectives marched the suspect to Preddy's car and pushed him into the back seat. Spence and Rabino squeezed in on either side so that he was huddled between them. Preddy climbed into the driver's seat and spun around. All four doors were left open. Preddy studied the man whose ebony skin was devoid of tattoos or any signs of bleaching.

"I didn't get a wink of sleep last night," said Rabino. "If you don't tell us what we need to know I'll make your life so miserable you'll want to move to Riverton City."

"Me no do nutten!"

Preddy flicked his fingers in front of Miller's distressed face. "Hey! You removed a gun from de red Camry. Dat gun was used to kill someone. Either you are de killer or you gave de killer de gun — which is it?"

The man's eyes widened and his lips flew apart. "Dat gun use kill somebody?"

"Riverton City dump, Mr Miller," elaborated Rabino.

The man stared at her and wailed, "Me never shoot a gun inna me life! Me did take it, yes. Me did just want to have a gun. Plenty bwoy have gun, but me never did a go shoot nobody."

"So what did you plan to do with it?" asked Rabino. "Use it as a doorstopper? We look stupid to you?"

"No ma'am," he mumbled. "Me couldn't keep quiet after me get it. Me tell all me friend dem dat me get a gun. Me don't know how dat news spread a road so quick. Even people what I don't even know come ah ask me about it!"

"What did you do with it?" Rabino turned slightly and stared into his eyes. "And if you're thinking about lying, really, don't. Play time is over."

"True talk," agreed Spence. "Murder is not a game."

The man rubbed his palms on his knees leaving wet streaks. "De gunman take it from me," he admitted. "Me did lean up right outside of a cookshop talking wid me friend dem. Next thing me know a motorbike pull up. Is one wicked bwoy dat! Him say de gun belong to him and me can give it to him or me can dead. Me give it to him quick-quick!"

"Who? What's his name?" asked Rabino.

"Me no know him real name. One ugly bwoy what bleach out and mark up. Devil Head me hear dem call him."

Spence shook her head. "Don't know dat name. Never heard of him."

"I have," said Preddy. "Devil Head. A man wid a lot of tattoos and two horns."

Miller seemed to brighten up. "Me don't know 'bout de horn thing, because him hair always cover up under hood or cap, but him have nuff tattoo fi real! All over him neck and hand! One shape like dem alligator me see a river."

"Crocodile," Preddy corrected him. "We don't have alligator. If you did stay in school you wouldn't make dat mistake. You going come wid us right now and look at some photographs."

"Spence and I are going to the Hip Strip, sir," Rabino reminded him.

"Yes, of course," he said quickly. "Call me later."

The fugitive watched in alarm as Rabino and Spence climbed out and walked towards their vehicle. "De woman dem going away?" Preddy kept silent and smirked at Deano Miller, who gulped. "A station we a go, officer?"

"Yes, straight to Pelican Walk." Preddy smiled at the man's desperation. "Relax. I'm not going divert anywhere. I'm not going shoot you or put you in a barrel and roll it off a cliff."

"Thank you, sir!"

"Not my plan at dis moment anyway."

CHAPTER 20

Detective Spence blazed along the Hip Strip, flying past the cafes, restaurants and retail stores. Forced to pause at a pedestrian crossing she scowled as a group of animated tourists took a leisurely stroll across the road, beach towels slung over their shoulders. She pressed the gas long before the last bare-legged visitor had both sandals on the pavement. Soon their destination was in sight and with a screech of tyres she pulled up outside the boutique. Rabino winced as the vibration ran through her body. The car came to a sudden rest across two bays, but Spence was not about to be troubled by parking etiquette.

"Well, you got their attention," said Rabino, staring up through the windshield at the two women leaning out of the window looking down at them.

"What we better get are some true answers. Not going play wid dat lying woman!"

"Any predictions about what she might say or do?" asked Rabino.

Spence shut off the engine. "Jump outta bed dis morning without even going online. I have an idea dat any tarot reading would predict a lot of lies and stress for de day."

Rabino retrieved her camera from the footwell and climbed out. "I don't think we'll be chasing Jacqui over fences or up trees though so it won't be that bad."

The boutique assistant held the door open. She seemed unsettled as if she had sprinted down the stairs. As the detectives walked past her she offered them her perfect smile. "Good morning, ladies. Nice to see you again. How are you?"

"Morning Marsha." Rabino was polite but did not return her smile.

Spence said nothing and made a beeline for the stairs straight past some customers who were inspecting the various racks of clothes. Jacqui appeared at the top, looking both regal and angelic in a long African print dress.

"This is unexpected, detectives." The businesswoman smiled at them. "Have you changed your minds about buying some of my pieces?"

Spence exploded. "We've changed our minds about buying anything dat you're selling!"

Jacqui frowned and massaged her fingers. "What do you mean?"

"You lied to us," stated Rabino.

"And when you done lie, you lie some more," added Spence loudly.

Jacqui peered over the balcony at a few customers who were looking up the stairs. She beckoned to the detectives to follow her into her small office and closed the door. She leaned with her back against it and faced the detectives.

"Did you spill something on your hands, or are they just feeling dirty?" asked Rabino.

Jacqui, who had not realised that she was wiping her hands on her sides, instantly stopped. She placed a hand to the curve in her neck and started rubbing it. "What is this about?"

Spence made no attempt to take a seat or make herself comfortable. "De night Judge Wrenn was murdered. Do you want to tell us again where you were?"

"Without the lies," instructed Rabino as she perched on the edge of a table.

Jacqui licked her polished lips smearing the red lipstick. She slowly moved away from the door and pushed a pile of plastic covered outfits from a wicker chair onto the floor. She sank into the chair, picked up a hand fan and began to use it vigorously.

"We went out to dinner, Lawrence and I. I told you."

"Look here, lady. Stop play fool," snapped Spence waving a finger in her direction.

"You're not a suspect in the murder, yet." Rabino stared coldly at Jacqui. "Judge Guthrie obviously asked you to lie. We want to know why."

Jacqui's fan began to work overtime. "I would never be involved in any murder. Never! And Lawrence was certainly not involved in any murder."

"What happened on Monday night?" demanded Rabino.

"What did he say?" asked Jacqui. She paused her fanning momentarily to gaze at Rabino.

"Dis is clearly not going to work," said Spence, moving towards the door. "Just lock up de shop Ma'am. We'll go to Pelican Walk and talk 'bout it."

"I agree," said Rabino. "Come on."

"I can't go!" Jacqui's eyes flicked desperately from one detective to the other.

"If you think we're going to be lenient with you, you're so wrong. You're going to end up with a charge of aiding and abetting a murder," warned Rabino.

"No! Look, Lawrence and I did go out to dinner. We went to the Houseboat Grill just like I told you."

"And had a lovely romantic meal, eeh?" Spence bored Jacqui with her eyes. "While our investigations place Lawrence Guthrie elsewhere dat night?" She opened her notebook and flicked the pages back until she found the relevant entry. "Run de times past me again. You say he picked you up around six-thirty or seven and took you home around ten?"

Jacqui did not respond and instead studied a bundle of fabric swatches on the table.

"What would you say if we told you we can definitively place him elsewhere around that time?" asked Rabino.

Jacqui's face turned sullen. "I would say place him there then, because I don't know what you're talking about. Let Lawrence speak for himself and he'll tell you what I'm telling you now. He's a loving, truthful, honourable man. He didn't kill anybody."

"You're still lying." Rabino began scrolling through the camera gallery. She stretched out towards Jacqui and placed the screen close to her face. "Lawrence is certainly a loving man. Truthful, honourable . . . I'm not so sure about that, are you?"

Jacqui squinted and removed the camera from Rabino's hands. "It's heavy, don't drop it," warned Rabino.

Jacqui held it away from her face and scrutinized the image at length.

"Use the right arrow and scroll along," said Rabino. "There are plenty more of them."

The woman obeyed, her forefinger explored the gallery. "When were these taken?" Her voice was barely audible.

"On Saturday, at the regatta down at the Freeport. He called her Bella."

"Regatta?" Jacqui continued to gaze at pictures of the busty younger woman wrapped around Lawrence Guthrie's neck. She passed the camera back to Rabino and rested her trembling hands in her lap. "He said he was going back to St Elizabeth for the weekend. Said he had to sort out some things with his wife as he's planning on moving out."

"Jacqui, tell us about the night Judge Wrenn was murdered," Rabino implored her.

Jacqui took a deep breath. "We did go out to dinner. At least that was the intention. He did pick me up and we got to the waterfront just before it went dark. Took the sixty-second journey on that quaint little raft across to the Houseboat Grill. We were shown to a table and ordered drinks, then he said he had to make a quick phone call and disappeared.

He came back and said something had come up. Apologised profusely." Her lips curled into a snarl. "He called a taxi to take me home and left me before it even arrived. I was back inside my house by eight-thirty."

Rabino and Spence exchanged glances.

"That lying John Crow," muttered Jacqui. "I can't believe he would do this to me."

"So he didn't tell you who was on the phone or where he was going?" asked Rabino.

Jacqui shook her head. "He just sounded irritated. I guess he went off to see this Bella. Gave me a big hug and kiss, said he would call me and then he was gone." She paused before adding, "He did call me that night, woke me up around midnight. Said he was in bed reading. Well, maybe he wasn't lying about that. Maybe he was in bed with her fast asleep beside him."

A knock came at the door and the shop assistant poked her head in. "Everything alright, Mrs Morgan? You need water or coffee or anything?"

Jacqui gave her a grateful smile. "No, thanks Marsha. We're alright. Just watch the customers for me."

The door closed behind the young woman.

"Lawrence still didn't indicate where he'd been?" asked Rabino.

"I didn't press him, Detective," said Jacqui throwing her hands up in the air. "The relationship is three months old. Men don't like to be questioned. If you start to press a man about what he's doing and where he's going or where he's been so early in the relationship he'll be gone in a flash."

"So that's where I keep going wrong," said Rabino dryly.

Jacqui continued, "I told him I missed him and suggested he get a good night's sleep."

"You should always question dem, Ma'am," said Spence shaking her head. "Whether de relationship is three months or three years or thirty-three years old. If dey get defensive or angry den you will have answered your own question."

Jacqui stared dolefully at Spence and said nothing.

"Look — if there's anything else you remember that will help us, whether about that night or anything Lawrence has said to you since, please give us a call," said Rabino heading towards the door.

"Dis is a murder investigation. He might contact you to try and get you to tell us another story," said Spence, following behind her colleague. "Don't get yourself involved in something dat could land you in serious trouble."

"Oh I won't, you can be assured of that," said Jacqui firmly. "Delete and block work just fine on my phone. I have absolutely nothing to say to Lawrence Guthrie."

CHAPTER 21

As Preddy drove along the highway deep in concentration, Harris watched him through the corner of his eye. "I was beginning tae get worried this morning," he said. "Station was deserted. Checked yer office, the evidence room, the interview rooms, naw a sign of anybody."

Preddy detected a hint of reproach in his voice. "Just had one or two distractions dat took longer dan planned. Had to stop at de court house. Spence and Rabino went to tackle Jacqui Morgan again as dey told you."

"Who was that skinny guy ye were showing out?"

Preddy increased his grip on the steering wheel. Until this moment he was unaware that Harris had seen Deano Miller's departure from Pelican Walk. "Just a would-be informant. I was hoping to get some leads on all dese guns we have circulating in de parish. Had him look at some photos to see if he could identify anybody."

"Learn anything useful?"

"Not really," lied Preddy.

Harris buckled his seatbelt. "I would've come with ye tae court. Ye should've called me."

"Didn't even believe dey would let me inside. Dey are agitating for a full blown strike down dere." He had provided Harris with as much information about Judge Guthrie and the Night Court as he thought necessary. "Anyway, at least we know where Lawrence Guthrie is right now. Looking forward to hear what he has to say."

Harris said, "Oleta Wrenn phoned, wanting tae see how things were going. I told her we were on it, but I couldnae give her any details. She seemed satisfied. Gave me a monetary value for the missing Samsung phone and the old coins. Reckons the coins are worth eight hundred thousand dollars."

"That's about . . . over six thousand US dollars," calculated Preddy keeping an eye on the vehicle in front. "Not a bad haul."

"Said her kids will be flying in from Canada tomorrow evening."

"Dat will be good for her." Preddy turned behind the judge's brown SUV. "Can't be nice rattling around in dat big house by herself even wid a great view."

"I'll say," agreed Harris. "And with the murder scene right in front of her, poor hen."

Preddy parked outside a plaza of shops and watched as Judge Lawrence Guthrie alighted from his SUV and walked towards a stationery shop. The detectives left their jeep and quickly caught up with him.

"Judge Guthrie, we need tae talk tae ye," said Harris. "Can ye spare us a minute, please?"

Guthrie turned around in surprise and acknowledged them with a beaming smile. "Of course, detectives. What brings you here? I hope you have some news about Everton's case?"

"Actually, we do," said Preddy.

"Good. You've caught me on my day off." He used a remote to lock his car door and began to walk. "Follow me, gentlemen."

Preddy increased his stride and overtook the judge before coming to a halt in front of him forcing the judge to stop abruptly. "On de night of your good friend's murder, you were at Night Court. You and a few of de Benbow Crew murderers."

Guthrie's eyes reflected his shock, but in seconds he regained his composure, "You mean 'alleged murderers' don't you, Detective Preddy? Still waiting on you officers to bring us some evidence that will secure murder convictions."

"Ye lied tae us," said Harris. "And now ye've got us wondering who the murderer really is."

The judge raised his eyebrows and looked from one detective to the other. "Surely, you are not serious? You have *got* to be kidding!"

"We're Pelican Walk. We dinnae kid." Harris was stone-faced.

The judge narrowed his eyes. "Hell! Maybe I need a lawyer before I talk to you."

"Was dat a question or a statement?" asked Preddy. "Do you need a lawyer before you tell us what we need to know?"

Harris took out his notebook and read, "Ye're naw obliged tae say anything, but . . ."

"Please, Detective Harris." The judge waved a hand dismissively. "We don't need that. I know my rights."

Preddy shrugged. "Your choice."

"You've got this all wrong," insisted the judge. "It is not what it looks like."

"Well, tae me it looks like ye lied about ye whereabouts. Met with some pretty nasty criminals — one of whom was Antwon Frazer, now deceased — and shortly after that yer best friend was lying dead on his verandah," said Harris. "Fancy that?"

The judge drew himself up to his full height. "Okay, so maybe I left a bit out of my statement. It was for a good reason. If you think I would get myself involved with any members of that savage gang you must be mad. I'm only acquainted with them in so far as I see them in court, other than Antwon Frazer who Everton swore was reformed. I've always trusted Everton's judgment. Maybe on this occasion he got it wrong."

"Let's naw blame the victim here," said Harris.

"I'm not, Detective," insisted Guthrie. "Everton was a great guy. He certainly didn't deserve what happened to him."

"You still haven't told us why de lies or what possible reason you had to dump your girlfriend and run to Night Court," said Preddy. "You were not deir lawyer."

"Look, when I got to the Houseboat, it crossed my mind that I might be on standby for the Night Court. I sometimes am. I rang the security desk at court. Their phone log will prove it. It was about seven thirty. They said I would be needed because Judge Bailey wasn't feeling too well. My first thought was to let the cases be postponed for another day, but we have such a backlog that it makes things worse. I asked the officer if any of the defendants were known criminals and he said yes. When he read the names out I just knew that I had to go see if there was any chance that we could keep these thugs off the streets even for a few months."

"And?" pressed Harris.

The judge shook his head. "It wasn't to be. The hearings didn't last long. There's this little thing called due process. I can't order the detention of people just like that. Some police officers certainly know how to waste court time."

Harris interjected, "Present company excluded, of course."

Guthrie conceded the correction. "The Trojan Street officers need reasonable cause and evidence to be dragging people to court, not a mere hatred of them or wish to annoy them. There was no reason to hold any of them. I had to let them go."

Preddy frowned. "So why did you feel de need to hide all dis, if it was so innocent?"

"I'm embarrassed to say, it's because I'm a snob." The judge held his head high and stared at Preddy. "Sometimes I can't believe that after my long career this is where I still am. I knew I didn't murder anybody so there was no need to admit that I have to work Night Court. Face it, Detective, you've been to daytime sessions and seen what it's like. There is some semblance of order, but in truth it's depressing. Full of the ignorant and the naive, and that's just the lawyers."

"Charming," muttered Harris.

The judge shrugged. "You asked for the truth and now you've got it."

"You left Night Court and where did you go?" asked Preddy.

"I went home . . . well, to the Ambassador West Hotel, Detective. I'm sure you've already checked that out. I was there by around eleven."

"You could have gone to Wynterton Park before you went to your hotel," stated Preddy.

"But I didn't, Detective." Lawrence Guthrie's eyes roved over Preddy. "So I'm a snob. Look down on me for that. I'm not a murderer. I went to bed and read a book just like I told you."

Preddy was unnerved that Guthrie remained calm and polite. He had expected a fierce denial or even abuse but not this seeming detachment. Maybe the judge had suspected that this day would come and had fully prepared for it.

"I know you have a job to do but I did not murder Everton Wrenn." Guthrie moved to step around Preddy who was still blocking his way. "Now, if you don't mind?"

"We cannae just take yer word for it. Everyone who comes on our radar will be investigated whether they like it or naw."

"Well, you're looking in the wrong place, Detective Harris." The judge shook his head as if sympathising with their predicament. "Everton and Oleta were my friends. Now that Antwon Frazer has been taken out in a hail of bullets I get elevated on your list of suspects? What about people who have actual motives? What about the one who was causing Everton grief polluting his waterfront with dirt? Mr Mexell. He has millions of reasons to want Ever out of the picture. Why don't you find out what he was doing Monday night?"

"It's very kind of ye tae point us tae the murderer," said Harris snidely. "Can ye tell us how he did it as well?"

"That's on you. And as the pride of Glasgow I'm sure you'll do your job." The judge felt around in his pocket for a handkerchief which he used to wipe the moist area above his lips. "Next time we speak my lawyer will be present. I wanted to help you find Everton's murderer, but all you've done is try to pin it on me. That's why murders never get solved in Mo Bay. When people try to help you, you use it against them."

"All we're doing, Judge Guthrie, is trying to find de truth," retorted Preddy. "We need all de help we can get, but you lied and had your girlfriend lie for you."

The judge froze. "Oh Lord, I need to phone Jacqui."

"Good luck with that," said Harris.

Judge Guthrie's expression switched to annoyed. "So, you've spoken to her already then? I should have known. Probably put the fear of God into the poor woman."

Harris smiled at him. "Let's just say I dinnae think ye'll be seeing much of her, but ye seem tae have a back-up friend anyway. Bella, I understand?"

The judge pursed his lips tightly closed and began to stride away.

Preddy stared after him. "Before you go Judge Guthrie, one question."

The judge paused and turned to Preddy. "What is it?"

"You mentioned you had lunch wid Everton Wrenn earlier dat afternoon at Catherine Hall. How did it go, was everything alright?"

"Yes, why shouldn't it have been? As I said before Everton was on top form and funny with it. We had a perfectly pleasant lunch, usual ribbing, and then we went our separate ways." The judge swung on his heels. "Now, we should do the same." He stormed away without looking backwards.

Harris glanced at Preddy. "What was that about?"

Preddy continued to stare after the judge's disappearing back. "Oh, I just wondered if he failed to tell us something about de lunch meeting too."

"And do ye think he did?" That trace of suspicion surfaced again in Harris's tone.

"It's a distinct possibility," replied Preddy as he headed to his car, aware that Harris's green eyes were on him.

* * *

Harris glowered as he climbed into the passenger seat. Raythan Preddy was a man with something on his mind that he had no intention of sharing. As Preddy backed out of the parking space Harris wondered if he should press him or wait for him to speak. He toyed with the idea of putting the radio on and tuning it to one of Preddy's favourite channels, Kool FM, but the deep frown on his colleague's face was enough to put him off. They cruised along the busy coastal boulevard in silence for a few minutes. Just before they reached the busy downtown shopping area Preddy swung a left onto a neglected side road. This was a short road leading to an unkempt area of beach that Harris had never seen before. It was mainly rocky with only a few metres of white sand.

Harris peered through the windshield at the unfamiliar scenery which would never make it into a Jamaica Tourist Board glossy brochure. Propped against an overturned dilapidated fishing boat were giant black garbage bags overflowing with beer bottles, plastic bottles and paper plates. Dried fish scales and a strong odour indicated that someone had recently been gutting fish. Styrofoam boxes lay on the sand with the half-eaten contents exposed to the fiery sun. A black drum used by chefs as a grill to cook jerked chicken sat partially covered with cardboard under an almond tree. Handwritten signs implored beach goers to take their garbage with them. There were no people in sight on land or in the water and Harris assumed this was a night-time party area.

"What's this place?" asked Harris as Preddy shut off the engine.

The driver's door slammed and Harris watched as Preddy crossed the rocks and walked through the sand, stopping a few feet before the water. Harris donned his sunglasses, climbed out slowly and followed him. Preddy picked up a small shell and threw it out to sea watching as it skimmed the water on its return home.

"What are we doing here?" asked Harris.

"Talking," said Preddy. He picked up another larger shell and threw it.

Harris waited for as long as he could bear. "The thing about talking is that people need tae move their lips, open their mouths, let words come out."

"So talk."

Harris could feel the blood rising in his face and for the umpteenth time he wished he could disguise it. "Cut the cryptic bull, Preddy. What gives?"

"Earlier, you sounded a bit peeved about missing people at Pelican Walk," said Preddy studying the horizon. "Yet everytime I look around, no you."

Harris ran a hand through his moist hair. "And?"

"And?" Preddy turned and faced him. "Sometimes you're wid Super. Sometimes you're hiding away in one of de meeting rooms all by yourself."

Harris licked his lips. "Sometimes I need tae find a quiet place tae concentrate. In case ye forget, the open-plan area can be noisy."

"Now who's talking bull?" said Preddy. "In case you forget, I've seen you sit down and concentrate when a jack hammer was being used to tear down a meeting room wall and everybody else fled to de canteen. What I haven't seen anywhere in de open-plan area, at any time, is dat little bronze coloured laptop you seem so attached to. I want to know what de rass you doing, man!"

Harris took a deep breath. He should have expected this. Preddy was a smart man and it was inevitable that he would have suspected that something was afoot. "Okay, listen tae me."

Preddy folded his arms across his chest and stood feet apart. "I'm listening."

"There's naw much I can tell ye, Preddy."

"You have my undivided attention, Detective Harris."

"I'm investigating, someone. Someone at Pelican Walk."

"Someone?"

In the distance Harris could hear a loud speaker, a man encouraging shoppers to enter his store for the best bargains. Probably counterfeit designer goods by the sound of the prices. His patter was interrupted by motorists who used their car horns to curse each other as tyres screeched. "A detective we think is dodgy."

"A whe' de rass you a tell me?" said Preddy as he glared at Harris. "Which detective?"

"I'm naw at liberty tae say."

"Tell me is who!"

Harris shook his head. "I cannae do that Preddy. I've told ye as much as I can. This is way above me."

Preddy sneered in disdain. "And suppose I ask Brownlow?"

Harris's eyes became slits. "Ye're naw going tae do that though, Preddy. We both know that."

Preddy picked up a rough stone and clenched his fist around it. "So dat's why you rushed back here from Glasgow? Thought you were here to solve murders, for the greater good of St James? Rass claat! You nearly fooled me."

"What the fuck do ye think this about?" blazed Harris. "Who said we need tae root out the bad apples? Boot out the people that are dragging down the JCF? Ye're the one pushing for action against corrupt cops. That's exactly what this is!"

"I see." Preddy almost spat the words. "Just like when you were investigating me last year?"

"It wasnae about corruption with ye, Preddy. They questioned yer methods. This is much, much worse."

"Go join MOCA or INDECOM if you want to fuck around investigating police!"

The veins in Harris's temples pulsated. He ignored the sweat that poured from his brow. "I'll stay right where I am and do the work."

Preddy squeezed the stone even tighter as he stared at the Scotsman. Both of his hands were now clenched and his chest heaved and fell. "Twelve detectives. Can't be Sasha cause she's on maternity leave. So . . ." He passed the abused stone from hand to hand.

The movements alarmed Harris. He whipped off his sunglasses and blinked as he tried to hold Preddy's gaze. "Would it help ye if I swore that it's naw Rabino or Spence? That's the truth, nothing tae do with them!"

"So, seven detectives. Which rass claat detective?"

"If and when there's something tae tell, ye'll hear it, I promise ye that."

Preddy turned, drew back his arm and threw the stone with all his might. It flew high through the air and travelled far out to sea. He continued to stare silently in the same direction long after it had disturbed the water.

"There's work tae be done, Preddy. Ye know it and I know it. Right now, we need tae find out who took out Judge Wrenn, agreed?"

Harris's question was met with silence from Preddy and with a harsh squawk from a curious snowy egret. The man on the loudspeaker went at it again, imploring unsuspecting customers to enter his store for unbeatable offers. The voice irritated Harris and he made a mental note to ask officers to investigate the store and its remarkable discounts.

"What will it be, Preddy?"

Preddy turned to face him, his jaw squarely set. "Back to work, Detective."

* * *

Oleta stood at her window staring into the distance at the White Heart breadfruit tree. It loomed above the houses, its broad green leaves failing to cover a bountiful crop of the succulent staple. It was the only breadfruit tree on the Wynterton Park complex and everybody who could reach the fruits helped themselves. If she did not get a few down soon they would probably all be gone within a day or two. Her children would fly in from Toronto tomorrow and they both loved roast breadfruit. Martin loved it freshly roasted while Maria preferred it roasted and then fried in coconut oil. Oleta preferred it boiled when almost fully matured as she enjoyed the slightly sweet taste. Everton had enjoyed it whichever way she prepared it and was always complimentary. Now she wondered if his over exuberance about her cooking was his way of apologising for having to be away from home sometimes, which absence she never begrudged as they were working for their future.

Oleta drew a deep breath. Everton used to do the picking as he was quite adept with the bamboo stick. She opened the side door and walked outside, down the driveway, heading towards the tree. The long bamboo rod leaned up against a nearby poinsettia tree and she frowned, annoyed that someone had moved it. The gardener had carved out a nook which the residents used to hook a chosen branch and snare a breadfruit. She looked around but did not see the gardener anywhere.

She retrieved the heavy bamboo and dragged it along the ground towards the breadfruit tree.

"Hi, Miss Oleta!" shouted a voice. "Wait let me help you!"

Oleta turned to see the gardener in the next-door garden with a soil-heavy machete in one hand and a bunch of weeds in the other. "I'm okay man, thanks!" she said. "Don't let me disturb you!"

She made it to the breadfruit tree and squinted upwards. With precision she jabbed at a branch and turned the stick until the branch snapped, trapping its target in the nook. Slowly she lowered the stick to the ground and unhooked the huge breadfruit that had matured from dark green to a lighter shade of green with tiny brown spots. Milky-white latex flowed from the stem. Again she reached up and secured a second large breadfruit. They were just ready for roasting. Everton was good at doing that too. She hated making up wood fires outside and tending to the breadfruits, not least because if you didn't continuously watch and turn them they would burn. Everton had put them inside the gas oven once, but the taste just was not the same. Breadfruits had to be roasted outdoors for that delicate smoky taste.

Oleta picked up a breadfruit in each hand and headed to the kitchen. If the nosey residents saw her lighting a fire now, in broad daylight, they would ignore her grief and report her to the strata manager. She would roast them outside when the sun had gone down and people were locked up indoors. There was plenty of saltfish in the pantry which she would soak overnight. The ackees and onions she would have to buy from Charles Gordon Market in the morning. She could not do much, but the little that she could do to help make her children's pain that less gnawing, she would do. Family was everything and always would be. She had never met Tuffy Frazer's mother, but she knew the woman would be suffering indescribable anguish similar to her own. To have your family destroyed was a terrible thing. Tomorrow she would buy a bouquet of white lilies and seek out the poor bereaved lady.

CHAPTER 22

Superintendent Brownlow entered Preddy's office uninvited. The detective looked up from his computer screen and forced himself to exchange his scowl for a look of surprised pleasure as Brownlow lowered his significant behind into a seat. The expression on his superior's face was hard to decipher. Whatever Preddy thought about Harris, he was pretty sure the Scotsman would not have mentioned their earlier confrontation. This was something else. He prayed that some other suspect connected to the Wrenn case had not been murdered. Preddy sat back in his chair and waited.

"So the Norwood nightmares are all over, Detective."

It was definitely a statement. Preddy had a feeling that the Super was just warming up. He decided against fanning the flames. "Not quite, sir," he replied.

"And yet, I understand you have not been near the psychologist? No, let me correct that. You were seen once and did not even complete the full hour."

Although Brownlow's voice was even, Preddy knew him well enough to detect that he was not in the mood for excuses. "Sorry, sir. I'll sort it out."

"Yes, you will." The superintendent spoke through clenched teeth. "Once a fortnight was the agreement. One hour of your time. You can and will find one hour of your time to go and talk to the psychologist. Do I make myself clear?"

Preddy drew in a deep breath. Each day might have twenty-four hours, but he needed at least twenty-eight to do everything he needed to do. "Perfectly, sir."

"Just remember that if you fail to keep your promises, other people might fail to keep theirs too — like the Commissioner," warned Brownlow. "He might decide you're not mentally fit to lead the Major Crimes team."

Preddy blinked. So, a not-so-veiled threat of being deputised to Golden Boy Harris had materialised at last. He was not surprised. Somehow, he knew that the brass would always keep this this lasso ready to throw around his neck and drag him to heel. He wondered if Commissioner Davis had given a second's thought to how Harris would successfully lead a murder investigations team while spending half his time seeking dirt on another detective.

"Am I talking to myself?" asked the superintendent.

"No, sir," mumbled Preddy. "I'm going to do my best to get to de counselling sessions, sir."

The superintendent shook his head. "You'll have to do better than your best, Preddy. You need to be at peak form to do this job. This is the highest profile murder we've had for a long time. All eyes are on Pelican Walk. I'm depending on you to get this right. Your team cannot function if any of you are in a disturbed state of mind."

Preddy spoke politely. "Harris seems to be managing to stay upright now."

The superintendent's appearance suddenly changed to one of concern. "Is he alright?"

"I would be de first to tell you if he wasn't," swore Preddy. There was silence as Preddy waited impatiently for the super to get up and leave. Brownlow appeared to be in no hurry to do so. The detective pointedly stared at his computer. "Well, sir, guess I'd better get back to my report?"

A shallow smile crept across the superintendent's face and his eyes hardened. "I haven't finished, Detective Preddy." He pulled his chair even closer to Preddy's desk. "You could have used more tact to deal with Judge Guthrie."

He should have known a complaint would have been raised. "Sir, Judge Guthrie is not an easy person to talk to. In fact, I would say him downright shady."

"I knew you were investigating the judge, but come on, man. We're trying to improve our relationship with the judiciary not make it worse. They complain that police reports are late or incomplete, that our witnesses can't be found, that we don't follow due process. Now this? I didn't think you would accuse him of murder to his face! Are you out of your mind?"

"He said dat?" Preddy straightened up in his chair. "He lied — about dat, and about his whereabouts on de night his friend was murdered."

The Superintendent frowned. "That complaint came from the Senior Parish Judge not from Guthrie himself. The general consensus within the judiciary seems to be that because a few of our major cases got tossed out last year, we're seeking revenge by trying to bring one of them down."

"Dat's ridiculous," said Preddy.

"Exactly what I said. It's all about perception though." The superintendent played with his pen while he studied Preddy. "What do you think will happen if they completely close down the Parish Court? What will happen if the unrest catches on and spreads?"

I'll be blamed, thought Preddy. He said, "It would be terrible, sir, but dat would not be on us. Look how many times we bring people before de court wid good evidence. De jury convicts dem and de judges give dem light sentences. Before we know it de same criminal is back on de street causing mayhem."

"I don't need a lecture, thank you," said the superintendent. "Don't speak to Guthrie again, unless you have solid enough evidence to arrest him for something. Not as much as good morning. And when I say solid I mean impenetrable,

Preddy. I mean unanimous verdict evidence. Do you understand me?"

"I understand, sir," said Preddy, before adding. "He
knows more dan he's saying though."

Brownlow slapped his fat palm down on the desk. "Then
prove it, Detective! Until you can do that I want you to focus
on the people who actually have motives for murder."

"I've never stopped trying to reduce de list of suspects,
sir, I can assure you of dat," replied Preddy curtly. "Every
member of de team is on it. I still haven't ruled out de
Benbow Crew, and I think we're close to finding de man
who killed Tuffy Frazer."

The superintendent leaned back, scowling. He made a
steeple formation with his hands. "Tuffy Frazer is the least of
our worries. His cronies probably murdered him."

"Dat's quite likely, sir," agreed Preddy. "De man who
killed Tuffy could know who killed Judge Wrenn and why.
It might be de same murderer who took out both of dem.
At de moment, we can't prove de two murders are related."

"So you think you've identified the person who killed
Tuffy?" asked Brownlow. "What was that, a tip off?"

Preddy kept his eyes averted. "Yes, sir."

"You bringing him in?"

"Still trying to locate him, sir, a guy named Devil Head,
real name Jevon Collins. I have some informers on de ground
looking for him," Preddy reported. "Apparently he mainly
comes out during night hours. Him not easy to find during
de daytime and him generally cover up from head to toe in
winter type clothes. Devil Head is a jogging pants, socks and
hoodie type. Skinny too, but I guess is all de sweating cause
dat."

"Devil Head," the superintendent repeated. "Lord help
us. I want this case wrapped up soon Preddy. And remember
what I said about Judge Guthrie."

"I won't forget, sir."

Brownlow struggled to his feet and adjusted his jacket.
"What about Nathaniel Mexell? Is he still under suspicion?"

"Detective Harris and I going try interview him later," Preddy advised. "I'm pretty sure Mexell saw Judge Wrenn dat night, but I don't know in what capacity."

"He admitted it?"

"He hinted at it. What I don't know is whether it was an innocent sighting of him, or if he broke de judge's neck. I just need to break him down, sir."

The Superintendent waved a warning finger. "I don't want to hear any more complaints from prominent citizens. Make sure that Detective Harris is kept abreast at all times."

"Why wouldn't he be, sir?" asked Preddy feigning innocence.

"When I saw him in the open-plan area this morning, he didn't seem to know where anybody was," said the superintendent. "Although he was quick to say he was pretty sure you were all following up leads on Judge Wrenn's murder."

Preddy absorbed this information and wondered what Harris would have said to Brownlow had he known that at one point they were trying to coax a gun thief out of a guango tree. "I'll correct de communication issue, sir."

"Good. You do that."

CHAPTER 23

Harris was relieved that Preddy's hostility had thinned out somewhat after lunching with Rabino and Spence. Although he believed that the female officers sensed the tension they had not alluded to it and kept up their usual amusing banter. The instrumental jazz music piping through the jeep seemed to be helping too. At the very least it prevented silence from enveloping them. Harris tapped the dashboard as soon as the black BMW X6 cruised past their vehicle.

"There's our man Mexell," he said.

Preddy immediately started the engine. Soon the detectives had left downtown Montego Bay and the roads gradually became narrower and more winding. The prevalence of concrete began to diminish as they headed towards the hills. Tall trees and lush plants occupied both sides of the roads, spared for the time being from the relentless residential development of the expanding city.

Harris sighed. With no evidence against Mexell there was little chance of getting a warrant for search or arrest. If this was Glasgow he would have found a friendly judge to sort out that little issue, but this was Montego Bay. He knew no judges personally and in the current climate, with such a fractured relationship between the two bodies, he was unlikely to make new friends. Not that he felt particularly inclined to befriend officials who regularly let suspected murders out on bail. In any event Preddy had insisted that they pressure Mexell by staying on his tail rather than resort to more formal policing methods and the Glaswegian could tell that Preddy was in no mood to debate.

"Ye sure ye dinnae want me tae drive?" asked Harris.

"I don't like your driving," replied Preddy.

"Say what ye feel, Preddy."

"We're not getting any new tyres. You love pothole too much."

"Well, I wouldnae say I *love* them exactly . . ."

"You're not driving dis car, Detective Harris."

At first the journey was uneventful, but after around ten minutes the sleek sports car in front began to pick up speed.

"He knows he's got company," said Harris.

"Rass," muttered Preddy and stepped on the gas. Had they been on the highway Mexell's sports car would have put the police jeep to shame. As it was, these roads were not meant for speeding and the powerful vehicle ran close to the grass verges as it screeched around corners. The brake lights were put into use every few seconds.

Preddy frowned. "I don't know why dat idiot doesn't just stop."

"Maybe Channer told him if ye see the police dinnae speak tae them without me around and he took it literally?"

"Must be trying to beat us to his house. Dis road leads into Irwin Village."

"If that's where he's going I cannae imagine why he's driving like this. It's naw as if he gets diplomatic immunity from being on his own lawn."

Preddy clenched the steering wheel. "No, but he might get to dispose of something in de car or de house dat he doesn't want us to see. He doesn't know we don't have a warrant."

Harris turned slightly to study his colleague. "What do ye think he's got?"

"You never know," murmured Preddy. "Mementoes. Some coin artefacts perhaps?"

"I warned ye, we should've got a warrant."

Preddy tooted his horn and lowered both side windows as he came parallel to Mexell. Harris leaned out and gesticulated to the driver to stop. The heavily tinted windows remained up as the driver raced along. The BMW pulled away again and the squealing tyres sent a cloud of brown dust into the air. Preddy stayed behind, for although the road was quiet there was always a chance of meeting an unsuspecting motorist travelling in the opposite direction. As Preddy rounded the corner he spotted the luxury car partially impacted in a ditch. He stepped on the brakes and drew the jeep to a halt beside it. Both detectives walked briskly towards the vehicle.

"You see, dat's where we would've ended up if you had de wheel," said Preddy.

Harris rapped on the driver's window. "Sir! Open up." The window did not budge. Harris cupped his hands and tried to see through the tint.

"Open de damn window before I mash it out!" demanded Preddy.

The window hummed as it retracted smoothly and the detectives found themselves staring into the angry face of Stephan Channer.

"Mr Channer," announced Harris in surprise. "Didnae expect tae see ye. Ye wouldnae stop for me, but ye'd stop for a mound of dirt? I'm hurt at the implication."

Preddy was taken aback for a brief moment. He peered at the licence plate. Yes, this was definitely Nathaniel Mexell's ride. "Your boss not going happy wid you," said Preddy shaking his head.

"What the hell is this?" asked Channer. "You need to stop harassing us. I'm going to make a formal complaint to the Commissioner, you watch. This is ridiculous!'

"Naw. What is ridiculous is ye racing through a residential area with naw concern for the bairns or the lasses walking on the roadside. Ye could have killed somebody."

The impact of the vehicle had drawn a few residents from their houses and they now approached the scene of the collision. One of them who approached more quickly than the others was none other than the vehicle's owner.

"Oh my God! What happened here?" asked Mexell crouching beside the front of his dented car.

"The damn police ran me off the road!" asserted Channer, arms flailing.

"Lie you a tell!" interjected a young man. He was no more than a teenager. He wore a torn T-shirt and saggy shorts which exposed his fake designer briefs. "A right dere on de wall me lean up when you come round de corner. De white man car was nowhere near you! Oonu must learn fi stop speed pon road! Oonu will kill off people and dem pickney."

Harris nodded in agreement. "What he said."

"Detectives, don't tell me you just happened to be behind Stephan because I won't believe it. Look at the state of my car! What do you want?"

"I think you know what we want Mr Mexell." Preddy spoke quietly but firmly. "De truth would be a good start."

"Don't talk to him Nat!" hissed Channer, glaring at Preddy.

Harris rounded on him, temples throbbing in his pink face. "Ye need tae shut up. I'll book ye for reckless and dangerous driving and I'll see what else I can add tae that."

"Carry him go jail, Kingfish!" shouted a woman. "And take way him Bimmer too! Dem too showoff 'bout yah, always a race pon road!"

"No lef de Bimmer give me," said another man. "Me will fix it up and drive it!"

The small crowd chuckled and continued to make comments about the scene before them, pleased to see road hogs being taken to task.

"Mr Mexell we need to go somewhere and talk," said Preddy staring at the businessman. "If you want to get a lawyer go ahead and call him, but we are going to talk."

"This is harassment!" shouted Channer. "This is not a police state. You cannot force anybody to talk to you."

"Just watch," said Preddy.

"Still a murdering thug," Channer taunted.

Preddy walked up close to the company secretary so that he almost stood on his toes. "You should be very careful what you say to a murdering thug," he breathed.

Channer's throat constricted visibly. He glanced at Harris who chose not to speak. Nathaniel Mexell's shoulder's sagged. "Follow me, detectives," he turned and started to walk towards his house.

"Nat, are you out of your mind?" asked Channer.

Mexell spun around. His voice was cold and flat. "You'd better call the garage, Stephan. There were a couple of guys crawling past here in a pickup earlier. There won't be a tyre left on the vehicle if it doesn't get moved. They can put it in my driveway."

The detectives followed the construction boss as he walked towards his property. Channer lagged behind talking urgently into his phone. Mexell's home was a two-storey terracotta coloured property which from the roadside appeared to be of a modest size. As Mexell led them through a side gate Preddy was surprised to see a large pool. The premises were deceptively larger than had first appeared. Two half-breed Alsatian dogs raised inquisitive heads as their master and his visitors walked up the drive way. One started to bark while the other gave the party a death stare. Harris hesitated.

"Ye sure those dogs will naw attack?"

"It's okay, they're chained," said Mexell. "They'll bite if they get the chance, but I promise they won't get the chance."

The men assembled under a turret-shaped gazebo with an attractive bamboo trellis lined with lilac flowering ivy. Mexell offered to get them cold drinks, which both detectives declined. Mexell sank onto a wooden bench and stared up at the inside of the thatched roof watching a spider expertly build its web.

"You saw Judge Wrenn dat night," stated Preddy.

Mexell closed his eyes. "I did not murder him, Detective."

"You said he was alive."

"Are you going to arrest me?" asked Mexell. He kept his eyes closed while massaging his temples.

"You may give us no choice," said Preddy. "You want me to read you your rights?"

Mexell stopped his movement and opened his eyes. "No need."

Preddy stared at him keenly. "Please, just tell us what happened. De truth."

"Nat . . ." began Channer, "they have nothing!"

Mexell lowered his eyes and glared at his friend. "Stephan," he said quietly. "Shut the fuck up."

"Go ahead, Mr Mexell," insisted Preddy.

"I didn't kill, Judge Wrenn. I didn't, I swear."

"We want tae know what ye did do," pressed Harris.

Mexell sighed. "I was there that night at Wynterton Park, on the water."

"Rass claat, man!" Channer could not restrain himself. "Why do you want to send us to jail?"

"We didn't murder anybody!" retorted Mexell.

Preddy pointed at Channer. "He was there too?"

Mexell nodded. "Yes, he was."

Channer was on his feet, moving effortlessly as usual. "I don't want you to speak for me, Nat. Don't you fucking dare speak for me!"

"I won't. You can tell your own tale, but we both know the truth."

Channer bristled. He folded his arms across his chest. "If you're going to interrogate me in connection with a crime I'll just exercise my right to keep silent. I have no intention of answering any questions so I won't waste your time or my money on retaining independent counsel."

228

"Fine. Dinnae open yer mouth," said Harris giving the lawyer his finest side-eye.

Preddy said, "Tell us what happened Mr Mexell."

"It's all so stupid really when I think about it," Mexell began. "Judge Wrenn had scared the hell out of me, to be honest. I mean, I know I bluster and talk a good talk, but this is a fledgling business. The house, the cars, the yacht . . . it's all about appearances. Money goes to money. I'm up to my eyeballs in debt, but the Falmouth project really took off. And then the Montego Hamlet development had been going so smoothly that I was quite confident in future projections. Had grand plans for another one at Green Pond in Hanover." He paused, remembering. "And then I got this letter from the Wynterton Park office."

"I've seen de file," interjected Preddy. "You got more dan one letter."

Mexell nodded. "Yes, there was correspondence going back and forth for about a year. Then I stopped answering questions, rather foolishly hoping it would all go away. A few months later Judge Wrenn came to see me . . . practically threatened me. Then I got this stupid idea in my head." Mexell stared at the subdued Channer as he said this and the man sank onto the gazebo steps. Preddy noted yet again the sleek movement, no hands.

"What idea?" urged Harris.

"To prove that the pollution didn't come from my development. I'll admit that I suspected it did. At least . . . I was pretty certain that my work was contributing to the issue. NEPA got involved with monitoring the water quality . . ."

Harris frowned. "NEPA?"

"De National Environment and Planning Agency, our environment protection body," explained Preddy.

"I was afraid the work on Montego Hamlet would really get shut down," continued Mexell. "But then I'd heard somewhere that if I could prove cross-pollution then maybe I'd get away with it. You know, what was it you called it again? Stephan?"

"Causation," grunted the lawyer reluctantly.

"That's it," said Mexell. "I wanted to throw a spanner in the works, so to speak. Get the matter to drag out for a year or so until the development was finished. I thought that if NEPA named NatMex as the sole culprit, Judge Wrenn would get his injunction and my site would be left to grow cobwebs." He wiped his damp fingers on his shirt before continuing. "You know that old tyre factory about a mile up the road, up by Lime Ridge?"

"I know it," said Preddy.

"You're going to be sorry you spoke," muttered Channer.

"We . . . I decided to do whatever it took to divert attention from my company. I'd dropped off some water samples at a lab to be tested, but I had it in mind that maybe that water was not polluted enough." He gave a sheepish look. "Thought about breaking into the lab and contaminating the water sample in there, but I realised that was a stupid idea. I mean, I know NEPA has issues with resources and funding, but I concluded that they'd never just accept my sample, they'd want to take their own."

Preddy's eyes widened and the hackles on the back of his neck raised at mention of the lab. "So you gave up on dis idea of breaking into de lab, or you just weren't able to pull it off?"

Mexell did not reply, but his eyes flicked to Channer and back.

"Dat wouldn't happen to be de private forensics lab at de top of Grove Street would it?" asked Preddy, clenching his fists at his sides.

Mexell noted the movement and determined that any answer to that question was likely to provoke the detective. Like many people who regularly followed the local news, he viewed Preddy as a dangerous cop. Mexell continued, "We heard a rumour that NEPA would be collecting samples on Tuesday. So we . . . I got on my boat on Monday night and went up river to the Lime Ridge tyre factory. There's a pipeline which stretches into the sea. I, um, made a small hole in it . . ."

Mexell covered his face with his hands so that only his lips were visible. "It's still there by the way . . . the hole. You might want to tell them to plug it before it really causes trouble."

"What time were you on de water," asked Preddy.

"It must've been eleven or going on twelve, I'm not sure." Mexell squinted as if looking deep into his mind. "God, what have I done?"

"Our pathologist reckons Judge Wrenn was killed right around dat time," said Preddy.

"Whoa! I swear I didn't do it!" Mexell thought for a moment before pointing at Channer and adding, "neither did he, Detective."

"He doesnae want ye tae speak for him," warned Harris. "Might be a good thing in the circumstances."

"I did not murder anybody," said Channer resolutely. "You can stick that in your notebook."

"Wait a minute," said Preddy. "Dere's something I'm not getting. Dat Bimmer was seen leaving Wynterton Park on Monday night. Who was in it, you or Channer?"

"Stephan was behind the wheel." Mexell glanced at Channer's sullen face. "I took the boat by myself the whole mile from the mooring near to the marine park — which is where it sleeps most nights when I can't be bothered to drag it on the trailer up here. I went from there up to Lime Ridge and back. Stephan drove the car to Wynterton Park, which is probably about mid-way between the two, so the view from that vantage point on the beach is ideal. The idea was that if he saw the marine police he could alert me and I'd throw my borer tool overboard."

"You pass any other boats?" enquired Preddy.

Mexell rubbed his chin. "Now that you ask . . . I think I did. When I sailed to Lime Ridge I saw no boats, at least I don't remember seeing any. When I was coming back I heard a noise. Thought I saw the shape of a boat behind me, but I wasn't sure. It was so dark. You know how it is, sometimes you see things in the dark that aren't there, but they seem real."

Preddy certainly knew that feeling well. It happened almost every night, but he was not about to share his personal troubles with a murder suspect. "Whereabouts was dat?" he asked. "Before you got to Wynterton Park or after you sailed past it?"

"Definitely before," said Mexell. "This happened before I got to where Stephan was."

"You know we're going to jail, right?" stated Channer.

Preddy walked towards where Channer was sitting and crouched down beside him staring stonily into his face. He whispered, "I guess de question is what is he going in for and what are you going in for?"

Channer looked nervous and drew back his head. "I'm not a murderer!"

"Maybe ye didnae intend tae murder him, Mr Channer?" said Harris. "Maybe he saw ye and wanted to find out what ye were doing on the beach at that hour. Called ye ontae his verandah. Maybe his death was an accident and naw intentional?"

"You two are out of your fucking minds!" Channer seemed to finally realise his predicament. "His verandah was well lit up. He was alive. I could see him from the beach, sitting on his porch, smoking. You know you can hear St James Parish Church clock from there? It was chiming midnight and he was alive. You will never pin this on me, because I didn't kill him!"

"Stephan did tell me he'd seen Judge Wrenn too, detectives," said Mexell. "He left Wynterton Park in my car and picked me up about fifteen minutes later down where I docked the boat. It was probably the first thing he said to me. 'Guess who's out taking in the night view? Everton Wrenn.' Why would he say something like that if he'd just killed him?"

Preddy rose from his haunches, but continued to stare down at Channer. "You did speak to him, Judge Wrenn?"

"I certainly did not. I backed up way under some trees and made sure he couldn't see me," stated Channer. "Got bitten by red ants too. That's what these marks are before you ask." He held out his left wrist and pointed at a few dried scratches. "When I heard about the murder the next day I was in complete shock. Couldn't quite believe it. Didn't want to believe it."

Mexell looked at Preddy. "Never really thought we could ever be murder suspects. I just assumed somebody broke into the judge's house to steal, found him unexpectedly out back, and killed him to prevent being identified."

Preddy looked from one man to the other. "I'm not sure dat I believe you — either of you."

"It's the truth, detective," insisted Mexell.

"Here's what you're going to do," said Preddy. "You're going to contact NEPA yourself and show dem what happened to de Lime Ridge tyre factory pipeline. I'll leave it to you whether you admit to sabotage or say it was an accident. Dey can decide whether to prosecute you or fine you."

Harris shot Preddy a warning look. "Maybe we should have a quick talk, Detective."

Preddy ignored him. "I'm giving you twenty-four hours to contact dem Mr Mexell."

"I will," whispered Mexell.

Harris's face was darkening red and the muscles strained against his skin as he bit his lip. Preddy ignored the challenge in the piercing green eyes and concentrated on his target instead. "Don't let me hear dat you've been anywhere on Grove Street either."

Mexell looked annoyed. "But there are plenty of other businesses up there, a great bakery . . ."

"Find somewhere else to buy your damn grotto bread."

"Outrageous!" muttered Channer.

"We'll find something to charge you wid, Mr Channer, don't worry," growled Preddy. "Even if it's only terrible driving. Watch and see."

As the detectives began to walk away Preddy shot a glance at his otaheiti red colleague beside him. "Your forehead going burst if you let your blood pressure go up like dat," he warned.

Harris glared at him. "So ye're worried about ma blood pressure? What about those two possible murderers? Mexell was co-operating. What about taking the opportunity tae see if we could look inside the house?"

"Didn't need to." Preddy kept his voice flat. "I don't think dey are . . . murderers, I mean."

"Naw?" said Harris in exasperation. He came to a stop and locked eyes with Preddy. "So, naw old coins detected by yer x-ray lenses as ye surveyed the premises then?"

Preddy stared at him unblinking. "No."

The two men stood facing each other. Preddy took a mint from his breast pocket and slowly unravelled it. He popped it into his mouth all the while keeping his eyes on the Scotsman's face. He crunched loudly.

Harris took a deep breath and spoke first. "It made sense since we were there tae try and have a look around the house. Ye have a way tae go about things that isnae like anything I've seen before."

"Anything else?" Preddy waited a few seconds. "No? Den let's get back to de car."

The mechanics had not yet arrived. Both the BMW and the police jeep remained untouched. The young man who had witnessed the accident jumped off the wall and strode towards the detectives. He stared closely at Harris. "Wait, how your face look so? Dem rough you up, boss?" he asked.

"Naw." Harris formed a deep ridge in his pink brow. "Thank ye for yer concern."

"Oh!" The youth seemed satisfied. "Cause me did a go ask how come Preddy is de Don Gorgon a Mo Bay and him let dem two man do you so!"

Preddy stifled a grin. "Detective Preddy."

"Yes, boss! Detective Preddy. Sorry."

"Sun hot," said Preddy, by way of explanation for Harris's appearance. "Nobody round here can't rough up any officer."

"See me make sure nobody no trouble de car, boss?" the youth offered eagerly, following behind them. "Me watch dem carefully, you know?"

"Thanks," said Harris and climbed into the passenger seat. The man leaned against the door staring at Harris in anticipation.

"You don't get it, do you?" asked Preddy, glancing at Harris as he settled in beside him. Preddy fumbled around in the glove compartment and then handed the youth two one hundred dollar bills. "Thanks, you hear?"

"Yes, sir!" said the youth.

"Dere are plenty of things I do dat you might not appreciate or understand, Detective Harris." Preddy started the engine. "Dat is probably one of dem."

"Och, I think I got that one alright," said Harris noting that the happy youth had reclaimed his seat on the wall.

"He'll wait on de mechanic and follow dem up to Mexell's and repeat de same lines," explained Preddy. "Someone will give him some more dollars. Bald tyres are better dan no tyres at all and I don't fancy a six mile trek to Pelican Walk in dis heat. Do you?"

Harris managed a grudging smile. "Or explaining tyre theft tae the superintendent."

Preddy turned on the air conditioner then did a U-turn. "Mexell didn't make up such an elaborate tale dat placed him smack bang on de murder scene. No way. He practically admitted to a crime, albeit not de one we're investigating."

"And Channer? Mexell has naw idea what he was doing at Wynterton Park!" Harris turned sideways in his seat towards the detective. "Channer could have strangled the judge before he drove out tae pick up Mexell."

"And told Mexell dat he saw de judge? And at de time of death?" Preddy shook his head emphatically. "He'd have said he never set eyes on him."

"Ye cannae second guess psychopaths," asserted Harris.

Preddy waved a hand at him dismissively. "Scottish psychopaths maybe."

"Och! Here we go. So, ye think Scottish psychopaths are different from Jamaican psychopaths? Ye've got tae be having a laugh. Whatever happened tae 'we have naw differences?'"

"You sure as hell never heard dose words come outta my mouth!" spluttered Preddy. He kept his eyes on the road and drove at a leisurely pace downhill. "White men are de craziest murderers. Pure serial killers. Dey leave from foreign to come colonize Jamaica. All dem do is come murder off we people." He wrinkled his brow and kissed his teeth loudly.

"Are we talking about centuries ago here, or now?" Tiny pinpricks of red invaded Harris's temples.

Preddy risked an accident by giving the Scotsman a lingering gaze and a hint of a smile. The veins in Harris's forehead lost their tension and a smile crept across his face. He shook his head and stared out the passenger window admiring the luscious greenery.

"Hey! What you say, though, you've got to agree wid me eeh?" pressed Preddy. "Your people were de worst murderers."

Harris decided to counter the taunts without aggression. "The Scottish were naw known for being mass murderers of Africans or Jamaicans."

"Please! Dey did it too, but dey had enough sense to know not to write down too much about it."

Harris shook his head, determined to stand up for his ancestors. "It wasnae us."

"English people kept all kind of notes, like dey well proud of it or something."

"Aye, well let's stick tae blaming the English, shall we?"

"For now." Preddy turned onto the main road. "I'll check my daughter's history book tonight."

"For my homework I'm going tae do some digging intae the background of Stephan Channer," pledged Harris. "Our murderer might be smarter than ye think, Preddy."

"Of dat, I have no doubt."

CHAPTER 24

Preddy glanced at his watch as he headed towards the evidence room and noted that he was around fifteen minutes late. He had not slept well and not even a giant cup of ganja tea had restored his energy. In addition to seeing the usual bloody flashbacks, he had also dreamed that Judge Lawrence Guthrie had placed his hands around his throat and tried to throw him into a hole in which lay Tuffy's body. Preddy had awoken for the second time that night with a start, sweating and breathless. A disturbed sleep pattern was not the sole reason for the delay in his arrival at Pelican Walk. Spartan temporarily derailed him, but even the parakeet could not be blamed. The accommodating bird had perched on Preddy's shoulder eating corn grains while listening to theories about why various suspects might have committed murder. When the food was gone he had stayed put offering gentle caws of encouragement if no solid advice. Preddy was late mainly because he had made a temporary diversion in order to tick a box for the superintendent who wanted him to share his thoughts with an actual human being.

Earlier that morning he had dragged heavy legs up the steps of the nondescript office that housed the police psychologist. The psychologist would no doubt sympathise while hearing all about Preddy's nightmares, but the detective had no intention of regaling him with it. Not today anyway. As soon as Preddy saw the doctor approaching the waiting area he put his phone to his ear, swallowed his mints and began a one-sided urgent conversation. The doctor folded his arms and leaned against the wall watching his reluctant patient talking to himself. Preddy made his excuses over his shoulder as he fled. At least the man could tell Superintendent Brownlow that he had turned up. It was not his fault that duty called.

Preddy could hear a muffled conversation as he pushed open the door of the evidence room at Pelican Walk. Inside were Spence and Rabino. No sign of Harris, which observation did not lend to warm feelings for the Scotsman.

"No word on Devil Head yet, sir," said Rabino, spinning around in her chair.

"Damn," muttered Preddy as he headed for the whiteboard. "We need to bring him in."

"Dem soon spot him, sir," Spence assured him. "If him was a daytime man we get him long time."

"So no one at all saw him last night?" asked Preddy.

"No, sir," said Rabino. "Our informants think he went to a dance in Discovery Bay last night and should be back today. We've got the main road covered by Highway Patrol from here to St Ann. Every station on the entire north coast has his photograph and description."

Preddy nodded. "Okay, good."

"The Dragon stout bottle that Mexell had at the regatta? And the cigarette? No DNA match to the stub picked up on Judge Wrenn's verandah," reported Rabino.

"Mexell has dropped way way down on de list anyway," said Preddy, circling the man's name. "I want to cross him off completely — he and his sidekick Channer — but Harris would burst a gasket so I'm leaving dem dere for now."

"The two of you alright, sir? You and Detective Harris?" asked Rabino.

"Sure," said Preddy keeping his back towards her. "Why you ask?"

"Well, yesterday at lunch the two of you seemed a bit, distant," she said.

"To say de least," added Spence with a meaningful glance at Rabino.

"Everything's cool." Preddy turned around and displayed his best poker face. These women knew him too well and he could have kicked himself for his lapse in demeanour. "Now, talk to me about de evidence."

"This is Judge Wrenn's cigarette stub," Rabino dangled an evidence bag in her fingers, "The only fingerprints and traces of DNA on the cigarette stub were matched to the judge and his wife."

"Oleta said she never touched de things," remarked Preddy.

"Guess she was speaking figuratively," said Spence. "You know how it is when people won't clear up after demself? You end up doing it for dem just so de mess don't drive you crazy."

"Wait a minute." Preddy looked at Rabino curiously. "What are we doing wid Oleta Wrenn's DNA anyway? And if we had such a thing as a fingerprint database I'd know about it."

"Lord knows we need it," said Spence.

Rabino looked slightly bashful. She fished around in her handbag and waved a packet of hand tissues in the air. "It was all over this packet, sir. When the lab said there were two distinct DNA samples, I decided not to get too excited because the trace most likely came from whoever lived with him. I was going to ask her for a sample, but then I remembered she had held onto my tissues packet while she was crying."

Preddy smiled. "Makes sense."

"I had so hoped it wouldn't match." Rabino shook her head. "Unfortunately, this cigarette wasn't smoked or touched by Tuffy, Mexell, Channer or Guthrie."

"Dat would have been nice," said Preddy ruefully. He circled a black marker around Guthrie's name and stared at it. "This man bothers me."

"You really think he could be involved after all, sir?" asked Rabino, peering around her superior's broad back. "We know he lied and was at Night Court . . ."

"Wid Devil Head," interjected Preddy.

". . . with Devil Head," continued Rabino, "but some people really cannot accept that their career is not where it should be. He could've lied just because he's an extreme snob like he says. Some people are."

"Maybe all him friend in St Elizabeth think him have a big shot court position in St James," sneered Spence. "If me was like him, maybe me woulda lie too."

Preddy smiled. "I seem to recall dat when you were a constable you were happy being a constable, never hinted at being delusional and never lied about it."

"Hah! Dat is what you think, sir." Spence grinned. "Everybody in my family thought me was running Pelican Walk single-handed, and is me arrest every St James criminal dem see pon TV news! Me never set dem straight at all!"

Her colleagues laughed along with her.

"Yeah, sounds like you," agreed Rabino.

Spence dabbed at her eyes. "Listen, you hear, you have to talk de talk before you can walk de walk."

"It's possible dat Guthrie is just hindering our investigation by being stupid, but we can't eliminate him," reasoned Preddy. "He said he had lunch wid Judge Wrenn Monday afternoon. Dat's confirmed by a third party. I'm going to stop by Mosino and see if anybody saw dem behaving suspiciously or overheard anything. Which of you coming wid me?"

"I've got a meeting with an informer, sir." Rabino glanced at her watch. "Have to go on the road and talk to him. See if I can get him to pinpoint exactly when and where Devil Head is likely to appear."

Preddy nodded. "You do dat."

"I'd promised to go see Oleta," said Spence. "She was asking' bout de investigation. I thought maybe a visit from a female would help put her mind at ease, but I can go wid you, sir, and go see her later?"

"No, dat's good. You'll get to meet her kids and assure all of dem dat we're working de case," said Preddy. "Not sure where Harris has got to. Anyone seen him?"

"He was by de canteen," Spence informed him. "I'll tell him you looking for him."

Almost on cue the door opened and a dishevelled looking Harris entered with a cup of coffee. "Had tae get ma tonic, sorry." He waved the steaming plastic cup in the air as he shuffled towards a chair.

"I know dat feeling," said Preddy dryly. His own tonic was cleaning up his system in a way that coffee could only dream of doing.

"Ye know, the strangest of things just happened," recalled Harris, balancing his cup on a desk. "Some officers in the canteen were suggesting that we'd lost one of the guns that Tuffy was transporting in the Camry."

Spence reached for a bottle of cold water and put it to her lips, allowing the water to trickle slowly down her throat. Rabino turned on the oscillating fan and leaned towards it turning her head from side to side with eyes closed.

"Oh," said Preddy, spinning around to clean some non-existent smudge from the whiteboard. "And what did you say?"

"Told them it was bull," said Harris blithely and took a swig of coffee. "Told them I'd tagged all the guns that came in the Camry and locked them away and we have them all." As silence filled Harris's ears he lowered his cup. "It *was* bull, right Preddy?"

Preddy turned to face him. "Every single gun dat was in de Camry is under lock and key," he said. "Every one."

"Och, good! Ye had me worried there for a minute." Harris took another large gulp of coffee. "Lord, this Blue Mountain stuff is great."

Preddy could not help but wonder where the Scotsman had been before he picked up the great coffee. He gave Harris the insincere smile of a gameshow host. "Well, drink up Detective, you're just in time. You and I are going to a casino."

Harris looked at his colleagues with suspicion. "Did I lose a bet or something?"

"You'll like it down dere," predicted Spence. "And no tarot reading told me dat."

"Why will I like it?" asked Harris. "You shouldnae believe everything ye hear about Scots being devoted gamblers who cannae walk past a betting shop."

Spence smiled sweetly. "Perish de thought."

Preddy closed the cover of an evidence file and pushed it into a drawer. "You can drive since de road to Catherine Hall is quite good."

"There ye go nit-picking about ma driving skills again."

Preddy snatched up the keys and handed them to the Scotsman. "Learn to avoid de potholes and learn to push out, because nobody going let you out unless we use a marked vehicle or start flashing lights."

"Seems a bit early tae be heading for a casino?" Harris hastily drained his cup.

"It's not Caesars Palace," explained Preddy as he headed for the door. "Much smaller scale. More of a gaming lounge. I'll fill you in on de way." Even as he spoke Preddy vowed to tell Harris only what he needed to know. "It's where Everton Wrenn had his Last Supper, with Lawrence Guthrie."

The Mosino gaming lounge was a relatively new entertainment venue on the landscape in the Catherine Hall district just over a mile from the downtown city centre. The area was a low to middle-class district, part residential and part business, each distinctive section separated by a long carriageway. On the residential side, the houses were built so closely together that many residents could lean over each other's walls and hang their washing on their neighbours' clothes lines. On the business side was a large plaza with a huge supermarket, bank and restaurant, as well as a window installation company. Adjacent to the plaza was the Montego Bay Sports Complex which hosted an array of sports and entertainment. Further along was the detectives' target: Mosino, a grand building with a high peaked roof and huge tinted glass doors. Above the entrance was a red and black symbol, a card pack spade that hovered over the name.

As Harris pulled into one of the well-marked parking spaces Preddy scrutinised the exterior carefully. He was pleased to see some CCTV cameras. The doors to the establishment were locked. Preddy cupped his hands over his eyes and pressed them against the glass. He could see movement within. He tapped the glass and pressed his badge against it. Keys rattled on the other side and the door was opened by a clean-shaved young man dressed smartly in black trousers with a spotless white long-sleeved shirt.

Preddy smiled at him politely. "Detective Preddy and Detective Harris, Pelican Walk."

The youth stood back. "Come in, detectives. How can I help you?" He used his best English reserved mainly for foreign clientele.

The interior was particularly spacious with the centrepiece a well-stocked bar, laden with local brews and imported alcohol. A glowing sign over the barman's head said G's Sports Bar & Grill. Plush bar stools were arranged around the granite bar top with TV screens high above the shelves. Plenty of table games: roulette, blackjack, horse racing. Colourful slot machines stretched for as far as the eye could see. Further inside were cubicle-like benches and tables arranged to resemble an American-style diner. More flatscreen TVs lined up along the walls. The background was muted beige which, set against the dark of wood, gave the whole enterprise a clean and inviting atmosphere.

"Naw bad." Harris studied the scenery. "Nice place tae hang out. Cannae remember hearing about it before."

"Try not to get hooked on it," warned Preddy.

"Aye, ye lose more than ye win."

A bartender with earphones firmly plugged in polished the drinking glasses and seemed not to notice the visitors. Two females were present: one was busy wiping tables, the other refilling condiment bottles. The young man who had opened the door stood patiently, watching the detectives.

"We're investigating de murder of Judge Everton Wrenn," said Preddy eventually. "You've heard about it?"

"Yes, sir. What a terrible thing to happen." A pained expression crept across the man's face. "And at a nice place like Wynterton Park too. If they can murder people down Wynterton, they can murder people anywhere."

"We're trying tae ensure naw one gets murdered anywhere," Harris said as he continued to survey the interior decor.

"We understand dat Judge Wrenn had lunch here de afternoon of his murder. You remember seeing him . . . dat was Monday de first of May?"

"Eeh hee? He was here? I didn't work that Monday!" He spun around and clapped his hands together, trying to gain the attention of the bar man. "He was serving that day. Aaron! Aaron! Come over here man."

The bartender continued to sway his hips and bob his head while concentrating on his task, oblivious to the visitors.

"It's okay," said an amused Harris. "We'll go tae him." The detectives walked up to the counter. Harris leaned over and pulled on the earplugs startling the man who almost dropped his glass. "Good morning tae ye, sir."

"Hello, sirs! Good morning," said the man, with a confused look.

"Pelican Walk police!" shouted his colleague from a distance, causing the two females to stop working and start watching them.

"Were you working here on de afternoon of Monday de first of May?" asked Preddy.

"Yes sir, I was here."

"We're investigating de murder of Judge Everton Wrenn." Preddy placed a photo of the judge in front of the bar man. "You remember seeing him here?"

The bartender rested his freshly polished glass. He picked up the photograph and stared at it. "Saw him on the news. He was here that day. I well remember him."

"Are ye sure?" pressed Harris.

The man nodded. "I'm sure. The very next day I heard that he was murdered. Couldn't believe someone I served, someone I stood right next to and talked to, could have been killed overnight. It was shocking, man!"

"You remember who he was wid?" asked Preddy.

"Yes, it was him and Judge Guthrie and another man. Judge Guthrie has come in here many times before, but it was the first time I'd seen Judge Wrenn in here. Before that I only used to see him on TV chat shows or the news."

"You said dere was another man?" Preddy quizzed him.

The bartender looked thoughtful. "I'm not sure who the other man was though. Can't remember ever seeing him before either."

"What did he look like? You think him was a judge too?" asked Preddy.

"Possibly." The man leaned his head to one side. "Looked a bit young though, had a big forehead. He was well-dressed in a suit just like them. I should go back a bit, though. Judge Guthrie and the man were in here drinking long before Judge Wrenn joined them. They only ordered food after Judge Wrenn arrived."

"Were there any arguments between the men either before or after Judge Wrenn arrived?" asked Harris.

"Well, not arguing. Judge Guthrie and the man were looking at some papers. I came over and wiped the table each time I brought them their drinks. I noticed they moved the papers to one side each time. I think they were job applications . . . CVs or something. Looked like they were discussing the contents so I wouldn't say they were arguing exactly. They seemed quite serious though." The man pointed. "They sat right in that corner over there."

Preddy stared towards the corner. "Strange place to come sorting out job applicants. Did you see any names on dese CVs?"

"No sir." The barman shook his head. "Actually, they held the papers pretty close to their chests when I was beside them."

"So you didn't get a look at dem even when Judge Wrenn arrived?" asked Preddy.

"No, sir. Those papers were put away before Judge Wrenn got to the table. Whatever they were looking at he didn't see them. I got to the table shortly after Judge Wrenn and it was cleared of all papers."

"Did ye naw catch the name of the other man?" Harris leaned on the bar. "Can ye remember?"

"I think they called him Patrick or Rick, something like that. He was tall and very thin. His forehead was long as I said, sort of like Rihanna. I love her, you see!"

"Bonny lass," agreed Harris. "What else can ye tell us about this Rick?"

"He was meagre — a thin guy. He had on a pair of those rimless glasses, that I do remember." The barman screwed up his nose. "Made his eyes look really large. They were all first names and shaking hands. Two of us attended to them. I went and got Judge Wrenn a Red Stripe. Later on their server brought them ribs and wings and fries. I followed up with plenty more drinks. They all seemed in good spirits, getting tipsy and louder, but happy."

Preddy scribbled away in his notebook. "Who paid de bill?"

"Judge Wrenn paid in cash, sir. Gave me two five hundred dollar bills as a tip to split with the waiter."

"Did they all leave together?" asked Harris.

"That guy Patrick or Rick left first. The two judges were here for about another fifteen minutes or so, then they left."

"Do ye know whether the judges left in the same car or took a taxi?" asked Harris.

The bartender shook his head. "I didn't go outside, sir. None of us did. In here can be quite busy. We just pocket the tips and move on to the next table. Only at night one of us might follow people outside. You know, like if it's a group of females, make sure they get to their vehicle. We open until 4 a.m. so you have to be on the lookout for lowlifes."

"Okay, thanks." Preddy stared at the tinted glass windows. It was not possible to get a clear view of the entire car park from inside. According to Tuffy's lawyer, his client witnessed a confrontation between the two men in the car park. If nothing was said in the bar, something must have been said outside it to escalate into a full blown argument. Preddy was no closer to learning what.

"De CCTV outside working?"

The man gave an apologetic grimace. "Yes sir, but those files have already been wiped."

"It would be good in future if you could keep de recording for a minimum of thirty days. Ask your boss to give me a call if him want to discuss it." Preddy handed him a business card. "You've been really helpful. If you think of anything else dat happened on Monday, please call me."

The detectives left the building and headed to their vehicle. On the way Preddy stopped and glanced around the parking area.

"So, what are ye thinking, Detective?"

"Just trying to work out what was going on here." Preddy continued his stride towards their jeep. "So Judge Guthrie is reading a handful of CVs. Why?"

Harris said, "Well, I'm pretty sure that men with names like Tuffy, Steely Vicious and Devil Head, dinnae get recruited via resumes reviewed in a posh diner."

"Quite. Maybe one was Judge Wrenn's CV for de Appeal Court post, although I can't think why it would be under scrutiny." Preddy shook his head as he spoke. "Or Guthrie is trying to recruit someone official without Judge Wrenn knowing? Wouldn't have thought Guthrie had de power to recruit anyone high up, maybe only a clerk? Maybe he needed Judge Wrenn's agreement and he refused?"

"Guthrie is likely tae lie naw matter what the truth is," said Harris. "It'll be hard work getting anything out of him."

Preddy triggered the car door open. "We need to find dat third man."

"So we're looking for a young skinny lad with a long forehead and rimless glasses. Rihanna's relative."

"Start by checking all de judiciary photos online. I'll do de same. We're looking for Patrick or Rick somebody."

Harris climbed into the driver's seat. "Sounds like a man who's hard tae miss. If he's there we'll find him."

CHAPTER 25

As he entered the lobby of Pelican Walk station, Preddy spotted a colleague he had not seen for a while. He stopped and spent a few minutes chatting with the affable detective from the Fugitive Apprehension Team. As Preddy looked into the eyes of Detective Tony Paulson he prayed that this man was not the subject of Harris's clandestine investigation. The detective bid goodbye to Preddy and waved at Spence as she entered the building.

"How's it going?" asked Preddy.

Spence shook her head. "Mrs Wrenn not in a happy state at all," she said. "She look so drawn in her face. My guess is dat she's not eating. Says she misses her husband bad-bad and never envisaged old age widout him."

The two detectives walked up the stairs and towards Preddy's office. "Must be terrible for her," he said. "I can't even imagine."

"De good thing is dat her children are wid her now. Dey just flew in from foreign so she have company. Nice people, two twenty-somethings Martin and Maria."

"Glad dey made it," said Preddy.

Spence nodded. "Oleta cooking up a storm. You want to see her a chop up chicken and a knead flour dumpling. De place smell like grater coconut. Make me hungry!"

Preddy smiled as he held the door open and let Spence go before him. She flopped down into a chair with her arms on the armrests and tilted her head back. Preddy closed the door and made his way to the window where he closed the blinds against the sun. He pressed the CD player and the low sound of rustling leaves flooded the room.

"Mmm, nice," she murmured.

Preddy smiled. "Make yourself at home."

"All of dem were asking about de investigation, but I told dem we were still following a number of strong lines of enquiry," reported Spence. She discreetly slid her feet out of her shoes, glad for the coolness that immediately engulfed them. "De son, Martin, said dat was detective speak."

"And he wasn't wrong," conceded Preddy as he sank into his chair. "You can't blame dem for wanting to know." Preddy stared at her curiously and wrinkled up his nose.

"If I didn't know you better, Javinia Spence, I'd say you've been smoking?"

"Your nose good, sir. Haven't touched a cigarette since my first baby was an embryo, though." She pulled at her braids and frowned. "And me hair not washing till weekend you know. Is her son was smoking. When him light up Oleta start tell him off, nicely though. She speak to dem softly like baby. She jump up and run go look ashtray for him." Spence kissed her teeth. "Before she make de big tough-back man go look him owna ashtray."

Preddy smiled. "Just being a mother."

"Eeh-eeh. When my girls turn teenager dem going run around after demself. Me not going do it!"

"Dat's what you say now. We'll see." Preddy grinned. "My parents did de same thing for me. Is an instinct parents can't grow out of. Besides she did say family means everything to her. I got de feeling dat she lives for her husband and children. Fetching and carrying for dem."

"Well, she never fetch and carry a thing. She eventually come out of de kitchen wid nothing and said she forgot de ashtray was stolen. Den she start to bawl and bawl. Maria hugged her. Martin said something about giving up de habit anyway and went and dabbed it out in de sink." Spence shook her head from side to side. "Don't know why him didn't just do dat in de first place."

Preddy's eyes twinkled as he watched her. "I'm going to remind you of dis conversation in ten years' time."

Spence grinned. "I bet you will too!"

Preddy put his hands behind his head. A frown appeared on his face. "Dat's really strange," he murmured. "Oleta actually said de ashtray was stolen?"

"Yes, sir."

"She still hasn't reported it as stolen. She formally reported de phone and de old coins and put a value on dem." Preddy stared at the ceiling. "It's an expensive piece. How she going put in an insurance claim for it, if it's not on de record as being stolen?"

Spence considered this for a moment. "Maybe she's been too preoccupied to deal wid it so far. It coulda just slip her mind?"

Preddy lowered his eyes to look at her. "It's made of black onyx and black diamonds, personally engraved and all. I've seen de box and receipt: five thousand US dollars. Strange something like dat slipped her mind."

"Wow!" Spence whistled. "As much as me love my husband, him woulda never so lucky!"

"I know how you mean," agreed Preddy with a smile. "Maybe after you married for decades you feel different though, who knows?"

"Hmm. Anyway, when Martin came back he started asking about de investigation again. I told him dat as soon as we were at de point of arresting anybody we would inform dem." She stretched out her feet, put her head back on the headrest and closed her eyes.

"Hard day, eh?"

"Dem people exhaust me, man! It not easy to deal wid dem question because dey want to hear dat we have a strong suspect" She opened an eye and glanced at Preddy. "So I guess we still no have nobody to arrest yet?"

"Not yet," mumbled Preddy.

"What is it, sir?" Spence sat up straight and stared at him. "I know you. Something is going on."

Preddy gave a wry grin. "I don't suppose you know anybody named Patrick or Rick dat works in de judicial system? Maybe from one of de many Parish Courts?"

Spence shook her head. "We don't have no surname?"

"Unfortunately not."

There was a knock on the door. Preddy could just make out Rabino's figure through the partially shuttered blinds.

Preddy raised his voice. "Come in, Kathryn."

"Oh this is where you are, madam?" Rabino pulled out a chair from a side table. She pushed her colleague's shoes out of the way and took a seat beside her.

"We were just discussing Patrick or Rick," explained Spence, using her toes to pull her shoes closer.

"Patrick or Rick Who?"

Spence looked at her colleague in faux admiration. "Dat's just where we reach, girl. A how you smart so?"

"Shut up." Rabino elbowed Spence in her side. "What's happening, sir? I can see I'm not going to get any sense out of this one."

"She was smoking," said Preddy with a grin.

"Really?" Rabino leaned closer to Spence and sniffed. "You started that foolishness again, lady? Since when?"

"Move offa me, man!" said Spence pretending to wriggle away. "Is Martin Wrenn, Oleta son, was smoking."

"Yeah, right," said Rabino.

"Anyway, I have no idea what his surname is and I can't tell you what he did or plans to do," Preddy informed her. "Not even sure what his first name is. Got de tip from Mosino earlier. I think dis man works in de legal field though. He was at de same lunch as Judge Wrenn and Judge Guthrie. I also think dat he might have some information about both men. Something dat might help our case."

Rabino looked at Preddy. "And we're not going to ask Judge Guthrie who he is?"

"We certainly are not going to do dat." Preddy shook his head. "De man is a damn liar. It's hard to believe anything dat comes out of his mouth."

"We have a picture of him, dis man Rick?" asked Spence.

"No picture," said Preddy. "Young though, dark-skinned, with a big forehead like Rihanna, rimless glasses. Dat's de description we have."

"Heh! Him can't hide," said Spence with a chuckle. "Dis man set foot anywhere inna Mo Bay, me will spot him."

Rabino shook back her mane and fanned her face with her hand. "I'll ask around. Speak to a few lawyers I know. See if they can shed any light on the mysterious Rick."

"Great," said Preddy. "Get anything about Devil Head from your informer?"

Rabino gave an involuntary shudder. "Some of these guys you really don't want to be interviewing even in broad daylight. Makes my blood run cold," she said. "He's pretty sure Devil Head is coming back tonight. He laughed at the idea that any gang member would ever strangle anybody though. They deal in bullets he said very proudly."

"Nice of him to make de admission," remarked Spence.

"He had a lot of sympathy for Tuffy," reported Rabino. "Denied knowing anything about Judge Wrenn's murder though. Said no one in their crew went near any judge that night. I reminded him that we have proof that some of them were in Night Court that night so were close to at least one judge. He conceded that point, very ungraciously I might add. Said court is the only place they ever set eyes on any 'pussy claat judge'. Went off onto a rant about police interfering with their domino games when they weren't doing anything wrong."

Spence shook her head and said, "Him friend dead and him a worry 'bout domino."

Rabino deepened her voice and said in broad Patois, "Me sorry Tuffy ketch him dead, but him too rass careless!"

"Friendship is a beautiful thing," muttered Preddy. "You know you have a gift for mimicry."

"I won't be doing the bleaching and tattoos I can assure you," said Rabino.

Preddy leaned forward in his seat. "Okay, so we need to get ready for Devil Head's return tonight."

"We'll be on the highway from six, sir," said Rabino. "I have a man watching his last known residence in case he comes back in the day."

"Call me at any time. I'll be ready to hit de road," said Preddy. "Tuffy's murderer must go to jail. No jungle justice going to happen on my watch. No Bembow Crew member will be judge, jury and executioner."

"Amen to dat," nodded Spence. "I am so ready for Mr Devil Head."

Preddy glanced at her. "And no shooting at him unless he poses a threat to life or limb."

"Me?" Spence raised her eyebrows, but there was a distinct glint in her eyes. "No, sir!"

CHAPTER 26

Rabino and Spence sat in their unmarked police jeep in the Greenwood community on the border of St James and Trelawny. The windows were down allowing the warm salty sea air to circulate and carry animated voices from a distant bar. The headlights remained off while the engine purred. The detectives awaited an old Land Rover Defender driven by their suspect Devil Head Collins whom they were reliably informed was alone and heading back to Montego Bay. The sky was dark and the road lighting not as good as it should be, but the detectives were listening to running commentary on the police radio and knew that the vehicle would arrive within a few minutes.

Rabino tapped the steering wheel with her well-manicured fingernails. "You know when Preddy first said he was talking to his bird, I thought it strange you know? Like something Harris would say because British people call women 'bird'. Couldn't believe he meant a real one!"

"Hah!" Spence chuckled. "You think him was talking Valerie? Spend too much time wid Harris eeh, white man traits rub off on him?"

"Speaking of spending too much time together, I'm glad to see they made it back from Mosino in one piece," said Rabino.

Spence nodded in agreement. "Me did think one of dem woulda end up inna bush somewhere."

Rabino smiled wryly. "Testosterone will be the death of both of them."

"You think is just dat?" asked Spence.

"Who knows, Preddy's not saying, but he's not fooling anybody," she replied. "Well, they'll just have to make nice or Super will make nasty."

"True thing," said Spence. She studied the steady flow of headlights whizzing by heading towards Montego Bay. "Super would go extra crazy if he ever found out dat de gun went missing. We have to get dis two horn devil."

"Murdering brute has got me so agitated." Rabino gripped the steering wheel. "Lord knows I need to do some yoga meditation."

"What, you into all dat chanting stuff now?"

"Not chanting, deep breathing and relaxation of the mind while holding a specific posture in a quiet place," explained Rabino raising her shoulders to demonstrate. "You should try it, you know."

"Girl, dere is nowhere quiet in my house. Not even de bathroom." She turned slightly to look at Rabino. "So, you and Clive not going make it?"

Rabino sighed. "Doesn't look like it and I'm tired of trying."

"You know de last tarot reading I got said a man I don't know well will surprise me in de coming days. You should get a reading, girl, see what is coming your way."

"Those things are so general," replied Rabino giving Spence a sceptical look. "The only man that's likely to surprise us is Devil Head."

"Make him try it!"

The voice on the police radio became louder and more urgent.

"You ready to do dis?" asked Spence buckling up her seat belt.

"Never been more ready. Let's go get him!"

As soon as the Land Rover blew past them on the highway, Rabino dipped the headlights and set off behind it. Gradually the distance shortened between Greenwood and Montego Bay. The journey would take an estimated twenty-six minutes and the plan was to apprehend Devil Head once he entered the city.

As they reached a dark corner with a blown streetlight the Land Rover slowed down and Rabino followed suit. They had covered less than two miles. The detectives watched as the driver stopped the vehicle beside a bushy thicket. Rabino pulled in across the road and shut off the engine. The moonlight provided poor lighting, but they could see the hornlike hair as the man exited the vehicle and walked towards a lamppost where he began to adjust the lower part of his clothes. The detectives alighted quietly and knelt in the long grass, guns drawn. Noisy crickets chorused close to their feet while a tethered goat complained bitterly about its plight. Devil Head glanced over his shoulder and seemingly noticed nothing. The detectives crouched and ran silently across the road in the shadows.

Rabino stared him up and down. "Nothing to see here, Detective Spence."

"Rass claat!" The suspect blinked rapidly and quickly adjusted his zipper. His right hand inched towards his waist. As it did so his sleeve was drawn back and exposed on his bleached bare arm was a carefully drawn crocodile.

"Let's see which one a we quicker," shouted Spence, pointing her gun straight at his forehead. "Gwaan reach, no? Give me a reason Mr Collins."

"Wait no lady!"

"Detective Spence is de name. Pelican Walk police."

His eyes widened as he focused on the gleaming steel. He raised his palms above his head. "Don't shoot officer! Wha' you see me do?"

"Urinating in a public place," said Rabino.

"You . . . ree . . . wha?"

"Pissing," said Spence.

Devil Head stared at her incredulously. "A dat you want shoot me fah?"

"Any reason would be just fine," said Spence.

Rabino took a few steps forward and disarmed him. "I'm Detective Rabino." She patted the pockets of his jogging pants as well as his hoodie. "Finish zipping up, man. You have nothing we want to see."

"You have him covered?" asked Spence.

"Sure," said Rabino, raising her weapon inches from the man's face. "Get down on your stomach, now! Lie flat."

As Devil Head obeyed, Spence handed her gun to her colleague. Spence removed her handcuffs from her pocket and dragged the fugitive's hands behind trying to secure them. He struggled violently and tried to wriggle free cursing loudly at the women.

Rabino chastised him. "What a nasty thing to say, Mr Collins. What would your mother and sister say if they heard you describe women in that manner?"

"Fuck off, bitch!"

"Nobody going fuck off and leave Mo Bay to you!" Spence attempted to affix the handcuffs again. "We'll fuck off when you and de rest of your Crew stop murder people!"

The detectives suddenly became aware that a vehicle was approaching and slowing down. Spence immediately lay flat on top of Devil Head's back. Rabino crouched down and trained her weapon on the vehicle while shuffling backwards out of the glare of the moonlight. The vehicle stopped. The door opened and slammed. Rabino squinted as she watched the tall man's approach. "Sweet Jesus!" she said.

"Close, but naw quite," said Harris. "Preddy compared me tae Him as well."

"I nearly put a bullet through you!" exclaimed Rabino. "More than one, actually."

"I hope we're just talking about tonight, and naw some other time?" Harris glanced at Spence who lay on top of Devil Head wrestling with his hands. She had secured one half of the cuffs on his right hand, but he was continuing the fight with his left. The fugitive managed to punch Spence in her side, but she ignored the blow and stuck to her task. Rabino placed the barrel of her gun against the angry man's temple.

"You feel that, Mr Collins?" she asked. "You want that to be the last thing you feel?"

The man stopped struggling. Spence grabbed his slumped limb and drew it backwards allowing her to secure both arms with the handcuffs which gave a satisfying click.

"Get up!" ordered Spence.

The man made no attempt to comply. Harris leaned down and hauled the suspect to his feet. Spence gestured to Rabino for the return of her weapon and quickly used the butt to deliver a sharp blow to Devil Head's scalp. "I going buss you rass claat head!"

"Aargh!" The fugitive tried to lean his body away from the attack.

Harris quickly pulled the bleeding man away from her. "Whoa! Stop!" he shouted as Spence stretched across him and delivered yet another blow.

Rabino reached out a hand and pulled her colleague back. "It's okay, Javinia. We've got him. It's okay."

Spence rubbed her rib cage, breathing heavily. "Piece a shit," she mumbled.

"Watch and see what a going do you!" screamed Devil Head. "Oonu police too love fuck wid people, you wait!"

"Quiet!" ordered Harris. "Now walk!"

"A who you?" screeched Devil Head and tried to shrug off the man's grip.

"Detective Harris, Pelican Walk."

A trail of blood ran down Devil Head's temple to his mouth and he spat it at his feet. His eyes scorched Harris.

"How you make dem do people so? De whole a oonu is blood claat criminal! How oonu can beat people so? A fuckery!"

"So ye're totally against beating people, but naw against murdering them? Funny that."

"Murder who? Who me murder?"

"Antwon Frazer." Rabino stared at him with contempt. "But I'm sure you could name a few more."

Harris pushed the man towards his vehicle, "Jevon Collins? Ye are under arrest for the murder of Antwon Frazer. Ye dinnae have tae say anything, but . . ."

"Go fuck youself, white bwoy!"

"Ye certainly didnae have tae say that," Harris scolded him.

Devil Head struggled in vain. "No put you dutty white hand pon me!"

"Yer a right fussy scrote," chided Harris. "I'm naw a fucking surgeon. Ye'll survive ma 'dutty white hand.'" Harris marched the belligerent fugitive in front of him. "And dinnae even think of telling me anything about wanting dry dumplings. We're done catering tae Crew members."

"What the hell are you doing here anyway?" asked Rabino as they strode behind him.

"I followed ye," admitted Harris. "I've been following ye all night."

Rabino did not hide her annoyance. "Why exactly?"

Harris shrugged. "Preddy insinuated I needed tae watch and learn. Naw sure if this is what he meant, but I'm watching and learning. There's been a lot of whispering around the station since this morning. Heard that ye were going tae 'take out a Benbow bwoy tonight.' I guessed that didnae mean a date."

Spence overtook them and stood in front of Harris's passenger door, hands on hips, eyes narrowed. "A we catch him. We going take him back."

"Och naw, Detective Spence." Harris shook his head firmly and made his body a barrier between the detainee and Spence. "Ye'll probably kill him and I think the brass will have something tae say about that — even if Preddy willnae."

"We'll follow you," said Rabino. She looked at Spence who had not moved then took her arm. "Come on. Let him take him."

Spence stared defiantly at Harris. "Why? He is not de boss."

"He isn't," agreed Rabino, quickly assessing the level of her colleague's irritation. "But I might be tempted to do something to Mr Collins that I shouldn't and somehow I don't think I could count on you to stop me?"

Spence exhaled and tore her eyes away from the Scotsman. She gave Rabino a reluctant grin as she followed her back to their jeep. Spence flopped down into the passenger seat.

Rabino climbed in and reversed the vehicle. "Good work, girl," she said.

"You too," murmured Spence. "Tell de boss him can go to bed. Lord know, me need to get to mine."

CHAPTER 27

Preddy sat in his home office drinking coconut water with a splash of white rum. Earlier he had microwaved last night's fish dinner and was now comfortably full. He was dressed in khakis and boots, ready for action. His bullet-proof vest was sitting on his desk, his holster beside it. No calls had come in from either Spence or Rabino and Preddy was growing impatient waiting for an update on the whereabouts of Devil Head. Every few minutes his eyes flicked at the time in the bottom of his computer screen. It was important to try and concentrate on other things that were bothering him.

The visit to Mosino was firmly on his mind. What were the two judges arguing about that had so incensed Judge Lawrence Guthrie? There had to be a motive to link him to the murder, yet unearthing it was proving a struggle. Tuffy's lawyer trusted Preddy and he intended to keep their conversation confidential, even if it meant annoying the hell out of Harris. Preddy frowned. He and Harris were being touted as The Answer by the straw-clutching Commissioner Davis, but Preddy knew just how such things worked in Jamaica. If things went well a beaming commissioner would push Harris

262

in front of the camera. If things went badly a scowling commissioner would send the media in the opposite direction, following a carefully laid trail of ginger-laced coconut drops straight to Preddy's door.

The detective sighed heavily. Thoughts of the third man had occupied his mind all day and now he could finally look into it. Who was Rick? He stared impatiently at the computer screen as the pages refreshed at their leisure despite the much touted 4G broadband service. He searched through the records of judges for the parish of St James without any luck. He then searched the other parishes until he had covered all fourteen parishes, but could find no one who matched the description. His phone beeped and he snatched it up quickly. It was a text message from his daughter Annalee, wishing him a good night. She should have long been asleep and he smiled as he texted her back as much while wishing her a good night too.

Before he had a chance to put the phone down it rang. Valerie.

"Hello," he snapped.

For a moment she was silent. "Boy, what a greeting. Is what happen? You no sound happy to hear me at all!"

"Sorry, baby," Preddy apologised, wishing he could answer the phone again. "Just waiting to go on de road. It have me a bit on edge."

"On de road where? What going on, Ray?" Her concern was evident and he mentally kicked himself for not choosing his words more carefully, but he had not been thinking clearly.

"Nothing to worry your head 'bout, baby, honest," he lied. "We just have to pick up a man dat needs to be under lock and key — for life preferably."

"Dat don't sound like no routine pick up to me?" she replied sharply. "Sound more like a murderer?"

Her voice was searching and Preddy found himself smiling. It pleased him that she was able to read him and understand his work. "Don't worry, baby. Him don't know we looking for him and him don't know tonight is de night."

He glanced at the bottom corner of his screen again. "Baby, I can't tie up de line. I'll call you in de morning."

"You damn well better," she warned.

"Before I even brew my tea," he promised. "Love you."

"Love you too, Ray. Please be careful. Goodnight."

Preddy turned his attention back to his scrolling. An advert for legal services popped up which he quickly closed while frowning. He needed to install a better ad blocker to deal with the frequent intrusion. The pages ticked over. Still there was nothing and nobody that fit the description. It was nearly eleven and he was getting tired. He placed his hands to his temples and kneaded, forcing his brain to think. If the man was a young man it was unlikely that he had risen to the rank of judge. It could be a judge's clerk, though why a clerk would meet a judge in a gaming lounge to run through CVs was beyond him. The dots just would not connect.

Suddenly a thought struck him. He opened a new tab and conducted a search on the recruitment of judges. Near the top of the search results was a link to the website of the Kingston based Judicial Services Commission. He read through their details. This was the body responsible for the hiring, firing and disciplining of judges. There were no photos of any of the named team of people who made up the august body, and there was no one named Patrick or Rick.

Preddy scrolled down to the bottom of the page and his heart stopped. A single line paragraph beside a small headshot caught his eye. The head of a young man with an elongated forehead, rimless glasses and large eyes. He could be Rihanna's brother. Alrick Douglass, Judicial Personnel Co-ordinator. The person to contact with all initial queries relating to the judicial service. Preddy sank back in his chair and drained the rest of his beverage. He would do just that.

His phone rang and he snatched it up eagerly this time while getting to his feet. Finally something was happening.

"We've got him, sir." The elated voice of Rabino sang in his ear. "Mr Jevon Collins A.K.A. Devil Head is on his way to Pelican Walk."

"You got him?" repeated Preddy.

"Yes, sir," she replied. "Spence and I apprehended him on the highway about half an hour ago."

"You never call me." It was a statement of resignation, rather than annoyance.

"No time, sir." Rabino hesitated before adding, "Detective Harris turned up. He heard the rumours amongst the guys that something was going down tonight."

"Rass," said Preddy through gritted teeth.

"He was a help though, sir," she assured him. "Didn't get on his high horse or anything."

"Yes, but I'm wondering what he might just let slip to Super?"

"I'm pretty sure he doesn't know the whole story yet, sir."

Preddy sighed. "Never mind, dat's for tomorrow. I'll deal wid it."

"Yes, sir."

Preddy sank back down, surprised by how relieved he was that his presence was not needed after all. Rabino and Spence were ace detectives, that he had always known, and no matter what he said Rabino would continue to blame herself for Tuffy's demise. Preddy suspected that all along the two women were determined to do the take-down their own way. "Devil Head came quietly?" he asked.

"As quietly as can be expected with cold steel against his temple," she informed him. "He had a gun concealed on him, but we relieved him of it. He was a bit . . . boisterous, had to restrain him."

"Look forward to hearing all about it tomorrow." Preddy smiled at the thought. "Well done, Kathryn. Sleep well."

"Yes, sir," she said. "You too. Goodnight."

Preddy put down the phone. One less murdering vermin on the road. He frowned as he wondered if it was indeed rumour that led Harris to follow Spence and Rabino or whether the Scotsman had lied and one, or both, of his team members were under investigation.

CHAPTER 28

Thursday, 11 May, 5.02 a.m.

Having slept at an awkward angle, Preddy's arms felt stiff when he awoke. From experience he had discovered that his nightmares were lessened when he slept on his stomach, using an arm as his pillow. It did not do much good for his limbs even as he restlessly exchanged them. The Norwood visions stayed away last night and for that he was grateful. He would need his wits about him today if he was to nail Everton Wrenn's murderer. He stretched as he rolled off the bed and whacked the top of the alarm clock to shut off the infernal noise. The trilling was instantly replaced by the audible ticking of the second hand. The outdoor security lights made tree limb shadows which bobbed and weaved on the ceiling. Through the window the distant tree-lined horizon was gradually turning light orange. He resisted the temptation to crack the windows, knowing that tiresome mosquitoes would detect blood and want in. At some stage he would get around to installing mesh protection.

A long drive lay ahead of Preddy and while it would have stood him in good stead to just take off before the sun rose, he needed some exercise before he faced it. He slid into track bottoms and trainers, pulled on a T-shirt and picked up his chronograph watch. His gun and badge remained on the dressing table. They were not part of his exercise ritual and he had never faced a need for them. It was still dark outside, but people would be on the streets. Montego Bay never really slept. Those who had never gone to bed would soon encounter those who were early risers. Whether it was people or animals or birds, middle night or break of day, someone or something could always be seen or heard.

Preddy's feet pounded the streets of Ironshore, a gentle breeze cooling his face as he settled into his running. A taxi driver tooted at him hoping for the first fare of the day. A young man pushed a wooden handcart containing a huge steel pot of steaming porridge to an intersection that would soon be busy with commuters. Preddy passed two street cleaners with their rakes, brooms and black bags, diligently removing the evidence of the previous night's escapades from the littered roadside. The detective acknowledged the workers with a wave. A male jogger ran in the opposite direction and nodded at Preddy who frowned and gestured towards his ears. The man did not appear to notice and Preddy turned his head to watch him go past. The detective briefly entertained the thought of going after him, but decided to continue on his way. He could not understand people who jogged with earphones. Yes, it must be nice to listen to music, but it was too great a distraction. People needed to be alert to their surroundings, to vehicles and to other pedestrians.

After a full hour Preddy returned to his apartment drenched in sweat, feeling energised. Within minutes he was out of the shower, and dressed in casual slacks and a printed shirt with long sleeves. An eager Spartan sat on the front window ledge demanding entry, his tiny green head moving up and down as he tried to catch Preddy's eye. The detective smiled and rolled up his sleeves to the elbows. He entered the kitchen and sprinkled some cooked rice grains into a saucer before approaching the window with it. The bird spread its wings and paced the sill, its movements becoming more eager as it watched the approaching food. As soon as the window opened it flew onto Preddy's bare wrist and started cramming away.

"Learned my lesson Spartan, nothing for you to wipe your feet on today," said Preddy as he walked the feasting bird to the kitchen and placed the dish on the counter. He filled the kettle as he watched it eat. "Wish I had your wings. Could do my trip to Kingston in a fraction of de time, looking down on de hills and valleys and sea."

Preddy gently pushed the saucer a few inches and put an empty mug in its place. "I would stay away from people if I was you, you know? Sometimes dey seem nice, but you never know what manner of evil dey will do. Clip your wings in an instant."

The bird paused guzzling to cheep questioningly before returning its attention to breakfast.

"Must be nice to have a stress free life," murmured Preddy and tickled its crest. "Why don't I fly away from it all? Because I remember what Mo Bay was like before de gangs formed. Can't let dem win."

Preddy put his phone on speaker and chatted to Valerie while inhaling the refreshing smell of steeped ganja leaves. He downed a long hot cup in between the conversation. After hanging up the phone he escorted Spartan to the window and locked it. He grabbed some hard dough bread and cheese, picked up two ripe bananas and headed for the door.

The drive along the picturesque coastline was relatively smooth. There were fellow drivers leaving western Jamaica and heading east for various destinations. Preddy soon left St James, crossed through Trelawny and entered the parish of St Ann, where he turned off at Mammee Bay, bypassing the bustling town of Ocho Rios. The Mammee Bay to Kingston leg of the North Coast Highway was a breeze. The controversial excessive toll charge to get to Kingston on the relatively new bypass kept most financially-challenged motorists away. Instead, those drivers followed the free scenic route through the three-mile tunnel of lush tropical ferns in

Fern Gully, down the winding Mount Rosser terrain with its spectacular views of St Catherine, across the notorious eighteenth-century built Flat Bridge, and followed the snaking Rio Cobre to Spanish Town, before picking up the highway to Kingston. As much as he missed the panoramic views, Preddy was thankful for the Chinese-built bypass chiselled through mountains which knocked nearly an hour off the previous travel time from Ocho Rios to Kingston. He had estimated that it would take him three hours to get from Montego Bay to downtown Kingston, traffic permitting, and he made it in just under that.

Parking was always an issue in the capital city whether you entered downtown or uptown. Here at National Heroes Circle it was even worse, since Gordon House, the home of the Jamaican Parliament, was nearby and no stopping was allowed in the vicinity. He thought about seeking permission to park from one of the many security guards, but decided against making his presence known to them. Instead he parked on a garage forecourt close to his destination after showing the gas attendant his credentials. Most businesses were accommodating to police officers, no doubt because the presence of law enforcement officials made them feel safer.

Preddy donned his sunglasses and strolled across to the National Heroes Park. The site had a long history before being transformed into a shrine for Jamaican heroes. It had once played host to Queen Victoria's Golden and Diamond Jubilees and had even hosted travelling circuses before becoming the centre of horse racing on the island. Now the park was a stunning landscape which included fifty acres of botanical gardens, a huge green space in an otherwise concrete jungle. The detective could not take the time to admire the impressive surroundings. He watched the target premises from a distance — the Judicial Services Commission. While he waited he dialled Rabino's number and left a message that she should expect him at Pelican Walk in the early afternoon.

At minutes to nine o'clock staff members began to appear. Preddy crossed the road and stood beside a fresh fruit seller as people stopped to buy plastic bags of diced pineapple and peeled oranges before heading into their offices. It was not long before he saw the young man, unmissable even behind aviator shades. He was smartly dressed in a grey suit and carried a brown briefcase. Preddy stepped in front of him as the man approached, blocking his assent up the stone steps.

"Alrick Douglass?"

Alrick took off his sunglasses and replaced them with rimless glasses. "Yes, can I help you?"

"Detective Preddy, Pelican Walk police, Montego Bay. We need to talk."

The man licked his thin lips. "You sure it's me you're looking for, Detective?"

"As sure as I am dat Kingston hotter dan Mo Bay." Preddy removed his own glasses and tucked them into his shirt pocket. "You were in Mosino having lunch wid Judge Guthrie and Judge Wrenn on Monday de first of May. You're going to tell me all about dat."

Alrick Douglass stretched a hand towards a side rail, missed it, and clutched at the bare wall. "Oh God! I know I should have minded my own business. I'm going to lose my job now!"

Preddy was startled by his reaction. While he had wanted to shock the man by swooping on him without notice the detective did not want to have a coronary on his conscience. "Come wid me, Mr Douglass. Let's go sit in de park and talk." He took the man by the elbow and steadied him on his feet. The two men crossed the busy road and followed a path through the colourful fragrant flowers in the park. They came to a stop under the nearest monument erected in memory of Sir Alexander Bustamante, one of Jamaica's seven national heroes.

"Please don't lie to me, Mr Douglass," warned Preddy. "Tell me exactly what happened."

"They'll fire me!"

"Dis is a murder investigation. You think is only your job you going lose if you don't talk to me? How do you think losing your liberty will feel?" The detective paused allowing this to sink in, and watched as Alrick mopped his brow. "I have a good idea what happened," lied Preddy, "but I want to hear it from you."

Alrick sat down on a white stone bench while Preddy remained on his feet in front of him. "I had a long weekend off and decided to go to Mo Bay. I've got family in the Bogue area and had planned to go down there for so long and never got around to it. I wasn't just going for the break though." He glanced hesitantly at Preddy. "I know you're going to think I'm a troublemaker, but I'm not. Not really. I just thought Judge Wrenn is two-faced and I should expose him."

"What did you do?" asked Preddy.

Alrick drew a sharp intake of breath. "I heard some people in the office discussing Judge Wrenn's upcoming promotion to the Court of Appeal. They were saying it was funny how Judge Guthrie was using Judge Wrenn as a reference in his own application for a Supreme Court role."

"So? Dey are friends? What was wrong wid Guthrie doing dat?"

"Nothing really. The thing is Judge Guthrie obviously had never seen what references Judge Wrenn was sending in on his behalf. There are five years' worth of so-called references that Judge Wrenn sent in. Each of them was so diplomatic yet condemning . . . passive aggressive I guess you'd call it. I decided that Judge Guthrie needed to know." Alrick studied his feet. "So I showed him copies of the applications and the attached references. My guess is Judge Wrenn was being spiteful to his so-called friend and I didn't like that."

A surge of rage ran through Preddy's body. "Or maybe Judge Wrenn just couldn't bring himself to hurt his best friend's feelings?" Preddy glared at him. "You showed him everything dat Judge Wrenn said about him?"

The chastened man hung his head and nodded. "Judge Guthrie called the office seeking feedback on his application. I suspect he probably called every year, although I have only been there two years. He was never given any feedback

— just told he was free to reapply next time he saw any relevant advertisements."

"And you decided it was your duty to go against de instructions of your employer?" Preddy did not try to disguise his disdain.

Alrick squirmed on the uncomfortable bench. "I tried to do it anonymously; you know, called him a few times and told him to get another set of referees. I didn't tell him who was spoiling his chances. One day I made a mistake and forgot to hide my direct phone number. He tracked me down and insisted that I tell him exactly what was going on."

Preddy shook his head. "And just like dat you told him everything."

"I was trying to help him! I was sorry for him. It's not fair when you're trying to get ahead and the people you trust are busy back-stabbing you." The young man's face took on a sullen look. "He had a right to know."

"And who made you de arbiter of deir business?" demanded Preddy. "Judge Wrenn is dead!"

"Judge Guthrie didn't do it! I know he didn't, detective!" Alrick removed his rimless glasses and wiped his entire face. "When I told him, he didn't react badly like I expected. He was very calm, friendly. Seriously, you would think he'd just been told that his shoelace was undone. We finished eating, he thanked me for letting him know. Said he would be changing at least one of his referees next time."

Preddy frowned at this. "When Judge Wrenn turned up, who did he think you were?"

"I didn't even know Judge Wrenn would be there. Nearly died of fright when I looked up and saw him walking towards us! I was panicking, trying to stuff the papers away. Man, I downed that bottle of beer so quick, my head was spinning!"

"Judge Guthrie was surprised to see him too?" asked Preddy.

Alrick shook his head. "Judge Guthrie obviously expected him and was cool as a cucumber. He introduced me as just a friend from St Elizabeth named Rick. Look, I agreed to meet Judge Guthrie at noon and that's what I did. While we were talking and drinking he kept saying a friend would soon turn up . . . never said it was Judge Wrenn though." Alrick frowned. "I did think that was a strange thing to do. He must enjoy danger or something. We talked shop over the meal . . . about bad music, politics, the weather. Then I left. The two judges were happily chatting away over a final drink when I left."

"Where are de job applications and references?" asked Preddy.

"Judge Guthrie has a copied set. The originals are back in the files upstairs at the office."

"Go get dem," ordered Preddy.

Alrick straightened up and looked aghast. "I can't just walk in there and walk back out with private papers! I'm late as it is. I'm supposed to be at my desk working."

"You did it before," sneered Preddy. "You have ten minutes, and den I'll just march right up to your boss and ask for dem."

Alrick quickly got to his feet. "Soon come, Detective."

* * *

Preddy placed the resume pages on the passenger seat as he made his exit from downtown Kingston. Whenever he hit a stoplight he glanced down at the papers, speed reading as best he could at a bad angle. Now he could finally attach a motive for murder to Judge Lawrence Guthrie. A Jamaican psychopath. He smiled wryly and wondered what Harris would think about that. Preddy believed Alrick that Guthrie had smiled and reacted with calm. That was just who the judge was: a man who wore an impenetrable mask. Yet with no physical evidence and no chance of a confession from someone as unhinged as Guthrie, Preddy had no clear idea how to reel him in. Superintendent Brownlow would have a stroke if Preddy dared challenge Guthrie without solid evidence.

273

Guthrie who swore he was at the Ambassador West hotel, all night, and whom the concierge had signed in.

A thought struck him as he motored along, barely adhering to the speed limit. He wondered if Oleta Wrenn suspected all along that Guthrie had killed her husband. Why did she not speak up? Was it out of some sort of loyalty towards the man who was Everton's best friend and almost part of the family. Maybe the two were having an affair and the expensive ashtray was an item he had coveted. One she had let him keep to prove her devotion. A deep frown etched in Preddy's brow. Oleta was still a handsome woman, but having seen Guthrie's two recent conquests he was not convinced that Oleta would be his type — if she ever was. So what was it that kept her from sending the detectives Guthrie's way? Maybe he needed to interview Oleta, bring her to the more sombre surroundings of Pelican Walk station and interrogate her there. Lawrence Guthrie was unlikely to disclose a thing, but if he wouldn't, maybe, just maybe, Oleta would.

CHAPTER 29

Thursday, 11 May, 12.50 p.m.

The capital city was a nice place to visit once in a while, but St James was Preddy's parish and Montego Bay was his heart. Nothing and no one would be allowed to ruin its image or endanger the lives of its residents, not on his watch. On re-entering St James, Preddy was flagged down by the Highway Patrol who quickly waved him on when they identified him. Preddy sped up again covering many miles of dazzling coastline until arriving in Montego Bay and heading straight to the Ambassador West hotel. The guestbook had been checked days ago by his officers, and Preddy knew that Judge Guthrie had not lied about staying there or about what time he had walked past the concierge. Preddy smiled at the female receptionist and showed her his badge.

"Good afternoon, Ma'am, I need to have a look at room 214," he said.

"Good afternoon, Detective," she greeted him through over-painted lips. "You need a room, sir?"

"Not at de minute. I just want to see what dat one looks like."

She turned her head over her shoulder. "Warren! Come here. Bring the key for 214," she shouted. "If that one isn't to your liking we have others, sir. It's a popular room though."

A large man emerged from behind the door leading from the reception area. "Hello, sir," he said and fumbled on a shelf. His tight waistcoat strained as he moved. Preddy nodded at him.

"This is Detective Preddy from Pelican Walk," she said. "He's not checking in. Just show him around 214 for me."

"Follow me, sir." They went up two flights of stairs, the guide panting heavily with each step, Preddy covering two steps at a time with ease. They walked along a corridor lined with abstract paintings by talented Jamaican artists. "We in trouble, sir?"

"Not at all," said Preddy, "unless you personally have something to confess?"

The man laughed. "No, Detective. Not me. I just hustle to make a living then go home at nights. I never go near trouble if I see it lurking."

"Dat's what I like to hear."

The man opened the door and moved back allowing Preddy to enter. Light flooded the room. It was a corner room with huge windows to the front and the side. From the front was a clear view of the shimmering Caribbean Sea. The balcony was small and occupied by two white chairs and a low side table. Preddy walked towards the side window from where he could also catch glimpses of the sea. Immediately below was a very tidy floral garden. He studied the window carefully.

"Dis window looks like it opens outwards?" said Preddy peering at the hinges.

"Yes, sir." The man moved quickly towards it and tugged at the locks. "They're a bit tricky, but all of the windows open. Sometimes we have to help guests to open them though." Using his shoulders to brace it he pushed a window, opening it to one side, and then did the same with the other pane. "It's a bit hot to have them open in the days. Guests usually prefer to have on the air con. In the nights mostly you'll see them opened. This is one of our nicest rooms." The man rubbed his now smarting upper arm.

Preddy leaned out of the garden side window. Secured to the wall was a spiral fire escape which ended next to a short tree which, despite being devoid of fruits, he recognized as an avocado pear tree. Well-trimmed green bushes were below interspersed with bold pink hibiscus flowers which surrounded the trunk. Preddy straightened up and walked towards the balcony windows.

"You need those to open too, sir?"

From his tone Preddy knew that opening them was the last thing the man wanted to do. Pushing heavy windows back and forth was no fun. "No man, dis is fine. I can see all I need from here."

"Well, what do you think, sir?" asked the man.

"He's a strong man, he could easily have left," murmured Preddy under his breath.

"Sir?"

"Nothing."

* * *

As Preddy entered Pelican Walk lobby he spotted Detective Spence. "Get Oleta Wrenn on de phone," he said urgently. "Tell her to come into de station right now."

"I'll try and track her down, sir," replied Spence with a questioning look. "Suppose she can't make it right away though? She could be anywhere?"

"Look, you have to get her here. Tell her it's to do wid her husband's murder, and it is. I'll need you to sit in on her interview wid me," he said. "We're going to discuss Judge Lawrence Guthrie."

"Alright, sir. Will do." She looked at him hesitantly. "Sir, we better talk 'bout Devil Head Collins."

"Yes, meet me in de evidence room in a minute." He bounded up the stairs with his stack of papers tucked under his arm. As he headed down the corridor he spotted the superintendent. Realising that there was no escape he greeted his superior.

"Just the person I wanted to see," said Superintendent Brownlow.

Preddy winced. The superintendent's words were spoken with something bordering on venom and Preddy's mind desperately tried to work out what was the likely cause this time. "Oh, sir?"

"Follow me." The superintendent headed towards his office with a wary Preddy behind him. The superintendent reached for the door handle then looked up at the person approaching. "Ah, Detective Harris. Another person I really wanted to see. Don't go past, come in please."

"Aye, sir."

Preddy glanced at Harris hoping to detect what was about to come their way, but he was unable to read the Scotsman. Preddy took a seat. Harris moved a leather chair from beneath a side table and placed it next to Preddy's. The superintendent closed the door and leaned heavily against it.

"What can you gentlemen tell me about Jevon Collins, alias Devil Head, and a gun that we lost?" Brownlow seemed to be making a sturdy attempt to keep his voice even. His eyes flicked between the detectives as if he did not care who gave the answer.

"Sir, I can explain all dat," said Preddy quickly as his stomach churned. "But what you really need to focus on is dat de gun is back in our possession and a murderer is in custody."

Harris's face was a picture of incredulity as he gave Preddy a deadly side-eye. Superintendent Brownlow's meaty jowls shook. "You have the audacity to tell me what it is I really want to know? Really?"

"Sorry, sir. I didn't mean it dat way," replied Preddy. "What I meant was . . ."

"What do you know about it?" The superintendent set his eyes on Harris.

Harris moved his chair a few inches away from Preddy's and half turned in his seat to study his colleague through narrowing eyes. "Naw as much as Detective Preddy obviously, sir, but I can assure ye we're on the same page."

The superintendent erupted. "A gun was stolen from our possession and used to kill Antwon Frazer, himself a murder suspect! How in God's name did that happen?"

Harris spluttered loudly and used a hand to cover his mouth. His complexion began to turn crimson. Brownlow looked at him with some concern. He moved away from the door and walked to his desk, stretching across it for a glass and a jug of water. "Here, drink this, Detective." Harris grasped the glass and gulped the cooling liquid appreciatively. Brownlow refilled it and Harris drank again.

Preddy licked his dry lips. He badly wanted a glass of water too, but knew better than to reach for one. "I take full responsibility for de stolen gun, sir. We retrieved it within forty-eight hours and . . ."

"Because the murderer dropped it on the crime scene!" said Brownlow.

"It is something dat will not happen again, sir. We have better processes in place."

The superintendent sat down heavily. "And why was I not informed of the theft in the first place?"

Preddy's lips opened and closed like a fish. Harris leaned forward and picked up a clean glass. "Water, Detective Preddy?" He poured without waiting for an answer. The gurgling flow of liquid pierced the silence. Harris handed the glass to Preddy who drained it in one go.

The superintendent pointed a stubby finger at Preddy. "You should thank your lucky stars we got that gun back before the media got wind! Make sure that I get a full explanation of the theft and the recovery for the Commissioner. I want every i dotted and t crossed.

"Yes, sir," said Preddy.

"Aye sir, a full report," said Harris pointedly.

Preddy moved to get to his feet. "I'll get onto it if dat's all, sir?"

"Sit!" The superintendent pushed back his chair and placed both legs on a stool close to his feet. "I've been informed by the lawyer for Jevon Collins that his client was already secured by handcuffs when Detective Spence beat him about the head with her gun."

Whe' de rass? Preddy had imagined many statements coming from the superintendent's lips but this was so out of place that it did not even figure in his imagination. "I wasn't dere last night, sir," he stammered. "Haven't had de full details yet."

Brownlow stared at him. "Get Detective Spence up here. Let me hear what she has to say."

The oscillating fan was of no assistance as the air in the room began to stifle Preddy. "I should speak to her first, sir."

"She can speak for herself, can't she?" raged the superintendent. "Javinia Spence is not an officer who has ever been reluctant to speak her mind. I want to hear what she has to say."

Harris pushed his ginger fringe out of his eyes. "She'll say the same thing I'll say, sir."

The superintendent's head immediately jerked towards him. "Oh, and what is that, Detective Harris?"

Preddy looked from Harris to the superintendent. He now wished that he had taken the time to speak to Spence about these sins that Super was now laying squarely at her feet. And now here was the foreigner about to throw her under the bus.

"That the amount of force used was reasonable in the circumstances tae secure the fugitive, sir," reported Harris. "He's a very violent man as I'm sure ye're aware. He attacked Detective Spence, punched her in the rib cage. She defended herself admirably, sir."

"So he wasn't securely handcuffed at the time?" pressed Brownlow.

280

The green eyes never wavered from the superintendent's face. "The clasps were naw fastened, sir. He was desperately trying tae get them off and, in ma opinion, he would have succeeded. She hit him tae prevent further injury tae herself. Once he was subdued she was able tae fasten the cuffs."

Preddy could hear his breath leaving his body and wondered if the others could too. This sounded like completely reasonable behaviour to him in the circumstances. He believed whole heartedly in self-defence.

Superintendent Brownlow concentrated on Harris. "You sure that is what happened?"

"Absolutely, sir," replied the Glaswegian. "Saw it with ma own eyes. Textbook self-defence."

"Okay, good." The superintendent exhaled almost as loudly as Preddy. "I'll let the Commissioner know that the allegation of police brutality is totally false."

"Totally false, sir," Harris echoed. "He's just mad that Spence and Rabino took him down. Doesnae want his crew tae know that females got him. Wounded pride and all that."

"So we've got Mr Devil Head Collins at last," stated Brownlow, relief evident in his tone.

Harris nodded. "He said some things that leads me tae believe he's never going tae give up violent crime. It's up tae the judges, but this guy needs tae be put away for life."

"I agree, de judges are a problem." said Preddy. "Way too many lenient sentences being handed out."

The superintendent sank back in his chair and threw his hands up. "What can we do, bribe them?" he asked, before quickly adding, "Don't answer that. Let me have your report later, Detective Harris. You can combine it with Preddy's."

"Aye, sir," said Harris, keeping his voice even. "I'm sure we can do that."

"If you can link Jevon Collins to Judge Wrenn's murder do it, and do it quickly," urged Brownlow. He waved a hand towards the door. "You're free to leave, Detectives."

As they left, Preddy headed towards the detectives open-plan zone without a backward glance. Harris quickly caught up and stayed two paces in front of him.

Preddy did not look directly at him. "Look, before you say anything, Detective Harris, as far as I'm concerned de fewer people knew about de stolen gun de better."

"I'm naw fucking people, Preddy, I'm yer partner."

"Point taken." Preddy quickened his pace trying to out-pace Harris who ensured that this did not happen.

"Where are ye going, Preddy?"

Preddy's eyes widened. "You asking me where I'm going?"

"I thought ye were going tae get a drink in the canteen?" Harris stopped abruptly forcing Preddy to do the same.

Preddy frowned and stared at him. "Look like de sun make you a get mad?"

"They have that guava and mango smoothie that ye like. Saw them delivering it earlier." Harris glanced at the watch on his peeling sunburned arm. "I reckon it will take ye at least fifteen minutes tae get yer drink and get back."

The two men stared at each other. A pair of luminous green eyes facing a pair of suspicious brown ones. Slowly, Preddy reached into his pocket and removed his wallet. He opened it and flicked at the cash studying the proud image of Nanny of The Maroons on a five hundred dollar note. "I'm going to be in de canteen for de next ten minutes, Detective Harris."

"Aye, Detective Preddy. The next ten minutes."

* * *

Exactly ten minutes later Preddy ran back up the stairs. The three members of his team were sitting together when he walked into their open-plan space. A silence he did not like hung over the usually noisy area. He studied them. Harris looked quietly calm leaning back in a chair with a sheaf of papers in his hands pretending to read, but Preddy's eyes momentarily caught his before he became so engrossed and he guessed the Scotsman had only just snatched up the bundle. Spence, completely still, concentrated keenly on her monitor. Rabino, not nearly as focused as the other two, glanced up from her paperwork for a split second to acknowledge him and then lowered her lashes again.

Preddy said, "So. Is dere anything about last night dat anybody needs to report?" Harris started to open his mouth but Preddy closed it for him. "Not you, Detective."

"I thought Detective Harris already gave the report, sir?" Rabino's face was blank as she chewed the top of her pen. "Sounded pretty good to me."

Preddy did not respond. His gaze was concentrated on the back of Spence's head. The heat of his glare compelled Spence to turn her chair to face him rather than be enveloped in the flames. Her expression was defiant. "Another version of de report is possible, sir. If you want dat one?"

Preddy shut his eyes briefly and counted to five. When it came to stakeouts sometimes the best laid plans went wrong. Sometimes situations like Norwood happened and you just had to deal with the unexpected. "No," he breathed as he opened them. "We'll stick to de one Brownlow is expecting." Preddy looked around the floor and spotted a spare chair near to another pod of detectives nestled in a far corner. Since learning that a detective was under investigation he had reduced his interaction with them considerably. The not knowing gnawed at him and he strode towards the men trying to avoid making eye contact with any of them.

Spence whispered, "Thanks, Detective Harris."

"It's naw as if Mr Collins has any brain cells tae damage anyway," murmured Harris.

Spence inclined her head graciously. "All de same, thanks."

"If ye think I've forgiven ye for the susumba surprise, yer wrong." His words came strongly, but a hint of a smile crossed his face.

Rabino coughed and jerked her head to indicate the rapid return of their leader.

Preddy rolled his chair towards them and sat down. "Okay, let's talk Oleta."

"She said she had an appointment in town centre and was on her way dere," explained Spence. "She asked if she could come in later. I told her it was to do wid Everton's murder and we needed her right now. She wanted to know if we had a breakthrough." She paused waiting for Preddy to speak, but when he did not she added, "I just said it was very important dat she come in."

"So she soon come?" asked Preddy.

"Yes, sir. She say by three o'clock."

CHAPTER 30

Preddy rose from behind his desk and shut off the sounds of nature CD as soon as Spence knocked on his office door. It could mean only one thing: Oleta had arrived. As the two detectives walked down the stairs towards an interview room, Preddy tried to put the Devil Head incident out of his mind. There were more important matters to preoccupy his thoughts than the whines of an injured murderer. Preddy glanced at Spence. "You ever get de feeling dat Oleta and Guthrie could be romantically involved?"

"No, sir." Spence shook her head. "She talks about her husband as if him was God Himself. I don't think dat lady has ever had eyes for any other man."

Preddy stared into the air. "Hmm, Guthrie is not just any other man though. Wonder if she would keep him secrets?"

"I never mention him name to her on de phone nor when she got here," said Spence. "She look well nervous though and went straight to de bathroom. Still, some people bladder full up when dem innocent just like if dem a hide something. I can't believe she would keep silent if Guthrie murdered her husband though. No doubt in my mind dat she love dat man to death."

As they entered the interview room Oleta jumped to her feet clutching her small leather handbag to her chest. She was dressed in a tailored grey skirt suit with her hair covered in a short neat black wig. She wore no make-up other than a hint of lip gloss. It was the first time Preddy had seen her dressed up and he silently admired the conservative business-like look.

"Detective Preddy, what's happened? You know who killed Everton?" Her words came blurting out as soon as she set eyes on him.

"Take a seat Mrs Wrenn, please," said Preddy gently, and waved his arm at her vacated chair. She slowly lowered herself down and sat perched on the edge. "Try to make yourself comfortable."

Oleta looked around the room. "You know, I've never been inside a police station before in my life," she declared. "Didn't know what to expect. Thought I might have to do fingerprints and a strip-search before I was allowed this far into the building." She gave an embarrassed laugh.

Preddy smiled at her. "No we wouldn't do dat to you here."

"Only to people under arrest or under suspicion of something," added Spence. "How are de kids doing? Shouldn't say kids — big man and woman — Martin and Maria?"

"They'll always be kids to me. They're fine, you know. I'm so proud of them. A tower of strength to me, both of them."

"I know de feeling," said Spence, giving her a broad smile. "Sometimes when I think about what going on in dis city, is only my kids keep me sane . . . even though dey also drive me insane."

Oleta chuckled and appeared to relax.

"I want to run a few things past you." Preddy leaned forward in his seat. "Sorry, dat I seem to have caught you heading somewhere?"

"Just into town, Detective, I'll still make it."

"You want a glass of water or something, Mrs Wrenn?" asked Spence.

"No, no." Oleta smiled. "Or I'll be back in your restroom again in two minutes. My system is not what it used to be at all."

Preddy decided to just go right in for it. "Mrs Wrenn, on de night your husband was murdered, did you see Judge Guthrie?"

Oleta's smile dissolved and her eyes flicked between the two detectives. "What do you mean?"

"I want you to think very carefully," said Preddy calmly. "Do you remember seeing him or hearing his voice at your house?"

Oleta squeezed her handbag so hard that her knuckles stood out. "I don't understand. Of course I didn't see Lawrence. I already told you that I saw and heard only Everton before I went to bed." She stared at Spence. "What's going on, Detective Spence? Do I need a lawyer?"

"You want one, Mrs Wrenn?" asked Spence politely. "You can get one if dat would make you feel more comfortable, but you're not being treated as a suspect."

Oleta's voice took on a curt tone. "I don't think I like your question, Detective Preddy. You asked me the same question before. Your inference is that I am a liar. Why on earth would I lie?"

"Actually, I was just wondering if you were mistaken," replied Preddy, studying her more closely. "Not calling you a liar. I never meant any disrespect."

Oleta seemed appeased. "Oh. Well, to answer your question . . . no, I did not see or hear Lawrence. He was not at my house that night, Detective. Lawrence would never murder Everton no matter what you might think. They were the very best of friends until the end." Her phone rang and she reached into her bag, glanced at the screen. "I have to be elsewhere, you know, so I hope this is not all about Lawrence?"

Preddy stayed on track. "I have good reason to believe dat dey argued dat afternoon. Did Everton mention it to you?"

"I don't know where you got that from, although I'm not saying they didn't argue." Oleta frowned. "Wouldn't be the first time they had a disagreement. Best friends do not agree on everything. They are work colleagues too and even work colleagues don't agree on everything. I'm sure that it's the same for you and Detective Spence?"

"Not to de point of strangulation, anyway," said Spence.

Oleta shook her head and tucked her bag handle under her chin. "Lawrence would never lay a finger on Everton. Whatever information you have is wrong. Somebody caught Everton on the verandah, murdered him, stole what they wanted and took off." Her voice rose. "You have plenty of ruthless criminals in St James to choose from, yet here you are focusing on an upstanding judge!"

"As I'm sure you understand we have to investigate all avenues to find who murdered your husband, Mrs Wrenn," said Preddy. "I'm sorry, we didn't intend to upset you wid de questions."

"Well, I am upset," she sniffed. "No wonder the Parish Court is shut. Watch and see if all of them don't shut down at this rate. Making a target out of the judges is a bad idea, Detective. Lawrence is not guilty." She got to her feet adjusting her jacket around her hips. "I think I've answered what you asked, detectives. If you need anything more, please call me."

Spence and Preddy rose too. "Thank you for your time, Mrs Wrenn," he said, and quickly moved to open the door. "We'll keep you informed."

"Thank you, Detective Preddy." Oleta bowed in his direction then turned to Spence. "I'll just use the restroom again before I go?"

"Sure," said Spence, smiling at her before leading the way. "I well want to go too."

Preddy leaned against the door and watched them walking down the corridor towards the restroom. A yellow 'cleaning in progress' sign barred their way, and a water-filled mop bucket was propped against the door as an extra warning to those who decided to ignore the sign.

"Lord man," grumbled Spence as she eyed the blockade. She beckoned to Oleta who followed closely behind her. "Come we go use de one downstairs."

"You sure we can't use this one?" asked Oleta.

Spence smiled encouragingly. "Is not far Mrs Wrenn, you'll make it. I promise!"

Preddy headed back to his office, closed the blinds, sank into his chair and switched on his soothing music. He reached for a pile of case papers on Judge Wrenn's murder and sat reading. An hour later he still had not changed his mind. His radar was firmly on Guthrie, regardless of Oleta's staunch defence of her husband's best friend. Maybe she really was unaware of what Lawrence Guthrie could do when he was not playing the legal nobleman act. Preddy began working on his report for Superintendent Brownlow. There was a knock at the door.

"Come in."

Detective Harris entered with a set expression that Preddy recognized immediately. "If you slam dat damn door, Detective, you and me will have a big problem," warned Preddy.

Harris inhaled and closed the door as quietly as his tense fingers would allow. "I tried tae let it go but I cannae. I'd like tae know why ye didnae feel the need tae tell me about the stolen gun? Even when I specifically asked ye, ye kept quiet?" Harris leaned against the wall and Preddy could tell that the Scotsman was trying to appear calm, but the tell-tale throbbing pink temples were a dead giveaway.

Preddy leaned back, clasped his hands together over his taut stomach and rested his elbows on his sides. "I already told you, de fewer people knew about it, de better."

"There was me thinking I was part of a team."

"Detective Harris, de gun is back, de murderer is in a cell. I'm de one who will face any consequences if de shit hits de fan," said Preddy roughly. "Is what do you?"

"What *do* me?" Harris's face had turned a darker shade of pink and a deep furrow was etched in his forehead. He appeared to be struggling to find the right words.

"Lord knows what you going do when you hear 'bout Kingston," said Preddy.

Harris was instantly alert. "What's in Kingston?"

"Let me see now: Devon House, Emancipation Park, Heroes Park, National Gallery, Bob Marley Museum, Peter Tosh Museum . . ."

"That's very funny, Detective Preddy."

"Tell me something, Detective Harris." Preddy sat forward. "Seems you want to pick and choose when you want to be part of de team?"

"Meaning?"

"Meaning, you never even show up at de regatta. Had way more important things to do, eeh? De rest of us were dere working together. Where were you?"

"As I told ye, I had a prior engagement."

"What? Refereeing de kids football game, really?"

Harris bit his lip. "Look, we have tae move forward, Preddy, agreed?"

"Doesn't seem like we're at a standstill to me," replied Preddy. He reached for his draft report and waved it in the air. "When I've finished writing my bit you can add yours to it, den I'll get it typed." The Glaswegian stared darkly at Preddy, who maintained his authoritative demeanour. "We'll be right where you told de Super we already are — on de same page."

Harris shook his head and reached for the door handle and opened the door before pausing. "Somebody else may have told the Super something else. Oleta Wrenn? I wouldnae be surprised if she hasnae lodged a complaint."

Preddy raised an eyebrow. "She seemed a bit put out, but I don't think she'll be complaining."

"Well she's lurking downstairs. I just thought maybe she'd made a complaint tae Brownlow or something. She looked a bit flustered."

"She left here ages ago. I doubt you would've seen her."

"Naw?" Harris spun around. "I'm naw blind, Preddy. Grey suit, cropped black hair. Walked past her in the front driveway."

Preddy started writing. "Well, she never made any complaints, or Super would have been in here already giving me what for."

Harris narrowed his eyes. "Guess we better be prepared tae stand together if anything does come of it."

"I agree." Preddy refused to look up at him. "Good afternoon, Detective Harris."

As the door closed, Preddy put down his pen and studied the peeling ceiling immediately above his head. He hoped he did not come to regret allowing the foreigner to interfere with the dynamics of his team, even if it had been in defence of Spence and Rabino. Preddy had concluded that the Scotsman had not lied when he said he was not investigating the women. There was no way Harris would have compromised the integrity of his secret investigation by intervening in Devil Head's arrest if he was trying to get dirt on Spence or Rabino.

The detective glanced at his watch. He did not want to see anyone, speak to anyone, sort out anyone's doubts or concerns and certainly did not want to listen to anyone's complaints, even the widow Wrenn. He would give it another hour then head home where there was no one to knock on his door, question his methods or set his nerves on edge.

CHAPTER 31

Friday, 12 May, 9.13 a.m.

Preddy stood at the whiteboard and looked around at the team who sat drinking steaming cups of coffee. The lower case spelling of Lawrence Guthrie's name had been rubbed out and replaced with large capital letters at the top of the board.

"If we believe Stephan Channer, den Judge Wrenn was murdered after midnight, not before," said Preddy. "Lawrence Guthrie swears he was in bed wid a book."

"When you've got motive and opportunity 'in bed with a book' sure fails as an alibi," suggested Rabino. "Having his career ruined, or thinking Judge Wrenn ruined his career is a definite motive." She read from a reference page that Preddy had shared with them. "I mean 'unfit to assume higher office' is a pretty harsh indictment from his best friend."

Harris stared at Preddy. "I would have liked tae have spoken tae this Alrick Douglass lad, maself."

"You may yet get de chance," replied Preddy. "He may eventually be called as a witness."

Spence piped up. "If you going back to Kingston me a come too, sir. Long time I want to go sit inna Heroes Park wid de butterflies and chill."

"Sounds ideal," said Rabino. "I'll come too and do a picnic." She placed the page on the desk in front of her. "So, Guthrie put down his book — too angry to read — climbed down the Ambassador West's fire escape and went and did the deed?"

"Works for me," said Preddy nodding. "Nathaniel Mexell thinks he saw a boat behind him dat night. Guthrie could have been on dat boat. Oleta seems to have a soft spot for Guthrie even if it isn't romantic. I'm not so sure dat Oleta didn't see him, despite what she says."

"Och, so the Oleta that saw Guthrie is the same Oleta that I didnae see?"

Rabino cast a confused glance at Harris. "Huh?"

"Never mind," muttered Harris.

Rabino scrolled along the photos on her camera album. "Ah, that's it . . . *The Falcon*. The boat Guthrie was in on Saturday."

"Yes, dat's de name I was trying to remember," said Spence. "Tiny boat, just big enough for him and him lady-love."

Harris took the camera and glanced at the photo before handing it back to Rabino. "We'll have tae try and locate it."

"Dere weren't any photos of boats in his courtroom chambers." Preddy wrote the name of the boat next to Guthrie's. "He probably hired it to show off for de day. If we can trace de owner we can find out if he rented it to Guthrie on Monday."

"Yes, sir," agreed Rabino.

"We have to speak to every homeowner de whole length of de coastline: from Lime Ridge, through Wynterton Park to de Doubloons," ordered Preddy. "See if anybody saw him. De judge will never admit to anything. We have to get him."

Harris ran thin fingers through his ginger locks and spoke emphatically. "Lawrence Guthrie is over sixty years old. I just cannae see him climbing down a fire escape in the middle of the night tae go strangle somebody . . . his best friend no less. Seems too much like hard work tae me."

Preddy stared at him. "I don't plan to be bedridden when I'm sixty, Detective. In fact, I intend to run a few marathons and spend way less time at my desk if I'm still on de job."

Harris remained unconvinced. "Surely Guthrie could have found an easier way?"

Rabino threw a sarcastic look in his direction. "Judge Guthrie could hardly suggest to Judge Wrenn that they go for a walk and slide a blade under his ribs could he? That would definitely be easier than hunting him down in the night."

Spence gestured her agreement. "When people vex dem no have time to think 'bout easier way and harder way to murder. Dem just murder."

"I just hope we're naw missing the bigger picture here. Let's naw rule out the others with motive yet."

Preddy folded his arms across his chest. "It's Channer you want isn't it?" he asked. "Channer and Mexell? Den bring me something dat makes more sense dan de explanation we already got from dem."

"I'll do ma best."

Preddy turned to Spence and Rabino. "In de meantime, go after de boat. I need to go down to de courthouse."

"Courthouse lock, sir," said Spence, getting to her feet.

Preddy frowned. "Lock up, completely?"

"Yes, sir. From yesterday dem swear say dem not working today unless every employee get police protection."

Rabino shook her head. "Boy, they're not asking for much then?"

Spence kissed her teeth. "And me sure know when dem sign up for court job de benefits never include each person getting a private bodyguard. No courthouse in de world provides dat."

"Detective Harris, you're wid me," said Preddy. He would not leave Harris to sneak off anywhere. Everybody in officialdom jumped to attention for foreigners. The judges in particular would not be immune to the presence of a white saviour.

Harris rose and stared at their leader. "I'm with ye."

* * *

As the two men headed out to the car park Preddy made a phone call and turned on the loud speaker so that Harris could hear. Judge Bailey answered the phone just when Preddy thought his call was being ignored.

"Yes, Detective Preddy?" The judge sounded curt and his voice came over quite loudly. "I recognized your number. Something tells me I should hang up."

"No, please don't do dat, sir." Preddy spoke humbly. "I need to ask you for a favour. Dat is, Detective Harris and I need to ask you for a favour."

Harris stood at Preddy's elbow listening. There was silence at the other end for a few seconds, before Judge Bailey said, "Going after judges like Guthrie instead of going after criminals that are ruining this parish, I'm not so sure I should be doing any of you any favours."

"Den do it, for Judge Wrenn," said Preddy. "I'm begging you on his behalf." More silence. Preddy was sure the judge had gone. He could hear the faint sound of instrumental music in the background and imagined the judge reclining on a sofa. "Judge Bailey?"

Preddy handed the phone to Harris who quickly put it to his ear. "Judge Bailey? Please talk tae me, sir."

"Hello Detective Harris." The voice instantly lost its aggression.

"We're relying on ye tae help us solve Judge Wrenn's murder, sir. Believe me we wouldnae do this unless it was absolutely necessary. Will ye help us?"

"Tell me what you need, Detective Harris."

"We need full access tae the court chambers ye share with Lawrence Guthrie. I understand the place is locked up, but we do need tae get inside."

When they had finished speaking and hung up their respective phones, Judge Bailey stared at his. Yes, he wanted to help the detectives with their enquiries into the murder of his deceased colleague, but he also owed a duty to his living colleagues. Judge Bailey picked up the phone again and made two calls.

* * *

295

Preddy spotted the court clerk as he parked in the almost empty car park of St James Parish court. She was dressed in jeans and T-shirt, but he had seen this woman before and her features were unmistakable. There was an eerie feel to the court area, almost as if it was a Sunday or a public holiday. Fridays were never usually like this. No cars, no crowds, no social conversations, just a lonely newspaper vendor who had dragged her stand in front of the post office in search of customers. Preddy appreciated being able to exit his vehicle without brushing the door of another one. Harris climbed out of the passenger side door.

"This way, sir." The clerk looked directly at Harris, after giving Preddy a hostile glance.

"Thank ye very much, Ma'am." Harris gave her a bright smile.

Preddy did not react to the hostility knowing that Guthrie would have wasted no time in stirring up the staff to believe that he was being unfairly targeted by Pelican Walk officers. Now the staff could feel justified taking out their grouses which should be more properly directed at the Minster of Justice; the man with the power and money to improve their working conditions. This woman was no doubt one of them that clerk Ivy Dixon had tried to convince to get on board with the police, without success. She spoke to the sole security guard who glanced at the two detectives with open resentment. The guard unlocked the padlock and rolled the steel sheet shutters up. The detectives followed quickly behind the clerk, up the stairs and down the corridor towards the chambers shared by Judge Bailey and Judge Guthrie. Preddy was a few paces behind them when he heard a distinctive voice. He looked at Harris who had heard it too.

"Ye have got tae be kidding me," Harris mumbled and paused mid-flight. He pressed his nose against the glass window and looked below. Judge Guthrie stood gesticulating at the security guard, clearly admonishing him.

"Shit!" said Preddy.

"Go on," urged Harris. "I'll try tae delay him."

The clerk unlocked the door to the shared room and stood back as Preddy pushed past her. She stared daggers into his back. "Excuse me, Detective!"

With a few strides Preddy was at Judge Guthrie's desk. He opened drawers and shuffled through them. He flicked through papers in the judge's filing tray. A glass jar with coins sat beside it. Preddy held the jar towards the light and shook it, examining the pieces as they moved around. They were all modern coins.

The clerk watched nervously. "Detective, you sure Judge Bailey said you could do that?"

"Close de door," ordered Preddy. "Now!"

The woman did as she was told and stood inside of the room watching the detective. Outside Preddy could hear the approaching voices of Judge Guthrie and Detective Harris. He lifted up a desk blotter which was not sitting firmly on the desk. Underneath were a few loose pieces of paper. The voices were now outside of the door.

"Get out of my way, Detective Harris!" snapped Judge Guthrie. "You have no right to be in here."

"We have Judge Bailey's express permission tae be here."

The door began to open and the clerk hastily moved away from it. Judge Guthrie was clad in Hawaiian shirt and long white shorts. On his feet were flat canvas pumps. He looked for all the world like an American tourist. His hazel eyes blazed as he glared at Preddy. Swiftly he moved towards him and made to snatch the papers, but Preddy held them high over his head.

"Give me my documents and get out, officer!" shouted the judge. "Who the hell do you think you are?"

"A detective, trying to get to de truth of a murder," replied Preddy calmly. "And in my right hand I'm holding de motive for murder."

Judge Guthrie stretched towards Preddy again. Harris said, "I wouldnae do that if I were ye, sir. Ye can get charged with obstruction or assaulting an officer."

Judge Guthrie stepped back. "I see. Fake charges? That's the plan is it?"

"You alright, sir?" asked the clerk anxiously.

Judge Guthrie rounded on her. "Why did you let them in here?"

The woman shrank back against the wall. "Judge Bailey said I should, sir! Said I should give them whatever access they need until he comes. He's on his way!"

"That old fool Bailey! I told him that I didn't want anybody in here," cursed Guthrie. He perched on Judge Bailey's desk opposite Preddy, hands on his knees. "I don't know what you think those will prove."

"Dey will prove what I had already been told. Dey will prove what Alrick Douglass will say in court. Dat he gave you dese papers." Preddy shuffled through them. "Your numerous applications. Judge Wrenn's many references. None to your liking."

Judge Guthrie smiled in a way which disturbed Preddy. His eyes began to sparkle as if someone had shared a good joke. "So I knew that Everton Wrenn was providing poor references. Will Mr Douglass say that I was visibly upset? That I flew into a rage? That I shouted and banged my fists on the table?" The smile grew sinister, as he waited for Preddy to respond. "Well, Detective?"

Preddy glanced at Harris and whispered, "Maybe our psychopaths are not so different from yours, after all."

"I'll say." Harris turned his attention to the judge. "Why did ye do it?"

"What was that, Detective Harris?" Judge Guthrie leaned forward and cupped his ear. "You are becoming a true lazy Jamaican detective. Zero evidence. Let's grab the first person we can get."

"Compliments like those will naw help ye."

"Tell us about Everton Wrenn," urged Preddy. "Tell us what happened dat night."

Guthrie chuckled. "I'm not going to answer any questions. If you want to charge me with reading my own personnel files then do so, although I'm pretty sure it's not a crime. Alrick Douglass might have committed some unforgivable sin as far as his employers are concerned, but I have not. Never paid a bribe, never paid for him to come to Mo Bay. Hell, never even bought Alrick a meal or a drink. Everton did."

"You think you're so smart," rasped Preddy. "One way or de other you are going down."

Judge Guthrie wagged a finger at Preddy. "No, I am not, Detective. That is not how the justice system works. That is how you would like it to work. That is why INDECOM will always be riding your back." He glanced provocatively at Harris. "Tell him, Detective Harris. Tell him what happens in Glasgow. You get evidence, you charge someone, there is a trial. That is how the justice system works in Scotland as well as out here, am I right?"

Harris stared at him with disdain. "Ye murdered yer own friend, and ye have naw remorse. This is just a joke tae ye."

"I can assure you it is not a joke," said Guthrie. "I preside in court every day, weighing up evidence, deciding who should win and who should lose. I never make judgments based on what I think happened. Whatever evidence is put before me — that's what I use."

The door opened and Judge Bailey stepped in followed by a breathless security guard. Judge Bailey looked at Judge Guthrie in some alarm. "Everything alright, Lawrence?"

"Yes, man! The detectives have what they want and they're just leaving." Guthrie walked towards Bailey and gave him a light pat on the shoulder. Not a trace of fury or animosity was evident in his voice. "It's fine, man. You did the right thing."

Judge Bailey seemed surprised at his colleague's demeanour. "You know they're convinced you're involved in Everton's murder, right?"

"Me and half dozen other persons. Don't worry about it. I'm not." Guthrie waved a hand dismissively. "Now, if there's nothing else, detectives, I really must get back to my sailing. It's so nice to have a break from court to do nothing for a while. All courtesy of the bungling JCF."

Judge Bailey looked sheepish. "Come on, Lawrence. It's not the police that caused this. Everton's death was the catalyst. Look from when we've been waiting on the Justice Ministry to implement salary increases and pay allowances. You and I know this is just an excuse to force an issue the government has been ignoring for years."

Guthrie bobbed his head from side to side and smiled. "I won't agree or disagree."

"What are those?" asked Judge Bailey staring at Preddy's hands.

Guthrie followed his gaze. "Just some papers, job applications and references that were submitted to the Judicial Services Commission," he replied. "You're welcome to them as I say, detectives. Our clerk will show you out if you can't find your way."

Preddy beckoned to Harris and the two men left the judges' chambers. Guthrie was not a man to be easily broken. Superintendent Brownlow and Commissioner Davis would be incensed if the detectives dragged the judge into the police station and they were in no position to charge him. Inside his car, Preddy gunned the engine and drove furiously back towards Pelican Walk.

"Steady on!" warned Harris. "And ye complain about ma driving!"

"Sorry, man," breathed Preddy. "Damn!" He banged the steering wheel.

"Definitely a psychopath," said Harris. "What the hell has he got tae laugh about?"

"He's right though, and he knows it. De evidence is circumstantial," said Preddy. "If we could find him wid Judge Wrenn's phone or his coins or his ashtray."

"The phone he was never going tae keep, naw matter how crazy he is," said Harris. "It's probably at the bottom of the sea. The coins and the ashtray he might hang on tae."

"And where do we find dem?" Preddy groaned. "I really hope Rabino and Spence are having better luck."

CHAPTER 32

Rabino and Spence spent hours under the blazing sun walking the coastline while dousing their parched throats with bottles of ice water. Eventually they located a boatyard where they discovered the owner of the *Falcoln*. Following a short conversation with the man, Rabino phoned Preddy and waited impatiently for him to answer the phone. He was with Harris interviewing boat owners further along the waterfront, but she could not see them from her location.

"We've confirmed it, sir," she said when he finally answered. "Lawrence Guthrie did have the *Falcoln* on that Monday night."

"Nice." Preddy gave Harris the thumbs up sign.

"Finally," mumbled Harris as he wiped his wet brow.

Preddy pressed the phone closer to his ear and listened.

"Guthrie didn't have permission, but apparently he's done it before, just taken the boat without asking," explained Rabino. "When it's brought up with him he always pays. Never argues."

Preddy frowned. "So de owner didn't see him take it?"

301

"That's right sir. Said he thought about reporting it stolen, until he checked with Guthrie who admitted to having it. Brought it right back and paid up. That's why he allowed him to rent it again for the regatta."

"Guthrie could have hidden a few stolen items on dere," mused Preddy. "A warrant going take too long. We need to get on dat boat right now."

Rabino hesitated before saying, "Er, slight problem there, sir."

The line sounded fuzzy and Preddy moved the phone to his other ear. "Oh, what happen?"

"Guthrie's got it. He's apparently somewhere near Pier One restaurant. Or at least that's where he told the owner he'd be going."

"Ah, he did say we had interrupted his sailing." Preddy felt a surge of adrenalin course through his body. He snapped his fingers in Harris's direction. "Okay, we're closer to Pier One dan you. We'll get on it. Ask de owner for permission to board de boat."

"What is it?" asked Harris as he adjusted his shades.

Preddy covered the speaker on his phone while waiting for Rabino to return. "We're going down to Pier One. Dat's where Guthrie is, on the *Falcon*." Preddy could hear loud voices through the phone, one of which definitely belonged to Spence, but he could not decipher what was being said. Eventually Rabino came back on the line and he could detect laughter in her voice.

"We have his permission to board. Go ahead, sir," she said.

Preddy was curious. "What was dat noise about?"

"Oh, I just asked him if we could board the *Falcoln* and search it. He said he wasn't sure that he wanted any police on his boat." Rabino paused and chuckled. "Detective Spence asked him if he was sure he renewed his boatyard licence. He said we can search the boat and even take it from Guthrie if we want to!"

Preddy smiled. "Okay, thanks. We'll take it from here."

Preddy hung up and headed towards the police jeep with Harris in tow. "Guthrie is sailing down by Pier One. We going get him off dat boat and search it. And we going bring him in to Pelican Walk."

Harris's eyes widened. His face was too red from the morning's sun damage to grow any redder. "Have ye lost yer mind, Preddy? I thought we already agreed we still didnae have enough tae nail him?"

"Nothing concrete," conceded Preddy, the superintendent's warning still ringing in his ears. He turned the vehicle onto the main road and stepped on the accelerator. "He was on dat boat on Monday night. Whether or not we find anything on de boat, I intend to throw him in an interview room and question him."

Harris glared at him, his temples pulsating. "Ye sure ye know what yer doing, Preddy?"

"We have to bring him in," insisted Preddy.

"Without a fucking warrant?"

"Without a fucking warrant or a normal warrant." Preddy refused to let his mind go anywhere beyond his goal. "Look, of course I'd love physical evidence. If we can get it, great. If not, dere are lots of circumstantial matters connecting Guthrie and I want him to clear dem up once and for all."

"And if he doesnae? What do ye think the Commissioner will do tae ye?" asked Harris in frustration. "If we drag him back tae Pelican Walk, find out that he's naw going tae admit tae anything and there's nothing we can stick on him, then what?"

Preddy crunched loudly on a mint. "Den I guess I'll be retiring to de cool hills of Mandeville wid my humble pension." He reached for his phone and dialled the marine police. He was too engrossed in his urgent conversation to notice that Harris was fidgeting uncomfortably.

"So we're going on the water, are we?" asked Harris. His voice came at a slightly higher pitch, which went completely undetected by his colleague.

"Yes. Let's pick him up!"

* * *

303

Pier One was a popular open-air seafood restaurant and bar located on a rocky outcrop on the downtown Montego Bay waterfront. Conveniently placed, it was far enough from the bustling town centre to make dining there a serene pleasure. A long pier at the end of the dining area extended out to sea harbouring many sleek yachts. The detectives were met by an earnest waitress waving a menu at them as they entered.

Preddy walked briskly past her, flashing his badge. "Police business."

Harris did the same giving her an apologetic smile. "Another time maybe, Miss."

They strode through the busy bar area where some patrons were perched on stools watching flatscreen TVs while others watched the barman expertly mixing unique cocktails. Tables spread with blue cotton tablecloths were occupied by diners seated on expensive wicker chairs. Tourists and locals of all colours were present their varied accents carrying in the light sea breeze. They concentrated on the aromatic plates of spicy whole fish and steaks in front of them. Occasionally they raised their heads to gaze at the passing boats. One or two glanced at the lawmen, but were too absorbed in their meals to notice anything untoward.

As Preddy strode down the pier, he swiftly assessed that the *Falcoln* was not there. He trained his binoculars on the sea and waved at the approaching marine police vessel. Soon the two officers were boarded and setting out to sea at a gentle pace. Harris steadied himself and swept the sea with his own binoculars. Eventually he spotted Guthrie at a distance.

"He's certainly making good use of his time off," murmured the Scotsman.

"Judge Guthrie!" shouted Preddy.

"Judge Guthrie!" called Harris. "A word please!"

The loud sound which pierced the air was the clear throttle of the Falcoln's engine as the boat gathered momentum.

"He's seen us," said Preddy. "Not interested in a chat. Follow him officer."

The captain nodded and turned the boat after Guthrie. As the police vessel moved from leisurely to gliding over the water at pace, Harris sank into a seat.

"Him not speeding, but him not going stop either." Preddy squinted at Guthrie's solid frame. "Dis man is strange. Is like him enjoy provoking people."

"Guess he doesnae have much fun in court so he gets his kicks where he can," replied Harris faintly. He lowered his binoculars and grasped the rail. "Besides he's still naw doubt annoyed at our wee confrontation. When it comes tae police, I dinnae think he's the forgiving type."

"Judge Guthrie!" Preddy waved his hands in the air as their vessel drew closer. "Stop! We need to talk to you right now!"

Judge Guthrie waved back blithely. "Thought you said everything you wanted to say earlier? You've lost your chance, Detective."

"It won't take long," lied Preddy. "We need to come aboard."

"I'm betting you don't have a warrant!" Guthrie bellowed. "You are not coming aboard this boat! Enough of your harassment, Detective Preddy. And you, Detective Harris, should know better. We are done talking."

Harris felt his stomach churning. He took a deep breath and tried to shake off the nausea. "We have reasonable cause tae believe ye can assist us with the murder of Judge Everton Wrenn," shouted Harris. "We have the owner's permission tae board that boat."

Suddenly the *Falcon* began to increase speed leaping across the water as it headed out to sea. The judge's cotton shirt billowed behind him as he moved further away.

"Ye have got tae be kidding me," breathed Harris.

"Stay wid him," ordered Preddy, gesticulating at the captain. "Don't let him get 'way."

Their captain obeyed and went after Guthrie who began showing off his nautical ability twisting and turning, manoeuvring the vessel in tight figures of eight. White swirls of foamy water were thrown up into the air. Harris doubled over and took deep breaths, while keeping his eyes firmly on the deck beneath his feet. Guthrie laughed loudly and waved at them, slowing down and speeding up again just as they caught up to him. Then it was as if the judge grew tired of his little game. He brought the boat to an almost complete standstill in the vast openness of the water and turned it to face the police craft. There was a slight collision as the police helmsman reacted slowly to the target boat's sudden swing.

"Careful now, this boat isn't mine and it's expensive." Lawrence Guthrie grinned displaying his white teeth. "Phew! Haven't had so much fun in years. That wasn't so bad, was it, Detective Preddy? Better than being in a stuffy old court house all day. We should do this more often."

Harris struggled to his feet and stared at Guthrie. "It was ye, wasnae it? Ye did it."

"No, I already told you. I did not murder Everton Wrenn."

"Ye called in the bomb hoax. Ye did it," murmured Harris. "Just tae relieve yer boredom."

"Ah that?" Guthrie's eyes twinkled. "Now why would you accuse me of such a thing, Detective Harris? And without even one iota of proof. You must admit it did indeed relieve the boredom though, whoever did it. People really should stop changing their smelly shoes in the court house and the security personnel should be more alert about what bags people enter with and what they leave with." He paused to glance at Preddy. "Wouldn't you agree, Detective?"

Preddy stared at Judge Guthrie wondering who the man really was. "You must outta your mind to do something like dat," said Preddy shaking his head. "Something badly wrong wid you."

"No, I'm fine." Guthrie inhaled a lung full of sea air and smiled appreciatively. "It's not as if you can shoot me is it, Detective Preddy? Then you really would have an issue with the justice minister, with the national security minister, with the public. They haven't forgotten the Norwood murders even if you conveniently have. You found an excuse for that, but you wouldn't have one for this."

Preddy gritted his teeth determined not to be drawn by the taunts. "We need to talk, Judge Guthrie."

Guthrie stood on tiptoes and peered into the police vessel. "Oh dear. You alright there, Detective Harris?"

Preddy continued to stare at the judge. "We're coming on board."

The judge shook his head, his expression one of polite regret. "You're not welcome aboard," he replied. "Five minutes to the shore, no more. I'll meet you there, detective."

Before Preddy could reply the judge had set off again making a beeline for the shore. As the police vessel followed behind Preddy kept his binoculars firmly trained on Guthrie. "Well, dere's no sign he's throwing any evidence overboard," he mumbled. "His hands are on de wheel."

Soon the boats were docked side by side at the mooring at Pier One. Preddy stepped from the boat easily. Judge Guthrie stood with his arms folded leaning against an iron bollard watching them.

"Your colleague looks like he needs a little help, Detective Preddy."

Preddy glanced at Harris, and cursed under his breath. Harris was sat doubled over, head close to his knees. Preddy wondered if Harris was up to one of his tricks and what this latest performance could possibly be in aid of. If the Glaswegian was trying to create a diversion he should have at least given an indication beforehand.

"What do you?" hissed Preddy.

"I'm fine," grunted Harris. He rose slowly trying not to look at the rippling sea.

"Try him with some Scotch malt whisky," suggested Guthrie failing to sound genuinely concerned. "I doubt if he can handle our Wray & Nephew whites."

Harris straightened up with some difficulty and climbed out under his own stream. He blinked twice and fought to steady himself. "Lawrence Guthrie . . ." he managed, before

307

swaying. Preddy barely managed to grab his elbow and stop him from falling.

"Ah, poor Detective Harris, you sound like a drunken sailor." Guthrie was enjoying the Scotsman's discomfort. "Not a fan of the sea then? I wondered why you didn't join us all for our lovely day at the regatta."

Realisation finally dawned on Preddy as he studied the foreigner whose colouring had changed from deep pink to slightly green. This was not a performance after all. Harris lurched forward and his stomach contents hit the sea just missing the police boat. Using both hands Harris propped himself up against the mooring bollard.

"There, well done, Detective Harris." Guthrie clapped his firm hands in mockery. "That was a sterling effort. Exactly what I would expect of a fine Scotsman. You're a credit to your country of birth."

"Enough of ye bullshit," whispered Harris. He inhaled deeply and exhaled slowly.

"That's not very detective-like talk," Guthrie tutted as he continued to smile.

Preddy turned to face the judge. "Lawrence Guthrie, you are under arrest for de murder of Everton Wrenn. You do not have to say anything, but anything you do say may be used in evidence against you. Do you understand your rights?"

"Yes, I certainly do. I was nowhere near Wynterton Park and I didn't kill Everton Wrenn as I've told you before." He glanced from Preddy to Harris and back. "That said, I did the one thing that would hurt Everton, cut him to the very soul, without inflicting any physical injury at all."

The detectives stared at him and waited. Guthrie looked straight at Preddy. "Do you remember those photos you were admiring in my chambers, Detective? You suggested they were my kids and I didn't contradict you?" He shuffled through the photo gallery in his phone camera and held the screen out to Preddy.

"I remember," said Preddy, with a swift glance at the youngsters' smiling faces.

"Only one of them is mine. The girl, Elise. The two boys are my Godsons."

"That's all very nice," said Harris, who had begun to breathe more easily. "We dinnae want tae see yer damn happy family."

"Ah, don't be so disagreeable, Detective Harris," said Guthrie pleasantly. "Look at this one." He scrolled again and waved another picture at them.

Preddy looked at it before handing it to Harris. It showed Oleta with her hand around her husband's shoulders, standing next to Guthrie with the two boys and girl kneeling in front of them.

"What is dis supposed to be?" asked Preddy.

"I showed Oleta that photo. She remembers us taking it. We had a great day on the beach — New Year's Eve." Guthrie's eyes narrowed. "I finally told her the truth. Poor woman. Those boys — they're ten and twelve, by the way — they're not my sons."

Preddy flinched inwardly. Harris stared at the screen again before handing the phone back to Guthrie.

"Yes, detectives. They belong to her wonderful husband."

"Everton Wrenn has two illegitimate children?" stated Harris.

Guthrie nodded. "Only he and I, and the mother of his children knew about it. The two boys don't know who their father is. Their mother just told them it was a man who left her for someone else. Swore she would never tell them the truth. It was our secret and I kept it for years. Would have taken it to my grave." His voice went from sugar sweet to bitter. "When I found out Everton was blocking my career — back-stabbing dog that he is — I wasn't going to keep his secret any longer. I was going to make sure he knew the pain I felt, the pain of betrayal by that person you most expect to have your back."

"Rass," breathed Preddy as his throat constricted. "Oleta."

Guthrie held up his palms. "Hey, wait now, Detective. She's had to put up with a lot from Everton over the years, but she's a kind trusting soul."

"Put up wid a lot of what?" asked Preddy.

"Ah, you must know how it is, Detective?" Guthrie gave him a conspiratorial wink. "Overnight training courses, conferences, workshops, whatever excuse was needed."

"Ye knew that Oleta had marital problems and ye said nothing?" said Harris glaring at the judge.

"I'm not necessarily making a connection between what she heard and what she did," said Guthrie lightly. "That's one for you."

"Ye told her all this, when?" asked Harris.

"Same day, Monday."

"You went to Wynterton Park dat afternoon?" asked Preddy. "After de Mosino lunch?"

"No, no. I sent her the picture by phone with a message. You'll see it on her phone . . . if she lets you touch her phone." He paused and waved a finger at Preddy as one would a naughty child. "Anyway, I told her to call me to discuss something she needed to know. She called me back almost instantly. Must have been around five o'clock that afternoon." He stared off into the distance, deep in thought. "She didn't believe me at first. Then I told her the children's birth dates and asked her to cast her mind back all those years ago to where Everton supposedly was on those dates. One of them was born on Christmas Eve. The other shares a birthday with The Honourable Louise Bennett. 7th September. Oleta cried down the phone. She cried a lot, so much so I wished I could hug her. And she shouted. Never heard Oleta shout before. Didn't even know she could."

"When you say dat photo was taken?" asked Preddy.

"Five months ago, New Years."

Preddy stared off at the sea, watching the distant catamarans. The widow Wrenn had lied to them about many things. She had kept up the facade yesterday as she sat with them at Pelican Walk. "Send dose photos to me," he demanded.

"Of course, Detective. Always happy to help," said Guthrie. "Oh and don't bother to check my phone number. I have more than one phone."

Preddy shook his head. As much as he would have loved to nail Lawrence Guthrie for something he could not. The man did not throw any stolen goods into the sea because he had none. He did not kill Everton Wrenn. Preddy's mind raced as he turned to Harris. "You *did* see Oleta Wrenn yesterday afternoon!"

Harris stood as straight as he could muster. "I said I did, and I wasnae mistaken. What is it?"

Preddy spun around to Guthrie. "Why you never talk before? You knew Oleta had a motive for murder and you never say a word."

Judge Guthrie remained calm. "You call it a motive for murder. As I've said to you before, lots of people have motives. It doesn't make them killers. Let me see now, I have a good motive according to you. Nathaniel Mexell has a motive too. Tuffy Frazer, Devil Head Collins, and their murdering crew have plenty of motives." He pretended to think. "Who else now?"

"Ye know I've met some lawyers who are right dicks, but ye take the biscuit." Harris's temples throbbed as his face slowly regained its natural pinkness. "Did Oleta Wrenn confess anything tae ye?"

"Not a thing, Detective Harris." There was a distinct sneer, bordering on contempt, in his tone. "You must know I would immediately tell you?"

"Let him be," said Preddy as he turned away from the judge. "We need to go find de widow." Harris stumbled along behind him.

"Oh, detectives?" called Guthrie after them. "Aren't you forgetting something?"

"To shoot your rass and fling you into de sea?" said Preddy.

"No." The judge smiled. "Am I . . . *de*-arrested?"

"Ye're *de* worst judge on *de* island," snapped Harris in Patois as he shuffled away. He tried to move quickly towards the car, but his legs wobbled as he went.

"You'll be a Master of Patois by year end." Preddy grasped Harris's shoulder and helped him along. This time

311

they were watched by curious diners as they passed through the restaurant. "You know, Super already believe dat you not well?"

Harris gave him a weak glance. "Come again?"

"Seriously. Dat little show of yours in de canteen de other day? After de Susumba Surprise? Well, Super has heard about it."

"Och!" Harris dabbed at his sweating forehead. "Well, there isnae anything for him tae worry about on that front."

"Dat's what I told him. Seemed a bit reluctant to let it go. Didn't really put him at ease at all." Preddy pursed his lips. "Might be time for you to take a break from dis hard work."

"He said that?" asked Harris breathing rapidly.

"Him worried dat you'll drop a ground at one of him party . . . in front of de Security Minister, no less." Preddy smiled broadly at the invalid.

Harris's stunned look began to fade and his lips curled slightly upwards. "Aw shit, guess I've gone and overdone it."

"Make sure you don't try out your Oscar skills wid de uptown crowd. Super will ban you from attending all parties."

"So, that's how tae get out of those things?" murmured Harris.

The police vehicle was now in sight. It seemed to be much further away than Preddy remembered parking it.

"Thought you'd gone to some big brunch one of de high command had laid on, instead of coming to de regatta. Dey like to have socials on Friday or Saturday at least once a month."

"I did ref the kids match and they were terrible." Harris managed a smile. "In the afternoon I went for a long walk around ma neighbourhood meeting the locals, checking out some properties for sale. Kathryn had given me a few real estate brochures so I thought I might as well go look at the properties."

"Dat would be Cinnamon Hill? Nice locals to meet. Nice monied locals, mainly expats." Preddy absorbed the information with no outward emotion, although again the idea that Rabino and Harris might be closer than he thought did run through his mind. He had never heard Harris refer to Rabino by her first name before, but now was not the time to probe. "So, you can't manage de Caribbean Sea?"

"Listen, I absolutely love the sea, believe me," said Harris. "Beautiful tae look at, great tae swim in."

"Why you didn't say something?" Preddy probed in a sympathetic tone.

"Guess I could have. Stubborn, I guess." Harris smiled and his cheeks dimpled. "I would have if I thought ye'd be at home sticking needles intae ma voodoo doll for naw turning up."

"No one use needles and dolls here, man." Preddy grinned and used the remote to open the car doors. "Here — we do obeah."

"Well, please can ye do neither."

"It's a deal." said Preddy. "I need to think. You can drive?"

"Probably, but I'm naw so sure we'll get tae where ye want tae go."

"You'll manage," said Preddy helping him in through the driver's door. "I have every confidence in you. Dere are no potholes on dis route. Head for base."

Harris carefully settled his frame on the driver's seat. "Back tae Pelican Walk, naw tae Wynterton Park?"

"Pelican Walk," repeated Preddy, fumbling for a mint sweet. "Here, it will help settle you stomach."

Harris caught the mint and started the engine.

Even in his shaky state Harris made short work of the main road. Preddy phoned Detective Spence on the way. "You and Rabino need to find Oleta Wrenn. Arrest her. I don't care if she's in her bath, arrest her and bring her in."

"Yes, sir!" said Spence. "But on what charge?"

"Murder. De murder of Everton Wrenn."

"Jesas Chrise!" There was a muffled conversation in the background and Preddy knew Spence was speaking to Rabino. "We'll head to Wynterton Park, sir, and see if she or her kids are dere."

"Where are you now?" asked Preddy.

"We just got back to de station, sir," replied Spence. "We'll just grab some box juice and turn right around again."

"No, don't!" said Preddy. "Wait."

Spence's voice reflected the confusion she felt. "Wait? You sure sir."

Preddy's mind ticked rapidly. Some things that had confused him were finally making sense. "Positive. Detective Harris and I will be dere in ten minutes. I need you ladies to accompany us to de ladies restroom."

As Preddy hung up, Harris glanced at him through the corner of his eye. "We're going tae the ladies toilet? I'm naw sure I'm getting this."

"You will."

"Ye think we can prove that she committed the murder?" asked Harris. "She has a motive, but so does Guthrie and we cannae prove he did it either."

"He's a liar, but so is Oleta."

Harris nodded. "On that we agree. But what makes ye so sure it was her?"

"Dat photo," said Preddy. "De one wid all of dem and de outside kids. You never see her hand? She had on her wedding ring."

Harris frowned. "So?"

"So, she told me she hadn't worn her ring in over a year. I assumed it was to do wid diabetes or something. She lied. Probably took it off in a fit of anger after Judge Guthrie told her de truth about her beloved husband."

Harris inclined his head. "So she lied about it. We still cannae tie her tae the murder other than by circumstantial evidence. It's naw as if the ring was found shoved down Everton's throat."

"I'll tell you what was not shoved down his throat and was not thrown into de sea," said Preddy, "de ashtray. A black onyx and diamond ashtray."

"So where is it?"

"My guess? At Pelican Walk." Preddy glanced at Harris's startled face. "If she didn't manage to retrieve it."

CHAPTER 33

As Preddy and Harris pulled into Pelican Walk car park they spotted Spence and Rabino pacing the courtyard looking out for them. Preddy grabbed a box of latex gloves from the dashboard, slammed the car door and walked quickly towards them, momentarily forgetting about Harris who bravely tried to keep step.

"To de ladies' toilet," demanded Preddy striding past and pulling on a pair of gloves.

Rabino raised an eyebrow as she spun on her heels. "And I thought Spence was joking!"

Preddy shook his head. "It's no joke. Dat allegedly stolen ashtray is dere."

"But listen here, me Jesas!" gasped Spence. "Why would you think dat, sir?"

Rabino echoed, "Yes, why?"

Preddy handed the box to Rabino who removed a few pairs of gloves and handed one set to each of her colleagues. Preddy ran up the stairs and they followed closely behind him. "She paid thousands of US dollars to get it specially

315

made for him," he said. "Black onyx and diamonds. Even in her anger she would never have thrown dat away."

"So she didn't throw it away, she brought it here?" asked Rabino incredulously.

"Not intentionally. She didn't know she was coming here when she put it in her handbag," explained Preddy. "Detective Spence diverted her from where she was going wid it, somewhere downtown. Remember, for most of de interview she sat wid de bag in her lap gripping it so tight her knuckles strained?"

Spence glanced at him. "I did notice, sir, but I thought it was just de subconscious action of somebody who has probably been de victim of a bag snatcher?"

"Nerves," said Preddy with certainty. "Even though she must have been relieved dat she got to hide de evidence first, she was still full of nerves."

"Dis way sir, not dat bathroom," said Spence turning down a corridor, forcing them to change direction. "Dis is de one she used when she arrived here yesterday." Spence pushed open the restroom door. "She used de bathroom further down before she left because a cleaner was in dis one."

"I still don't see why she would have put it in here, sir?" said Rabino.

"Unless she crazy," muttered Spence.

It was an empty four cubicle stall. Preddy pulled at the paper dispenser and opened up the top. He felt around inside. "Remember she said something about thinking dat she would have been searched and fingerprinted before she was allowed through to de interview room?"

"I remember," nodded Spence. "Thought it was a joke?"

"No joke," said Preddy shaking his head.

Spence placed her hands on her hips and stared at him. "She desperately wanted de restroom as soon as she came into reception. I didn't accompany her . . . just pointed de way. I was chatting wid Officer Wilson until she came back."

"She panicked," stated Preddy. "She hid dat ashtray in here."

316

Spence's eyes grew wide. "She really wanted to come back in here after de interview. De cleaner was inside and blocked de door."

"I get the picture." Harris nodded. "That's why she was lurking around when she should've been long gone. Fuck! It could've been in the bin and went out with the cleaning lady. Either with the rubbish bag or in her pocket."

"Oleta wouldn't mad put it inna no bin!" said Spence. "Anyway, de cleaning woman is an honest lady and she knows to look out for things like people drying deir hands and dropping rings and bracelets in de bin. She even found a full purse in here once and returned it. Dere is no way she would leave here wid an expensive ashtray."

Harris lifted the lid of the toilet tank and peered into the clear water. "It's naw in here."

"You alright, Detective Harris?" Rabino looked at him closely. "You look a bit greenish?"

"Just a wee touch of sea-sickness," replied Harris forcing a smile. "I'll be fine."

The detectives carefully examined the other tanks. They felt around behind the toilet bowls. They peered inside the huge keg used to store water when the precious commodity failed to emerge from the pipes. Harris checked the floor for loose or broken tiles. He then ran his hands along the wall looking for the same. Rabino put her fingers into the liquid soap dispenser and felt around. Spence crouched down and peered under the wash basins.

Preddy grew increasingly frustrated. "She hung around here for at least half an hour waiting for de cleaner to finish her work so she could go back in and get it."

"Maybe she did get back in after the cleaner left and retrieved it, sir?" said Rabino. "It's not here."

Harris grabbed a paper towel and patted his perspiring brow. "Naw, she was still loitering with intent. We looked at each other. I nodded at her and she took off. I thought maybe she'd just made a complaint to the Super and was embarrassed about it."

Preddy frowned. "Once she left she couldn't just walk back in here, stroll past de front desk and head up de stairs without Officer Wilson giving her permission."

Rabino said, "So let's go talk to Wilson."

Harris cleared his throat and leaned his shoulder against a wall. His strength seemed to be returning in the excitement of expectation which showed in his reddened features. "I really hate tae blow ma own trumpet or anything, but we do have a few tasty surveillance cameras now." The other detectives turned in silence to stare at him. Harris did not bat an eyelid and kept his face poker straight. "These ones can actually identify people. Just in case ye thought we had the same old grainy shite we used tae have."

Spence suddenly exploded into laughter and Rabino joined in. Preddy felt the tension seep out of his muscles and found himself laughing too. Harris grinned and shook his head.

"Come on," said Preddy. "Let's go see what we have on disc."

They dashed back down the stairs past a few startled colleagues who were on their way up. Soon they were huddled in front of the TV monitors, a cluster of which were arranged in a small room adjoining the canteen. Harris checked the position of each camera, filling them in on which one covered which angle of the lobby and the corridors. He searched the surveillance hard drive and pointed at a screen. "There she is. That's when she was leaving."

"Dat's her alright," agreed Preddy. "Clear as day."

They watched Spence wave Oleta goodbye. Within seconds of Spence disappearing from the lobby Oleta reappeared. She said something briefly to Officer Wilson who barely lifted his head from whatever he was reading. She headed back upstairs.

"She really came back in," breathed Rabino.

Another camera picked up Oleta hovering outside the target restroom door. The cleaner came out and the two women appeared to acknowledge each other. Oleta entered the restroom. The cleaner put her things in the storage cupboard next door and then walked off in the opposite direction.

"That's it for the outside then," murmured Harris. "Naw cameras inside the restroom."

"Wait look," said Preddy. The door opened almost immediately and Oleta reappeared. She stood with her back pressed against the bathroom door looking left and right.

"A wha' she a do?" mumbled Spence.

Suddenly, Oleta moved towards the cleaning cupboard and pulled on the door. She pulled and tugged at the padlock. An officer walked along the corridor and Oleta went back inside the bathroom until the man had passed. She exited and resumed her struggle with the door which would not budge. A few seconds later Oleta headed down the stairs again, and was picked up on another camera pacing around the station's front entrance.

Preddy leapt to his feet and ran from the room. He came to a halt outside the cleaner's cupboard and grabbed the rigid padlock which he tried to break with his bare hands. The sinews in his arms pressed against his shirt, but the padlock remained solid. "Who have de key?" he asked.

"Just de cleaner and her supervisor, I think," said Spence arriving at his shoulder.

"Neither of them will be back until tomorrow morning, unless we call them," said a breathless Rabino.

Preddy looked around him in frustration. "Dis has to open up now!"

"I'll get a dumbbell from the gym." Harris took off running in the opposite direction and soon returned with the apparatus.

Preddy hoisted the cast iron ball to shoulder height and brought it down on the lock which splattered. The weight also made a huge impact in the metal door which swung open. Inside, were five shelves. On them were some boxes, reams of tissues and soaps, a dustpan and a few brushes in various state of disrepair. Everything was shuffled aside and prodded under Preddy's desperate hands. He stopped and stared at the back of the second shelf from the top. He reached in and pulled out a padded brown envelope that did not resemble anything used in the JCF. It felt heavy. His breath came in quick spasms as he opened it and peered inside. He turned the envelope upside down and out slid a small box which he recognized on sight. He smiled as he held the box up for the other detectives to see.

* * *

"Playing Devil's Advocate here, Oleta will probably say she must have absentmindedly picked it up on the Monday morning and it's been in her bag forever," suggested Harris. "She'll say she didnae know it was there and then panicked when she realised she had it. She was too embarrassed tae tell us so she hid it."

Spence shook her head. "She say dem thief it. Dat's what she said when her son, Martin, wanted it."

"She had plenty of opportunity to formally report it stolen and never did," said Preddy pacing the floor of the detectives' open-plan zone. "In a way you could say dat her honesty was her undoing. She never had any intention of filing an insurance claim. It's worth a small fortune and she would have needed a police report to give de insurer for any claim."

"So what was she going to do with it?" asked Rabino.

"Maybe she was going tae try and pawn it, though I dinnae know how much money she could hope tae get," said Harris. "It doesnae look like the sort of thing ye could easily pawn around here."

"So she's not a fraudster, but she is a murderer." Rabino looked thoughtful. "What a lady."

"We could give her one last test," murmured Preddy.

"Och, what do ye have in mind?" asked Harris.

Preddy stopped pacing. "Check if she's home. She'll be needing an excuse to return to Pelican Walk and retrieve her property. I guess she's wondering how long to leave it before she finds an excuse to come back. We won't let her search for an excuse, we'll offer her one."

Officer Timmins came around the corner and walked towards the group. "Oh, good, Detective Preddy. Super looking for you. Him waiting in de conference room."

"You never see me," said Preddy striding past him.

"I never see you?" repeated Timmins hesitantly.

"Naw. Ye didnae see any of us," added Harris winking at the officer.

"Didn't see any of you," echoed Timmins frowning. He swiftly drew back to avoid being knocked over as all of the detectives rushed past him and headed for the lobby. "Bwoy, Super always quarrelling say dis place can empty out too quickly pon Friday and now I have to go tell him dat I don't see nobody! Is now him going mad!"

As Preddy drove with Spence at his side, he cursed himself for having dismissed Oleta as a suspect so soon. After nearly two decades on the force he knew that the relatives always had to be looked at first. Instead he had let Oleta's age and seeming disability cause him to treat her as a victim. Oleta who reminded him of his Sunday School teacher. Her motherly appearance was disarming. He had ignored a major clue: a broken nail that she said happened when she cradled her husband's body.

"Damn!" Preddy snapped out loud. "Me shoulda do better."

Spence read his mind. "None of us could have known, sir. She's good dat one. Really good."

"I thought it had to be a man," he said. "Don't even know why I had dat fixed in my mind, except dat strangulation is just not a female crime."

"Not an everyday female," Spence pointed out. "A very angry female. When you well-vex is like strength grow inna you hand! Sometimes I well want to kill Mikey. And dat is only when him leave him dirty socks around de place. If I ever find out dat him have a next woman and pickney!" Spence contorted her face and mimed squeezing somebody's neck.

"I bet you would do it too," said Preddy, "have a little episode, like wid a certain tattooed Crew member."

Spence flicked her head to stare out of the passenger window. "No idea what you talking 'bout, sir!"

He smiled wryly as he glanced at her side profile. "Of course not, Detective."

CHAPTER 34

Friday, 12 May, 4.48 p.m.

Harris and Rabino arrived together at Wynterton Park first. On Rabino's instructions the barrier was propped up until Preddy's vehicle turned onto the drive. The detectives parked outside of the Wrenn's villa next to the red Camry. Maria Wrenn opened the door to Preddy's ring. She was a slender young woman casually dressed in shorts and vest. She recognized Spence immediately. "Oh hello, Detective Spence. Has something happened?"

"Hello Maria." Spence smiled at her. "Dese are my colleagues. We can come in?"

"Of course, please do." Maria held the door open and took a step backwards. "Mom! Mom! The detectives are here!"

Oleta Wrenn appeared from the kitchen trailing the odour of seasoned meat. Her apron was smeared in flour. "Oh hello, detectives. I was just cooking dinner."

Preddy stared at her. Oleta was a smart lady, but how smart was the question. She was certainly no criminal mastermind. A sixty-something high school principal. She had seemed so shaken and withdrawn when he had first met her.

Now, no doubt buoyed by the presence of her children, she seemed cheerful and content.

Oleta shuffled uncomfortably in the silence. "Detective Preddy?"

"Sorry, my mind was elsewhere," said Preddy snapping out of his stupor.

"It's the lovely smell of that food," offered Rabino.

"Aye, it is mighty distracting," agreed Harris inhaling deeply. "What is it?"

"Oxtail," said Oleta proudly. "Oxtail and butter beans with Irish potatoes."

"Sounds great and smells better," said Preddy keeping his eyes fixed on the widow. Her hands now did not look swollen and he wondered if she had a medical condition at all. Maybe all along her previous disability had been self-inflicted. "We think we're making good headway on your husband's murder."

A young man walked into the room with a cigarette dangling from his fingers. In the other he held a saucer with some traces of ash. He was naked from the waist up, his belly protruding over his shorts. His eyes did a quick scout of the occupants. "Hello folks."

Oleta looked up at him. "This is my son, Martin," she announced. "Martin, you already know Detective Spence. These are Detectives Rabino, Preddy and, erm I forgot . . ."

"Harris," the Scotsman nodded politely. "Sean Harris."

Martin drawled, "We've got a full house. Glad there's a lot of you on the case." There was a distinct twang in his voice, though unlike his sister, he maintained a hint of a Jamaican accent.

"Oh, we're always out in full force when we're after a killer," Preddy assured him.

"So you got the guy who killed our dad?" asked Martin as he inhaled a lung full of smoke.

"We have some photographs back at de station," said Spence. "We were hoping Mrs Wrenn could come wid us. See if she can identify our prime suspect."

Oleta's face brightened and she wiped her hands on her apron. "Sure, give me a minute."

Maria looked at Spence. "Not now though, surely, Detective? It's gone five o'clock. You're talking in the morning, right?" She walked over to her mother and put her arms around her shoulders rubbing them gently.

"Well, it doesn't matter . . ." started Oleta.

"But Mom, you're cooking!" protested Maria.

"Oh, it will soon be done," said Oleta sounding slightly peevish. She patted her daughter's hand and gave it a soft squeeze. "You two can share it out."

"Come on, Mom," said Martin childishly. A frown appeared on his forehead. "You've gotta know we'll make a mess of it."

"It would be great if we could wrap dis up tonight," urged Preddy, while thinking that the adult children were spoiled brats. He had thought they would have jumped at the chance to see their father's murderer identified. "Who knows, we might even be able to pick up de killer."

Harris said, "Actually, Detective Preddy, tomorrow morning may naw be such a bad idea." Rabino raised her eyebrows and turned to look at the Scotsman. Preddy frowned darkly at him, but did not speak. Harris continued, "We can get a couple of bereavement counsellors in tae see ye too . . . The very best. Mr Brownlow and Mr Davis. Mr Davis in particular is very enthusiastic in his calling, but he's naw available today. They'd both welcome the chance tae see ye tomorrow."

Spence snorted and reached into her pocket for a handkerchief, mumbling an apology.

A slow smile crept across Preddy's face. "Dat is true. How's nine o'clock tomorrow for you?"

"Whoa! That's early," grumbled Martin. "I want to come too. I want to see the person who killed Dad." He dabbed out the ash remains in the saucer.

"And me," added Maria.

Martin stared at Preddy as if he was a nuisance. "Can't you guys just bring the photos here?" he asked.

"No, no," said Oleta before Preddy could speak. "They can't do that. What's wrong with you? The evidence must stay in a secure environment. It's better we go to Pelican Walk."

"You'd make a good detective, Mrs Wrenn," said Preddy.

"We'll say ten o'clock, then?" suggested Harris.

"Ten is good," said Oleta while wiping her hands on her apron.

"I can come and pick you up if you like?" offered Rabino. "It's no trouble."

"It's okay," said Martin. "I'll drive the Camry. Mom doesn't like to drive, but I don't mind. Besides, I want to practice on Jamaican roads and there's less traffic on a Saturday. Need to learn to dodge the potholes."

"Ye and me, both, apparently," agreed Harris.

Oleta smiled. "Yes, my son will drive. We'll see you in the morning, detectives."

"I look forward to it." Preddy bowed as they left.

CHAPTER 35

Commissioner Davis and Superintendent Brownlow sat squeezed together on uncomfortable plastic chairs staring at the surveillance monitors. Both men were used to softer, more lavish seating for their ample behinds. Detective Harris hovered over their shoulders, his eyes focused on the centre monitor. Preddy stood next to them watching expectantly.

"Keep your eyes on de top right screen for now, sir," ordered Preddy.

"What am I looking for?" asked the commissioner, propping up his glasses on his nose.

"Dat's de lobby area. You can just see de corner of Officer Wilson's shoulder. You'll see everybody who enters," explained Preddy. "De left screen picks up de area beside de first floor ladies restroom and de janitors' closet. De one to de right picks up Interview Room 2 where you'll soon see Detectives Spence and Rabino."

"I haven't even had a coffee yet," grumbled the superintendent, wriggling in his seat and finding no comfort. "This better be good, Preddy."

"It will be, sir." Preddy assured him. "Spence tells me dey are looking for a parking space."

"Who is looking for a parking space?" asked the commissioner. "I have things to do. Should have been heading for Frenchman's Cove right now."

The joys of the weekend on a private estate in Port Antonio when you are not a hard-pressed detective, thought Preddy. "Judge Wrenn's murderer, sir," he said.

The commissioner and the superintendent stared at each other. The commissioner turned to Harris. "Judge Wrenn's murderer? He confessed?"

"It would be nice to know what is going on in this place for once," mumbled Brownlow.

Harris managed a smile as he shot Preddy the side-eye. "Amen tae that."

"How comes I never heard about his confession?" demanded Brownlow.

Harris returned his gaze to the monitor. "Ye really should do as Detective Preddy says, sir."

Preddy said, "It isn't a he, sir."

Commissioner Davis stared keenly at the monitor. "Well, I can see a woman entering now with a bucket and brush. Don't tell me one of the cleaners did it?"

Preddy looked at the screen in alarm. "Me rass!" he shouted as he ran through the door.

In Preddy's absence, Commissioner Davis aimed his discomfort at Harris. "What is going on with Preddy?"

It was a question Harris had asked himself many a time without getting an answer. At least this time he knew exactly what was going on. Harris grinned and pointed at the images on screen. "That's him there. Dinnae worry, sir. He's just making sure the cleaning lady doesnae go anywhere near the ladies room or the storage cupboard. The cleaner isnae guilty of anything, sir." He paused as if considering the veracity of this statement before adding, "Well, naw theft or murder anyway. She could give the taps a wee bit more attention though."

* * *

Oleta Wrenn crossed the threshold of Pelican Walk police station with Martin and Maria at her side, each holding an arm. Rabino greeted them in the lobby and escorted them up to the interview room. Inside sat Spence with a closed manila folder on the table in front of her. Spence rose immediately and shook the hands of her guests. Rabino showed them their seats. Maria and Martin took theirs quickly. Oleta hovered awkwardly, before smiling at Spence.

"My bladder acting up again," she said apologetically. "I'm just going to pop to the restroom before we start."

"Of course," said Spence placing her palms against the table as if to help herself up. "You want me to come wid you?"

"No, no, Detective," Oleta smiled. "I remember. I'll find it." She spun around and quickly walked down the corridor.

Rabino closed the door behind Oleta and took up a seat beside Spence who promptly opened the folder of photographs and turned it around to face Judge Wrenn's children.

Oleta moved purposefully. Outside the door of the ladies restroom she hesitated and looked up and down the corridor. A female officer exited the restroom and held the door open for the widow. She smiled her thanks, but did not go inside. Instead she pretended to be searching for something inside her handbag.

As soon as the officer had vanished Oleta propped her handbag over her shoulder, pulled open the cupboard door and reached up to the penultimate shelf. She felt around for a while without looking. Then she drew back and peered up at the shelf. She moved forward again, rising on tiptoes. She stretched her arm even further back and rustled behind some tins of floor polish. Eventually her hand came out with a padded brown envelope. She closed the doors.

"Glad you found what you were looking for, Mrs Wrenn," said Preddy. He was leaning against the wall behind her.

Oleta's face registered her shock. She held the envelope close to her chest and began to move backwards slowly while never taking her eyes off the detective.

Preddy gestured at the packet. "So, what's in de envelope?"

Oleta did not answer. She shook her head from side to side. Suddenly, she whirled and ran back towards Interview Room 2. Preddy moved quickly behind her. The four occupants of the interview room looked up when the door crashed open.

"Welcome back," said Spence eyeing the woman with disdain.

"We were just showing your children some photographs," explained Rabino. "They say they've never seen these boys before."

"Mom, what are they talking about?" Maria pointed at a photograph on the table. "Who are these boys?"

Martin clutched a photo in his hand. He held it up and pushed it towards his mother's face. "This can't be right Mom? Tell me these guys in the photo are not my brothers?"

Preddy appeared behind Oleta. "Tell dem who dey are, Mrs Wrenn."

Oleta stared at the photo. It was the one she now hated. One of herself, Everton, Lawrence and the three children that she had known to be Lawrence's, until two weeks ago. She sank into a chair and said nothing. Her handbag fell to the ground, but she made no move to retrieve it. Preddy pried the envelope from her fingers and opened it. He removed the box and handed it to Martin.

"What is this?" he asked, stretching out his hand.

Maria craned her neck and looked. She took it from her brother and opened it, removing the onyx ashtray. The diamonds sparkled under the florescent lights. "Mom, what does this mean?"

Oleta began to cry. Tears streamed down her cheeks and rolled under her chin.

"That's Dad's!" Martin snatched the object from his sister and looked confused. "The murderer stole it. Where did you find it?"

"Your mother found it," replied Preddy quietly. "Right where she put it."

Martin moved from his seat, a look of incredulity covered his face. He stared at his mother. She avoided looking at him. She was as still and silent as the day the detectives had first visited her. "Mom? What did you do, Mom? Talk to me." He moved closer to her. Took both her hands in his.

Oleta mumbled, "They are not Lawrence Guthrie's sons. They're Everton's, from another mother."

"It's not true," breathed Maria. "This is some mistake."

Oleta looked at her daughter through glazed eyes. "Your father ruined our family. Ruined our plans for our lives."

Maria pushed back her chair, stood up and stared at her mother. Her incredulity matched that of her brother's and tears began to impede her view.

"I loved him! He betrayed us!" wailed Oleta. "All that hard work building our home and family."

"You killed Dad? Oh my God, you killed Dad!" Maria spluttered.

"All these years your upstanding father has been nothing but a liar and an adulterer! He ruined our family. Those two young boys are your brothers." Oleta clutched her cheeks. "I thought he and I shared the same vision, but he was off making a second family when I was making a home."

Maria shook her head from side to side as if in a trance.

"I didn't want this to happen, but if it wasn't for me you would have nothing," whispered Oleta. "He was going to put those bastards in his will. That evening, I found a document he was drafting by hand, hidden among some papers in his safe." She paused, took a deep breath before continuing, her voice filled with malice. "Your precious father was planning to give his whore and his bastards a share of our hard earned money. Our money! Your money!"

"No! Tell me you didn't do this!" cried Maria.

"I didn't plan to, I swear." Oleta stared at her. "He came back from work quite late that evening. I'm not even sure where he'd been. Probably drowning his sorrows somewhere after he rowed with Lawrence. I was glad he didn't come home as it gave me some time to do some digging around."

"Oh my God!" Martin sounded as if he was choking. He placed the ashtray on top of the folder. He squeezed his mother's hands and she clutched his. "You see what's written on it, son? It says 'For Ever' and that's exactly how I thought it would be." She gave a snort of derision. "I was going to try and find someone to extract the diamonds for me. Had an appointment to see a jeweller yesterday when I made a detour to come here. Black onyx is said to protect you from harm so I wanted to keep it. Thought I could do something nice with the diamonds. Diamonds are forever."

Martin seemed to regain his composure. "Don't say anything else, Mom. We need to get you a lawyer."

Oleta pulled her hands from his and waved at him dismissively. "I'm sorry, son. I don't care about any lawyer. I loved him and I killed him. That's what I'll say in front of the lawyer or without one."

"But you confronted dad about . . . about the children. He attacked you, right. It was self-defence," stuttered Martin.

"He did not attack me." She shook her head defiantly. "We barely spoke a word throughout dinner. I said nothing about what I knew. He could see that something was up, but I don't think he suspected I knew the truth. I went upstairs to our room. He went on the verandah to smoke. I was getting more and more agitated while I waited for him to come up. I decided that I was going to confront him about his dirty little secret. He didn't come up, so I went down." She clenched her fingers. "His phone was on the table. I've never looked at his phone in all the years we've been married. I scrolled through the messages. There were many under the name 'Workshop Supervisor.'" Oleta snorted then fell quiet as if she was reliving the pain of reading the messages again.

"Where's de phone?" asked Preddy.

"Floating halfway to Honduras by now," she said. "He was in his chair. Bottom perched at the edge, leaning back with his head against the back rest, snoozing. It was like he didn't have a care in the world. In that split second, I hated him."

Maria burst into tears and used her hands to cover her eyes. Martin slumped back into his chair.

"I used my walking stick, rammed the bottom of it into his neck. He sprung forward against the table. He lay there gasping." Oleta inhaled. "I knelt down and put my hands around his throat and squeezed and squeezed again. Squeezed my pain."

Maria got up and ran through the door screaming. Oleta got to her feet as if to follow, but Preddy promptly blocked her. "No way."

Spence stood up. "Put your hands behind your back."

"Do you have to do that?" croaked Martin.

"We do. You can give her a hug if you want to, but that's it." Rabino stared at his distraught face and her tone became more gentle. "I'm sorry, Martin. I suggest you find her a very good lawyer."

* * *

Preddy headed to the surveillance quarters where he found a delighted Commissioner Davis and Superintendent Brownlow still being supervised by a triumphant Harris.

"If I didn't see it with my own eyes, I wouldn't have believed it!" beamed the commissioner.

"Dat's exactly why Detective Harris invited you here, sir," replied Preddy.

"But ye can still make it tae Frenchman's Cove in time for lunch," said Harris.

Preddy heard the cheeky inflection and managed to suffocate a laugh that was straining to emerge from his throat.

"Yes, that can wait." The commissioner, unaware of the Scotsman's slight, rubbed his hands together in delight.

"This is great work, detectives!" said Superintendent Brownlow. "What did I tell you Commissioner? Didn't I tell you they would do it? I knew they would work well together."

"Teamwork is definitely our thing," said Harris holding Preddy's gaze.

Preddy resisted the urge to roll his eyes. "I guess we can get de Parish Court open again on Monday morning, sir?"

"Of course! Of course!" babbled the superintendent as his jowls jiggled. "We'll make it known immediately that the judge's murderer has been caught."

"Yes, that needs to be done right now!" agreed Commissioner Davis. "I'll get on to the media unit and set the train in motion." He took out his phone and began scrolling through his contacts. "Now where is that number?"

"I'm sure I have it," mumbled Brownlow, whipping out his own phone and bringing it close to his face.

"You have the mayor's number?" asked the commissioner.

"Yes, man," replied the superintendent. "Must find the minister's too."

Preddy took a step backwards and gave an almost imperceptible gesture towards Harris who followed his lead. They edged away from their superiors then rotated and quickly headed down the corridor.

"Leave dem to do deir back patting," grinned Preddy.

"Phew! Those two do make a tight environment feel even more claustrophobic," said Harris.

"You know dey love your company though?" teased Preddy.

"Aye, well naw today." Harris wiped his reddened face.

As they walked along the corridor Preddy stole a glance at him, this foreigner who was on his patch, investigating a fellow detective right under his nose. "You going tell me what I want to know?" he asked.

"About what?" asked Harris coolly.

"About de price of tinned ackee."

"Scandalous," said Harris shaking his head. "Saltfish prices are holding steady though."

The men eyeballed each other for a few seconds. Preddy sighed and glanced at his watch. "We can give it half hour den collect Spence and Rabino and go look some food," said Preddy.

"Where do ye suggest?" asked Harris as he walked alongside him.

"We can try dat place near de Freeport dat seems so popular. De Houseboat Grill. Never been dere myself. Rabino says it almost hidden by de mangrove trees, which may be why I've never noticed it." Preddy waited, expecting instant resistance, which did not materialise. "Don't know what dey serve, but we can check it out."

"Sure, I'm game for that."

"Yes, apparently it's moored about thirty feet out to sea, and you have to get on a little raft to get to it."

The footsteps beside him came to a sudden halt. Preddy looked over his shoulder and grinned. "Anything wrong, Detective Harris? You're looking a bit . . . off-colour."

THE END

ACKNOWLEDGEMENTS

Special thanks to my brothers Duane Lennon and Guy (Coza) Lennon for their unwavering support and for much-needed supplies of Aspall and Merrydown, without which this book could not have been written. My gratitude always to the people I can always call on for advice and encouragement: Sharon Thompson, Gwendolyn Thompson and Juliet (Lavern) Ingram Reid. Thanks also to my publisher Joffe Books for keeping the faith.

To my returning readers, thanks so much for following the series and I really hope you enjoyed this instalment.

ALSO BY PAULA LENNON

PREDDY & HARRIS
Book 1: MURDER IN MONTEGO BAY
Book 2: MURDER UNDER THE PALMS

Thank you for reading this book.

If you enjoyed it please leave feedback on Amazon or Goodreads, and if there is anything we missed or you have a question about, then please get in touch. We appreciate you choosing our book.

Founded in 2014 in Shoreditch, London, we at Joffe Books pride ourselves on our history of innovative publishing. We were thrilled to be shortlisted for Independent Publisher of the Year at the British Book Awards.

www.joffebooks.com

We're very grateful to eagle-eyed readers who take the time to contact us. Please send any errors you find to corrections@joffebooks.com. We'll get them fixed ASAP.